Brothers in Arms with Benefits

Rukis

Brothers in Arms with Benefits

Production copyright FurPlanet Productions © 2024

Text Copyright © Rukis 2024

Cover Artwork and illustrations © Rukis 2024

Published by FurPlanet Productions
Dallas, Texas
www.FurPlanet.com

Print ISBN 978-1-61450-641-6
Electronic ISBN 978-1-61450-642-3

Also by *Rukis* from *Red Lantern*:

Legacy Dawn (Book 1)
Legacy Dusk (Book 2)

Heretic

Illicit Alliance

Kindred North (Book 1)
Kindred South (Book 2)

Off the Beaten Path (Book 1)
Lost on Dark Trails (Book 2)
The Long Road Home (Book 3)

Red Lantern — The Crimson Divine (Book 1)
Red Lantern — Conviction (Book 2)

HeartTheft

Dubiously Canon

Content Warning / Disclosure

This book is part of a collection of novels in the *Red Lantern* universe, a Historical Fiction setting that is not intended to be analogous for the real world, at any set point in time. The characters, places, events, religious practices, and cultures in this world are also not intended to be compared to reality, either past or present. It is a fictional setting, and the opinions and thoughts of its characters are similarly fictional. These animal people are not role models. They are flawed, frequently wrong in their assertions, and morally bankrupt — as is their world.

While my writing is inspired heavily by history, my own lived experience, and the lived experiences of others, I do not personally find that drawing analogies between an anthropomorphic society and our human world is always helpful. Red Lantern is meant first and foremost as entertainment and to inspire creativity, open-mindedness, and empathy for those around you.

This book contains themes some may find uncomfortable or hard to read, including:

Violence, Sexual Content, Mentions of Religious and Familial Abuse, Substance Abuse, and Consensual Non-Consent Situations

If any of these themes are particularly upsetting to you, this may not be the book for you.

Table of Contents

Foreword

By Rukis

Brothers in Arms With Benefits is a collection of short stories set in the *Red Lantern* universe, a Historical Fiction-Inspired Anthropomorphic world written and illustrated by Rukis.

This collection chronicles the evolving, tumultuous relationship between two of the leading characters in that series, Crown Admiral Luther Denholme and the Privateer Admiral Grayson Reed. Each of the following four stories takes place at different points during the timeline of the Red Lantern series, and while they can be read on their own with no context, you'll appreciate the story far more if you're versed on the novel lore.

The suggested reading order for Luther and Grayson's stories, if you're interested in getting to know the series through them, is as follows.

Heretic
Luther Denholme's origin story

Illicit Alliance
Grayson Reed's origin story and the first series of misadventures the two characters engaged in together.

Brothers in Arms With Benefits
This book of short stories!

Red Lantern – The Graphic Novels

Rules of Engagement

Rules of Engagement

I was two days into the festival on Elrados, and he still hadn't shown.

The island was small and poor enough to hold to its sovereignty. A free port in all ways that mattered. Ceded decades ago to a powerful and numerous tribe of ocelot traders with a substantial fishing fleet that kept trade and currency flowing through the otherwise far-flung speck of land they'd laid claim to. Hardly what was due to one of the original nations of people who should have rightfully still inhabited and owned the mainland of Carvecia, but they'd carved out something unique for themselves here that even we pirates and privateers had failed to hold on to in the southern seas, and that was rare in our modern world.

Freedom. Independence. Their own customs, alive and still practiced despite the scattered presence of Amur Missionaries.

I saw the distant flag, red and emblazoned with those bloody moons, hanging on the horizon like a pall over the otherwise colorful, diverse festivities taking place in the city streets. The Amurescan Quarter, separated from the rest of the city with literal walls, intentionally drab. They'd built their steeple higher than any local tabards or totems, also intentionally, and I imagined, with malice. Literally looking down on the port of sin they were hoping to convert.

But here, on this island, they were relegated to the outskirts. The overgrown forests of invasive bamboo and local palms and cypress. Let them fight the green wild for space, let them suffer the tropical maladies they refused local medicine for. Let them strive in vain to convert a populace happier and more prosperous in their freedom than they'd ever be under the stifling weight of the colonial heel or their tyrannical religion.

But damn the thing, I kept looking towards the Amur end of town, towards the small port that hung the Empire's flags, because I expected if he came, it would be through that pier. I knew not on which ship, probably just a passenger vessel....

Enough, I promised myself when I turned again on my paw, focusing on the warmly-lit, already loud villa at the end of the dirt road I was walking. There were pole lanterns hung all along the way, draped in hanging bunches of local flowers, and tattered ribbons in all hues tied from the branches of the cypress. They fluttered in the perfectly-cooling breeze of the approaching evening, scrawled with the wishes of those who'd hung them. They were for no one's eyes but the spirits of luck who might grant them, so I avoided reading them.

I was not a man of faith, but superstition? I was still a sailor. I didn't want to spoil someone else's wish. Bad form.

Pausing near a limb low enough for me to reach, but not one of those fully covered yet, I hesitated before withdrawing the torn ball of fabric in my coat pocket. I'd scribbled it at the last minute this morning after thinking the better of it for too long now. It wasn't as though anyone meaningful would ever read it, and even if they did, they'd hardly know who it belonged to, but....

It was just so bloody pathetic. I mean, even for *me*.

This wasn't a battle of common sense like my usual bad decisions were. This was a battle of wills against my own personal self-condemnation. My respect for myself hung in the balance. I didn't even believe in spirits, least of all that one would fulfill *my* ridiculous wish. Even writing it on this torn bit of red cloth had felt like speaking its truth into being, and that was nearly more than I could bear.

It took a lot to make *my* ears burn. But here I was, clutching the damned thing in my palm so tightly my claws were digging into my paw pads.

"To hells with it," I growled out, unfurling the crumpled cloth, quickly looping the upper end in one of my personal go-to lazy-man's knots, and releasing it like it scalded. I turned from it quickly and fled, not even wanting to read the words in the flash after they were hung. I beat a hasty retreat back to the path.

I shoved my hands in the pockets of my costume jacket and finally produced the last pieces of my 'disguise': a white pair of fingerless gloves and a matching white porcelain half-mask I'd be wearing tonight. It covered the upper portion of my face and muzzle and was adorned with a sweeping pair of pointed, shepherd-like ears, taller than my own. It was a bit reductive, I suppose, wearing a canine mask when I was myself a canine. But it was a statement piece. I hadn't gone nearly so all-out as some of the denizens I'd seen approaching the party. No dye or powder in my fur, no wings or extra appendages. My costume was essentially just a mockery of what I normally wore. Or rather, what the gents across the pond normally wore. Almost no one here would understand what it meant, and that was fine. It wasn't *for* them.

And it wasn't much of a disguise. I was well-known enough in these parts that I'd be recognized by some, owing mostly to my mane. It was in a rare state this year… loose, well-groomed. Not yet grown out enough to be dreaded. But I'd managed at least to incorporate some of my family's jewelry in the occasional small braid and that was enough. There were not many black wolves with turquoise in their mane and my particular swagger. I'd not be entirely anonymous tonight, but I'd been to this function before, and most were good enough to keep up the illusion.

The Feast of Possession was an ancient holiday turned modern excuse for a debauched masquerade ball, which I think the ancients would have approved of honestly. I'd never attended a traditional festival for the holiday, but apparently it hadn't been much different generations ago, before colonial influence. The ocelots who practiced it would don personally-decorated masks, loose robes that would obscure their spots and figures– which they also sometimes decorated in interesting ways, a precursor to the costumes they'd recently adopted– and do what all good peoples did when they celebrated: eat, drink, dance, and whatever other… activities… suited under the cover of anonymity.

I could see why the Amurescan Faith took such issue with the celebration, don't get me wrong. It was believed if one truly surrendered their being to the festival, they would become possessed by a spirit of luck and grant the wishes of those fortunate few who caught their interest. The colorful ribbons and flowers were meant to tempt them to honor the requests.

In reality, I think quite a lot of people *would* be possessed by spirits and grant *someone's* wishes tonight. But I wasn't just here for a lot of free-flowing local booze and a good time twixt someone's thighs. For once.

Today marked over a year since I'd last seen Luther Denholme on the eve of my would-be execution. I'd spent much of it off the water doing a little catching up with my family, enjoying a fling with an Amur widow whose association had been mutually enjoyable... and mutually agreed-upon to be a passing fancy... and leaving the running of my fleet to an interim Captain. Rook seemed glad to be back on the Dawn Roar, grumbling nonstop about our 'leaky bucket' of a capital ship being more trouble than she was worth. But then, that's something she and I shared in common, and I'd never besmirch her cracks and maladies so cruelly.

I'd been back in the saddle as Admiral now for three months, and for some reason, I'd expected once I was back out on the water, the Amurescan pirate hunter who led the Cerberus fleet would have shown himself in some form or another.

Having to flee his guns would not have been my preferred method of reacquainting ourselves, but it would have been *something*. Instead, I'd spent most of those three months practically waggling my ass in his backyard, on the routes I *knew* he patrolled, and I'd not seen hide nor hair of that three-headed flag.

Of course, just because you didn't *see* the Cerberus Fleet didn't mean they hadn't found *you*.

It was odd to think the man was actively sparing me, but I could find no other reasoning for his absence at this point. I'd accidentally sunk a gunship protecting an Eastern Tavesi Cartel fleet just a month back, seized nearly every piece of cargo they'd been carrying– I had taken my time, even– and nothing. The crew was happy and rich, my purser was less angry at me on the regular, the time spent on the mainland meant my girl was in good-ish repair, for once...

... and I was bereft.

I played with the beads in one of the short braids tumbling over my shoulders as I entered the gala grounds. Most of the festivities, including the dancing, would be outside or in an open hall, on account of the warm nights. I'd brought a Chartruc coin as a means of passing through into the inner, more private sanctum of the main house or availing myself of their courtesans on retainer, but I wouldn't bother trading it in unless I had need for privacy tonight. And that was seeming less and less likely.

I knew the Cerberus Fleet would be moored in Arbordale for Crowning Day because they always had him on patrol when the Lords' ships came in. Luther may not have been popular at court (and my widow friend had confirmed this suspicion of mine), but his King and lordlings liked to have their nastiest, most lethal guard dogs nearby on short leashes whenever they were traveling and worried for their safety.

I'd left a letter for Luther with a trustworthy, highly reliable courier who I knew would most certainly have seen to it my invitation was received, once he docked. Other than being intercepted by someone in his own fleet, he *should* have gotten it. Elrados was only two days' sail from Arbordale in good weather, which we'd had. Crowning Day had been two weeks ago. Unless they'd had him immediately ordered out for some other reason… the timing should have worked out.

Lord. I felt like I was in boarding school again, finding out the other canines in my dorm thought I was dirty because of my mane. Had it all meant nothing? I wasn't a child anymore. I was not desperate for friends. Perhaps I should have left well enough alone and enjoyed the memories of the brief, unlikely partnership we'd shared bringing down Roccosal. It had been rough seas enough without looking to rekindle the storm.

But I'd just never met anyone else like him, and I was convinced I never would again. The tribal wolves spoke of the concept of 'brothers across mountains', referring to kinship not unlike the bonds of family, but between those of different clans or drastically different beliefs. I already had a wide array of strange, diverse comrades amongst my crew and out in the world.

But I don't know. This was different.

I spent the first hour at the party just drinking in the sights and sounds, without interacting. I'd come alone and without the guest I'd hoped to meet here, so I wasn't sure where the night was going to take me. I considered the gaggles of obviously-foreign mariners— you could pick them out easily enough, despite the costumes and masks. Rough hands, scars, smelling vaguely of brine and nearly always armed. Minimal masks if any, some just cloth, here likely on invite from their Captains or trade contacts, making the most of the booze and music. There was a lively string quartet probably accustomed to finer functions playing, and the mood wasn't right just yet, but I was certain in time there'd be dancing.

The spread of food was tempting me, wafting smoke from the grills and the sumptuous scents of fruit and liquor, beckoning from the open hanging gardens. I'd yet to visit except to fill my rations cup with local rum, and really... I'd have to consider eating soon, or that would catch up with me.

It would keep me busy a spell.

Two hours and a light meal in, and I stood near one of the emptier verandas. I'd still not had it in me to strike up conversation with any of the many interesting, costumed faces that decorated the grounds. To my left, a local ocelot woman spoke in hushed tones with a canine gentleman pretending he wasn't married for the evening. He was most evidently *very* married. She likely didn't realize the slim silver collar he wore beneath his cravat denoted as much, given it wasn't a local custom. Likely she wouldn't have cared. Tonight, after all, they were spirits.

Sitting out by the heavily-planted carp pond to my right, three youthful mouse girls giggled over their pints and passed a pipe back and forth, their feet dangling partially into the water. The fish nibbled at bits of sweet bread they tossed to them. A horned man walked the grounds along the opposite edge of the water gardens, an eerie phantom of dark red and gray-blue, his mask a twisted black visage of a devil that lent him a more macabre appearance than most guests here. He had that slow walk that suggested he was imbibing something more than just liquor tonight.

The people-watching was good, and if not for my mounting disappointment, I might have enjoyed the evening on its own merits. I'm not certain what I'd expected, really.

Maybe it had all meant much more to me than it should have. I'd fixated on the image of the man I'd built up in my mind for months while imprisoned, after all. Perfect circumstance to build an unnatural and unhealthy obsession with someone. Someone who had good reason to reject *any* continued relationship with me, given how we'd met. I'd thought his machinations to see to it I escaped execution were a sign the fascination and regard was mutual, but it could very well have been a sending-off. A farewell to an unlikely, *temporary* relationship of convenience.

"I'm a fool," I told the fish because no one else was in earshot to hear me.

"Dejection is so unnatural a visage on you, it disheartens me to see it more than that offensive costume."

I glanced briefly at devil-man, who was apparently not so high that he couldn't speak cryptically to a stranger, and I tossed him an offhanded, "You presume to know me so well."

"Utterly. I rose from the grave with you, after all."

That's when I recognized the voice.

I choked on my tongue, shoving my mask up for a moment to improve my vision, but there was no denying it when he did the same, tipping back the black, horned, twisted mask of Ciraberos, the Amur devil himself, to reveal his own natural mask of black fur. And those gold eyes.

He was smiling *that* smile– like he was three steps ahead of you all the time, even when you hadn't made up your own mind, somehow– and winked once at me before lowering the mask again. "We are meant to keep these on, I think," he said.

When I tell you I snapped that mask back on *so* fast. And not at all because my eyes were prickling with something that felt suspiciously like tears. God, I was such a pup. I had never wanted to know my friendship was desired in return so much before *in my life*. And now he was here, and that meant…

…what *did* it mean?

"You're here," was all I managed, stupidly.

The man– the cattle dog– in the half cape and dark doublet, adorned with the horned mask of Ciraberos, merely gestured back out towards the lantern-lit gardens and offered me his arm.

I glanced at it, throat run dry, before quickly and with a slightly shaking hand finishing off the rum and juice in my measures cup so I could affix it to my belt. Then I asked, while tentatively reaching, "You don't like being touched. I mean… Amur don't, in general. But you, especially."

"I wouldn't offer if it wasn't in earnest," he assured me, nudging me with his elbow expectantly. "Better than braced together in a coffin, aye?"

I huffed with a smile and took his arm as though I was a damsel going for a spin with a would-be suitor. If he didn't care, I'd enjoy being coddled. It was a secret pleasure of mine. Or not-so-secret, really.

"Taking a turn in a shadowy garden with such a devious gentleman," I swooned. "How untoward."

"I am completely unknown in this port of call. No one here is acquainted with… how *devious* I can be."

I laughed, but his 'joke' said a lot more than its shallow meaning. He was telling me not only that he felt safe enough to eschew his propriety here on an island he was a true stranger on, but that his 'deviance' was not known here. I now hated I'd chosen that word because I knew in this context what he was implying by it. That's not how *I'd* intended it.

We walked into the privacy of the dimly lantern-lit gardens, full of the branching shadows of imported flower bushes and palm fronds, interrupted in our solitude only occasionally by the faceless shadows of others moving through the maze, similarly seeking privacy. It felt illicit. Somehow more than our first meeting had been, and I couldn't say why. My heart was beating an erratic drum. Why was I so worked up?

"I knew I'd find you near the water," he was the first to speak again.

"I… don't mean to be so predictable," is what I said. What I wanted to say was how I'd waited near the cliffs on the northwest end of the island for the last two evenings because the spot reminded me of that mountain we'd climbed together, and a shared moment of kinship etched into my dreams that he'd probably never thought of again. But some part of me, some pitifully lonely corner, had hoped he'd meet me there, instead of at the party I'd invited him to. Sooner. So that we'd have more time.

It was also by the water. That's what I'd *wanted* to say.

He was here. That alone should've been enough.

"You really are somewhat predictable for someone so chaotic," he chuckled, "or perhaps I just understand you too well, now." He was not showing a single sign of the anxiety and trepidation I was feeling at seeing him again. He was all ease and friendliness. It felt like our dispositions had swapped. Maddening.

"Ciraberos?" I managed at some point after that. "The Amur Devil? Really? The *namesake* for your fleet? A little on the nose, wouldn't you say?"

"You were watching me from across that pond for a good five minutes, and you didn't pick me out," he noted. "I gave you time, even."

"I thought you were wandering the haze of the Divine," I coughed. "Stalking about like that. You were waiting for me to recognize you?"

"Don't count yourself lacking. We're just circling one another as we always do," he said in a casual tone. "As usual, I got the drop on you. As usual, you did not realize you were under watch. It's nostalgic, really. Amazing how we fall back into our regular rhythm, even on dry land."

"Bastard," I breathlessly chuckled. "What can I say? I'm out of practice. You've not hunted me in so long. Odd how we keep missing each other, aye?"

It was intended as a probing barb to test the waters. I expected, given how he'd reacted to everything else tonight, that he'd just laugh it off. Give me nothing. No answers. I'd be left to wonder as I had all these months if he was truly off his game, or he intentionally avoided me.

He stopped walking. I hadn't expected that. When I turned, he tipped his head at me, his expression covered by the mask. Even without it, he could be so subtle when the gears turned in his brain, anyway. It was always hard to deduce where the man stood.

But he was still for a moment. It read like concern. When he spoke, it *sounded* like concern. "Do you not…" he paused, then pressed on, "… remember? Do you… believe me a coward?"

I balked. "No. Hells no. I know better than to doubt your nerve. Or ability, while we're on the subject. If y'wanted me, you'd have me, and instead it's been open season—"

"Was that not the deal?" he asked, confused.

My mind went blank.

"The whole bloody ordeal on Dokuro," he pressed on. "Is this not our agreement then, fulfilled? Do not let me think I have been negligent in my duties, and you *haven't* made the most of it."

"Oh…." I stammered.

"Do you know how many excuses I've had to cook up to avoid altercations with your fleet?" he asked me exhaustedly. "I don't personally give a damn about your particular trail of wreckage this season; the Eastern Tavesi Cartel and their bloodstained penal colonies are best run out of business— I hope you send all their rotting gunships to the bottom, if I'm being fully honest— but the Crown and several of my Captains are none too happy. I'll hear of it from the Board of Admiralty when I come home, mark my words. But that was the *deal.*" He stared at me through the sockets in his mask, and there was *nothing* cutting the intensity of those eyes. "I hold to my word."

My heart was on *fire*. He *had* been sparing our fleet. And he was talking to me like he had when last we'd parted. Informally, for him. Man to man. Like there was something there. Like everything we'd gone through still mattered to him. I hadn't imagined it.

He wanted to know that the effort he'd put in meant something to me. That I'd recognized it for what it was. He sounded almost *hurt* that I'd thought he'd not keep his word.

I *was* a fool, but not for the reason I'd thought.

"Thank you," I said because summarizing everything else I felt right now seemed like it would simply be too much. And Luther valued brevity. "I don't know why I thought we'd go back to chasing each other with cannons, but I suppose some part of me must have missed it, is all. Man likes to feel wanted, you know?"

He sighed, tapping a hand on the pommel of his sword. "Oh, you're wanted, alright. In most civilized nations for one crime or another."

I gave him a shrug and a guilty-as-sin smile that I was certain he'd see despite the mask. At length, he visibly rolled his eyes and slowly returned the smile.

"Fine pair we make," he muttered, offering me his arm again. "I've never communicated so poorly and so well with someone all at once. It's confounding."

"Any one twist of fate could turn the tables on which of us is the criminal, you know," I pointed out. "I've contracts for my work, remember. And your nation has enemies."

"Aye, but my loyalty's to *one* nation, wolf," he said. "That's the thing about making enemies. When you take contracts across the board, all the world's your enemy. You've no respite at any port, not for very long, anyway. It's foolish. Where do you lie your head? At least I've a home to return to."

"The sea is my home," I said, still smiling, his words not chilling me as he'd perhaps intended. I knew my truth, even if it didn't make sense to him.

He didn't quip back at me, at that. I think I even saw a dash of envy flit over his expression. Maybe it did make sense to him.

"What's all this, then?" he finally spoke again after a prolonged silence. Blew out a breath and arched an eyebrow, I think. Looked me over again, gesturing at the white dog mask, splattered in red. The red-stained, white gloves. The red coat, bedecked in gold buttons and fringe. I'd fancied it up, but it was a good crack at an Amur navy Admiral's coat, I think. "A mockery?"

"A statement," I clarified. I'd intended it as a barb, obviously. But suddenly, I wasn't so sure. "If it *offends* you, that's the point—" I said quickly.

"The bloodstained Amur Navy," he clucked his tongue. "No, wolf. I'm not so easily offended. Bit of a thinker though, isn't it?"

"You got it," I pointed out.

"You know Klaus Richter was a white shepherd."

I stopped dead in my tracks, my heart freezing. I pulled up the mask again. "I didn't," I stammered. "Oh, god. I'm sorry. That wasn't intentional—"

He was laughing. Low, barrel laugh. Deeper and thicker than you'd think for a man of his size. "Under-confidence also doesn't look right on you," he said, crossing the few steps between us and tugging my mask back down.

What a horrific mistake. It isn't even that I hadn't known, I'd done no end of research on Luther when I'd set out to blackmail him. His association with the dead Admiral was *not* a well-kept secret, and I'd known of Klaus while he was still alive. We'd never met, but I knew the man's *breed*. Stupid. Careless.

But Luther wasn't hurt. He wouldn't conceal it if he was, either. It would do him no strategic value to hide something like that from me. He wasn't so brittle, I suppose, but....

Now I felt like shit.

"You're lucky the wound that took his life wasn't to the head or hands, or I'd have *your* life," he joked. I think.

"I believe you," I said with a swallow. I left the mask to rest propped up over one of my ears in case I might need it later, but I was now especially sick of wearing it. I went to unshoulder my coat next, but he stopped me with a hand on mine suddenly.

"Keep it on," he insisted, his voice so very low, a rumble like distant thunder. "Red suits you."

"O-oh…" I said uneasily, slowly shouldering it back on. My unease was not due to what he'd said. Rather, how he'd said it. As I'd opined on since I'd met him, Luther could be maddeningly hard to understand. And now was one of those times. He seemed at once relaxed here, more casual than I think I'd ever seen him. But in the few moments where his eyes were focused on mine and he was looking up at me, muzzle to muzzle, there was some kind of calculation going on there. I knew that particular intensity in him. It's how he looked when he was figuring you out.

I really wished whatever he was trying to see in me, he'd just spit it out. I was having enough trouble understanding myself of late. If there was something particular he wanted to puzzle through, maybe we could take a crack at it together. I had no doubt the man might be better at figuring me out than I was.

This was part of it though, wasn't it? The reason I'd wanted to see him. He was challenging. A real adrenaline rush. A true peer. I think we even complimented each other's stupidest impulses. Which… wasn't a plus. Lotus had once told me we needed to be separated by an ocean for the safety of the world, and I think she'd meant it.

The point is, it was possible whatever it was he was trying to figure out, it was staring us both in the face. Something obvious, but a blind spot we shared. But asking would mean communicating effectively. And that didn't sound like me.

His ears were rigid, I realized suddenly. I'd drifted off while we walked. Lost in a mire of my own thoughts again. My family used to say my head was full of air, like billowing sails.

I bumped him with a toss of my tail, hitting him mid-back due to our height difference. "Rude to ignore your suitor for the evening."

"You've been lost in thought since I complimented you. Overthinking something, no doubt," he said without missing a beat, not even bothering to turn his gaze back towards mine. Just making accurate assessments that cut me to the bone again.

"I thought I'd just leave you to that," he continued, then tugged his arm and my grip on it. "But come forth and help me find our way out of this maze. I hear music."

"They've been playing all this ti– oh," I paused, twisting my own ears up, "yeah, I guess the main ensemble's gotten underway. They're probably in the Grand Hall. Windows are all open tonight, so we're hearing it even out here."

He made a bit of a face as we walked. "They don't worry about insects?"

I chuckled. "The insects were here on this island before the Ocelots settled in, and they'll be here long after all we civilized folk are a thing of the past. Most islanders accept them as a fact of life, rather than shutting themselves into stuffy, sweltering homes like you Amur do."

He still seemed displeased by the idea. "In Amuresca our greatest enemy is no foreign nation. It's the damp. Older than time, that foe. I can't *imagine* leaving my estate open to the elements for so long in this humidity."

"Lord, I keep forgetting you're an elevated nobleman," I remarked. "Gotten accustomed to your fineries, have you?"

The cattle dog only turned briefly to flash me a fanged grin. "Live poor as long as I have, and you'd understand how enticing all those creature comforts can be."

"Oh, I remember," I snorted. "I'm on the opposite trajectory, remember? Don't see much in the way of accommodations other than my cluttered and very *damp* cabin these days."

"It's still the finest cabin on your ship," he reasoned. "Or, I'd imagine it is, anyway. Not that I've ever had an invitation." He almost sounded coy when he said that, and I was briefly proud of him for the bullshit flirtation. He was usually painfully *sincere*. "You know, I really should get more than a distant view, someday. I've earned a private tour, at this point."

"Of my ship or my quarters?" I asked with a smirk and a lean down.

He turned his muzzle towards mine unfettered by the proximity, glaring good-naturedly. And yes, there *was* a difference, especially when you knew his glares well enough.

"Someone needs to teach you a lesson or two about tempting dragons," he said, quoting something from an old poem, I think. I was well-read enough, but it all jumbled together over time. The cattle dog struck me more as the sort of person who had a few favorite books or authors and read them once a year.

"I know m'not welcome on yours, and I got a good enough look the first time around anyway, but you're *always* welcome on my ship, Luther," I sighed, knowing the offer was pointless. At least for now. Maybe someday. "Although this past year, I've had my paws on land, roving the East Coast's lake country and a number of my Father's wealthy contacts," I admitted. "So, been indulging in quite a few creature comforts I used to enjoy, all said. Rubbin' elbows. Got to tap the well for contracts sometimes."

"I'm a Navy man, I wouldn't know. My 'contract' is whatever I'm commissioned to do."

"The debonair ne'er do-well act rings a lot more true these days with that story of me slipping the noose going around, too," I chuckled. "I should thank you. Met a hell of a lady, thanks to all that."

He stopped suddenly when we were about two feet from emerging into the lantern-lit patio outside the open doors to the Hall. Turned on me. And asked, placid and particularly unreadable, "Another woman?"

"Mate, I don't know how to tell you this, but the rumors of me being a rakish man-whore are *pretty* fair."

"Do any of them even matter to you?"

I felt– even though his face still betrayed nothing– that he was weighing what I said here very heavily. I wasn't sure what he wanted to hear, though. For the novelty of its rarity, I went with the truth.

"They all mattered to me," I said, "to varying degrees. Some were just good company, some comrades in my profession or trusted souls. Some I'll see again, some I won't."

"You're never going to wed?" he asked, while looking out towards the patio. People were pairing up here, likely to dance inside. Nearly all men and women together, obviously. Although I spied at least two women arm-in-arm.

"Likely not, no," I confessed. "I'm not the marrying type, as they say. And I wouldn't want to tarnish a woman, or even potentially endanger her, with a legal association to a known criminal."

"It's just as well," he murmured. "Best not to be married to a woman you seem to regard more as a passing fancy or a friendly acquaintance than the love of your life."

"I suppose you'd know," I said, eyeing him.

"My marriage to Delilah offers us *both* protection and the life we want," he said. "It's mutually beneficial."

"But she's not the love of your life."

He looked uncomfortable for a beat, before relenting, "Not in a romantic sense, no. But I do love her, and I regard her very fondly as the mother of my children and an equal partner. We've a comfortable arrangement that suits us both, and," he pointedly looked at me, "that's as deep as I'll go on the subject."

I smiled, glad I'd gotten anything out of him. Even the whole of the time we'd spent together on the hunt for Roccosal, I'd not gotten him to open up much about his marriage or his wife. He seemed to prefer to keep that part of his life private. "I'm glad it's not a loveless marriage," I told him sincerely. "I considered in your position that it might be."

"I'm fortunate," he said ruefully, "compared to others… very fortunate in that regard. Delilah and I were lucky to find each other."

I nodded, looking around the large patio for where we might refresh our drinks or sit, if we were to take our leisure out here for a spell. Listen to the music, maybe watch some dancing through the window. Sounded grand, compared to the night of loneliness I'd been facing not half an hour ago.

"So, no chance of this recent flame making a decent man out of you, then?" he snuffed. "You speak like you were quite taken by her."

"And you're speaking like you want to make sure," I said, arching an eyebrow.

"Would mean a lot less trouble for me if you gave up on all the thieving and murder," he said wryly.

"No such luck, I'm afraid!" I announced chipperly. "No. *God*, no. It was a mutual parting of ways, I assure you. Didn't leave *this* one heartbroken. She was bloody sick of me near the end, in fact—"

"– can't *imagine* why."

"We were both eager to go our separate ways, although we parted amicably enough," I continued. "I to the sea; she wanted to leave the lake country before the winter storms came in. I doubt I'll see her again, but she left me with fond memories. I hope I left her with some, as well."

"I'm sure you did," he admitted, and I felt his eyes on me for a moment even from my side. "You can be charming and engaging, in your own way."

I clapped a paw over my heart. "That's *twice* now you've flattered my ego tonight. I may just die happy. Honestly what has come over you?" Something occurred to me then, and I turned to him, grinning. "Oh, you dour lad. Have you found yourself a fellow, then? Shall I congratulate you? Is that why you were asking *me*?"

He didn't bristle or sputter, as I expected. He was still wearing his mask, so whatever reaction I might have tried to discern, it was made all the harder. But his tail was a traitor, and it gave the slightest sway and dip, which in canine language, meant… shyness? He was being *shy*?

Oh, I had to dig deeper.

When he spoke his voice all but confirmed it. Quiet, reserved. Self-aware. "I'm not certain," he confessed. "Perhaps it's just a passing fancy or a 'trusted soul', as you said."

"That's not so bad, you know," I said, dropping my voice to a kind pitch. "Not every attachment needs to be the soul-rending passion that destroys your life for the lack of it."

"I have trouble… reigning in my passions," he cleared his throat. "But I'll try to remember that. It's good advice." He exhaled slowly, staring back out into the warmly-lit, glowing windows of the Hall. "I am in no doubt of my own attraction– I know myself well enough. But it would be a fraught match, and I'm not certain what he wants. That's a factor I must consider when I have more information."

"Ugh," I groaned, "stop talking about your designs on someone like it's a bloody war game. I know you're an eccentric genius and all, but goddamn. Be normal about this, if nothing else."

"I don't know," he shrugged. "He's eccentric, too. Maybe he'd understand."

"Right," I rolled my eyes. "Hell would freeze over before a man like you could have anything but an aggressive, strange, *awkward* courtship with another aggressive, strange, awkward man. I'll stop fishing, I swear, because I know we've got a history of me usin' information like this against you, but I have to assume… also a seaman, given you've been at sea all season?"

"Mmhh," was his somewhat annoyed response. He was beginning to sound more irritated in general, and I had to assume it was because I was probing too much. But what can I say? I was jealous.

Another man might mean someone like Klaus Richter, who'd take him so deep into the Empire's bosom that we'd be mortal enemies again in no time. I wanted him to be happy, but…

Not at the expense of having him for an enemy again.

"*Try* a more standard approach," I offered. "I know you're sea-poisoned in the brain, and he might be too, but people appreciate the basic gestures of flirtation, no matter who they are. Uh-ah… hang it all, I don't really know what works with men… probably not flowers. Well, maybe. They're a sign of virility here amongst the ocelot islanders, you know. Men wear them too. Anyway. You obviously share a common interest, so… talk about that."

"Mnh-hm."

"Make excuses to find time together, just the two of you. A bit of privacy never hurts, and I suppose that's even easier amongst two men. Less concern for propriety."

"Alright..."

"Any excuse for good times, you know... merriment... spent together. That can open doors. Sharing a drink, a meal, a dance... do your men dance together?"

"Do yours?" he asked curiously.

"Luther, I have men who bunk together," I chuckled. "It's not a Navy ship. The men get good and drunk and dance together sometimes, aye. At port we usually bring women on, but sometimes you're at sea, and it's only th'lads, and the lads want to dance."

"And if he's being particularly stubborn and thick-headed?" he asked impatiently. Uncalled for, if you ask me. I was just trying to help him.

"Be direct," I said. "I know that's a risk for you, given the secret life you have to lead, but for you to even consider an attraction to a fellow, I'd have to assume you feel safe enough with him to... be yourself. Trust your gut. I'd say worst case, it's a no and things are a bit off between you afterwards. I flirt with near everyone in my circle—"

"Oh, is that so?" he asked drily, even though he bloody well knew the answer.

"—so that's just how *all* o'my relationships go," I continued, undaunted. "It's not so bad. Makes life interesting. Besides, only a fool would let something like a pinch of tension between ya ruin the camaraderie you've got now."

The man gave a long-suffering sigh. Emphasis on *long*.

"I know I'm not exactly the most glowing example of courtly behavior," I prattled on— and I *was* prattling now, no denying that, "but you could receive my advice less bitterly, you know. Man to man, I'm genuinely trying to help you out, mate. I know we've got different quarry when it comes to would-be paramours, or... no, wait. That sounds wrong, the way I put it. 'Targets' would be even worse, somehow—"

Hands fixed themselves on my tasseled shoulders and turned me the few inches necessary to face him. I drawled off whatever it was I'd been trying to re-phrase, finding myself face to face with the man. He'd taken his mask off, turning it backwards over his cloak hood, so that he could look me in the eyes. Anxiety spiked, uncertain what this was, why he was looking at me so seriously all of a sudden, and then he–

–bowed, shallowly but sincerely, no mockery I could detect. And offered me an outstretched hand.

I took it before I knew why. Metaphor for my whole life, really.

"What's this, now?" I asked, charmed. I was certainly sporting a dope's smile by then. He was acting so *strangely* tonight. I just couldn't help it.

"A formal request," he said, slowly straightening and nodding a shoulder towards the Hall behind us. "To dance."

"B-wha…?" I laughed through the question, rendering it more of a noise of befuddlement. "Really, truly, and actually?"

"And whatever other synonyms you can cook up," he confirmed. "Do you accept?"

"Are you bloody kidding me? Of course I do," I exclaimed, grinning. "Y'think I'd turn down the chance to do something that outrageously bizarre? With *you?*"

"I don't see what would be so unusual about it, least of all here," he said, glancing around. "On a night like this? That's the point, is it not? To say to hells with tradition, tonight we need not play our usual roles. Besides, you said it's not uncommon on your ship. Two men."

"It ain't that, mate," I hummed, leaning down closer to him and dropping my voice. "It's who we are out there on the water… and I think you know that."

In a silent answer to that, he reached up and slowly re-affixed his mask. Then gingerly, careful not to tangle it in my mane– but good lord, the stuffy bastard was *actually touching my mane*– did the same for me.

"… you're right, of course," I agreed after he'd finished. "Hang it all, aye? C'mon then, devil. Let's dance."

"You certainly have a flair for the dramatic," he muttered as I took his arm again, and we made our way towards the Hall.

"You know your way around the dance floor, I take it?" I asked, as we emerged into the cacophony of light, sounds, and scents, some recognizable, some exotic, *all* intriguing. Especially to two canines.

"Don't expect mastery, but I've enough experience to muddle my way through a few, thanks to my wife," he confirmed.

The massive hall was attached to the gardens and a hot house on one side and was clearly meant to be used in precisely this way: open-air celebrations and gatherings. The ceilings here were as tall as what would be the second story in the rest of the villa and were strung with massive, chained lanterns that could obviously be lowered to be polished and lit. At some point before the festivities, they'd hung streamers, multicolored glass beads, and the fabric leavings of many hues of cloth and ribbons from the garment district. I think the Ocelot family that owned this place was in trade in textiles. Some pigments were only manufactured and dyed right here on these islands, including the deep indigo blue I liked for my tunics. It matched my eyes.

There were tables in here, but not many, pushed to the sides of the hall where people could take their rest and enjoy some of the carafes of wine that were the only foodstuffs on offer in this particular wing. Large, heavy, deep red curtains adorned nearly every wall, pulled and tied aside into great billowing cascades that reminded me of a theater. They were probably meant to cover the enormous windows during the colder months, but with every window open tonight, they made for a lot of small, darker alcoves along the east wall, which I'm certain some folks were taking advantage of.

The wind and string ensemble that had previously been outside was now situated in a corner of the room with a slightly raised dais, and the lilting, fine, almost whimsical melodies of a courtly dance hall took me back for a moment to the many functions I'd attended in my youth. Claustrophobic, uncomfortable affairs that I might have enjoyed more if not for the constant hovering of my family over me, worried the 'excitement of the evening' might cause me to seize. More often than not, it simply kept me from being a part of what little enjoyment was to be had at a formal event.

Not tonight, I told myself silently, and whatever part of my body the disease answered to. *Please not tonight.*

When we got to the floor, the crowd was chattering and talking in between songs, the players taking a quick respite. It gave us a chance to second-guess ourselves, which was only a brief dash of anxiety for me, genuinely uncertain why the cattle dog would want to, well… do this. With me. But I wasn't about to ask and have him re-think whatever impulse he'd had. What a memory this would make! And a tale when I was in my cups at the dining room table with my boys. They'd never fucking believe me, of course.

When the players began to take their seats again and folks started drifting out onto the floor, we hit a snag. Or rather, he seemed to think we had.

"Uh-I..." he paused as we began to reach for one another's hands, and both briefly came at it from the same side. He cursed quietly under his breath before admitting, "They're going through each of the acts of the Harvest Moon's Dream. I don't know the female part well, it's... reversed, and completely different in the refrain, if memory serves."

"I know both parts," I assured him with a smile, switching arms and taking his in mine, underhand. "Did this one a lot as a kid with my older cousin."

He looked me up and over before commenting, "But you're taller."

"And you've never seen some little terrier gentleman swinging an arm over a stooping deerhound lass's ducked head?" I countered.

He guffawed into the crook of his free arm, still smiling when he came away.

"We'll manage," I assured him. "And I think my manhood can take it."

"I've been in doubt of many things with you," he said as we took to the floor, "but never your manhood."

"Oh, my manhood has taken its share of abuse and bullying..." I said with an intentionally mocking tone at my own expense, "... humiliation, *neglect*, lord, so much neglect..."

"That's a real shame," he said, barely keeping his countenance together, trying so very hard to remain straight-faced as we took up our positions.

"... but it always bounces right back, more resolute than ever!"

"The dance is starting," he said around a cough, concealing a low brow laugh. He was still smiling when our hands met to form the arch for the first movement. "You're making it hard for me to keep my poise."

"I'd rather you be happy than poised," I said dismissively, as I easily ducked under our hands and spun into the first turn. He led confidently, as I knew he would. "Your laughter is a rare reward, and I consider it a personal talent to coax it out of someone so severe, but so obviously, sorely needing it."

"You do make me laugh," he confessed quietly. Soft enough I had trouble hearing him over the music and footsteps around us. "I..."

He didn't pause in his words because of the dance. He just seemed to swallow whatever he was going to say, lost for a moment. Maybe trying to decide how to phrase it. I don't know. It was strange but endearing.

"Thank you," he finally settled on. "You're right. I could use more good humor in my life. A lighter heart."

"I'd be able to talk you out of your dour moods more often if we had a relationship that wasn't separated by two oceans and a line of ironsides," I said, chuckling mirthlessly.

"We stand on opposite ends of the law, even still," he said pointedly. "*One* of us would need to cross that divide, and duty and honor bind me—"

"Not so much that you weren't willing to keep my company when we were hunting Roccosal," I said, dipping into the second refrain and coming up to grip his hand again after the spin, my coat-tails and booted spats brushing past his. It was notable only because until then we'd both been handling our footwork with care, not so fluid and practiced as some, certainly, but well enough. In my case because the dance was coming back to me... in his, I had to imagine, because he practiced his footwork for other, more deadly reasons.

We were distracting one another. Dancing closer than we should have to hear each other's voices. Our words were approaching more of the sparring tone I knew so well with him in the past.

"That was an exceptional circumstance," he reasoned, tilting his head, the lantern light flashing in the gold of his eyes. "A mutual enemy, attempted blackmail, I wasn't certain I could trust you out of my sight just yet. It took the planning, travel, and execution of that caper, plus you and I trading a life debt back and forth before I really ever felt I could."

"Trust me?" I grinned, my ears perking.

"Only a fool would trust you," he scoffed, "but to trust that if we parted ways, I'd not have a dagger to my heart the moment I turned my back? Yes."

"Ah," I clutched both of his hands in mine, or rather, was clutched, and we pulled in for the closest full-circle around one another. When the motion was at its zenith, I tipped my muzzle down and said, "So, you trust me with your heart."

Even through his mask, I saw his eyes narrow. The first sign I'd crossed a line. Where the hell those lines lay, I could not tell you. I seemed to stumble over them like tripwires, rarely knowing what I'd said that would set off his more aggressive nature. This had been innocuous, a teasing joke. But when our hands brushed one another again, I could feel the warning even through his touch. His claws tightened on my knuckles. Not enough to hurt, but that wasn't the point. It was a warning shot.

"Why do you say things like that?" he demanded. "If you don't mean them."

"It was a question, mate," I reminded him. "I meant to get an answer, that's all."

"You don't actually want me to answer it," he growled. The couple dancing to our right, the mouse in particular, caught the growl and shied away from him.

"You're scaring the other dancers," I pointed out, lowering my voice.

I could feel in his countenance how frustrated he was, and I was genuinely trying to ease it. But I also liked seeing the man flustered. Those two facts were at war with one another, and the conundrum was delightful, I won't lie.

"If I told you right now," he pressed out, "that I would consider… trusting you… to that extent… what would you even do with that? Joke about it?"

"I'd be honored by it," I said in a single breath. "And then, I'd ask you again why there must be so much in the way of us having a real friendship."

"You are a *criminal.*"

"You're a criminal when it suits you," I said fearlessly, lifting my muzzle a moment. "The very nature of who you are is criminalized in your home nation. Look, we both have convictions. You keep asking me to set aside mine, but I'm *not* asking you to set aside yours. I'm just asking if the blood-soaked Empire you've sworn yourself to really *aligns* with those convictions of yours. And if not, why it has your loyalty."

I saw a flash of his fangs, not directed at me but his own lower lip, as he bit back something. He moved into the next motion, silent for a spell, before finally coming back with, "A friendship, then? That's what you want?"

"It would be a start, being able to call you that," I said, inclining my head down at him as we drew close again. It did not escape my notice how this dance had us retreating from and drawing close to one another again and again. Poetic.

"To what end?" he asked tiredly. "We cannot be long in one another's company without it being a literal national scandal."

"You came to this place to be with me tonight of your own volition despite that fact," I said, attempting through my words to let him know how much that had meant to me.

"Aye, I did," he said tensely. "And here we are at square one again. Barbing and baiting one another, arguing while we literally dance around the subject at hand."

I laughed because he was being so *serious* and because it's one of the things I did when I was nervous. "What's the 'subject' again?" I asked. "Sort of lost the thread."

"You cannot possibly be this obtuse," he said, blinking rapidly. "You invited me here tonight, which marks the *second* time you've issued me a private invitation for a meeting between us, I'll point out. I refuse to believe this isn't just another of your games, and I don't appreciate being *toyed* with if it isn't."

"Right," I clucked, "you prefer to be the only one toying with your prey."

"If I saw you as prey, you'd be dead," he promised me with no malice, just infinitely serious, factual belief in his abilities to do just that. It sent a chill down my spine, but I'd long since found the man's threats more... exciting... than frightening. "Why did you even send for me to come here? What is all of this about, really?"

"I swear to you, there isn't some ulterior motive," I promised earnestly. "I just wanted to see you again."

"Why?" he pressed, for some reason not content enough with that. What more did the man want from me? I was telling him the truth, and he was pushing back against me like I was hiding something.

Wait, was I hiding something?

"Because I'm... fond of your company?" I said, certain that was obvious, but saying it nonetheless.

"Why here?" he asked, tugging me in tight suddenly until our noses nearly bumped. It was far closer than the dance required, and he held me through what should have been a turning step, breaking the line of otherwise mostly orderly dancing. No one cared at a function like this, but it made us stand out for a few seconds, which I assumed he'd want to avoid, so I tried to hurry us back into the next movement. "Why during a festival such as this? Did you only wish to meet with me when we could pretend we were each someone else?"

"I'm not ashamed of wanting to see– or be seen– with you," I said, narrowing my brows. "That's *your* issue, remember? Trying to spare *your* honor and *your* reputation doesn't mean I'm embarrassed by you or anything about you."

"You don't have the same concerns I do," he said bitterly. "The same declarations of heresy and scorn leveled at you for something you cannot help."

"No, I wouldn't know a bloody *thing* about how that feels, would I?" I raised my voice slightly as our line neared closer to the instruments. I was glad for the din, as it would mostly mask our conversation from anyone nearby. "Being accused of possession, of demonic corruption of my mind *and* body, and how cursed, and broken, and *unfortunate* a soul I am from the time I'm a wee pup–"

His posture and ears fell back, his tone going with it. "I'm... sorry. I... I'm just unpracticed at this, frustrated, and I'm not thinking clearly before I speak."

"You're frustrated?" I whuffed out humorlessly. "You keep asking me the same questions over and over again as if you're expecting a different answer. Believe it or not, I didn't want to spend m'whole night with you arguing, mate. I know that's our usual fare, but..."

"What were you hoping we'd do together tonight, then?"

He'd asked it in another growl, but this one was different. Smoother, quieter, meant only for my ears. My stomach clenched, a pulse of tension going through me. I tried to literally laugh it off.

"Well, I know what my men would think this rendezvous was about, if any of them knew I was here meeting you tonight," I said, grinning lasciviously.

He did not take the bait with annoyance or anger this time. Instead, he merely arched an eyebrow and asked during one of the pauses as we waited for the other dancers to move around us, "You're here alone? You never travel alone. Is that safe for you? Given..."

"I informed the Captain of the passenger ship I took to come here," I said. "Just in case. I know the man, vaguely. I stayed with him and his deckhands for the last few days. And I… had some doubts, but ultimately, I knew you'd come. I knew I wouldn't be alone for long. I know you'll look after me if my health fails me tonight."

He tilted his head, staring at me through that dark mask for a few long moments, before asking, "Doesn't that mean you trust me with *your* heart?"

I smiled warmly. "I suppose it does."

He blew out a breath. "It's so easy for you, isn't it?"

"You've known I was easy since the first day we met," I crooned at him. "Don't act all surprised, now." I took the opportunity of one of those close pull-ins to press into his personal space and place a hand on the small of his back. It was a part of the dance reserved for married couples, but most of the people here were doing it regardless. Because most of them had designs on one another. Thus far, Luther and I hadn't partaken of that, preferring to keep a more respectful distance, as we would have at a formal event.

I expected a shove or a jostle, of course. Like before. Like always. He always rebuffed my flirtation and goading. Save that one time….

But he didn't. Instead, his own hand– and with it, his ironclad grip– found the small of my back, just above the split in my coat that made way for my tail. When I made to step into the next turn, he held me there, unmoving. I watched as the other dancers proceeded, and we once again were the odd men out. I might've said something about it, but he spoke first.

"It's easy for you," he said, "because it isn't real… to you. It's entertainment, it's a *joke*. A laugh had at my expense because the way I feel for other men, to you. Though you might not hate it, you do find it absurd."

"No, mate," I tried to assure him, "just because I don't fancy men th'way you do doesn't mean I think of your feelings as absurd."

"Then why can't you take this seriously?"

"I'm laughing mostly at myself," I assured him. "It's not that men flirting or courting is ridiculous, it's just… it's because it's *me*. I'm a buffoon. I'm a fool. It's the thought of a man of your stature having to put up with a fellow like me that entertains me. I mean. Imagine. Not for nothing, cattle dog, but you could do *better*."

"I wish you thought more well of yourself," he said, voice threadbare. "Do you really think me so egotistical as to assume I am so far above you?"

"Mate, I'm pretty sure I pissed on both of us when I seized in that box. When we met, I was shitfaced and tied to a bed. I'm an ill, loathsome, no-good blighter. You *could* do better, I promise ya. Y'got this flame you're chasin' in the Navy–"

"How is this not mocking *both* of us, again?"

"I can't help how you take it, but I'm not intending to mock you," I insisted. "I'm just… naturally flirtatious, and I mix it with my humor out of habit. And anyway, nothing I've said isn't true. It's just," I had to correct myself before a huff turned into another nervous laugh– because that's what they were now, pure nerves, "easy to interpret so much'a what transpires between us as…."

He shook his head. "You can't even finish the words."

"I'm trying not to 'joke' about it, or whatever it is I'm doing that's pissing you off so much. It's just a real mess in my mind, mate. Hard to put to words."

"It wouldn't be so fucking confusing if you meant half of what you said," he snapped.

"I *do* mean it! I mean every bloody word!" I insisted, lost. "I wanted to see you tonight. Terribly so. That's why I invited you here. I did so on this eve because I knew we could meet anonymously, and that matters to you. I *do* trust you, with my health, with my heart… fuck, how could I not trust the man that saved me from the gallows? You've held my life in your hands, and I dove through bullets with your lifeless body in my arms into enemy territory, I've *seized* trapped in a pine box with you, and we hold secrets between us no other rotten soul in the world knows. Memories that'll light up my brain in the last few fleeting seconds I'm alive. You, and a sunset after a night of rain, in one perfect fucking moment of shared awe at the majesty of the world… that might be the last thing I ever remember, Luther."

I was out of breath by the time I was done, and when I spoke again, hoarse. "If that isn't worth something, what is?" I asked quietly.

The dance had ended, I realized belatedly. We'd long since gotten to the last refrain, and soon after we'd stopped, the others around us had begun to dissipate off the dance floor, amidst polite clapping for the players and the renewed thrum of conversation all around us.

Luther removed his mask slowly and pulled it round to rest to the side over the hood of his cloak. The Hall was only lit from above by the lanterns, and we were near the farthest end where the light was dim and shifting with stray color from the streamers overhead. Despite being the only two men dancing together on the floor, despite our muffled arguing, there seemed to be a mutually agreed-upon pact here amongst the party-goers. Keep your nose in your own business. No one would recognize us here. No one would know us.

"I wish you understood how your declarations absolutely rend through me," he whispered fiercely. "You don't understand… you don't even see… what words like that *mean* to a man like me. You just feel, openly, and share of yourself, openly, without fear. Never mind the consequence, or the fool I'd be to accept them." He swallowed thickly. "You don't even know what you're offering."

"Make me a counter-offer, then," I said, my hand lingering on his coat. "Rules of engagement. How is it you think we ought to go on with one another?"

"Rules of engagement," he repeated, his eyes beginning hidden calculations. Risk, reward, cost, payoff. Whatever dangers he was considering.

"Aye, you're the one who prefers to plot your life out like a war plan," I muttered. "Just trying to put things in terms you'd appreciate, since we're having trouble communicating, it seems."

Something heavy settled against my chest, pressing into me. It took me a moment to realize it was his palm planted between the lapels of my coat, against my sternum. When I tipped my muzzle down, his eyes locked onto mine, and without the mask there, it was inescapable. He had me.

I found myself moving backwards at his direction. The guidance was clear, but subtle, our outfits doing much to conceal the way I was being manhandled towards the nearest alcove of dark cover. I realized in the seconds it took us to pass the few other bodies in this wing of the room, but before my back hit the wall, that I was being led to one of those invisible pockets between the massive folds of gathered, crimson curtains. Private, but still so very, very public.

My instincts rose, as we reached the unyielding sensation of cold stone against my back– I could feel it even through my coat and tunic. I was cornered, enveloped on all sides by thick, muffling red velvet, only somewhat concealing the continued sounds of strangers all around us. A dim flicker of light past his shoulders and the triangles of his ears was all that lit this sanctum he'd boxed me into. I could still see him exceedingly well, though. Just enough light for canine eyes. But little enough that I could see the hint of shine in his irises. Red.

I let my breath out because I hadn't realized I'd been holding it, unsure what any of this was or what I should say, do, assume. I knew what would be expected of me if a woman had led me off like this, but....

"You wish for me to be direct?" he asked, his deep voice quiet, but as firm as the wall against my spine. "Fine. I'm accustomed to being in command these days, and some men do better with discipline than a soft hand. Just know up until now, I was trying to be *kind*."

"Well, you *know* my feelings on 'discipline'–" I began in a breathy voice.

He cut me off. "First. Do not engage in flirtation or lurid talk with or about me unless you have the temerity to follow through on your offers," he said. "I would think you would have learned that already on Dokuro, but maybe you need another lesson." His hand eased up off my chest for only a moment, then he hooked his fingers around the edge of my waist belt and *pulled*... the only remaining inch left between us closing. He'd moved, too, his thigh now firmly between my legs. It was the beginning of a grappling lock I knew from experience and too many restless afternoons spent aboard a small sailing vessel with him and Lotus. She'd been all too enthusiastic to encourage the two of us to wrestle for her enjoyment. I'd lost more than I'd won and nearly always come away with bruises, but it had been worth it for the memories.

Right now, he had that thigh wedged right where I would be feeling a whole lot of pressure if this was– again, with a woman– but...

Actually no, parts of me *were* waking up, albeit warily. Alright. New thing to consider later. Confusing right now, but worth returning to when I wasn't so–

"I mean," I hiccupped back a breath of air, smiling unsteadily, "I'll try anything twice. Three times just to be sure."

"Second," his grip tightened on my belt, the leather creaking in his palm, "answer this *straight*, no deflecting, no baiting me, just tell me what's in your heart, so I can settle this for myself... and move on."

I held my breath.

When he asked, he sounded more tired than demanding. Like he was expecting to be let down. "Why did you send for me to come here? To an anonymous event on an island no one would know us on? What were your intentions? Is this really about friendship? Because... you have been driving me mad, *all night.*"

"Oh," I uttered quietly. The man's meaning finally sunk in.

"What do you want our relationship to be, Grayson?" he asked, blinking slowly up at me. "I have been asking myself that since I got your invitation, and after two hours spent here with you, I am still not sure."

I hung my head slowly, the fur along his brow tickling my nose. "I'm not sure, either," I finally confessed, lost. "Can two men like us be close... in *any* way?"

"Perhaps in rare moments," he said hesitantly. Wary as a man with a blade to his throat. Even he realized the odds. "Stolen time. I would make it, find it, if you were likewise inclined to, but as to what shape it would take...."

He was silent. Far too long. The urge to speak, to say *anything* to fill that silence, was absolutely clawing at my throat.

"Are you... likewise inclined?" he finally asked.

"I... don't know," I eventually stuttered out. A bubble of a laugh, the wicked thing, not intentional nor born of any real humor, nearly derailed me doing the one decent thing here– answering the man. I knew his predilection. I should have *known* what this invitation might signal to someone. Someone I'd been so intimately connected to in the past.

Of *course* he was confused.

And I wasn't faring any better.

"I just wanted to see you again," I said plaintively. "I didn't think... I didn't have a plan, mate. I don't *feel* this way about people, near ever. Normally I'm content to part with those I find a kinship with, and know if we're meant to see each other again, we will. But I just couldn't bear it. It's been a year. Have y'ever felt this way? Like there's a tide towing you back towards someone, and you don't stop to ask 'why not'? I just know we're meant for something."

His eyes were the color of the moon. All I wanted was to remember that color, if nothing else from tonight.

"Yes," he said, his breath warm on my whiskers. "I've felt that way before."

Oh, shit, my mind reeled. *He* wasn't uncertain, that was for damn sure. My thoughts stumbled like a drunkard through every dashing contradiction. What was I considering? Was I going to discard a lifetime of my previous conceptions of myself and see where this led? Was that *wise*? Was it what I'd actually been hoping for, all night? Is that why I'd felt this insatiable urge to provoke the man, despite knowing the cruelty in that, despite thinking it ludicrous he'd ever actually call my bluff?

He had once before. But we'd been so new to one another then, so wildly reckless with how we treated each other and antagonized one another, it was... it had just been a bit of fun.

Hadn't it?

I'd never felt any real, sustainable attraction to another man before. Was he an exception, for some reason?

God, he was so close. We'd been closer in that coffin, sure, but not like this. Not with our hips slotted together, his claw-tips hard against the inside hem of my trousers. Just above my navel now, keeping some decency in his touch, as forceful as it was. Too high on my body to feel how I was reacting to him— to this whole situation. He couldn't understand how his domineering, demanding presence, and the firm crush of his thigh between mine, was driving me to distraction. It would be all too easy for him to discover, though. If he worked his paw down just a bit further, if he shifted just-so, if he loosened my belt....

"This isn't a game," he growled, not angrily, but his voice was so *low* right now. "Maybe to you, but not to me. This is usually the part where things get serious, in fact."

I swallowed again. The things this man would *do* to me, if I gave him the all clear. The reality of how *close* I was to opening that floodgate, to all the potential chaos it could bring, I just had to....

"I'm going to do this one more time," he said, voice even and calm. "But I want you to know that this time, it isn't some petty punishment for your antics. It isn't to put you in your place. It's real."

I had felt things were headed this way for some time— since he first pushed me into this quiet, hidden spot— and our noses had been near brushing through the whole of the last few minutes. It was nothing, a bare inch of movement for him to connect our muzzles... finally... in the kiss we'd been working up to. But I'll be damned if I was prepared for it, nonetheless. No more so than I had been the first time, even though I'd felt this one coming.

He'd said it would not be like the first, and he was a man of his word. The first— and only— time we'd done this in the past, it had not been a kiss. It had been an attack. An aggressive clashing of muzzles, teeth, and tongues... that last bit mostly on my part. I would always still count it as a kiss because it was worth that much for bragging rights alone. But it wasn't the genuine article. Because Luther... as I was being educated on, right now... did not kiss like that. Not when he meant it.

This was the real thing, and I hadn't been prepared for how *gentle* it would be. How he'd cup the fringe of my jaw and urge me into it, tipping my frozen form into the roll of his muzzle, the slow curling of his tongue over mine, as it moved past my fangs. Bleeding moon, he'd even worked his claws through the fur along the nape of my neck, fixing into a guiding, firm grip at the base of my mane.

I would have given him anything in that moment. It didn't matter, none of it mattered. Not my convictions, who we were, the fact that we were both men... nothing mattered in comparison to the utter relief, the heavy, settling catharsis, of being treated with such care, with such *passion*.

I wasn't sure what I wanted between us, but it was safe to say I wanted this. This feeling of knowing I mattered, of showing him *he* mattered. I didn't think this is how I'd find it... and maybe... maybe this was the wrong vessel. I still wasn't sure. There were so many reasons left that this wouldn't work, couldn't work, or shouldn't work. But right now, it was good. It was *so* good, and I didn't even consider it ending, not for a second. We'd just do this, until such time as we figured out what the hell else we were supposed to be doing.

I was thoroughly blind, deaf, and dumb, renewing each roll and sup of our muzzles with increasing vigor, when he finally wouldn't let me anymore and eased back. I was left with my jaw hanging open.

"Lu…." I licked at my teeth, slumping against where he was holding me. "Y'can't just leave it there, mate… y'can't…."

But when I leaned back in, his eyes were sharp, and his words stopped me where our breaths intertwined.

"If you initiate, this isn't a joke anymore, wolf," he said, voice solemn and clear. "It's real. And we need to start treating it as such."

Panic overwhelmed me. Fear, not excitement but real, gut-wrenching fear. My mind spun through the possibilities, the disastrous consequences, contended with the reality of not just the physicality of all of this, but how it would doubtless change the course of our lives. He was asking me a serious question, and I wouldn't get more of what I wanted until I answered it. And lying to appease my needs right now would carry heavy consequences.

I froze.

And he saw it.

"… no," he said softly, slowly leaning away, his brows lifting. "The answer is no, then?" He didn't sound shocked or sad, just painfully unsurprised.

"I-I'm not," I stumbled over my words, "sure? I'm just… I know I wish us to be closer, and I understand I've… I've sent the wrong signals, I've unwittingly fished you along, and it's right you're– we're both confused–"

"The 'wrong' signals," he closed in on the worst part of what I'd said.

"I'm just saying words, mate," I said helplessly. "Don't go holding 'em against me, now. I meant that I've been treating you how I treat most folk I want to be closer with, but until now most of those folk've been *women*, so–"

"You think I don't understand what this confusion is like?" he asked plainly, pulled back enough now that I could see all his features. He looked sympathetic, actually. Not condemning, as I'd thought. Not angry.

"You've never seemed confused over your wants," I said. "Not on this subject."

"Not in a long time." He shook his head. "But I remember being thirteen… fourteen… fifteen… even my twenties, time to time. Contending with this inner war between my desires and my self-repulsion, second guessing if it's earnest or degeneracy, bulwarked always by shame and the fear others would know and judge me for it. Then the confirmation of all your fears... when they do."

I knitted my brows. "I'm not repulsed by the thought, mate. Quite th'opposite."

"As liberal and open-minded as you are," he said with a flash of fang when he smiled, "you're not any more immune to the social pressures around us, the way we were raised, or the worry of the very real danger and condemnation out there. You can say you're bolder in the face of it than I– and maybe that's true. But you're not unaffected by it."

"Fine," I agreed with a grit of my teeth and a stiff groan, as I tried to ease my hips into a less precarious position. But despite his trepidation, he hadn't let me go, yet. I was still very much pinned, and any movement was only making my current condition worse. "But that's not why I'm... uncertain... now. You're just so *intense*. M-maybe... maybe if we just fooled around a bit, I'd get a feel for it and decide whether any of this works for me, y'know? You're askin' me if I'm *serious*, and I don't really *do* serious, whether it's men or women–"

He sighed. "You're drunk, in any case. I don't know why I expected a real answer. I couldn't hold you to it, regardless."

"I am barely tippin', mate. I'm *fine*." I objected. "And if you think you've had anything but the rare sober discussion with me, I've got bad news for you."

He caught me by surprise– for the third time, damn it all! And leaned in to kiss me again then, his whiskers and breath a bare tickle before our muzzles were open to one another once more. I didn't question it, just soaked it in, my eyes slipping upwards and closed, a whine edging on a groan rumbling between us, answered in kind by him, as I abandoned any and all decorum and let the subtle motion of our breaths answer a burning need for friction in my lower extremities. I was grinding against him to the barest degree, but with all our layers of clothing between us, I wasn't sure he even realized it. Anything more than this would've been new territory for me, but kissing other men wasn't exactly new... nor was a helping hand. It's just there was usually a woman involved, somewhere.

And none of those men had been Luther Denholme.

I was edging myself into some sort of blissed-out oblivion, and it truly didn't occur to me how much I'd let the mixture of tension, excitement, physical domination, and the rawness– the possibility– of something new, wind me up until I felt with a certainty like missing a step and falling that the floor was coming out from under me. It was too late by the time I'd realized it. I gasped into the kiss and everything sharpened to a fine, blinding point for but a moment, before the ephemeral waves of my own body's relief washed over me, sending me to shuddering.

I'd never been more glad for the layered, heavy, suffocating outfit. If I'd been in my usual wear, I'd have one coat over perhaps a surcoat or light shirt, and trousers. Maybe leather on a good day. But I'd done up the theme of the costume by wearing all the needless smallclothes and layers the Amur Pedigree insisted upon. And it was all that was protecting my shame– and the slick now coating the inside of my smallclothes– anymore. Surely, he'd still feel….

He seemed too absorbed in the kiss. We were still locked in it, although I felt him drawing away, and not just our muzzles now, but his pressure was easing off my body, as well. No, no, no… it should have been what I wanted, especially given what had just happened, but….

His muzzle parted from mine long enough for his palm to stroke up over my cheek ruff and hold me there while he looked at me. Made sure I looked at him. When he spoke his voice was heated, but quiet.

"I don't fool around where lovers are concerned, wolf," he said.

"Bullshit," I said, my voice coming out more hoarse and thin than I'd wanted it to. Thankfully the man had never heard me cum before (at least not to my knowledge, but we'd shared a ship together for a while, so who knew) or he'd perhaps realize why. Instead, he merely arched an eyebrow at me, and I pushed through, finding my voice to explain, "Stop acting like you're some courtly protagonist from a romance rag– you hire prostitutes! It's how we *met.*"

He sighed. "You aren't literally a whore, Grayson."

"I just don't see why this's any different, is all."

"Because…" he took a moment, "… you are who you are, and I am who I am. And I intend to see you again, work together again, perhaps… sail together again."

I held my breath. He *couldn't* know.

"You don't seem certain on what you want—"

"You have *no* idea how off you are, mate. I never really know what I want, but right now—"

"—and I won't endanger our already fraught kinship any further on a lark. It's *because* I value what we are now," he insisted, looking at me intensely. His gaze drifted after a moment though, unlike him, to a spot on the floor between our feet. When he spoke again, it was far quieter. Meant only for my ears… as if anyone could hear what we'd been saying or doing back here. "And… because the first man I was permissive with was far less amenable to my second-guessing myself and took liberties beyond what I was ready for. It put me off entrusting control to another to this day."

My ears fell back. "Mate…" I said sadly.

"If you find yourself earnestly drawn to me in that way, in time, perhaps we revisit this," he said. "Soberly, in good conscience, and with no leverage between us. But not with panic in your eyes. Not with quaking in your arms. I won't have it that way. I won't have the weight of a mistake that grave between us."

I flexed my claws against the tile floor, duga canine into my lower lip, and looked away from him. "Why is everything with you so bloody difficult?" I nearly whispered.

"I'm in the right here, and you'll realize it in time," he assured me, his fingers drifting down my arms as he finally stepped away from me.

"I realize it now," I assured him bitterly. "You're always damnably right. Where are you going?"

"To avail myself of the pleasantries on offer here," he said, staring out past the curtain into the warm light and drifting, merry sounds of the dance hall and villa beyond. "It's rare I have a chance like this, you know. The anonymity, the lack of a minder, or duties to keep me busy…"

"All the gorgeous, liberated men," I coughed.

"Indeed," he agreed with a slight smile. "Do you mind if I abscond for a few hours by myself? We can arrange to meet afterwards. I am not abandoning you, I just—"

"No, I get it," I said ruefully. "This is awkward."

"You and I are often awkward together. It's not that."

"I actually find it rather easy to be around you," I confessed.

"It is an agony to me that so much separates us, out in the world. I want to know you better."

"… I was just going to say that I thought you might also wish to blow off some steam," he reasoned. "Get a load off, and we'll both be more at ease when we reunite."

I laughed breathlessly, although he couldn't have known why. "You can't have meant that as crudely as it came out."

"I'm a sailor as well, lad," he smirked. "I surely did." He turned crisply and waved a hand at me as he headed off out of our curtained hideaway. "There are endless throngs of beautiful women here. Find me once you've disappointed as many as you please."

"Bastard," I grumbled, slumping back against the wall. The final insult hadn't been necessary… I already liked him plenty.

* * *

I moved through the villa in a fog, following that. Found my way at some point, almost accidentally, to a wash room and a basin I could somewhat tidy up at. It seemed rather pointless, honestly. It was nearly dry by then and staining the inside of my mockery of an Amurescan Naval outfit with my shame was fitting in a way I couldn't quite put my finger on.

The haze clouding my mind, divorcing me from any meaningful interaction with the party at this point, was comprised unsurprisingly of every intense moment I'd just spent narrowed into that quiet, suffocating linen den with Luther. We could have made a memory there that would have changed the course of history, I was convinced. Not to mention our own personal fates, irrevocably.

Every time I met a new, enchanting pair of foreign eyes or took notice of a charismatic person of interest in a new port, each new conquest with a woman whom I could convince somehow I was worth her time… there was always an apex moment of the night I'd think on for years afterwards. My cousin had once told me I would never marry, would never settle down, because I was the type who loved all the world too much to give the whole of myself to any one person. A very charitable way of saying I was loose and noncommittal. But the longer I lived, the truer it rang. With so many incredibly diverse, compelling, beautiful people out there to meet, to know, carnally or otherwise, it was unthinkable to me that I might give up all the rest for one, and one alone. And I genuinely did not think that would ever be challenged.

But Luther did not strike me as one who would tolerate the shifting, unstable soil of shared fidelity. He was too severe and, moreover, too wounded to portion out his attachment as I did. I could see glimpses, when he let me, of the life that had led to the bulwark the man had constructed around his heart. I could not rationalize— would never dare even try— to fight the cattle dog on his principles for the sake of slaking my own curiosity and wants.

But now they were *there*, and there was no denying their volume and the intensity with which I yearned to have answers.

I gazed around the hall I'd found myself in, smaller than the main dance area. More private. I was still in the guest wing, but the doorway in this piano room led into the warm light of the inner quarters. A boar protected the doorway, draped in red and wearing a fiery-colored mask. He was there to assure the guest rooms were only occupied to capacity and to prevent anyone from bothering those already using them. The family that owned this villa brooked no violation of the terms of the holiday. It was as important to them as propriety in Amur society.

I didn't care about being recognized, but I was feeling oddly raw and exposed, given the events of the night. Not to mention randy. The lasciviousness eating away at my coherency had become an intense frustration, as my mind spun through not only recent events, but those that had not played out, and my imagination was running riot with what I'd been denied. I felt nearly sick from the thoughts assaulting me, and what they said about my shameless, feral brain, residing beneath whatever civility normally kept me in check.

It wasn't that I was ashamed of my natural curiosity and lust, not even where another man was concerned. More... that he was a friend. Or at least, I wanted him to be so. And the visage of him my mind constructed in these imagined fantasies could not possibly be accurate or respectful.

But then, I didn't know for sure, did I? And I likely never would.

That right there was the kernel of frustration. I could tolerate being told 'no' when it was something I'd be able to pursue at some future date or a pleasure I'd tasted once before. But the *unknown*. The unknown was what drove all sailors to their end. And so, it would be here, if I did not answer that call inside.

Luther may have known himself, may have been assured of his own truth, but he didn't know me entirely as well as he thought. It wasn't a disastrous, awkward row between us that would drive us apart, we'd had our share of that and nothing had taken. It was this– this frustration, this gnawing open question– that would drive me to make some kind of far worse, hurtful mistake. If not with him, then with *someone*, I... I needed to know.

I needed to know. That was all there was to it.

My subconscious had been stirring this pot of thoughts for what had probably amounted to an hour by now, as I drank deeper from my measures cup. I barely knew what, anymore. I'd been refilling it in each room, with whatever was on offer. The world was getting fuzzy around the edges, but there was no denying where my eye-line had fallen and rested for some time now.

A small group of ocelots, denizens of the island no doubt, sat collected on a chaise lounge by one of the large, open bay windows in this piano room. The room itself had become a collecting spot, rather like a bend in a gutter, for people filtering through the party. It was somewhat crowded and buzzing with chatter and laughter, removed from the stronger odors of the dining tables and the overwhelming noise of the string ensemble and dance hall. It was the perfect place to mingle and talk, while still being surrounded by enough voices that your particular conversation would be drowned out for all but the closest to hear.

Which is why the prostitutes had chosen to gather here.

I was absolutely certain the three felines, draped in silks and inexpensive but eye-catching jewelry, were here working. For one, they weren't wearing masks, and, as denizens of the island, that was notable. They wanted their wares– namely their beauty– put on full display.

One, the most voluptuous and mature of the two women, was already leaning partially against the larger, heavier-set figure of a harbor seal. A man with money, but still a working sailor, by the look of him. Probably a merchant.

The other two ocelots were young but not overly-so, lean but soft around the edges like they led easier lives than many of the workers and fishing families here. Their coats were distinctive, especially around the eyes, in a way that suggested they might be of the same clan or even siblings. One male, one female, the latter of which had adorned her chest with nothing but jewelry. Or, well, actually... that was both of them. The male had piercings somewhere beneath the soft, pale fur on his chest, as well.

... and he'd just caught me staring at them.

I blinked, surreptitiously trying to look elsewhere for a few seconds, before feeling more than seeing his gaze draw mine back in his direction. His eyes were wide and golden-brown, hard to ignore. He had a river of spots down the center of his forehead, banked on each side by wider black bands, and two inky black stripes along either cheek, following the curve of his sleek, handsome face. Gold adorned his nose in a small bead, peppered his ears, and dripped down his forehead in a chained crown. He wore bracelets and anklets of a similar hue and a long, elegant lavender silk sarong, fringed in gold.

I was admittedly particularly attracted to the color gold today, but it was a safe bet that many mariners were, and the intentionally thought-out lure was working. As I watched, the fellow leaned over and subtly elbowed the female feline to the left of him, whose slender neck and ears snapped quickly in my direction with interest. Within moments, the both of them were smiling at me.

It was as plain an invitation as ever I'd seen. They were here looking to ply their craft, and I was considering a shift in my life's course that might lead to profound and lasting consequences... so why not?

I swallowed, as I drifted across the hall towards them. I'd never hired a molly boy before. The closest I'd say I'd ever come was the fennec fox I'd had on when I'd first intended to blackmail Luther and a few times when we'd had one or two visit our ship. Men weren't unknown in my bed, but that had more to do with my desire to share and double up— or more so— in my pursuits with women.

I considered the man before we were within speaking range, once more. I liked felines. I especially liked felines with spots, although don't ask me to explain that one. There was something more predatory about it, I suppose. Like the dappling on some sea beasts. I was a man who desired to be at the mercy of my partners, and cats did that for me in spades. Especially big feline ladies.

This fellow wasn't particularly large or filled-out. I probably had a head on him, if not more. But that didn't exclude anyone really, it was just a pattern of mine I'd noticed. I'd say in other cases it came down to personality, but that wouldn't matter much with a pro. He was beautiful in the regard most would appreciate: clean and fit, well-groomed, well-dressed. And when he stood, at last, he moved with that sultry grace I so appreciated in felines. His figure even sported some curves, with a slightly rounded belly and hips and a softer chest, accented by what I was now certain were gold piercings on dark areolas, barely concealed by his puffy fur. The ocelots on this island were growing in their thicker coats, readying for the somewhat colder seasonal storms ahead. He'd be fun to pet.

But everything– everything about the woman to the left of him– answered the siren song in my heart to a greater degree. She was similar in appearance in most ways, save slightly darker eyes, and a more curvaceous figure in all the places I was most drawn to. She was small-chested, but I still very much would have liked to get my paws on those. And maybe I would. The choice hadn't been fully made yet, after all....

I took the coward's way out, as I drew closer to them. They came first, stepping up to me and extending a hand, which I hesitantly received. He opened his mouth to say something, and I just blurted it out, before he even had a chance to attempt to charm me.

"Do you two beauties ever work together?" I asked.

It was crude. Blunt. I may have been drunker than I thought. But all the two ocelots did was glance briefly at one another as though I'd asked for nothing more scandalous than directions before the woman replied, "Of course, Admiral. We'd be overjoyed to grace your bed tonight."

They knew who I was. It wasn't surprising, but it briefly caught me off-guard. They clearly wanted me to know that they knew who I was, as well. As if to say 'you're known, so take care'. I was a criminal, after all. A well-received criminal in a place like this, but all the same.

That also meant they knew I had money and explained why they'd been so positively-inclined over catching my attention. It's not like that offended me. Commerce was commerce, regardless of the profession, and that's exactly why I was here, after all.

I cleared my throat and fished out the chartruc coin I'd had in my pocket all this while, holding it up for the two of them to see. Their eyes widened marginally, the rare currency apparently registering with them.

"The family and I are business relations," I explained. "We go back a ways. I can get us past the guest wing into the upper chambers, if that suits. At that point the silver's yours, and the room's yours once I leave for the night... I don't intend to sleep here. Whatever use you deem it fit for within reason. The family won't mind so long as you're discreet."

The male ocelot smiled at me and bowed his head to press his nose to my ring finger, elegantly. "Camilo," he said in a soft purr. "I am yours for the eve, sir."

"Let me guess," I glanced at the woman. "Camila?"

She laughed lyrically. "He's heard this one before."

"You're not actually related, are you?" I asked warily. "I come from too many lineages of cousins marrying to find any novelty in siblings kissing."

She shrugged, smirking. "Some like to imagine. No... different islands, in fact. And we're more than happy to engage with one another for your viewing pleasure or both be of service to you, at your leisure. Please feel free to fully communicate your imaginings for the evening, and we will endeavor to fulfill them."

I sighed, offering an arm to both of them. "Alright," I began, "here's the thing..."

* * *

I'd long been in the graces of the family here since a good trade we'd brokered together and the elimination of a troublesome rival cartel. The latter of which I'd only had a hand in, but enough of a contribution that they considered me a lifelong ally. The trade of the dead chartruc currency for one of the upstairs suites was a secret known only to their trusted, but a yearly tradition. Tonight, I'd gotten one of the smaller family rooms, likely meant for one of their children when they'd been young. But it was elegant and spacious enough for the three of us, including the four-poster near a balcony veranda. The moon was out, the sky was unobstructed, I recognized the constellation overlooking us, and the night insects sang.

Distantly, I could hear the lilting strings of the musical ensemble and the joyous noise of the party in full-swing.

It was perfect. The most fitting setting I could have dreamt up to learn something new and exciting about myself. But despite it all– and the beauty and graciousness of the two felines I'd be sharing it with– I couldn't chase off the feeling of wrongness. Like I was meant to be here with someone else.

That ship had sailed, as they said. Hopefully not literally. But honestly, it was worse somehow to imagine he was here, perhaps a room away, enjoying the company of another. Physical jealousy was not a feeling I was accustomed to, and I didn't like it.

"You seem distracted, Admiral," a whispered purr tickled my ear as arms slipped around my midsection from behind, under my coat. The unusually thicker, huskier tone of that voice being male sent a bit of a thrill through me, if only from the newness of it. Or perhaps because it reminded me of him… it was dreadfully hard to tell how any of this was making me feel, just yet. And it probably wasn't going to get much clearer as we went, I realized with some dismay.

I began to shrug out of my coat, and I felt him help me, peeling the garment away from my body. At the same time, Camila– the woman– slid in to rest against my chest, her hands replacing Camilo's where he'd left searing little trails of contact.

"Apologies," I said and meant it. These two were plenty alluring and plying their charms quite effectively, and they deserved my attention. "I've had… an eventful evening already, and I'll admit my mind is drifting."

"Well, we can't have that," Camila said, her claws catching on each button rather intentionally, as she slowly dragged them down my tunic. Her jewelry caught in the flickering lantern light from the wall, her cinnamon eyes pinned on mine as those fingers deftly worked my belt free. She glanced down once only briefly, her nostrils flaring. She'd probably caught a trace of the scent of me and what had befallen my trousers earlier, although she was good enough not to comment on it. She'd never know how sad a condition that had truly been… probably assumed I'd just gotten into it with someone else at the party.

Which I suppose I had, not that *he'd* ever know he'd brought me off.

"How is it a fine fellow such as yourself is without company this late in the evening?" Camilo tutted from behind me, boldly running his fingers through my mane after he'd helped me out of my second layer, straightening them out from the erratic tangle they often became when I disrobed.

I caught a brief, meaningful glance from his female companion at that, not meant for me to see. Her eyes said 'change the topic', clearly having caught on to the fact that I might have left a previous partner early and attempting to warn the male ocelot he was wading into troublesome waters.

"–although I shan't admonish anyone for enjoying the festivities first before retiring for the evening–" he tried to course-correct.

"It's fine," I said in an easy tone to let them know I wasn't offended. "Came here tonight without much of a plan, and I can't say this is an unwelcome way to spend it."

"I have to admit I'm pleasantly surprised to be involved," Camilo said, tracing his touch 'round my ribs as he joined his female companion in front of me, the two of them looping an arm around one another and pressing cheek to cheek with a purr and a flick of their tails, as they swayed forward against me. "We spied you from across the room for a time, and Camila considered heading over there once or twice… you're rather famous in these parts, you know."

"It would have been worth trying just to say we spoke with you," Camila said, blinking her long lashes up at me. She had powdered, deep blue shadow over her eyes, whereas Camilo had red. Their jewelry matched as well, each with their own personal touches to their outfit.

They were both achingly beautiful. Fuck, why wasn't I able to concentrate? I'd curse myself later for not being more present.

"If I'd known you'd fancied the stamen as well as the flower, I'd have come with her," Camilo said. "I suppose our gossip is… out of date."

I forced a chuckle. "Well not entirely, perhaps. You wouldn't mention trading gossip about most clients, I'd wager."

"You're an information broker as well as a Privateer," Camila reasoned. "You know the game. Besides," and here she smiled, tapping her claws against my collarbone, "I hear you're fond of a little… teasing."

"A sailor without an easily bruised ego is a rarity," Camilo twirled one of my dreads around a finger. "It speaks well of you. Not poorly."

"It bruises just fine," I assured him with a sigh. "I just enjoy the ache."

Camilo put a bit of pressure on my chest, and I realized I'd drifted towards the bed. I let him bowl me over like a sack of wheat, the soft mattress hitting my back and sending a long, relieved breath out of me. I hadn't realized how much I wanted to lie down.

But they had. Gotta love prostitutes.

The two slinky felines crawled over me, each shimmying out of their wispy sarong as they did, revealing their tender parts beneath. Camila was everything I usually anticipated, and that was normal. Comfortable. Camilo...

I hadn't expected he'd be partially erect, I won't lie. But I suppose it was... flattering? If unfamiliar. It's not like I hadn't seen the whole range of the male sex aboard a ship as diverse and as full of men as the *Manoratha*. I'd even gotten up close and personal once or twice, while sharing a woman. But there was something slightly different about staring down even a relatively small set of equipment like that when he was straddling you.

I was still dressed below the waist, at least in my smallclothes. But I was tenting and had been for some time. The presence of Camilo was not putting me off, at least not entirely. That wasn't surprising, of course. The fact that the both of them were here was rather confusing things. But it also set me more at ease, so I wasn't about to ask her to leave. Being alone with Luther, even up to and including the rise in the passions of my body, and the culmination of all that excitement and confusion... had contributed quite a lot to the panic he'd clearly seen in me. And I didn't want to panic with these two. I wanted to figure this out.

I hadn't told them what I wanted yet, though, so they'd been ginger about doing much other than crooning over me, touching me in polite areas or over my clothes and touching one another. Which is what they were doing now, putting on quite a show for me, as promised.

"If you're tired, we've a few routines you might enjoy watching," Camilo said as he craned his lady friend's neck back to run a tongue up her pulse point. One of his hands was already massaging the breast she wasn't touching herself.

"No, ah..." I stammered, then rallied. "Actually, if I might... confess something. I'm not usually... that is to say, you understand the phrase 'know thyself'?"

"We speak the same language, sir," Camila said around a slight laugh.

"Right, sorry, I'm just... nerves, you know."

"We know," Camilo said, rubbing a free palm up my thigh, perilously close to the edge of my smallclothes. My dick twitched when he squeezed the meat of my inner leg, and I decided that sort of settled it.

"Well, I'm trying to," I swallowed, "know myself. Here. I'm, ah, hoping to learn if I'm meant to... expand my horizons. As it were."

"Oh, spirits," Camilo suddenly loomed over me, his mouth slightly parted, eyes hungry. It was intimidating, despite his size. My dick twitched *again.* "Am I your *first?*"

"Ha," I huffed out, "that is a... complicated question."

"Shall I get to my knees, then?" he offered, waggling his hips with a lurid, playful grin. His sex swayed between his thighs, the sight causing a spike of anxiety to course through me. "Get right to it? You'll forgive my saying so, but you seem... prepared."

"That's hardly an insult requiring forgiving," I pointed out, chuckling nervously. "But... n... no? I don't think so. It's not that I doubt my ability there, it's just that... to put it bluntly, from behind, I'm not certain my mind would know the difference. It's not as though I haven't had a woman from the rear before."

"It's different," he assured me with a sly smile, "but alright... in the deep end, perhaps a bit too far for a first-timer. Or is it that you'd rather have me another way? Or...."

"Don't overwhelm him now," Camila said in a soft tone, crawling up beside me and nuzzling beneath my chin. "Let's ask something simple. How do you prefer it with women, handsome?"

"Ah... if they're of a mind, with them on top," I said, the confession coming easily. "Honestly, was rather hoping you two would just take the reins, and I'd see what worked... what didn't... that's how I most prefer things overall."

The two of them looked at one another for a moment before Camilo asked her quietly, "Should I...."

"Talk about the deep end," she shook her head, ending that idea— whatever it was— before it was even aired. Then she looked back down at me and stroked my cheek. "How about this, sweet lad? Camilo will entreat you to a cascade of his most pleasing affections, while *I* watch? And kiss you."

I considered her offer, and simply nodded. It made sense. Nay, she was a genius. It was like easing down a line slowly. A bit of what I knew, but the fellow would be doing all the most pointed work, which meant…

… well, it meant I'd have less doubts about what I wanted when this was all done. Hopefully.

Camilo's hands worked at the fastenings on my smallclothes while Camila tipped my muzzle against hers and found eager purchase. My heart was hammering with anticipation, my body was buzzing with nerves, and I was almost too anxious to lift my hips properly and help the poor feline out in getting the accursed undergarments off.

I felt her curves against my chest as she loosely looped a leg around my midsection, and I worked an arm under her so I could hold her closer, while I played with her tongue. I loved the feel of feline tongues… everywhere. Canine muzzles tended to be deeper, which was better to feel the edge of teeth all along my length, the dangerous sensation had always gotten to me something fierce—

I was thinking about him again.

I blinked my eyes open hazily when I felt a soft, warm palm closing around my length. I wanted to really *see* him, know it was him. Camila leaned down to nip and nibble her way down my neck, through the layers of my fur, somehow precisely finding my jugular. Cats were incredible.

I groaned and splayed my knees out so I could better see the lad down there doing his work. He had my cock in his palm, and while it was still somewhat jarring that he just… wasn't whom I expected to see there… it still looked good in his grip. His eyes said he agreed, and while I knew much of it was practiced, it was nice to be appreciated.

"Oh, Camila, you're going to want to make the most of this when I'm through with him," he rumbled, licking his dark lips. His paw had crept round underneath, slender fingers slipping below my sheath, and my heart briefly jumped, but then they were merely cupping my sac and rubbing it gently.

I'd thought, maybe… I mean I knew what men did together. Some men. I knew what I'd pictured the cattle dog doing to me….

It was supposed to be satisfying to some. I think most of the women I'd had under the tail had been either just indulging me or fibbing. But who can say. Enough men I knew swore there was something to it. And the idea of fully submitting to someone that way... it *was* intriguing. I'd sort of fooled around on my own, unsuccessfully, and once toyed with a strap, but neither I nor the woman I'd been with had really known how to find pleasure that way.

Camilo seemed more interested in having me in his muzzle, and that felt... safer. For now. Something I knew I enjoyed, but bridged with the pleasure-giver being a man? Good place to start.

On an impulse, I sat up just enough that I could reach the feline fellow with my palm and brush my knuckles over his cheek, toyed briefly with an earring, and traced one of those inky patterns of black. He smiled at me and kept eye contact as he leaned down and slowly wrapped his muzzle around my tip.

It didn't exactly light me on fire, but then this was a familiar act. And the wet heat of his mouth felt nice. I held Camila a bit tighter to me and recognized her nuzzling at my chest, but I kept my eyes trained on him for now. Watched him bob shallowly, while his distinctively more masculine hand stroked my base. Even soft and pretty and pleasing as he was, there was no getting around the fact that he was a *man*. It was strange. It didn't curdle my gut or repulse me, but it felt... odd. In a way that was hard to define.

I was hard and staying hard, but even as he slowly adjusted to my girth and took me deeper, I felt as though I were floating on my pleasure, not being taken away with it as though by rapids. This was enjoyable... it felt... good. Like a massage, and his cupping palm beneath was adding a lot to it, honestly. I liked having my balls fondled, I was more sensitive down there, and not everyone thought to.

The way his spots followed the curve of his bent back and flowed upwards into the round shape of his rear as it wagged slowly back and forth was... an admirable view, too. I think I honestly might have liked mounting him. I'd probably be able to get off too, if I really pounded the lad. Maybe later.

But I couldn't shake the feeling, the whole while, that I'd enjoy it more with Camila. Or... someone else....

This had been a solid plan, I told myself. The only issue was, I hadn't considered the additional confusion of my mind constantly drifting not only to the thought of the woman in the room... but the other person I would have preferred to be sharing this room with tonight, instead. Even if trying any of this had been disastrous, it was his company I'd wanted.

The many distractions dancing through my head, as well as the occasional reprieve so Camilo could relax his poor jaw, and I could enjoy another long kiss with Camila, saw to it that for once... I lasted. And lasted. These two were probably used to long haul clients, and they didn't know me well enough to realize that was unusual for me. And I was enjoying myself, there was no mistaking that. But it was relaxed, drawn-out, and lacking the sharp edge of excitement I'd felt earlier.

I could probably do this again, I came to feel, with another man involved in the future. But, I wasn't sure it was something I would seek out specifically. I felt an odd sort of... pride, though? In myself. For trying. Maybe this wasn't it, maybe I just wasn't made this way, and that was fine, and now I knew.

Something had passed between the two ocelots that I'd only vaguely caught out of the corner of my eye, a gesture shared between them. When I blinked hazily down at Camilo, he was returning to sucking me off, but with a renewed sort of purpose in his eyes. And a knowing look up at his fellow where she was gathered against my chest, nibbling on my ear.

His touch slid under my sheath again, but my attention was diverted, watching him take nearly all of me down his muzzle— no small feat! I was about to compliment him on just that, when I felt his probing touch on my taint, wetted presumably by his own saliva or my slick. I whined audibly and dug my toes into the bedspread.

And he pressed *in* with his finger, just a bit, while swallowing me down. There, finally, the waters got rougher. My vision went white hot, and something thrilled up my spine. I grunted desperately once or twice, wondering but not having the words for why this was at *all* different than the times I'd tried myself or the strap... maybe I was just worked-up enough this time that it was all it took?

He wasn't just pushing in though, it was like he was... curling... that one little slim finger. Before I could really think over how or what he was doing, he'd doubled the pace of his muzzle, his free hand stroking on the bottom where he couldn't swallow around, and my body was finally giving in, careening past its stasis.

Camila kissed me and moaned along with me while Camilo worked his magic. I tried to watch him through my orgasm, tried to force myself to experience it as though he were the only one there, to see how it felt to empty myself down a man's throat....

But it wasn't just Camila who was sharing that room with us. My thoughts simply weren't there. And it wasn't either of the ocelots I imagined as I released.

I'd wanted to know myself, and I'd certainly learned something, alright. Camilo was pleasing, as was Camila, and over the next few hours, we'd enjoy ourselves in various ways. But Camilo could have been there or not been there, and the night would have played out much the same. As it had many other times when I'd had men in my bed. It wasn't men on the whole I was interested in.

It was just... the one.

* * *

I didn't usually drink to excess on unfamiliar liquor because it had a tendency to give me vivid, sometimes disturbing dreams. Especially when I was sleeping in an unfamiliar place, as I was tonight.

I awoke damp, stiff, and sore, with the colorful mirage of my waking dream still dancing through my thoughts. I'd been home, or somewhere like it. The place I *used* to call home, anyway. Either the musty, storied halls of Ashrond Academy, where I'd wiled away most of my teenage years and an embarrassing amount of my twenties... or one of the many gilded ballrooms, stacked floor to ceiling with tapestries and paintings of my family estates. I could almost smell the brandy and mulled wine, the rich food, and the familiar fur musk of my family members. Not just my father, but the ones I'd truly lost. Too disgusted by my turn in life, outright anathema to me now... or dead.

It felt like another man's life, like a novel I'd greedily digested in my youth without taking the time to enjoy it thoroughly. I was beginning to forget the names and faces. Even my own. The wolf I'd been then was as unfamiliar to me now as a stranger.

I blinked, finding my eyelashes were sticking together, but inconveniently, my eyes were filling with tears despite that. I forced them open, snuffing in a long breath, wet in my nose as well. By the time I had shouldered back my jacket enough that I wasn't trapped by it and I'd managed to right myself into a sitting position somewhat, I was wiping a full trail of salt water off one cheek.

"Night treated you poorly?" a concerned voice asked to the left of me.

It didn't shock me to hear him, this time. I hadn't even needed to look that way to know he was there– his presence was what had woken me. A relief, really, given the memory-scape I'd been traversing. His scent filled my nostrils, stronger this morning and tinged with someone else's. My fur prickled enough to let me know his heat lay inches away from me. Likely sitting on the bench beside the stone patio I'd chosen to sleep on. Not the most optimum choice for a bed, but I was more used to sleeping outdoors, either on planks, cobblestone, or worse the older I got. I was restless at night, and when the overwhelming urge for sleep finally hit me full-force, I preferred not to fight it and just lie down wherever I was. Better than missing my window and spending a sleepless night somewhere more comfortable.

"Grayson," his baritone came closer now, and I could feel his hand, halting, inches away from my cheek ruff. "Look at me. Are you well?"

He sounded concerned, so I finally forced out a gravelly reply, "Yes, no, I mean… I'm fine, lad." I wiped my face and sniffed roughly again. "Not… the night. Just, dreams. You know how it is. M'mind's not always kind to me when it's at rest. Remembers too clearly."

He let out a slow breath before leaning back and giving me space. "Unfortunately, yes, I do know."

I leaned a bit in his direction, looking up at him where he sat on the patio bench. It wasn't actually morning, but it sounded like it might be getting close. The night insects had begun to retreat, and the distant tropical birdsong from the rainforest around us was growing. The sky was violet and the stars were dimming, the moon nowhere in sight. The pond was still and beautiful before us, save the occasional ripple of fish searching for the skittering water bugs.

He looked more relaxed than I felt, dressed-down and stripped out of most of his costume now. Just the light poet's shirt and his britches. No spats, even. His clothes and possessions sat wrapped in a ball of his own jacket at his side, his fur was charmingly askew, and he smelled vaguely hungover. Like liquor, musk, and a headache.

Headaches have a scent, if you don't know. Words would fail to describe it, but if you knew it, you knew it.

The fact that less than a dozen people in the world yet living probably ever got to see him with his guard so low occurred to me and briefly made me feel special. Then... sad. When that sun came up, we'd part again for who knew how many months. Years.

Fuck, maybe this had all been a rotten idea.

But then, almost timidly... although you'd never catch me using that word out loud to describe anything he did... I sensed the man's hand go lax and drape casually down beside me again. Close to where I was leaning my head against the cool stone of the wide bench leg.

I shuffled a bit, so that his claws were vaguely brushing against my cheek. It was plausibly deniable, like every goddamn thing between us. But I let my eyes drift closed and enjoyed it. For just a moment, I could live in denial and pretend this was how I'd woken up.

He broke the illusion by intentionally brushing me with his knuckles. It was an affectionate touch, truly and without any ambiguity. It would have meant nothing coming from any one of the boys on my crew who regularly embraced, nuzzled, or slept beside me under tables. But it was him. And it was devoid of aggression, or clashing egos, or some convenient excuse for why we needed to close our physical proximity. He was just petting me because I was there and feeling like shit.

And he cared about me. I didn't know how to define what we had, but the man was a sphinx, and that made every facet of our relationship hard to understand, so maybe I never would. At least I'd know it wasn't a figment of my imagination, now.

"So, how *was* your night?" he asked casually. Casual, but odd.

I dragged a breath in through my nose slowly in, then out. And humphed, not opening my eyes or bothering to move. "As if you don't know."

"I was being polite."

"*You* don't smell like whoever you spent your evening with," I said, annoyed.

"You learn a thing or two about how to conceal your shame when you seek your pleasures in the shadows as I do."

"How maudlin," I snorted, wobbling my head more into his palm.

He gave an amused noise before scritching my brow. "How'd they treat you, then? I half expected to find you under a pile of warm bodies somewhere."

I opened my eyes slowly, staring off into the pond until they unfocused. Memories of Camilo flittered through my thoughts, but nothing stuck.

"Nothing makes any more or any less sense," I finally settled on.

He hummed thoughtfully. "It can be like that."

I looked up at him again finally, and his hand slipped away, his gold eyes standing out in the first soft glaze of the dim morning light. "I half-expected you'd have fucked off by now," I admitted. "You never said goodbye the last time we parted."

"Circumstances didn't allow it." He shrugged. "But for what it's worth, I'm sorry. I'll try to remember you need that assurance from now on."

It was a barb with no sting. I just smiled. "Please do."

"Where are your things?" he asked suddenly, glancing around me. "You shouldn't sleep outside so exposed like this...."

"Oh, everything I brought fit in my pockets," I explained, stretching my back stiffly and rummaging around in the coat I'd been using for a blanket. "And it's all... there. Bit of coin, that shell I liked, my oil– oh!" I chuckled victoriously as I produced a few small, wrapped mints.

"... you carry oil?"

I tossed him one, and the bastard caught it despite the lack of warning. He turned it over in his palm as I said, "Great for hangover breath. And yes, Luther, and not just for my pistol."

"What else do you use it for?" the man had the gall to ask.

I arched an eyebrow up at him as I popped the mint in my mouth. "You decided not to find out. Remember?"

He stared at me, apparently gobsmacked by my answer, and it was only then that I realized an absurd amount of fur was forming a cowlick on the right side of his neck. Then he began to laugh in a rasp. "Fair play, I suppose."

"The rest of my things are in town," I chuckled, "why do you ask?"

He stood and offered me a hand up. "Let's collect them together. I've got somewhere I'd like to take you."

"… and I need my belongings for this, why…?"

He smiled. "You'll see."

* * *

I drank about a gallon of water as we walked from the villa into town, refilling my canteen twice at public wells along the way. Luther availed himself of the same, including once at the wellhouse near the entrance of the long, winding road up to the estate. I took the opportunity to try to spy my flash of red amongst the trees, but it was impossible. It's not as though I believed in the myths, anyway. It was just hard not to wonder, you know?

He rejoined me before long, downing half his canteen in a few swigs. I watched him with a whistle, remarking, "Someone's walked and pissed off a night of heavy drinkin' before."

He swallowed heavily, clearing his throat, before remarking, "You really do bring a kind of unique charm to any conversation, don't you?"

"Drives the ladies wild," I grinned.

He snorted a laugh, and that got me bubbling up in chuckles as well. We both made our way back to town, less sure-footed than we'd taken the trek to get here. The sun still wasn't up, but there was enough light to see the short road and the silhouettes of the buildings in town by.

It didn't take me long to gather my rucksack after ducking into the rooming house I'd briefly stayed in. The place was like a battlefield of fallen partygoers, sleeping off the night, barely a twitch or snore as I stepped over them. One extremely tired-looking woman barely looked up at me from the bar as she finished off cleaning the last of the glasses she'd presumably been left to handle with no help from her fellows. She was a raccoon, so already sporting dark circles, but I could tell from how bloodshot her eyes were and how exhausted her stiff motions were that she'd been working all night.

"Ey, lass," I said, digging in my pack for a moment before fishing out a handful of coins and plunking them down on the bar. "Thanks for being the last one standin' and mannin' the fort."

She slowly looked up, first eyeing the pile of gold coins— five crowns, hardly a fortune when you ran a fleet, but likely life-changing for her— and then me, something like fear or awe dancing across her gaze.

"You a spirit?" she asked in a hushed voice.

Explaining I was actually a hungover Admiral of an infamous privateering fleet, an ex-blueblood, and that I probably had twice that in crowns rolling around loose in my rucksack seemed like it would just make me seem more suspicious than what she'd assumed, so instead I held a finger up to my muzzle and whispered a quiet, "Shhh."

She stared at me the whole way out. When I made it to Luther I was grinning and laughing quietly at myself, and he gave me the expected 'what now?' look, but I just waved it off. Boasting about good deeds was gouache.

Instead of heading back towards the Amur section of town, which is where I'd thought he'd want to spend our morning, we moved towards and began to walk along the coast. I preferred it, but it begged the question....

"Where are you taking me?" I asked— huffed, rather— as we made our way up over the rocky, overgrown northern point of the isle. The view of the sun just beginning to tip its way over the sea's horizon was stunning, so I didn't mind the hike, even if I wasn't in the best state for going off-road right now.

He didn't answer. Only glanced once back at me and kept scaling up the small ridge we had to walk over to follow the beach. I began to suspect what this might be, and it tickled my heart to think on it. There weren't many high points on this island, but I'd picked a spot somewhere near here to wait for him when I'd first arrived. It had reminded me— albeit at a much lower elevation— of that place we'd watched the sun rise together in the Shanivaar. Had he remembered that moment as fondly as I had?

The thought warmed me more than the rising sun. And I became more and more certain of it as we trekked. But then I saw....

I gasped out loud, stopping to catch my breath on one of the smaller dune hills, staring out across the... 'bay' would have been too kind. An inlet, at most. There were a few smaller fishing boats moored here or just resting in the distant sands of the edge of the tidal forest, where the tide itself wouldn't reach. But amongst them, one boat stood out. For its size as well as its distinctive design.

"Look at that beautiful little Cutter," I admired openly. Her sails were taken in, and she had her anchor down in the shallows, in a safe, deep blue eye farther out from the inlet. The reefs here were minimal, so she was in no danger. All the same, it was clear she'd been moored with care.

"A lesser man would've called her a Sloop from this distance," Luther remarked.

"You can see the second forestay from here." I shook my head. "Beautiful lass. Cherry timber of some sort... I'd love to get a closer look."

He gave me that knowing smile.

"Oh, shite," I swore, "it's not–"

"She's mine," he confirmed. "At least for the season or until I decide to sell her. Honestly, it'll be hard when the time comes, but she can't come back across the pond with me."

"She could," I said insistently. "In the right weather, with the right hands–"

"I'd love to live in a world where you and I could sail the seas for leisure," he said ruefully, "but that is not the age we were born into, wolf."

I swept my gaze across the inlet as the sun started licking fire into the waves, the heat sinking into my body, gathering in my cheeks and ears. Or maybe that was me. Maybe it was him. It didn't matter.

"So," I asked finally, "when did you find my bloody ribbon? How?"

"Well, I sailed here alone to avoid my minder or any bothersome people from my fleet or... otherwise," he said. "And earnestly, I considered asking you if you needed a hop back to your fleet, wherever she's berthed, regardless."

"'I want to sail with him again,'" I said the exact words I'd written in my wish, scrawled on that cloth I'd hung from the tree. "Come on, man."

"It was fate, it seems," he smirked slowly, side-eyeing me, "or 'spirits'. However you choose to see it."

I made a frustrated noise. "You're not going to tell me, are you?"

"I told you, you're predictable," he said cryptically. "For someone so chaotic, I don't know... perhaps we move along the same currents. I always figure you out, somehow. I can always find you."

I laughed. "That was a more ominous truth just a few years ago."

"It means I'll find my way to you whenever you've need of me or I've need of you," he said. "No matter what separates us. Or at least... I hope it does. Allies I can rely on are scarce. People I can be myself with… even rarer."

I continued to look out at the sight before us and the gorgeous, if admittedly small, sailing ship. She'd be easy enough to crew with just the two of us, especially in the good weather we'd been having. Three days at sea if we took our time. Three more days with him.

Something occurred to me, though. I'd been on my share of sloops and cutters, and this one seemed more designed for performance and speed than crew quarters. The cabin, even from here….

"Luther," I asked, while looking her over from our perch, "there more than one bunk in that cabin?"

He sighed. "No."

"Didn't think that one out, ey?"

"I did not," he confessed.

I gathered up my rucksack, grinning. "Welp! Shall we?"

LIFELINE

LIFELINE

The Manoratha Fleet, docked for a brief time in Treneval, is celebrating after their highly lucrative take-down and subsequent liquidation of the Lancaster Cartel. While living the high life at a rented-out Social Club in the Pier District, Grayson Reed's festivities are disrupted by the appearance of an old 'friend' and very much uninvited guest – Admiral Luther Denholme. The only thing stranger than the Admiral's sudden arrival to a building full of men who very much would prefer him dead is the fact that he came alone, unarmed… and shitfaced. It isn't often someone catches Grayson Reed on the back foot, but this night promises to be one he will not soon forget and sets a chain of events in motion that will shape both men's lives and affect the lives of thousands more.

* * *

The staircase clattered noisily beneath the heavy, rushed footsteps of my boys and I, our overgrown claws clicking on the hardwood. I'm pretty sure I found every single poorly-nailed-down board on my swift descent, of which there were many. Normally, I might have watched my footing more carefully, especially when I had reason to expect there might be trouble – or a troublesome person – ahead. Not that I'm not a fan of making loud noises, mind you, I just tend to prefer the element of surprise when I might be walking into a fight.

But see here's the thing. This aging, enormous, port-side Social Club was our penthouse, *our* place of respite for the next week at least, and I should have had no cause to sneak around in it. We'd rented the whole of it out, legal-like and all. Fully paid up-front, and I'd made sure the owners got coverage for damages in advance, since I knew my men, and there were *very* likely to be damages, when all was said and done. For the time being, this place was our fortress, not some public rooming house.

Was nothing sacred? For once, I wasn't even looking for trouble. Couldn't I just bloody *relax* every now and then?

This was the third day we'd spent here, and I'd only just woken an hour ago, so I was annoyingly sober. The fact that this was happening during the scant few hours a day I tended to *be* sober was absurdly unlucky. I wouldn't have taken odds on that.

To be honest with you, I had no idea what time of day or night it actually was; this was Treneval after all, the weather just about any time of year could be summarized with the word 'grey'. For color, temperature, light, and overall 'mood'. Why the Amurescans had chosen such a dreary, dismal, frequently storm-wracked port as one of their primary places of commerce and society, I could not make sense of. The simple answer was geographic location. Just like them to prioritize practicality over pleasure.

But whatever time of day it was, I'd only *just* rolled out of bed (and the arms of a mink who'd gotten too drunk the day prior to do her job), and I hadn't had a chance to chase last night's drink with anything other than a pounding headache. It took a lot to get me in what you might call a 'foul mood', but I was rounding that corner.

"How did he even get in here?" I demanded of the boar on my right, who only shook his oversized head.

"Still haven't figured that out."

"Our best guess is through the kitchen," the rat ahead of us – I think his name was Jeffrey – said as he fished a key ring off his belt and thrust one of them into the locked door at the bottom of the staircase. The jangling made me wince and tip my ears back.

Really needed a drink.

"That's where he came strolling out from, anyway," Jeffrey continued, glancing back at us. "And a few of the boys said they propped the door out to th'back open last night, let out some of the heat after dinner."

"I take it no one thought to shut it afterwards, let alone lock it," I grumbled.

"Well," Jeffrey paused, "what with all the women came by last night. . ."

"Yeah, yeah," I moved in beside him, grabbing around him for the door handle. "Out of the way. I'll handle this."

"You sure, Adm'ral?"

I let out a ragged sigh. "I've handled him before. You're absolutely certain it's him? There are a few thousand cattle dogs in Amuresca, I'd wager. If I dragged my ass out of bed for some bum who crept in off the street to filch food –"

"It's him," a man from further up the staircase whom I couldn't see insisted, raising his voice so he'd be heard. There was quite a crowd gathered on the landing above by now. I'd had to push my way through them on the way down here.

For some reason – through what I'm sure had been an epic scuffle I'm only sad I'd missed – they'd managed to corner the intruder in the cellar. Which was, if bleary memory served, a large, dirt-floored basement primarily used for storing old furniture, vegetables, and casks. We weren't supposed to break into any of the booze down there, but the fact that my men had forced our party-crasher inside and then locked him *in* with keys they somehow had access to... well, it suggested I'd be paying even more damages down the line. May as well have bought the place outright.

"I remember him from Dokuro," the sailor affirmed. "Hard to forget those eyes. Goddamn... demon, that one."

"I'm sure he gave you hell," I muttered, pausing near the door and steeling myself. "Where'd *his* boys get to? They bail?"

I felt, rather than saw the uneasy looks that passed between my men after that question. When I turned to regard them again, the same man spoke up, "He came alone."

"Bullshit," I said defiantly, "we're in *his* territory. Why would he've –" I stopped myself short at that.

This was Luther Denholme we were talking about. It was actually entirely possible he'd come alone; for some purpose that would make terrifying sense once he explained his reasoning to me. Some gambit I didn't know of, some master-stroke he'd lay out before me as my world unraveled and I scrambled to catch up.

I was not prepared to deal with this shit right now. I just wanted to go back to *bed*.

I didn't bother asking if he was armed. I just braced my shoulder against the door, gripped the handle, and called back to my men, "Stay outta this. Last thing I need is one of you all getting trigger happy and murdering a fucking Crown Admiral in an Amurescan port."

"We know," Jeffrey insisted. "That's why we locked'im up. We didn't know what else to do. None of us want to fight our way out of these waters, Admiral."

"Good, because we wouldn't make it past the bay. I'm betting he counted on that, too," I realized aloud. Might explain why he wasn't worried about coming alone. I twisted the knob, shouting once more, "If I start hollering, just send a few of the biggest lads in. *No killin'!*"

A chorus of 'yessirs', and then I stepped inside, shutting the door firmly behind me with a backwards kick. Resting my hands on my hips, I didn't immediately bother with the hilt of my saber, even though I *had* come armed. This was Luther. And despite what the public perception of us was, even amongst my own men... he was *not* in fact some sworn blood enemy of mine.

I hardly knew what the cattle dog was to me, really. A friend? I hope he saw me that way. I think he did. I think *I* did.

But given the nature of our interactions over the years, given our diametrically opposed careers, we'd been both predator and prey and everything in between to one another. The sands our relationship stood on were constantly shifting, and I actually hadn't seen him in over a year now. A lot could change in a year. It had for me. I'd nearly lost my flagship to the Black Flag fleet this past season, and the Black Flag Admiral – one Heinrich Richard Cross was pretty tight with the Denholmes, or at least he had been with Luther's stepfather. I knew Luther worked alongside Cross from time to time, but as to whether or not they were friends... let alone friends who might swing one another's favor for or against someone like me...

Impossible to say. In all our encounters, I'd never thought to ask Luther about the nature of his relationship with Cross, the old Shepherd. And maybe I should have. *He* was definitely our enemy – the last battle between my *Manoratha* and the Black Flag fleet had been bloody on both sides. I think we'd given as well as we'd got and there was no telling what condition his ships had been in afterwards, but he'd nearly sunk my girl to the bottom and all souls aboard with her. We'd barely limped out of that one.

I needed to know these things, is the point. It was part of my job – no, part of my obligation – to my men.

I couldn't afford to be as reckless with their lives as I was with my own.

Shit, maybe we shouldn't have been here at all? While my ships were technically on a legal contract right now, we had enemies a-plenty here, some of them like Cross, incredibly *dangerous*.

My spirits lifted as I began to walk down the central line of shelves, peering down each row looking for the cattle dog. Maybe that's why he was here. Maybe this was just a friendly warning. That'd be damn decent of him. And you know what? I'd listen. To hell with our plans in Treneval, if Denholme was being courteous enough to look out for me, give me a head start away from trouble, I wasn't about to spit in his face. It would explain why he was here alone, why he'd come himself, why he'd felt the need to slip in unseen-

There were a few lanterns hung from the ceiling down here, but not enough to fully illuminate the place, in my opinion. Not for an underground space. Were I outside or were there any windows or doors letting in natural light, it'd be enough for me to see by regardless of the weather or time of day. But in between the rings of flickering orange were dead zones, usually in the corners near the end of each rows of shelves, where even a wolf's eyes couldn't see through the empty pitch. It was in one of these that I found him, and if not for his legs lying slumped partially in the light, I might have missed him. His eyes flashed once when I grabbed for the lantern above, tipping it towards him. Gold pin-pricks in the dark. A demon indeed.

"Bloody hell," I took a step back, my nose just now catching the sharp scent of iron in the air, in addition to the stale, lingering smell of most cellars – old wood, tar from the barrels, mold. And... whiskey. Definitely whiskey. Well, at least I now knew what they'd broken into down here.

The iron, though, that was blood. Unmistakably. Fresh blood, too. Not very much, but...

"The great Luther Denholme," I said with as much bravado as I could, putting up an air of strength. Whatever his game here, I didn't need him seeing how tired I was. "How in the hell did you let a couple groggy lads get the better of you?"

I hooked a finger around the top ring of the lantern overhead, easy enough in a cellar meant for shorter species, and held it out in his direction.

The man was a *sight*. I felt the air leave my lungs in a punched-out huff.

He looked like he'd aged ten years since the last time I saw him, thinner and gaunter all around, but most noticeable in his cheeks and the deep pits in the hollows of his eyes. His nose was bloody and had stained the simple white cotton shirt he wore beneath a frayed brown coat. He had none of his finery on, no blood red coat, no cravat, not even a sword that I could see. In fact, if he was armed at all, I couldn't tell. A knife, perhaps, hidden somewhere on his person. Maybe tucked into the side of his leather spats or beneath the coat somewhere. I couldn't imagine he went anywhere completely unarmed.

But there was nothing in the cattle dog's slumped, lifeless posture, or in the air surrounding him, that read as intimidating or dangerous. And for a man that exuded intimidation as easily as most men breathed, that was saying something. He looked ragged, hazy-eyed… almost sickly.

In short, he looked like I felt. In fact, if I didn't know any better, I'd say he was hungov-

Wait.

He tipped his head up slowly towards me, pupils sharpening marginally at the sound of my voice, but they were blown-wide in the dark, lacking the predatory edge they generally had. Luther had this intense way of looking at you, as if he was analyzing you, sizing you up, *all the time*. In all the years I'd known him, I'd seen him exhibit a range of emotions, but his gaze had never lost that focus.

Without a further word, I crossed the space between us and knelt down in front of him. He sniffed noisily, sucking blood back up into his nose – the work of one of my boys, no doubt. And he opened his muzzle as if to say something, but I gave him the chance and the words just… never came. Just a slow, labored exhale. Which confirmed what I'd suspected, once I breathed it in.

"LADS!" I raised my voice, as loud as I could with my throat still thick with sleep as it was. I turned my gaze back down towards the cattle dog as the door was thrust open noisily somewhere back the way I'd come and asked far more quietly of him, "Can you walk?"

He pushed himself up, palm grabbing unsteadily for one of the wooden shelves nearby and clamping around the edge of it for purchase. I had about a split second to warn him of what he should've noticed already – that there wasn't much other than gravity holding it in place – but mostly what I got out was, "Don't —" and then the plank gave way and flipped up on one side. I don't think it'd ever been nailed down; it was just a flat piece of wood resting on slats.

But it had been the only point of support he had, so with a clattering crash that I'm absolutely certain half the house must have heard, I had the extraordinarily rare privilege of watching one Luther Denholme laid low by sub-par shelving. Several glass jars of preserves rolled off and littered down around him, thankfully without breaking (glass jars and bottles are tough, let me tell you, did you know you could beat someone to death with one?), and he slumped back down against the wall, nearly to the ground. But by that point I'd caught his shoulder and leaned over him both to steady him and block him from the prying eyes of the men I'd called in.

"Pull it together," I whispered fiercely, a few inches away from one of his ears. "C'mon, up…" I moved a paw beneath his shoulder, beginning to heft him. Thankfully, he was a smaller man than I was and lighter now than I remembered.

What the hell, what the hell…

"Can you walk if I drag you along?" I asked him, still lowly. He blinked back a wince against the encroaching glow of the lantern but nodded.

"Admiral," I felt a paw settle on my shoulder, heavy and with retractable claws. I recognized the spots immediately. "Seems like you handled him," the leopard said, sounding only marginally concerned once he took in the sight of him same as I had.

"Taarush," I sighed. One of my trusted men… good. But there were a few others with him, Jeffrey included, and he was a new-ish hire. I didn't know him all that well, yet. "Yeah," I confirmed, "knocked him stupid. You lads must've softened him up for me, eh?" I raised my voice at that, so the others heard me clearly.

There were a few nervous chuckles of assent, followed by one bold man raising his voice and asking, "So why's the Cerberus bastard here?"

I cleared my throat, thinking quickly. "Didn't really get to that," I said, sounding as forcibly bored as I could manage. "Wanted to set the record straight about walking in on our territory this way, bold as brass. I don't care who the fuck you think you are, cur." I directed that at Luther, who still hadn't spoken, but at least seemed to be listening to me now. He was leaning on me heavily for support, but I had my paw clamped up beneath one of his arms in a way that at least *looked* like he was being man-handled. "We're here legal-like," I continued, then louder, "ain't that right boys?!"

A bevy of confirming shouts went up, a bit of bluster and profanity, about what I'd expected. Taarush was looking at Luther oddly, though. He'd probably smelled it by now, just as I had when I'd finally gotten in close enough. It was downright embarrassing that the men who'd forced him down here hadn't realized what was actually going on. But then, they were all as brutally hungover as I was, if not worse.

Luther was *incredibly* lucky he'd come here when he had. Last night, he'd've been torn apart.

"But the Admiral and I need to speak now," I continued, "so here's what I need from you lot. Clear the hall up there. And one of the sitting rooms... get me somethin' to drink while you're at it. Us. Get *us* something to drink," I corrected quickly, even though that was clearly the last thing Luther needed right now.

"Y'want us to clear out the boys upstairs in the main room?" Jeffrey asked, uncertainly.

I knew why the request confused him. It wasn't often I conducted business – of any kind, legit or black market – behind closed doors. I had a policy of allowing my men, regardless of their rank, to weigh in on decisions that affected the fleet, so long as they were present for said negotiations. We were Anarchists, sure... but that didn't mean I didn't believe in the power of a public forum. Also, having an ever-present flock of my boys around me served as a means of intimidation, protection, and was extremely off-putting to more rigid men – like say, Amurescan Pedigree Lords – who were not accustomed to people they considered low-brow lessers having any say in negotiations. For all these reasons, I rarely met alone with anyone, save the women I took to bed. And... not even then, sometimes.

But this was different. And I couldn't explain to them *why*. Many of my men would feel understandably betrayed if they knew I was sparing any concern for a pirate hunter, a man who'd frequently made our exploits less profitable or too risky to even undertake. We'd even traded shots once or twice, although I don't *think* we'd killed any of each other's men. Yet.

"Just do it," I commanded, stone-faced. I didn't have the energy or the creativity to concoct a lie right now. I'd come up with something later.

I felt the air grow colder, that palpable aura of discomfort settling in more heavily. Thankfully, no one questioned me.

Goddamn this man. We'd been having a good month… I didn't need morale issues right now. But I didn't want to run the risk of someone doing something absurdly stupid while they thought they had the chance of it. Denholme had put himself in a hell of a spot here.

I wasn't used to being the one stuck with cleaning up someone else's bad decisions. This just wasn't me.

Taarush stayed at my side, which I was grateful for because although Luther had lost a bit of weight and wasn't as large a man as either of us, the cattle dog was still… dense and hardly someone I could princess carry up a narrow, rickety staircase easily. Having two men to help support him seemed to do it, though. We made it into the main hall, which Jeffrey had obediently cleared as asked, and I took him into the nearest sitting room from there. There were quite a few of these rooms meant for smoking, entertaining smaller parties, and whatnot. We'd converted most of them into bunks or, as my men so elegantly put it, 'fuckin' rooms'. This looked to be the former, the single table and chairs all pushed closer to the fire, heaped in blankets and discarded clothing where the men taking up residence here had passed out last night.

I settled the cattle dog down in one of the chairs, then went about bundling up the various linens over my arm and tossing them all into a corner, away from the still-smoldering fire. It was low, but still… stupid. Sailors should have been smarter about that.

"Bloody… children," I grumbled, balling up someone's shirt and tossing it off the arm of the couch I chose to drag closer to Luther with a squawk of wood on the floor. "Going to burn the damn place down."

Taarush had paused in the door and was saying something quietly to a man outside, before fetching a pint bottle from whoever'd gotten it and setting it down on the edge of the table for me. "Will that do, sir?"

I uncorked the bottle and sniffed it, confirming it was rum. I didn't really drink much else in the mornings. "It'll do," I said, "but Taarush, get me a Brukicker tonic." I glanced briefly at Luther, "A double. And two cups."

He nodded, shutting the door with a gentle click behind him as he cleared out. It really hadn't been a slam or anything approaching it, but I saw Luther wince and tilt his ears back all the same.

"You look like you skipped 'drunk'," I informed him curtly, tipping the bottle back and swallowing, embracing the burn with a relieved sigh, "went straight to the hangover part."

"Feels... that way," he confirmed, voice rough and disused.

"How long?" I asked, drinking again.

He moved his head slightly at that, eyes slim slits when they finally settled on me. "I don't..." he mumbled, "...unh? What?"

"How long've you been on a bender?" I asked more descriptively. "You look like *shit*."

"Oh," he seemed to understand, finally. "I... no. Just... the night."

I gave him a wry smile. "How long's that 'night' lasted, bud? Or've you lost track?"

"I've been sick," he said, eyes slipping closed for a few moments.

"Look, if you're gonna be sick, just try to be quiet about it," I sighed. "My boys don't seem to realize you stumbled in here shitfaced like some drunk off the street yet, and it's in your best interest they don't comprehend how vulnerable you are right now. Not all of 'em are as good-natured as I am, and you'd be a hell of a feather in a Privateer's cap –"

"No," he insisted with a little more vehemence. "Not... sick from drink. *Sick. Seer's Fever.*"

That got my attention *real* fast. And it explained a lot.

I leaned back against the tattered cushion of the cheap couch. "Oh, hell," I breathed out softly. "Are you... through it?" Come to think of it, everything about his condition could just be the result of the physical effects of the Fever. "Are you even drunk? Wait, no, I definitely smelled whiskey on you –"

"Drunk, too. And not... I don't have it. Inoculated," he pressed his knuckles to his muzzle, clearing his throat and sniffing noisily again, although I think that had more to do with his bleeding nose than any symptoms. Sympathetically (and as one who'd had his fair share of bad punches to the nose) I got up and rummaged about the room for something he could use, settling on a bar rag someone had left on the table.

"How long ago?" I asked, handing it over to him.

He took it slowly, inclining his head in a half-nod of thanks before pressing it to his still bleeding nose. "Finished the course... two weeks ago," he tipped his chin back slowly, his whole posture going lax in the chair. "You don't seem worried," he noted.

"I'm not. I know how inoculations work," I sat back down heavily. "I really ought to get me'n the boys treated. We don't go near the Southwest seas often, but," I paused. "Wait, is the Fever ripping its way through the Navy, now?"

He shook his head slowly. "It is thankfully rare. For now."

I blinked. "Then, why – isn't it a rough course to put yourself through just because? It *must* be. You're…" I gestured at him. "I mean no offense, but holy *shit*."

"I know," he grunted. "Not a'my best, for sure." His chin tipped further back, eyes fixed on some point on the ceiling. "It's been… a *month*."

"Yeah, well getting fucked up on whiskey on top of all that couldn't have helped," I pointed out, feeling *so* unnatural chastising someone else for drinking to excess.

"Wasn't the plan, exactly." He spoke with his eyes closed, his brow pinched as if fighting back dizziness. Or nausea. Hard to say. "Usually know what I can handle."

"You lost weight," I pointed out. "Guessing you were on bedrest for a while –"

"Mnh," he confirmed.

"Not exactly in peak physical condition, mate. What the hell were you thinking?"

"I s'pose I wasn't," he admitted quietly.

"Thinking?" My muzzle twitched, this whole scene setting me ill at ease. I didn't like seeing him like this. "That isn't like you."

He didn't respond. At all. Only stared ahead into the fire. And sure, he was drunk. Apparently recovering from a rough inoculation process that I'd heard could actually kill you same as the disease it was intended to protect you from, if you weren't tough enough to endure it. He'd gotten his face kicked in by a few of my boys, dragged up and down a flight of stairs I'd gotten winded taking, and I was only a bit hungover.

But this was Luther fucking Denholme.

"What. The hell. Is going on?" I annunciated, reaching out and grabbing him by the lower jaw to turn him to face me.

"Too much," was his simple answer.

"Why are you *here?*" I tried to get him to look me in the eyes. "Why are you," I gestured vaguely at his condition, "in this... state? Why are you alone? Where's the wolfhound?" I realized belatedly at that point that he was without his shadow. That man was essentially his minder, or his personal bodyguard, I hardly knew what to call him. But I could count – twice now – that I'd *ever* seen them apart.

"Johannes is... unwell," he said, barely above a whisper. I hardly knew what that meant, but it sounded *bad.*

"Inoculation take poorly for him?" I guessed.

He shook his head. "He is grappling with his demons."

"Well, that's spooky as fuck, mate," I said, curling a lip. "What does that even mean?"

"I..." he paused like he was trying to form words in his mouth, but it took him considerable time. A quicker wit than this man, generally, you could not find. This couldn't be all the drink. "I cannot burden him now," he finally said. "He is with his family." Then after another considerable pause, so quiet I barely heard it, "If I were kinder, I would leave him behind. But I need him..."

I decided to leave that one alone. Sounded like they'd had some kind of falling out or something, but that really wasn't my business. I most certainly did *not* consider the wolfhound a friend or comrade or whatever (my thigh ached in remembrance of the bolt he'd put through it; the bastard could rot in hell for all I cared), and it really had no bearing on the situation at hand.

"Fine, but you've got other people who ought to have been looking out for you," I reasoned. Not that I'd *ever* thought the cattle dog couldn't handle his own damn self, he was worldly and clever enough to make his way in just about any port. But life can lay low the strongest of us – as was evidenced here – and if I'd had the month from hell, I know at least two dozen of my men would've intervened to prevent me from doing something as fool-hardy as stumbling off drunk, despondent, ill, and unsupervised into enemy territory. Maybe one or two of those, but all at once?

He was once again staring off into space, like he was very carefully considering what I'd last said to him.

"Not... really," he said at length. But I'd forgotten what he was replying to at this point.

"What led you to my doorstep?" I asked. "Is there something, I mean," I bit back the urge to sound snappish. "Is there something I can do for you?" I went with instead.

I couldn't bear to be an asshole to him right now. I didn't even want to risk hurting his feelings, truth be told. Normally I could handle a crying drunk, but the thought of seeing this man in particular weep was… it made my chest hurt just thinking about it. And he looked that bad, like he might very well be on the verge.

An impulse I can't explain led me to cross the few feet between us, grab him by the shoulders and shuffle him bodily to sit on the couch beside me, rather than across from me in that rickety chair. I felt like I'd get more out of him this way. But right off, he mostly seemed bemused, grabbing at one of my sleeves to stabilize himself as he plopped down. Wincing *for* him, I quickly reached down and tugged his tail to the side; he'd nearly crushed it sitting on it.

"Do you…" I paused, thinking on my own drunken exploits in the past. He seemed to be on the downslide, so he'd probably been worse when he'd first arrived here. And he didn't have a whole lot of answers for me, so…

"Do you even remember why you're here?" I asked him, letting a long breath out slowly.

His eyes moved to mine, almost pleading. "No," he finally confessed.

Blessedly, then came a knock. I didn't bother turning, but called out, "Come in!"

The leopard entered, albeit briefly. Taarush, always professional, only took one glance at the two of us, likely to assure for himself that I was still in no danger. He seemed unworried and set two tin cups and a taller glass down, filled to the brim with an ochre concoction. The pungent smell was an old friend to me now, and that looked to be a freshly-mixed batch based on the way the ingredients hadn't begun to separate yet. I'd have to thank the cook later.

"How are the men?" I asked him before he left.

"Curious," he responded simply, "but calm. All's well, sir."

"Thank you, Taarush."

He nodded at me, then took his leave.

"Good man," I muttered as I stood, pouring a bit of the rum into both cups, then splitting the Brukicker tonic between them. I handed it over to Luther, who curled his nose at the scent, but otherwise took it without further question, likely familiar with it, or something like it.

We sat in silence and forced it down, and apparently some of the man's resolve was still there, because he downed his faster than I did mine. I clapped the cup back on the table and waited for it to kick in, the popping of the fire the only sound in the room for a time.

"I'm flattered, by the way," I said after a long while.

"Hnh?" He glanced my way. It might have been a trick of the light, but it seemed like his gaze had sharpened marginally. Or maybe it was just because we'd been staring into a fire.

"That you came to me, of all people, when you were blackout drunk," I filled in. I flashed him a light smile. "I'm hardly a deep man, but that's gotta mean something, right? A drunk mind... something, something... a sober heart? I don't know," I laughed.

"Don't laugh," he said softly.

"And why not?" I snorted. "You have a problem with my laugh?"

"You've a good voice," he said, once again with the enigmatic answers I couldn't make sense of. "And a good laugh. It's not that."

"I'm just glad I've got you talking," I said. "Go on then. Explain it to me. Why can't I laugh?"

"Because it's nothing to laugh off," he answered simply. "It's the truth. In my fugue, I came to you."

"You have to be the only man I know who uses words like 'fugue' when you're hungover," I said dryly.

He glanced down at the empty cup. "This is working."

"You were verbose even before," I waved a hand, "once I got you talking, anyway."

"Was...confused," he confessed, whiskers twitching as he continued to stare down into his cup. "I still am."

"That'll happen," I said ruefully. "You don't drink like this often, do you?"

"I did more when I was young," he murmured.

"It's a wonder you survived your youth, then," I arched an eyebrow.

"I wasn't trying to."

There was that pain in my chest, again. Everything about this was worrying.

"Luther," I leaned in close, forcing him to look in my direction. He seemed momentarily startled by my proximity, but didn't flinch again when I cautiously placed a hand on his shoulder. His expression was… 'fragile' is the best word I can think of, and it's still not quite right. Everything from his stooped posture, his too-narrow shoulders, the light, involuntary shivers of his muzzle and the *deep* circles beneath his eyes… it felt like he could crumble beneath my paw.

"Grayson," he said, haltingly. The fact that he'd used my name – not my *surname* – was the first indication I had that this was going to be bad. Very, very bad.

"It's alright," I eased him on with a light squeeze of his shoulder, my blunt claws sinking into the fabric of his jacket. "I'm listening."

"A… man came to see me," he began, with a shuddering breath. "A man from my past. A lover of mine, from a long time ago."

"Alright," I said, simply nodding. I didn't dismiss the gravity of what he'd just put to words; those words could have seen him hanged in the Treneval square, simply because this man from his past and this lover were the same person. Years ago, I'd unearthed this secret of his and tried to use it against him. To my everlasting shame. But we'd gotten past that, and now he was trusting me with this. That was big.

"He's moved on," he said hoarsely. I didn't miss how he gripped his cup a little tighter. "I'm happy for him," he continued, and to his credit, he earnestly sounded it. "But, despite that, he came to me… cared for me, while I recovered."

"Good of him," I said.

"Cruel," he countered softly. "I'd come to believe – to make peace with the fact – that he'd left me behind because there were no mutual feelings between us. But, then, he does this. He comes to me, when I'm at death's door. Cares for me. He *cared* this much for me, and he still didn't want to be with me. He said he couldn't…" he swallowed; the action so evident beneath the fur of his throat that I could almost feel it in my own. "He didn't want to move on, until he'd made peace with me. He was asking for me to release him from *my* heart, from any remaining obligation he had to me. So that he could be happy in his new life, with no regrets."

"I'm sorry, mate," I said with utter sincerity. "That's fucking awful."

I wasn't about to chastise him for falling in love in the first place. It wasn't an illness I'd ever been afflicted with (thankfully), and that was by design, but I couldn't fault those who fell victim to it. Luther was a passionate man, I'd only known him a few hours when I'd first learned that, and he was in the unenviable position of having to hide those passions for the sake of himself, his partners, and his family. It was hard enough that his predilection for men limited his opportunities but based on what little I knew of his personal life, he'd also had lousy luck. Death, fear, and misfortune had befallen those few I knew of, so hearing that he was mourning another missed chance at happiness was no surprise.

Coupled with the inoculation, that was a double-blow that'd knock most men on their ass. But at least it was something I could understand. Maybe something we could solve.

"You just need to chase his memory off with someone new," I reasoned, shrugging. "You know I've got a few lads on my crew —"

"Trust me, that's the last thing I need right now," he muttered.

"Oh, come on," I said. "Maybe not *now*, not in your current condition, and it ain't gonna be some whirlwind romance, but it doesn't always have to be that way, y'know. Sometimes you just need to shake the water off," I straightened up, putting an arm up over the back of the couch and leaning closer to him. "I happen to know a few men'n particular who fancy the same sorts of leisure activities you do *and* are all too eager to make poor life decisions."

He let out a 'hah' of breath that might've been a laugh if he were in any condition for one. "I don't have the time, I'm afraid."

"You just need to sober up, get a warm bath, maybe take another week to recover. We'll be in port all month —"

"I sail in three days."

I stalled, opening my mouth to ask the obvious question. But then the pieces started to fit together on their own.

"Oh, fuck," I said aloud.

Seer's Fever was a horrible disease from the Dark Continent. It drove men mad, made them see things, thus the name. As bad as it was though, it could be relatively hard to catch. The only people who tended to get it were sailors who actually went to that accursed southern continent and the people who had relations with them. Family, whores, whomever. You didn't get this disease casually.

I'd seen a few cases over the years in my fleet, but it was rare. Not one of the ones we worried about, because we didn't traffic much in the southern seas. That was contested territory, and more importantly, an active warzone. The Amur had been fighting a losing battle to maintain control over their flagging Colonies in those unbroken lands for two decades now. They'd made an ill-fated attempt to colonize the continent the same way they'd tried to do with Carvecia, where they'd met with – and eventually lost to – rebellion. And now they were dealing with a similar situation with the natives of the Dark Continent, except *they* were being more… proactive about it. They'd never welcomed the Amur incursion, had fought them tooth and nail from the outset, and now the continent and all the waters surrounding it were a whirlpool of death and carnage that few escaped from. Yet in defiance of all logic, the bloody Amurescan King was clinging to the idea that they could prevail and bend the place to their will if they only threw enough bodies at it.

The inoculation, the old flame coming back into his life to make peace with him, his Second-in-Command abandoning him to spend time with his family…

"I'd heard you were in port," he said, as if just now remembering it. "I don't remember how I found out… exactly where you were," he spoke like a man stumbling through his patchy memory. "I suppose I must have wanted to… talk? To say goodbye, maybe." He flicked his gaze over to mine, eyes wider and clearer than they'd been so far. "You've been a friend, Grayson. Almost unwillingly, at times, but… I don't know what else to call what we have."

I swallowed heavily. So, there it was. He'd said it. "You can call it that," I said. "I think of you that way."

"Hnh," he hummed, almost contentedly. It was the first moment of peace I'd seen wash over his features since he'd come here.

A low growl, coming on like the distant rumble of thunder, disturbed the companionable silence that followed. It took me a few moments to realize it was coming from me, unbidden. Luther's brows rose, concerned.

"Fuck you, man," I managed to get out, the growl an undertone to every word. "I knew…" I hissed, clenching a hand over the back of the couch, feeling the cheap fabric against my claws, "...I knew if you were walking into my life right now, it'd be to drop somethin'... shattering on me. Some uncomfortable truth that'd tip me upside-down and set me reeling. That's what you fucking *do*."

"I'm... I'm sorry?" He said, sounding like he wanted to mean the apology, but was still confused. He was so lost – had been searching for every word and trying desperately to explain himself since he got here – and it was honestly a wonder he'd followed along with our conversation as much as he had, given his condition.

But I couldn't help it. The anger had come, finally.

"What do you expect me to do with this?!" I demanded, staring him in the eyes, our muzzles inches apart so that if he chose to look away from me, he'd have to make a real conscious effort to do so. "Wish you good fucking luck?!"

"I-I don't know," he admitted. He wasn't looking away, at least. He'd never been a coward. Steeling himself visibly, he reminded me, "I don't know why I came here. I really don't. I'm only guessing it was to wish you farewell before I left. I don't remember where my head was at when I was drinking."

"What the hell happened?" I demanded, swiping my free hand through the air, out in the direction of the dark blue windows beyond and the distant sprigs of masts silhouetted against the early dawn or late dusk, I still wasn't sure. "How – why are you sailing out to war?!"

He set his jaw. "It's my duty," he replied stoically.

"Hang that!" I belted out. "You're a *pirate hunter*, Denholme! Not some lapdog to your bloody Colonizer King. I feel," I huffed out in sheer audacity, "like the biggest fucking fool... *reminding* you who you are! It would be better for me and mine if you *forgot*."

One of his eyebrows raised, and there came an inkling, a hint, of the dry snark I knew him for. "Would it, though?" he asked pointedly.

"I mean, fine," I confirmed, "you *do* poach my competition more often than you've been a thorn in my side specifically. We've brokered a few good deals over the years, too. But you have to admit, they were far more beneficial to *you* than *me* – more bloody protection rackets than anything."

"Well," he closed his eyes for a moment, "you won't need to worry about me for a while."

"If ever again," I said, the growl back in my voice. Despite what some might call my 'explosive personality', I didn't actually like to growl at people. It was too rough for me, too angry. Not my style. I felt like I didn't have any control over it now, though.

He didn't respond to that, but he did finally look away from me. Which I took as a tacit agreement.

"You know damn well," I said, aghast, "that taking your fleet there is suicide. How are you letting them do this to you?! It can't be for the Crown's endorsement – you've been *kicking ass* these last few years. You're bloody infamous, man… my men call you a 'demon'. Most everyone I know in my trade is *terrified* of you."

"The flattery's unnecessary," he insisted, with the barest hint of a self-satisfied smirk. The one he usually wore like a second skin.

"I know I'm not the only Privateer you're on the take with," I said, trying not to sound as petulant as I felt about it. I'd been his *first*, at least. I'd always have that. "Are you hard-up for some reason? Whatever this commission is paying, it *can't* be worth it. Look, I just got off a job that paid absurdly well. What do you need?"

"It isn't about coin," he assured me, then brought his eyes back to mine, the firelight catching in them. "Although it's… surprisingly good of you to offer."

"Fuck you," I said good-naturedly. "I'm a great guy. And yeah, it's been a bit tumultuous, but I'd call us 'friends'. Comrades, for sure. Right?"

He nodded, silently. I didn't miss the way his shoulders lifted, either. There was a lightness in his eyes, that 'peace' I'd seen earlier, every time we'd confirmed this simple fact. It was stunning, really, how much of an effect it seemed to have on him. Maybe give some credit to the alcohol, but still, heartbreaking to think it might've just been a rarity in his life. In anyone's life.

I had *so* many people I considered friends, across the world. Dozens of bosom buddies, just in this one building. People I trusted with my life. Knowing I could count the Cerberus Admiral among them was nice, but… hardly as profound as it seemed to be to him. Treneval was *his* port city, he had a place of residence here, it's where his ships docked most of the time in between hunting seasons. With the wolfhound occupied elsewhere, was I *really* the only one he could think to come to at his darkest moment?

"So, if it's not about the commission," I pressed, "then why the hell are you letting them pull you into that maelstrom? You've never concerned yourself with those waters, before."

"It's the legacy I inherited," he said, voice laced with misery. "Lucius Denholme founded that Colony for the Crown. He later regretted it, told me about how he'd gotten pulled into the politics – it hardly matters why, now," he shook his head. "Serwich is Denholme land technically, even though it's no boon to me. I collect nothing from it; with the losses they suffer every year in the ongoing conflict, the place has never been profitable. Although that hasn't stopped the Crown from taxing it."

"Give it up!" I said as though it were the most obvious thing in the world. "Let the Crown inherit the responsibility. Just give up whatever claim your family has left on it. It isn't worth it."

He huffed. "I tried. No one wants the burden of protecting it, the Crown is content to continue collecting their due and leave the management to my house. Which I let my Seneschal handle, and honestly, if that's all there was to it… fine. But it's gotten much, much worse there over the last few years. The natives are growing more and more warlike, some kind of plague is making its way through the populace –"

"Seer's Fever?"

"Not just that," he sighed. "There are so many new diseases there, Grayson. I hired on one of the best Physicians willing to take the trip, I'm hoping we can do something to alleviate people's misery. Anything."

"That place is a hell for canines," I shook my head, the coins and beads in my dreads clicking against one another. "We were never meant for it. It should be left to the natives, it's their land. Even the natural order is rejecting us."

"I don't disagree," he muttered. He leaned, his back sliding down marginally against the mostly-flattened cushion of the old couch. I felt the scruff of his neck brush past my knuckles where they rested and resisted the urge to reach out. It behooved anyone to remember, Amurescans weren't nearly as open with their affections as those of us in the free world. Especially between men.

Honestly, how they survived on so little physical contact… it boggled the mind. Just the fact that Luther and I were sitting as close as we were now, our knees occasionally knocking together, would've been high scandal amongst his peers.

Just… stunningly stupid.

"So, let it go," I repeated, emphatically. "Send aid, send your Physician, hell, send firearms if you think it'll help."

"They need more than that right now," he said, rubbing a hand between his eyes. "I've had agents there for a few years reporting back to me – those that survive, anyway."

"Fucking hell," I snarled.

"I've even paid off a few men in your profession for intel," he continued. "The waters are ripe for Piracy, given the chaos. There'll always be vultures, opportunists, in situations like that… but for the right price, they tell me what they know. It's worse than the Garrison there thinks it is, or worse than they are choosing to report, anyway."

"I know," I said. "Word gets around. Some people do business with the lizardfolk, you know. Those that don't shoot on sight."

"Oh, I'm well aware," he said. "They have gunpowder now. And did you know that some of their soldiers can fly?"

I took a long breath in and out. "Yes, I've heard. So, that's not just some fanciful story about… war kites, or something?"

He laughed mirthlessly at that. "No. Though I wouldn't put that past them. No, there are creatures there – intelligent or beasts, I'm not sure – who can fly, for limited times of the day. And they've recently been engaging in this tactic of dropping cauldrons of boiling pitch, sometimes with gunpowder charges, on ships' sails."

"Mother of –" I nearly bit my tongue. "What the hell are you *thinking*, man?!"

He shrugged, helplessly. "The Crown will *not* send any additional vessels to protect Serwich or the shipping lanes. They don't have the firepower to defend their supply lines, and I'm talking even just *essential* voyages. I've shut down most exports, which isn't making the Crown happy, but it's all I could do to stem the bleeding. Grayson, they are *trapped*," he emphasized. "The people there – most of them are just workers and their families, a lot of them were sent as part of a sentence for minor crimes –"

"They turned Serwich into a bloody *Prison Colony*?"

"It isn't some posh city," he explained, voice growing more and more strained with a desperate edge. "They built the Fort first off for the Pedigrees, then let the settlement spring up around it, but they've never spent any 'unnecessary' resources to reinforce where most of the populace lives. I have little to no control over how the Colony is run, unless I am *there* asserting my authority. The Pedigree there do as they please and their primary interest is getting as much lumber out of the rainforest and as much silver out of the mines as possible. Bringing in new labor is less costly than protecting the workforce they already have. The terrain is impossible to tame, the natives can appear and disappear into it like ghosts, hell, they can *fly* over barriers."

"I get it," I held up a hand. "You want to whip the place into shape, to protect the people there. But Luther," I leaned in, "can you? I mean no offense to you whatsoever, and I'm sure the fools running things there right now are utter *bastards*, but are you sure you can do any better than they have? Running a Fleet and running a Colony are two completely different skill sets."

"I know I can't," he said quietly.

"Then… what –" I sputtered.

"Serwich is lost," he said, with dead certainty. "They've just not realized it yet. There's an alliance of tribes, an army massing, amongst the Cathazra – the natives. One of their tribal chieftains, an 'Elekk', they call themselves. A war leader. They're pushing back into the east coast. Two colonies have fallen to them already. Serwich will be the third."

I was starting to hate the fact that I'd sobered him up. He still looked and sounded like hell, only now he was making sense.

"Even with my fleet there, we… are just so severely disadvantaged," he sighed softly. "My Captains are confident, because we have the Fort, and we still hold the bay. They discount the natural advantage the terrain gives the natives and refuse to realize how entrenched they are, because they don't recognize their forms of architecture and style of war, yet. But they will soon. They believe if worst comes to worst, we'll be able to fall back and rely on our superior firepower."

"And will you?" I asked.

"If we abandon ninety percent of our populace?" He narrowed his eyes. "Sure. We could hole up in the Fort. For a while, anyway. What we *need* is a larger force. I *cannot* make the numbers work the way they are. I've been pleading with the Crown for over a year now. If they want me to protect their assets, I need assistance to do so. But every time I've tried, it's the same answer. Nothing additional can be spared."

"They're stretched thin," I said. "Tryin' to hold onto half the world will do that to you." Something occurred to me, then. "What about Cross?" I asked. "Piracy's rampant down there, like you said. And I'd thought your fleets were working together a lot, of late. Couldn't he spend a season down there with you?"

"Well, he might have been able to," he cleared his throat, "if *someone* hadn't shot his ships full of holes. They're in dry dock, you know. Might not be worth salvaging, at this point. He is *livid*, by the way."

"Man came after *me*," I pointed out. "I wasn't about to let him sink me without a fight."

"I don't blame you," he assured me. "Your scuffles with Cross have nothing to do with me, and honestly, I'm not sure he would've helped me, anyway. He hates politics even more than I do, he's no friend of the Crown, and I don't think he would've wanted to put his fleet on the line to protect their assets."

"Wait – is this maybe why you're here?" I asked outright, turning to look down at him. He was normally shorter than me, but slumped as he was now, it was much more pronounced.

He blinked up at me, still sleepy-eyed and ragged. It was *so* hard not to put a hand between his ears and at least smooth back the fur. "What?" he asked simply.

"You don't think you might've come to me for help?" I said pointedly. "I'm another man you know with a fleet –"

"I don't want anyone else pulled down into this nightmare with me," he insisted, immediately. "I wouldn't ask that of you."

"I don't expect you would," I assured him, "but you've got to put yourself in the mindset of a depressed drunk –"

"I'm not 'depressed,'" he insisted.

"Oh, not in the *least*," I drawled out, rolling my eyes. "You just got wasted –"

"You do that constantly, regardless of your mood."

"But you *don't*," I stabbed a finger into his chest. "And you didn't let me finish. You got wasted, stumbled out into the night looking for some kinda lifeline, with your usual stalwart wolfhound gone missin' and all… found your way to my doorstep, *broke into* my place –"

"My memory's not all there," he coughed, "but I'm pretty sure the door was open."

"You coulda' *knocked*."

"I… think I was trying to find you, specifically," he said, sounding more certain by the moment. "Bypass your men. I'm a lot stealthier in my mind when I'm drunk."

"You're lucky you're not *dead*," I said. "I was on the third floor. You never would've made it all the way to me without running afoul of my boys."

"Mmh," he dragged a breath through his nose. "Not alone, either. You were bedding a… mink, last night?"

"No, actually," I said irritably. "I mean, yes. She was there. But we never really got that far – it doesn't matter. Look. You find your way to me, blackout drunk, you practically cry on my shoulder about a lost love –"

"I did not," he insisted.

"Fine, you were a big damn man about it," I bit back my frustration. *Amurescan men.* Good fucking *GOD*. "You just went through a rough battle with one of the world's worst illnesses. You had to make peace with an old flame, your… Second-in-Command, your fucking shadow, can't support you right now, I'm guessing your family can't be with you either –"

"Delilah is angry with me," he said quietly. "She doesn't want me to go."

"Smart woman," I growled out. "You should listen to your wife, Luther."

"I don't have a choice," he said, voice hoarse. "Someone has to protect those people."

"You are *going off to war*," I emphasized, "against a group of people you hardly understand – and I know you, man – that has to *terrify* you. You can't out-maneuver an enemy whose moves you can't predict."

"No," he agreed shakily, "I can't."

"You're depressed," I said. "Scared. It's alright to admit that, no-*stop*," I reached forward with my free hand and grabbed his opposite shoulder, turning him towards me forcibly before he could look away again. "*STOP* … with this false bravado bullshit. You think I can't see through it? You think I don't know how it feels to put up a front to my boys when we're in deep?"

"You don't hide who you are," he said, his words almost a challenge, like he dearly wanted me to confirm for him that he was right. Was he envious of me? "You're the freest man I know," he said, his voice coming from his gut.

"You think I don't get barked at and challenged by my boys?" I laughed. "You think I don't have to put up a strong façade sometimes?"

"No, I…" he trailed off. "You have your own demands with your fleet, I'm sure."

I couldn't help it. The sentiment had always been there I think, it just chose this moment to boil out.

"You could've been one of us," I said.

His eyes widened.

"You *should* have," I put more force into the words, "been one of us. Luther. You *still* could. You and I? We'd be fearsome together."

I saw it the moment he tried to shift away from the point, the forced smile, the huff of breath. "As proposals go, you could stand to work on yours –"

"Who you are," I growled out, "*everything* you are… *we* would have accepted you. Valued you for the things that matter, for your *mind*, your skills. Everything else? Everything that's made your life a living hell amongst your countrymen, your… blood, your past, your choice of bed partners… none of that would matter in my fleet. You want to be *free*?" I dragged my arm from where it was looped over the back of the couch, settling a paw on his back, pulling him in closer. "It is literally yours for the taking. You just have to let go of all this," I gestured out the window.

His gaze hadn't left mine, but his irises were shaking. His whole body was shaking, I realized. It was subtle, barely a shiver. Like someone with a bow drawn taut, straining.

"It *pains* me to watch you suffer," I stated openly. "Your Crown does not deserve your loyalty. You are *too good* a man to be thrown onto the pyre of their pointless war. Leave all of this. Get out now while you can, before you *die* for them."

He opened his mouth, and I cut him off. "Your family will be *fine*," I insisted. "Hell, we can relocate them if you want. Carvecia. Mataa.

Anywhere. They're about to lose you, anyway. And do you really think the men in power won't still hate you, if you give *all you have* to defend this territory, and *fail?*"

"It doesn't matter what my countrymen think of me," he said quietly.

"I'm glad you feel that way," I said, not believing him, "because if they knew who you really were? The man you truly are, the man I know, they would *loathe* you. And you *know* it. You live in fear of the people you protect, man. People call me insane sometimes, but your life? Your life is the craziest con game I've ever heard of. And for *what?* How have they earned your fealty? What has your country ever done for you?"

He was silent for a long, long time.

"It doesn't matter," he said at long last, "if my country loves me. I'm accustomed to unrequited love."

My breath stopped. I couldn't find the words to tell him how achingly sad he was making me. No one made me *feel things* like this. *God damn him.*

"I'm a protector," he said softly. "It's all I've... ever wanted to be. The only thing that makes me feel whole. I don't need them to recognize it. Or even you. I just want to make the seas safe. Free. It's the only place of respite I've ever found."

"For what it's worth," I choked out the words. "Thank you. I know that matters very little, coming from someone like me –"

"It does matter," he assured me.

"There are some unbelievable monsters out there," I said. "In my trade. Knowing you're out there, it... honestly does comfort me. I understand what you're fighting for."

He nodded, slowly. "I hope you'll forgive me, then," he murmured. "The people in Serwich need help. I'm going to do all I can."

"You're going to *die* there," I said between my teeth.

"Maybe," he agreed, smiling bitterly. "But I have to try. I have to. No one else is coming to their aid." He lifted his muzzle some, then breathed out a quiet, "Oh."

"What?" I asked, trying to swallow around the pain in my throat.

"Your eyes are blue," he said. "I just noticed."

"Bastard," I breathed out, staccato. "We've known each other how long now?"

"I… try not to linger long when I stare at other men," he admitted. "Especially with those who… know." He glanced aside at that. "I-I don't want to unnerve anyone. Assumptions are easily made, tempers can flare. I have to be careful."

I felt my brows knit, anger rising again. "You can stare at me all you like, mate. I don't fucking care. I can't *imagine* how exhausting that shit must be. Please, *please* don't worry about that, with me. I'm fine. Nothing about being around you 'unnerves' me." I lifted my eyebrows, conscious of how angry I might look right now. "I… I want to… damnit," I gave a 'tch' around my back teeth, "I know I said I don't mind you looking at me, but would you just… *please* stop looking so sad…"

He shut his jaw self-consciously, uncertainty moving over his features. "I-I'm sorry. How am I –"

"Why did you come to me?" I insisted, even while knowing he still had no answers. "You won't let me *help* you."

"That isn't your responsibility," he assured me.

"It ought to be someone's," I ground out, my paw on his back balling in his jacket, the other gripping his shoulder a little tighter. "I… shit. I just want to…"

He continued to look up at me, lost. I had nothing for him. No answers, nothing I could offer. Except…

A frustrated growl tore its way out of my muzzle, and throwing caution to the wind, I pulled him the few remaining sacred inches we'd kept up this whole while, like a barrier. His head fell in between my shoulder and jaw, our hips pressed together, his side against my side. His whole body went stiff, but before he could push back, I used the arm I'd had behind him to loop around his waist, pulling him more firmly into the embrace. He was weak right now, but he still could have fought back if he'd really wanted to. And for a moment, I thought he would. I felt him poised to push back, to disentangle us-

But then he just… gave way. All at once, he began to uncoil. His shoulders loosened, his body went heavy against mine, his muzzle bent into the crook of my neck, and the finale – he let his breath out in a long, slow sigh. I felt it all the way down my chest.

I moved my arm a bit, slipping it up beneath the hem of his already bunched coat, so my hand was splayed more comfortably around his hip. I could feel the heat of his pelt beneath the thin cotton of his shirt. For some reason, right now, that was immensely reassuring. I'd had more than one of my men bleed out in my arms, like this. A warm body – regardless of whether they were a friend, a lover, or something in between – was always a comfort.

"Is this alright?" I asked, most *certainly* too late.

The only noise I got out of him was a quiet, "Mmhh," that sounded… accepting? My guess was confirmed a moment later when he nodded shallowly and leaned against me with what must have been his full weight. I shifted a leg and vaguely readjusted my arm to get comfortable, but otherwise made it clear I wasn't going anywhere.

I did my absolute best to just hold him like that for a while without fidgeting or saying anything. I didn't want to push my luck. But I'm just not good at sitting still, and my hands tend to start moving first, before the rest of me. I settled with gingerly moving my fingers in semi-circular motions against his shoulder at first, then slowly shifting my paw up through the scruff of his neck. I had been fighting the urge to smooth out the unruly, damp fur there since he'd arrived. I set to it slowly, easing into the idea of anything beyond the embrace with careful measure – because even being held seemed to be an adjustment for him.

"Your fur is a nightmare," I muttered, noting how much coarser it was than my own. "I've often thought you must not take good care of it, but… it's just like this, isn't it?"

"Luckily, I'm not so hung up on my vanity as you are," he muttered against my collarbone.

I gave a belly laugh at that. "Bullshit," I countered. "I might preen over my fur, but I've seen you without a shirt on. We just prioritize different things."

"Fair," he agreed, his tone gone tranquil and lethargic. I briefly entertained the possibility that he was coming down from a lot of booze and what must have been a truly exhausting night – he might actually just be falling asleep. I wasn't entirely sure what I'd do if he passed out here, let alone in my arms, but I quickly decided waking him wouldn't be an option. I'd just have to move him elsewhere in the house and keep him from the men until he'd slept it off…

He dragged in a breath through his nose, then let it out slowly. "Your shirt," he murmured.

"Hm?"

"It smells like you," he observed.

"Well, it's mine, so it ought to," I huffed.

"You've a tendency to smell like whatever you're drinking," he said, "or smoking. Or that oil you put in your dreads… or whatever woman you're currently seeing. It makes your scent hard to pin down."

"Not intentional," I shrugged, then smiled a bit. "Sounds like it bothers you, though."

"I'm a dog, Grayson," he cracked his eyes open for a half a second, before shutting them again. "You're canine, you should understand. I commit people to memory that way. Some scents you can associate with people, but yours are… hectic. Always changing. It's hard to pin-point your own, beneath it all."

"I understand," I assured him, tapping my own nose. "I guess I'm just not as hung up on it as you are. Also, if I want a whiff of someone, I have no issue just sticking my snout all up in their business. I guess you're rarely this… close with people, huh?"

"Very few," he said quietly. Then, a moment later, his voice tentatively curious, "Is this normal for you?"

"With other men?" I guessed.

"With… people other than those you bed down with," he said carefully.

"You mean friends?" I clarified. "Yeah. I'd say so. I mean, I don't go embracing strangers, unless I'm drunk. And that usually doesn't go well. But with my closest men, this wouldn't be all that unusual. If they needed it. If it felt warranted. Is it helping?"

A beat of silence. Then, a simple, "Yes."

"Good. I'm glad," I said, content to leave it at that. There really wasn't any need to complicate this. Obviously, physical affection between two men could have other context for someone like Luther, but that wasn't… this, and I saw no reason to compare or connect one to the other. I moved the hand on his hip to rub at his lower back, comfortingly. And for the first time, he pressed in closer against me, of his own will.

"If you can't protect these people..." I said, feeling his body stiffen expectantly. But I had to get this out. "Then, you should get them the hell out of there."

Silence. Which meant he'd already considered that.

"I know it's something you've run scenarios for in your head," I said, resting my chin on top of his head, "if even I've landed on it as a possible solution."

"An evacuation," he said quietly. "It would be... unheard of. Moving an entire population at once like that."

"Could you do it?" I asked.

He shifted slightly, breathing in and out deeply, once. I could practically smell him burning lamp oil, running the possibilities over in his mind. "Not as it stands," he finally said. "Even with the vessels they have on hand in the Serwich Bay – and I'm working with out-of-date information, mind you – we just don't have the capacity. Not if I want the warships to be fully operational. I'd have people crammed to the gills on the gun decks, we'd be running lower in the water, there'd be morale issues, obviously..."

"Unhappy men are better than dead men," I pointed out.

"None of this even addresses how I'd get my Command Staff to agree to an evacuation," he continued, "let alone the Pedigree Landlords of Serwich. That's... a dozen, at least... very 'well-bred' men with a lot of their resources invested in that land. Imagine the conversation where I attempt to explain to them why we have to abandon the Colony. Cede it willingly back to the natives? I'm going to show up on their shores with four brimming warships, and a flock of seasoned Navy men, including five Captains who've been cutting their teeth on Pirates for the last five years. The Lords are going to expect *results*. My Captains are going to expect results. They refuse to accept how hopeless our situation is, there. If I come to their aid, only to tell them the plan is to surrender their investments and shell the place out –"

"Wait, five?" I was counting on my fingers. I was fairly certain I knew all of his Captains.

"Johannes is technically a Captain," he filled in. "Since the Crown appointed me an Admiral, officially. I was only an acting Admiral, before."

"So, you'll have him on your side, at least," I pointed out. Then paused. "Or will you? What happened between you two?"

He made a quiet noise of discomfort. "It's not… entirely my story to tell," he said weakly, "but he's not… not handling the idea of returning to the Dark Continent as well as –"

"Don't say 'as well as I am,'" I said, horrified at the mere notion.

"Mmhh… well…"

"That man is a *rock*," I gasped. "At least, the few times I met him he was. I didn't even know he'd been to the Dark Continent. What the hell happened to him there?"

"That's the thing; he doesn't like to talk about it," he said darkly. "I've gotten bits and pieces. It's the only subject I've ever seen shake him so badly. He very nearly begged me not to bring him along. But he's a Templar, and Lucius left him with the care of the Cerberus fleet. He'd be turning his back on every duty he holds sacred if he refuses this mission, and he *still* considered it. Whatever his experiences there when they founded the Colony, they… damaged him. The Physician calls it 'Soldier's Fatigue.'"

"I've heard of that," I said softly. I felt, rather than saw, the way his ears had begun to quake as we spoke. I moved the paw I'd been uselessly trying smooth back his bristly nape with and cupped his ear, rubbing it between my thumb and forefinger.

He groaned, almost sounding *irritated*. "That feels better than it has any right to," he muttered.

"I'm good with my hands," I shrugged.

"How is it you just… *do*… these things?" He asked almost in wonderment, "So casually?"

I shook my head, chuckling. "What d'you mean?"

"You cross every boundary – I haven't even done things like this with most of my *lovers*," he protested, while simultaneously tipping his other ear. I didn't miss the gesture.

Smirking, I switched to the other. "It's no skin off my back," I pointed out. "And I know this sort of thing helps me when I'm down."

"Yes, but with *women* I'd wager," he said, voice slightly muffled by my shirt.

"Mate, sometimes it ain't about feelin' randy," I said. "Sometimes you just want someone to reach out. And you don't need to be fuckin' to reach back."

I saw his eyes open to slim slits, his features slowly going lax, like my words had plummeted him deep into thought. Before he could get lost in it, I said, "I'll help you."

"Hnh?" he rumbled.

I gave a long sigh, closing my eyes and carefully considering my words before finally landing on, "I want to help your people."

He opened his mouth, and I cut him off, "Not your bloody Pedigree curs – your *people*. The people livin' in that Colony; none of this is their fault. And I know that's why you're risking your ass, too. There's what – a few thousand souls there?"

"Roughly 3,400, last I heard," he said, voice coarse around the edges. "Grayson, I can't ask this of you –"

"You're not gonna ask," I informed him, taking on an authoritative tone, "you're gonna *demand*. A'least, that's the story I'm telling my men. You pulled my ass out of the fire a few times now, I'd be hanging from a noose on at least one occasion if not for you."

"We had an arrangement then," he insisted.

"Just shut the fuck up, man," I growled again, but there was no malice in it. "Listen. I'm not helping you *hold* the place. I'm not killing lizardfolk to make your King richer."

"Then what –"

"Evacuate the populace," I said. "You *know* it's the only option. We've been going back and forth here for too long – I can tell what it is you want to do. I know you well enough by now. It's the only way you stop the bleeding. Put this nightmare behind you. Otherwise, you'll be fighting for this hell-hole 'til the day you die, which… could be sooner than we'd both like."

"*Every* Pedigree Lord will be against me," he said with certainty.

"That's what you'll need the extra firepower for," I asserted. "Look, you can't always reason your way through things with people – especially if they're arguing in bad faith. That's the point in the conversation when I pull a fucking pistol; sometimes it's just how you have to handle things. The Lords there don't have the might to push back against you, if they did they'd've used it on the lizards by now. I know dealing with your Captains'll be tricky, but you'll have your man Johannes, right?"

He nodded, seeming more and more settled by the moment. "Yes. He'd agree to this. I'm certain of it."

"And you'll have me," I jerked a thumb back towards myself. "Just set the wheels in motion. I'll come calling when you need me, and I can bring supplies… powder, rations. Provide escort. Just won't agree to gettin' sucked into your war. Support *only*, alright? So, you'll need to have a plan ready."

"That could take time," he said, considering.

"I've got business here to handle, anyway," I assured him. "And if I'm taking the Fleet into an active warzone, I need to get my big girl ready for it. And the men…"

"Shit," he swore, "I'm so sorry. I'm…" he looked torn, "…I really don't want to turn you down. You've no idea what this would mean to me –"

"Trust me, I do," I muttered.

"– but is this going to throw your Fleet into chaos?" he asked. "It's going to be hard enough selling my Captains on the idea of hiring on Privateers, your men would need to *behave*. If you're going to be making landfall in my Colony, even briefly –"

"Mate," I said, "I *guarantee* you my men have better morale than most of yours. They can be a bit wild, but a job's a job. Speaking of, I'm tripling my rate for this nonsense. Bloody… flying, flaming oil buckets? Fuck."

"Whatever you need," he said, his voice quiet, but laced with the sincerest gratitude I think I'd ever heard in my life. When I turned to look down at him, I nearly gagged.

"Ugh," I shoved him away at last, playfully. "Stop that."

He smiled slowly. And it was fragile like before, but earnest. "Grayson," he said, my first name still sounding so unnatural coming from this man who'd always been so formal with me in the past. But I guess now, this was how we were. "Thank you," he said, gripping one of my hands and squeezing it tightly.

Slowly, I let the irritation slip away from my features; to be honest, I'd been faking it. Luther might have been resistant to the sorts of affection I found second nature, things as simple as embracing your fellows when they were torn down, making friends easily, *talking* about the things ailing you… but I was similarly unused to the gifts that he could bestow so easily. Gratitude. Loyalty. Respect.

I guess we'd both have to expand our horizons a little.

Smiling rakishly, I clapped my other hand on his back. "You're welcome. And you can thank me again in the Southern Seas. Every fucking day until this is over."

He gave a tired, crooked grin, "I'll do that."

Between Wind and Water

Between Wind and Water

Crucially, and by some rare twist of fate, I was neither drunk nor remediating bottle-ache that morning. It was uncommon for me to be sober, but especially so since we'd made landfall on the Mataa'atel a Shanivaar: The island that was, more and more each day, looking to be the gravesite for the beating heart of my fleet, and I daresay... my own.

My beautiful, ailing old *Manoratha* listed like a wounded and dying leviathan in the abandoned inlet on the northwest end of the island. We were aground on the sandbar, so she'd hopefully tip no farther nor sink. But grounding her there was as much as admitting defeat. If there were a dry dock large enough for her on this island, I'd afford her that dignity, but there was none to be had.

She was the ship that I'd at once saved from destruction and been saved by in return almost half a lifetime ago. My soul's reflection, my home, my reason for being... and the thing I treasured most in the world. I may have very well sacrificed her for, I was increasingly realizing, the one and only priority I apparently ranked higher than her survival.

The *person* I treasured most in the world. Apparently. Good fucking god, if there was a litmus test for that, this'd be it.

I was sober because I could not help but be so. Sobering realizations have a way of doing that to you. I could push back against it mentally, verbally even, since I had someone to talk to. Thank fuck I had a wise-beyond-her-years friend and confidante in Shivah, who didn't mince words on this subject and talked me through many a night spent angry and confused. For once, I was glad to have a woman in my life I was enamored of, who despite some mutual attraction I think, was thus far immune to my charms. All these years, I'd overlooked how useful the perspectives of female friends might be without romantic entanglement complicating our bond. What a fool I was.

What Shivah and I had was, at present (and I still had time to fuck that up, mind you), based almost entirely on mutual respect. Not lust, which I'd learned by now clouded my senses. I had trouble thinking and communicating clearly with a woman once all of that entered the equation. My long history of being fished along, duped, humiliated, and eventually burning bridges with most of the women in my life proved that painful truth in so many ways.

Shivah was my friend in the way a man would be. That wasn't because she bound her breasts or had pretended to be one for some time on my ship. It was because, to put it simply, I was at last realizing the folly of my ways in all matters romantic and trying to remind myself to see her as a person first. Regardless of what I wanted with her, it was *so* obvious to me now that a woman had finally put her foot down and made me wait, made me earn her trust, that we had to build our relationship as comrades first — anything else later. Like I would with a man with no thought for whether I'd get them in bed or not.

Like I had with Luther.

Fuck, Luther. Goddammit. I didn't even believe in god. The cattle dog had me cursing a fairy tale deity. *That's* how frustrated I was. Somewhere between considering ending the most important friendship in my life and realizing I couldn't, didn't, want to live without him. How the hell was I meant to meet in the middle between those warring feelings? Both were valid. Good arguments could be made for either, and I had made those arguments to Shivah.

She was still angry at the man, and she had a right to be. But she seemed to understand, despite how little time she'd been in both of our lives, how much we meant to each other. And she had a lot of empathy for keeping problematic, dangerous friends in your life, even when the rest of the world was questioning your sanity.

So, she'd been neutral on the subject of Luther, at least when talking me through my own feelings. She was pretty clear on her own where they concerned the man. I wanted that kind of clarity, too. I wasn't used to being this turned-around on an acquaintance. Usually when things got complicated with someone, I just… left. See: any relationship I'd had with a woman that hadn't ended mutually, which was at least half, probably, if I'd bothered keeping track.

But this was different. No matter our history, our often deadly back-and-forths, no matter how many people had told me to steer clear of the Cerberus Admiral over the years (and there had been plenty to do just that), we somehow kept circling back around to one another. And now, thanks to that, we were here.

I didn't know how to feel. The man would be the very end of me. Nearly had. Why wasn't that enough?

With Shivah's help, I was plotting a course through these tumultuous waters. At least trying to. I had begun to string together sentences. What I'd say to him when I was finally ready to be honest.

Because what we had now? Right at this moment? Was unsustainable. Utterly. Anything could pitch us over a crevasse into… I knew not what. It wouldn't take much. And whatever we were when we were over that edge, there'd be blood, or tears, or both.

I'd begun to unravel, slowly, achingly, how I might ease into the conversation with him. Perhaps in between our chortling and banter, our easy companionable drinking games and nights on the docks together. I knew he wanted to say more, too. There was just so much in the way.

My destroyed ship.

His nearly life-ending injury at Serwich.

The enemies hedging us in on all sides.

Secrets. Fuck, *so* many secrets.

The men we surrounded ourselves with, opposed on both sides to our now obvious and undeniable friendship.

Our futures, uncertain even in the best outcome of all of this.

But until we spoke on any of it, we were still friends. And clearly, we were both cowards, because that's how it had stayed. For over a month now that we'd been on the island. I just needed a little more time. A few more sober days to get my head screwed on straight, to script what I'd say to him when the moment came.

Of course, I'd forgotten. Where Luther is concerned, I never get my way.

The knock at my cabin door woke me from a fitful, headache-ridden second attempt that morning to make up for the hours I'd missed last night, mostly to no avail. It was just as well.

It had been short, two raps, firm but polite. So, I expected Magpie or someone else of that disposition. If I'd thought it was one of my rowdier boys, I wouldn't have answered, just yelled through the door at them to leave. I wasn't up for that right now.

I'm glad I didn't do that.

I slept nude most of the time, but last night I'd left my britches on when I hadn't found I had it in me to take the extra time to strip out of them. They weren't my leathers, anyway. My fur had still been wet from a late-night swim in the bay, so I'd just put on something comfortable. For the best, as it turned out, because I'd often come to my cabin door without bothering with clothing when I was in the privacy of my own quarters. Whatever man dared disturb me knew the risk of that. I didn't give a fuck if it was one of the more proper fellows, not that I had many of those.

But it wasn't one of my own men, as it turned out. It was Luther.

I had to blink and adjust my vision against the strips of sunlight filtering through from behind him on the stairs just to be sure I wasn't imagining things. But I was eye level with those dark triangular ears. The distinctive untamed roughness ran along the back groove of his skull, and the eyes, there was no mistaking those eyes. Luther's gaze was golden yellow like a wolf's, wilder than his domestic peers. Intense, always intense, unknowable calculations happening behind them at all times. Staring up at me.

He shifted a foot. Unlike him. He was nervous.

Oh shit. Oh *shit*. This was it. He was here first thing in the bloody morning. This had to be it. Something between us was about to capsize, was about to change, and he —

"You look tired," he said in that deep, but roughened voice of his, always with an edge like he'd been shouting recently. It had gotten more pronounced over the years. Wear and tear. His voice was like his body, betraying the ten lifetimes of turmoil he'd somehow packed into one.

I sighed, leaning against the door and running a hand through my dreads. "That isn't a compliment, you know."

"It wasn't — I was trying to express concern, not compliment you."

"Well, why not? You wake me this early, it's the least you could do," I said, snuffing through my nose as I wiped my hand over my face.

"I suppose you're right," he agreed for some reason. He didn't generally agree with my ridiculous demands unless he was humoring me.

He shifted his feet again, putting a hand on his hip and looking me up and down for a moment. He was dressed down in a simple black cotton shirt over doeskin leather britches. He didn't even have a sword with him, just a long knife on his hip. His streetwear. Low profile today, I guess. The black shirt made him look smaller, and he was already a smaller man than I was. It almost lent him an unassuming air, if you didn't know who he was.

"What should I compliment then?" he asked, very seriously.

My shoulders were beginning to lose some of the tension that opening the door to his face had first brought on. This just felt like more of our usual sparring. Early in the day, which was odd, but maybe he just wanted some company.

"If I have to fish for what I want to hear, it loses some of its novelty," I explained. "They need to come from you, unspoiled."

"Ah, I see," he nodded sagely. "Alright, then. Well…" he peered past me a moment, "…your quarters seem… more orderly than usual. Still cluttered, but… more organized."

"I've been tidying up," I said. I had been. I couldn't set to rights the rest of my ship, so it was some sort of desperation ploy for control, I suppose. Also, the whole cabin was listing, and many things had already fallen and broken or rolled across the room, so some part of it was triage. Save what I could of my treasures.

None of it would matter in the end if I had to abandon her, though.

That thought sunk into my stomach and instantly spoiled what little good mood I had going. And there with it came the unmistakable ulcer of anger gnawing at the back of my guts. I was good at keeping my anger in check, usually. But it rose like bitter bile even as I suppressed it. Eventually, I'd lose that fight.

My inner war with my feelings had made for some awkward silence. And I was standing in the doorway, blocking it entirely, so we were still at the opening juncture of this odd visit. He was obviously aware that things were strange between us, because he cleared his throat and looked past me again. Polite. Asking without asking. The obvious social grace now would be to let him in.

But fuck that. The least I could do was play with him a little.

"I asked you to compliment me, mate. Not my room."

"Oh," he said, giving me a curious look. A slight narrow of his eyes like when he was looking at a map. Now *I* was the subject of those calculations. They seemed to say 'what are you doing?' I could all but see it in his gaze. "Alright, fair enough. Where shall I start?"

"You're more an expert on complimenting men than I am," I pointed out.

He sighed. "If I had any modicum of skill in the charm department, I'd have better luck holding on to partners, I'd wager. I'd settle for even a fraction of what you can bring to bear."

"Good start," I said, nodding. "Now tell me how handsome I am. Tell me what you find appealing about me, specifically. How have I 'charmed' you?"

This was an old game of ours. Sort of like tag or chicken. I'd poke him, prod him, flirt with him, and get him to chase me down. Always right up to the ledge, because I liked to be chased, you see. Moreover, I liked watching him get frustrated with me. Even angry. I was like a bloody child when it came to Luther. From the day I'd met him, it didn't matter what kind of attention I got, good or bad. I just wanted his attention. I wanted his eyes on me. Staring daggers, gazing warmly, drunkenly, or one of those painfully rare, real smiles.

I just wanted to be with him. Why did it so happen that the closer we got, the more damage we always did to one another?

This part of the game? It always ended the same. Either he got irritated with me and pushed me away or the one time he'd called my bluff. But that had been *one* time, and it had never happened again.

Until today, I guess.

It wasn't like last time. It wasn't some aggressive, putting-me-in-my-place sort of gesture. It wasn't snide or patronizing. It was *so* much worse. He took me seriously and put his all into it.

He paused a moment, roving those gold eyes up and over me again, and for some reason the weight of his gaze hit me like a physical thing. Like he was looking me over with a different lens.

I felt self-conscious suddenly.

"You are… effortlessly masculine," he said, each word punctuated with a little bit of breath, letting me know he'd thought through each of them very carefully. "I don't think you understand how appealing that is. How appealing it is in a man, specifically. To me. It comes so naturally to you. You don't need to put on airs or falsify confidence, you walk about like some feral jungle cat, slouched and lazy, but I know... I've seen... you can bring your brawn and your grit to bear when need be. And not just physical ability, by the way, but your *mind*. You're smarter, more educated, more worldly, and more capable than you want people to know. You play the clown. And people seem to buy it. Even those close to you. I doubt half of them realize the depths of your knowledge or your competence. But I know. I've seen it."

He brought in another breath slowly, then let it out, crossing his arms over his chest. "The academics can say what they will, and I don't particularly care what anyone else thinks on the subject to be honest, but to *me*, to me that's what a man should be. Capable, durable, smart... but he shouldn't give a bleeding fuck whether people know that or not. I've always respected that about you."

I was stunned. I'm pretty sure my jaw was open. I didn't know how to respond to that. Who would know how to respond to that?

"You're also kind," he said, much quieter for some reason. His ears dipped marginally. "Too kind, sometimes. I worry."

"...worry?" I finally managed. "About what? That I'm... what? Too soft for all this?"

"I think that may have been true at some point," he reasoned. "But, no. Not anymore. You soldiered through that part. And it didn't come easily to you, like it does to some of us, so that must have been unpleasant. But I don't worry you're too soft for the demands of your fleet, let alone those I make of you. You've long proven yourself there."

"Then what?"

"I worry I take advantage of you," he said.

My guts ached. My chest ached. Because he may have been right, honestly. But confirming it did no good. Why did everything with this particular man have to be like this? He could make my heart sing, pay me perhaps the most flattering and earnestly-meant compliment in one breath, and then strip that feeling off like a bloody, clotted bandage in the next and rend me to the bone.

I set my teeth inside my muzzle and felt my eyes get cold. I know he saw it.

"Why are you here at the crack of dawn, Luther?" I finally asked.

"I need to talk to you," he said, both hands at his sides now. He was reigning in the physical signs of his nerves, but I could feel them all the same. I knew him too well by now to be fooled.

Shit, this really was it.

I closed my eyes a moment, leaning my forehead against the door jam. "You bastard," I muttered. "Did you have to beat me to it?"

"What?" he asked suspiciously.

"I was working up to this," I cursed under my breath and stepped back from the doorway, finally making room for him. "Come on then."

He followed me inside, but didn't go far, stopping near my dining table and gripping the back of a chair. He looked over the uncharacteristically clear surface, save the books I was disinterestedly flipping through last night and a cold cup of tea, half-full so it wouldn't spill. I had to make a habit of drinking half of whatever was in my cup now before putting them down on any surface, being as nothing was level, and I'd been too absorbed to finish it after that. Not with the books. I'd read them dozens of times before.

"Something's..." he trailed off, then seemed to realize, snapping his jaw and his gaze up to me quickly. "I assumed you were hungover this early in the day, it only smells of *stale* booze in here. But you're not, are you?"

"No, mate," I shook my head, wincing for a moment as it throbbed. "Stone-cold sober. Have been for days."

"Oh, hell." Now he wasn't masking the worry in his voice. "Are you ill? Is it your condition?"

"I needed to think," I muttered. "Clearly. But get on with it. You came here to talk. Talk."

I sat down on the edge of my bed, curling a few of my dreads in my hand, working the twists with a finger like I did every morning. I watched him grip the chair a little tighter, then nod. Fuck it, if he was going to start this off, maybe it'd be easier.

Luther was better about confronting his feelings head-on than I was. Not that he *handled* them any better, just... he didn't dawdle as much. I fully thought I knew how he'd begin this, too. I'd been waiting for that hammer to fall for weeks. He was either going to tell me he was going to put up the coin to save my ship or he wasn't. And then he'd explain his reasoning. Very logically. Concisely.

"I need…" He shook his head a moment, closing his eyes. "I need someone to stop me from making a mistake. A very emotionally-driven mistake that I *know* I am on the cusp of making. You're the first person, the *only* person," he amended quickly, "I could think to talk to about this. I can't discuss it with Johannes."

"Alright," I said uncertainly. Where was this going?

He glanced aside a moment, and I saw one of his fangs chewing at his lower lip. "I want," he began, "and… that is to say I *want*, I have no firm plans yet to… but…"

"I'm enjoying watching you struggle with your words," I admitted. "It's rare as Northlight. But I haven't got all day, man."

"I want to abduct someone," he finally spat out. "Have him taken off the island to safety. Steal him, as it were."

That hung in the air between us for about five whole seconds. The dying embers in my little iron stove popped and crackled, and the waves lapped outside in the bay and sloshed at the creaking, heaving bosom of my ship. Somewhere distant, seabirds were fighting over something on the beach. Footsteps thudded outside on the decks, the men going about their morning duties. And Luther moved his weight from one foot to the other, his claws splayed on the back foot, against the listing of the room.

"We're nearly at a fifteen-degree tilt," I said, looking pointedly at his splayed paws. "Hard to stand, is it?"

He tested the floorboards a moment and looked out the one window in my quarters where the curtains weren't drawn. "Feels more like thirteen degrees," he said.

"Aye, it varies," I sighed.

"But, so, these thoughts I've been having —"

I sighed even more loudly. "My ship," I enunciated, "is stuck in a shifting sandbar, listing at thirteen —"

"Maybe fourteen —"

"*Fuck*, man!" I shouted, getting to my feet. I couldn't help the outburst. "You're missing the goddamn point here!"

It was Luther, so if he was taken aback, he didn't display it. He just stood before me and stared the few inches up at me, waiting. Letting me yell it out.

"My ship is nearly derelict!" I exclaimed. It felt odd yelling at the cattle dog, but also… good. I was purging something from inside that I had needed to let out for a while now. But he'd been maimed, under attack, indisposed… "That's my mast cracked in half on the shore there," I pointed out that one window. "You had to walk past it to get to me."

"I am acutely aware of the condition of your ship," he assured me.

"Then why the fuck are you coming here to talk to me about your personal life, about the jackal you've been fucking —"

"You know about him," he said sharply. There was that edge. "His name is Amon, by the way."

"Aye, I know about him," I muttered, sitting back down with a stiff creak of my knees, clutching my hands over them.

"The last time we spoke, you were asking where I'd been slipping off to like you didn't know," he tested me. "Did you know then?"

"Cut to the heart of it, mate." I growled. "You know I have you followed. You don't protect yourself well. You never have. Someone has to watch your ass or you're gonna get it handed to you. If I can have you followed, spare a thought for who else might be."

"Is anyone else…?"

"No," I said with certainty. "Ariel made sure of that. You have no idea how much I protect you. I've even put up with the wolfhound once or twice to collaborate on your behalf."

"You understand how your felines stalking me at night is a rather difficult favor to thank you for?"

"Did I ask you for thanks?" I bit back. "Or even consideration? I don't do this shit for gratitude. Our fates are intertwined, in case you hadn't noticed. What comes down on your head comes down on all of us." I bit the inside of my mouth irritably. "You know he has a drug habit, right? Nasty one. And a contract a mile long."

His eyes widened, and he leaned forward. "You have information on his contract?"

"I know it's considerable," I said. "Quite a few others' debts rolled in, too —"

"Wait," he put up a hand, sighing. "I… I shouldn't know this. I shouldn't find out about it from you, anyway. I'd rather he tell me. We probably shouldn't talk about any digging you did —"

"We shouldn't be talking about any of this!" I flared up again. "Why are you here?! Why come to me, of all people, about *him*?"

He opened and closed his mouth once, tipping his ears back before quietly asking, "Who else would I go to?"

"You're talking to me about your *dalliances*," I huffed, "rather than the dozen other more important things we've been avoiding discussing since you woke up?!"

A pall of something, maybe guilt, passed over his features. But he schooled his expression quickly. "I take it you mean… wait. Since Serwich? Not just today, but since I woke up from my injuries?"

"Yes," I said desperately, hoarsely.

"Your ship wasn't damaged yet, then. That was before the drake attack," he said with the tone of someone trying to work through someone else's words. Someone, namely, who was being illogical.

Fuck, this was worse. This was so much worse. I thought we'd both been avoiding talking this shit through because we were both trying to maintain our friendship. But this was… he honestly hadn't even been aware. He was here to talk to me about his whore.

This felt like karma for every woman I'd ever neglected, whose feelings I'd ignored or misunderstood, for every lover I'd abandoned in a cold bed, shoved off that morning without so much as a letter. Maybe I deserved this.

My teeth felt dry, and I licked the backs of them. I felt that rising pain in the back of my throat and the sting in my eyes. I didn't do well sober. This had been a mistake. It hadn't brought any clarity to my thoughts; it had just made the misgivings I'd been nursing for months now unavoidable and loud.

I heard Shivah's voice speaking lowly to me, my head in her lap, her paw stroking through my dreads. *Is he worth all of this to you?*

"Grayson?"

He was looking intently at me now. God, he could tell, couldn't he? I felt stripped bare. The uncanny ability the cattle dog had to see through

every situation had *never* felt more threatening than it did to me right now. Not even when I'd been on the other end of his cannons.

"I don't think I'm up for this," I said, inwardly cursing how weak my voice suddenly sounded. "I think you oughta go, mate."

He was stunned into silence, or at least that's what I hoped, watching him stare at me with that lost look. His eyes briefly darted around the room, as if searching for someone's help. But of course, it was just the two of us there.

His gaze landed back on me, but specifically on my mane for some reason. And he latched on to something. Something I'd forgotten was there, if briefly.

"That's," he paused and leaned forward a moment, as if making sure, "that's… mine. Isn't it?"

I was lost for a spell, reaching for the spot he was looking at, until my fingers found the familiar silk tied 'round one of my dreads. One of the thicker ones, so I could find it easily. Toy with it when I felt the need to, which had been a lot lately.

"Yeah," I said quietly, holding it tightly in my palm. "How'd you know? It's just a strip of fabric."

"I recognize the color and the triangular cut at the end," he said. "It's distinctive. When did you…?"

"When you were," I had trouble saying it, finally stammering out, "dying. During the evacuation, when the northern fox was first working on you, and… no one knew if you'd bleed out. I'm sorry I stole from you, alright? But I figured no one would fucking care. They stripped you out of everything you were wearing, and the ties for your spats were just… they'd tugged them out so loose to get them off of you. This one was just sitting on the floor getting dirty, and… it was already bloody, and I didn't…" I took in a shuddering breath, trying to center myself, "…you didn't *see* yourself. I really thought you'd die right there and then and… I didn't… I realized I didn't… have anything of yours… other than your goddamn *contract*."

I was spiraling, my voice was half-choked, with anger or sadness. I couldn't say. The memories were crimson flashes of dread that had burned themselves into the back of my skull, revisiting me in my nightmares, featuring in more than one pre-seizure delusion by now. He couldn't know — even I didn't understand if I'm being honest — how much that day had made me suffer. I had already decided to forgive him, then and there, when I'd pled with him on what we all thought might be his death bed.

I'd told him then, when he was unconscious and no one else was around to hear it, that I'd forgive him for what he'd put me and my fleet through at Serwich. For the lies, for the carnage at the rookery, for willfully keeping something so fucking *awful* from me, and dragging me down with him in his depravity, making me a party to something I'd expressly told him I wanted no part of. All of it. If he'd just… live. I had no god to plead with, so I'd offered it to his unconscious body instead. My unconditional forgiveness. If he'd just cling to life.

I'm not even certain he'd heard me. He'd never said as much, and I was too embarrassed to ask. It may as well have been a prayer for how logical or thought out it was. Let alone how likely it was to work.

But he'd fulfilled his part of the bargain. And whether or not he'd heard me, I was not about to go back on my word. It wasn't that I was honorable. It's just… I may not have been the religious sort, but I was still a sailor. Superstition ruled the seas. I'd bound myself to that promise in that moment. I was afraid if I broke it now, I'd lose him again. And I knew the panic, the sudden clasping pain in my heart like claws had a vice grip in my chest. It was worse than any seizure, worse than any death I'd witnessed before. Even seeing my men die under my command. Even the day I found out my father had died, and I couldn't attend his funeral under penalty of arrest.

This man had a power over me I was still coming to terms with. Still trying to understand. I hardly knew what to call it. I'd never had a friendship like this, and I had comrades who'd been on my crew since the very beginning. This was… this was something else. Something that frightened me with its intensity.

But he didn't think of me that way. He hadn't even considered the heartache I'd been going through with my ship. He was dealing with his own fleet, his own turmoil within the ranks, and, apparently, his relationship with this local boy. A year ago, hell, even less, back on Serwich, I would've smacked him on the back with an 'attaboy' and helped him abscond with his newest infatuation.

I was caught between my anger at him and… something else. Something I dared not put words to. He needed to leave. Right now.

I felt something and, impossibly, looked down to find Luther's grey, speckled palm cupping mine. He slowly uncurled my fingers, revealing the dread I was clutching within that I'd tied his spat laces into. He was looking at it like it was a thing of wonder. It wasn't even that crimson color he liked so much anymore. I hadn't cleaned the blood from the silk, so the red was stained dark in places and always would be. It was the only red I wore in my mane. Red was not a color we in the tribes wore unless it was temporary. It was meant for war. For battle.

My relationship with Luther had always been a combative. And every day he'd fought to stay alive after that creature had nearly cleaved his body in twain, after he'd lost more blood than *any* man should be able to survive losing, I'd seen all of it as a battle. I was wearing it for him while he fought. And since then, I just hadn't been able to remove it. I told myself many things. That it was a reminder of the lives we'd taken to facilitate that escape. That I might remove it once he noticed it. That I'd laugh it off, then. Return it to him with a joke and a smile.

I stopped lying to myself eventually. I'd threaded it into the fur of my dread by now. It would have to be cut out, and I'd cut my mane for Luther once already. I'd not be doing so again unless our friendship ended. So long as I stayed at his side, so long as he remained at mine, so long as we survived our companionship together, it would stay with me. I'd die with it in my mane. I was resolved.

I swear, the man was spooky. It was like he saw through you. He read my thoughts like a book.

"I don't remember much from those weeks," he said, the rough pad of his thumb brushing back and forth over my knuckles, and then over the red silk and the exposed bits of my mane it was wrapped around. "But I recall… your voice. Vividly. The words elude me, but… you were there. Frequently. Weren't you?"

"As often as we were able to come alongside," I murmured. I snuffed wryly. "Let me tell you. The wolfhound didn't like it one bit. And he wouldn't let me —" I cut myself off.

He hunkered down, nearly crouching to be at eye level with me where I was sitting on the edge of the four-poster bed. "What?" he pressed. He hadn't let go of my hand.

"... stay with you," I mumbled. "Through the night. You had some hard nights. Your ears were so cold, and your gums were so pale. You wouldn't stop shaking. They were worried your broken collarbone was poisoning you inside or something. Every word of it sounded horrible, and you *looked* horrible, and they would just... leave you *alone* at night. They'd put the bed heater under the blankets and insist that was enough, that you wouldn't be cognizant of who was about enough that you'd care for company. And all I could think was that you were going to die, and you were going to die *alone*, because these stubborn jackasses were too hung up on decorum to let you have something as basic and humane as companionship in what could've been your last fucking moments. I-I... kept waiting to see that black flag at half-mast each morning. You'd die mortally wounded and alone, completing this fucked-up self-fulfilling prophecy you've doomed yourself to, because you think you deserve it or some shit. And we'd never talk again, never bicker, you'd never call me out on my bullshit, and I'd never see you smile or laugh at me again. And I'd never get to tell you how *fucking angry* I was with you!"

For my dignity's sake, I'm glad he chose that moment to break my tirade, with a quiet, "Shhhhh...." He leaned in against me, offering an arm around my shoulders. I shoved at it, but not hard. Not nearly hard enough to discourage him, anyway.

"Don't fucking *shush* me," I grumbled, trying to cover the unshed tears by pushing at him again and turning my head away. "I'm not a goddamn pup, and you're no school marm."

"I pity the school marms that had to handle a young you," he said, a false lightness in his tone. But he was trying to inject some of our usual good banter into what was swiftly becoming a flaming wreck of a morning. So, it was okay.

"Fuck you," I laughed miserably between my paws. "Like you were such a treat as a schoolboy."

"I didn't go to school," he said.

"Fucking idiot savant."

He hummed out a noise. "Mmhhh... more of a prodigy, really. I only took to a few things in life, but I wouldn't say I'm simple-minded overall. Just... under-educated. Until I wasn't."

"And I'm over-educated and most of the world thinks I'm a bloody dunce," I threaded my claws up through my dreads, scratching at my scalp and dragging in a wet breath through my nose. "What a pair we make."

He chuckled. But it was tempered, quiet. He was looking at me with a softness, a worry in his eyes that was so unlike him, I wondered for a moment if I was dreaming. Any time now, I'd snap my eyes open and be alone in my cabin.

"If I convince my fleet it's worth it to fix your ship up, Grayson," he said quietly, "you'll continue being a part of this. You know that, right? They'll expect you to stay on contract with us. All the way to Amuresca, until we're in safe waters. They'll use you as a shield just like they did on the way here. They'll sacrifice you for the good of the Cerberus ships. They'll expect the *Manoratha* to hold the line against enemies who show no quarter. Enemies that were never yours to begin with. And then when, if, we get home, they'll turn on you. Even *my* fate in Amuresca is uncertain at this point, I didn't… I didn't think you'd want any further part in this. It's already gone so far beyond what you'd agreed to."

"What choice do I have?" I demanded.

"Couldn't you repair her with the king's ransom I paid you in Serwich?" he asked. It wasn't harshly-spoken, just… he earnestly seemed confused.

"You paid me almost entirely in silver, mate," I reminded him.

"That's what the Serwich mines produced. It was the most valuable commodity we had."

"Do you know how long it would take on an island this size to convert that to usable currency?" I pointed out. "The Huudari don't trade in it unless you use moneychangers, and there are all of three of those on this island. They work out of Clan holds, all of them. We're not likely to get a fair market rate, and even if we could, that silver is dispensed amongst the entire crew, now. I'd have to demand they all hand over their portions to fix a ship most of them rightfully see as having been damaged by our *allies'* decisions. Our contractors. I'd have a mutiny on my hands if I don't stand up to you."

"Hmmmm," he hummed in agreement. "I see now. I'm sorry. Your crews' dynamics should be more familiar to me by now. I assumed you kept the silver with your purser."

"We were in Serwich for months," I shook my head. "The men needed living wages. And anyway, we're a communal profit-sharing company, now. Have been for a few years."

He gave an appraising look. "Does that work? That'd be anarchy on an Amurescan ship."

"We're Anarchists, Luther," I barely managed not to roll my eyes. "It's not just a three-syllable slur. Not for us."

He smiled weakly. "I suppose so."

We sat in silence for a bit, his arm still around my shoulder, the warmth seeping through his shirt to sink into my fur. Into my muscle, my bones. Just as I'd wanted to do for him, while he was lying there dying.

"Did you really look for that flag every morning?" he asked, staring off into space now. It was relieving at least not to have his eyes on me for a little while. Too much. Too intense.

"...yeah," I admitted.

"My coat belonged to Klaus Richter," he said rather suddenly. A moment later though, he explained it. "He died in it. I... did clean the blood. And had it tailored. But only so it would pass the Navy Standard. I wanted to wear it... to remember him. In honor of him."

"I never knew," I said, not hiding my surprise. I'd dug into Luther like a moon-eyed student over the years, and I'd never heard any of this.

"No one but Johannes, my wife, and Lucius Denholme ever knew," he said quietly. He tipped his muzzle down a moment, eyes distant, unfocused. "Sometimes I think I can still smell him on it, but... I know. I know that's insane." He moved his eyes, only his eyes, back up to mine. "It never occurred to me someone might do the same for me, some day. Eerie. But, also, I suppose I'm honored. Thank you for telling me that."

"You're welcome," I murmured. "Didn't have much of a choice once you recognized it though."

"I'm sorry I worried you all that time," he said.

"Sometimes I couldn't sleep so I'd just... wait for dawn's light on the nest until I could see your fleet," I said. "Hoping they wouldn't raise that flag. Sometimes, I'd fall asleep up there."

He mock-gasped. "That is *so* dangerous."

"Oh, please," I muttered. "Like you haven't."

"Have you ever lain on the shrouds to watch the stars?"

I smiled a bit at him despite myself. "Bit difficult at an angle."

"Well, you hook your feet in."

"There is no way you get away with this kind of behavior anymore these days," I said. "Not on an Amurescan ship. Maybe as crew. Not as Command staff."

"No," he agreed. "Stories from my wild youth."

He was leaning into me marginally more, the half-embrace becoming a true one. Every extra inch of his body heat that pressed into mine was significant. Amurescans, and perhaps especially Luther, were unbelievably guarded about touching, gestures of affection, or violating personal space in any way. They were an unhealthy people, if you asked me. Rigid and touch-starved, probably all weaned too soon, just an easily-irritated, miserable lot. Luther and I had managed over our acquaintance to share more contact than most men would allow themselves in his culture, despite our time together over the years being short. We gravitated towards one another like we were seeking it. He had quite literally been seeking me when he'd come to me for help with Serwich. And while I'd been open to the idea of basic physical comfort from the start, same as I would be with any person I was this close with, it was oddly relieving to see him loosening up and allowing himself the same. Not strictly because I wanted to touch him. Although….

Best not to entertain those particular thoughts and curiosities right now.

"Being with you is so easy," I murmured, feeling helpless. I was uncoiling, relenting to him against my better instincts. We had swayed into one another again, and it felt so *right*, so comfortable, so… exactly what I had wanted. But nothing had been resolved. As ever. "I forget myself," I continued, solemnly. "We were supposed to be fighting. Arguing. Now here we are. I can't ever stay angry with you for long, and… and I really fucking *should*."

"I'll convince my fleet to repair your girl," he said. "But that isn't really what all this anger is about, is it?"

"It *is*," I said vehemently, "or, well, I mean, partially at least. Hell, man. It's been a *month*. You could have talked to me about it, explained what was holding you up, told me everything you just did. We could have hashed this out earlier."

"I was afraid if I said anything," he spoke, his jaw trembling minutely for a moment, "it would seem like I was coming to you, begging for help again. That wasn't my finest moment, and… look what it's wrought."

"Oh, you mean the fact that you, your crew, and all the damn colonists are *alive* right now?" I growled out. "Crying shame, that. You wouldn't have made it out of that scrap without us. Don't play tough."

"I'm not denying that," he insisted, his blunt claws pressing into the fur around my bicep. "I would never. We owe you *everything*. You'll never hear it from the other Captains. Let me apologize for their pride on their behalf, but don't think I don't recognize it."

"I know," I muttered. "And yes, for the record. Do what you have to do with them. Convince them. The amount of lumber we need to repair her, let alone the shipwrights we'll need to hire, none of that's gonna come cheap on this speck of an island. It'll take months and more coin than we have. And we obviously can't earn much of anything here with the two brigantines unable to get out past the lizards patrolling the reefs."

"Lord no don't risk that," he agreed. "They'll tear your little ladies apart. Earnestly, I'd thought you'd want to wait us out. We'll either have reinforcements eventually or we'll muster the willpower for a blockade run. You'd be clear to leave once they chase us. Leave the *Manoratha* berthed for a while, drum up a loan or earn some coin with the rest of your fleet —"

"Just," I waved a paw through the air, "stop. Stop. I'm not abandoning you, Luther."

His shoulders slumped; I could feel it through where he was holding me, as well as see it. It was either resignation or relief. I couldn't tell. "All of them were *so* certain you were done with us," he said breathlessly after a pause. "I had almost begun to believe them."

"Wishful thinking," I snorted.

"It's how they'd prefer it," he agreed, shaking his head. "Bloody fools, all of them. We need you so terribly right now. More than ever."

"Damn straight," I asserted, enjoying the validation shamelessly. We'd earned it, after all.

"I need you."

He'd said it so quietly, I thought I'd imagined it. I had to physically turn to look at him to confirm I wasn't just fabricating things I wanted to hear. But when I faced him, I found he was staring at the floor. He had a guilty little tip to his ears, an awkwardness that was palpable in the stiffness of his arm. So… he probably really had said that.

"When…" he trailed off softly, still refusing to look at me. He cleared his throat. "When this is… over? However it ends. If you're determined to stick it out to the end, for whatever reason, I won't stop you. I don't *want* to stop you. But you mustn't follow us as far as Amuresca. Whatever grace I'm afforded there, if I even make it that far, they will *not* afford you. Especially if your ship is damaged, if your fleet is depleted, or God forbid you are aboard one of my ships when we make port —"

"Yeah, I'm not making that mistake again," I assured him darkly.

"I am barely holding down morale as it is," he sighed. "It's tenuous, I won't lie. I know some of the captains are talking mutiny. It's likely, even if we do escape this place, that I'll lose my command. I may even be detained and… worse. I don't know that I'll be able to protect you."

"That's bullshit," I snapped. "You did your damned 'duty'. The colonists at Serwich should've been the priority all along, and you couldn't have held the Colony regardless of what you did! Just explain to them what you were up against —"

He was shaking his head. "It won't matter," he assured me calmly. "It isn't just that I failed to protect and hold the colony. I went against the orders of the local magistrate and the pedigree landowners, and I overstepped when I hired you and shelled out the silver reserves to do it. It was as good as embezzling."

"Fuck them!" I snarled. "Fuck them *all*! How are you so bloody calm about this?! They're going to tear your life apart, ruin your family's name, take everything away from you — your ships, your rank, possibly your *freedom*, and you're just… you're just —"

"Well," he said, his voice oddly light, "that's… all of that… is in the unlikely event I survive this ordeal. Which, let's be honest…"

"I am not putting my fleet at risk for your sons-of-bitches Captains," I shifted my whole body finally to face him, reaching over and grabbing him by the shoulders to force him to face *me*. He only twitched for a moment at the contact. He was getting better about that. "Luther. Look at me. Please," I pleaded.

He did, eventually. It was so odd seeing this particular man having trouble maintaining eye contact, and I wasn't entirely sure why.

He didn't back away from challenges or conflict. What about this was getting to him?

"I am doing this for *you*," I said, pushing my voice out with all the intensity I felt. "I…" I gritted my teeth, my eyes darting to follow his wandering gaze. "I need you, too. Alright? I am *not* doing this so you can plan for death or some kind of noble sacrifice. To hell with that. I put my ship on the line for you! Show some fucking respect for what I nearly sacrificed. Don't throw it away."

"There is nothing for me after this, Grayson," he said, boxed in by my hands now, unable or unwilling to escape. "And you know it's me the Cathazra want…."

"There's your family." I splayed my palms. "They'll be waiting for you after this."

"They are better off without me."

"Fuck you, no they aren't," I hissed. "And you know your wife would say the same. What about this boy? You came here saying you wanted to save him —"

"Man," he corrected me. "And no. If anything, I would ask *you* to stow him away. Get him as far from here and the people who own him as possible. Hell, make him a part of your crew. Just… get him out of this life. I think whatever's ahead for him, it's bleak."

"I'll do that," I said quickly. "Fine. It's not like I don't have Divine addicts on my boat already. But a request like that, he must mean a lot to you, right?"

"I…" he was blinking rapidly, gaze moving about. "I don't know. I've only known him a few weeks. He's sweet-tempered, but cagey. He doesn't like me getting overly involved, which makes him smarter than me, I suppose. But he clearly needs help, and I… I think I mostly feel… angry about his situation *for* him. It feels like he's given up. And I know I've got the connections to help him even if he won't ask for it."

"Luther, I will browbeat the svelte lad into leaving this place with us if it will make you happy. Just say the word," I pressed.

He smiled sadly. "Even if you did, we hardly know one another well, yet. And how would we ever live together? Your head's in the clouds, wolf. Doesn't mean I won't take you up on your offer. Just, keep in mind I only want to help him, not force him into some commitment with me. I'm not sure either of us want that yet."

"Then live for *me!*" I raised my voice enough that it echoed off the walls inside my cabin. This time, I *did* take him aback. "Bloody hell, you're a stubborn son of a bitch." I clutched his shoulders tightly. "Live for the people who love you! Stop being so goddamn selfish. Think of us, if not yourself."

It took me a few heartbeats to realize what I'd actually just said. Luther, judging by his expression, had put the pieces together immediately. On the plus side, I had his complete attention finally. He was staring at me in stunned shock, his irises lost in a sea of gold glinting pale in the morning sunlight.

"Did you…" he began, softly, "…mean —"

"Yes," I said solidly. It was like jumping off a ledge into the whistling winds over crystal blue waters. Now that I'd done it, there was no room for regret. It was liberating, really. I just had to hope the fall wouldn't kill me. "There's no use being a coward about it," I almost laughed. "I fucking love you, alright? I'm counting myself amongst that number, whether you want it or not. Goddamn. Do you think I would've done all this, risked all this, if that wasn't the case?"

"I don't know," he admitted. "I have very little experience with the subject. At least, being on the receiving end."

"Oh, to hell with you," I muttered. "I *know* men who are unloved. *You* are not unloved. And what about me, huh? You think I'm a bloody expert on the subject? I hardly knew what this was, for years, outside some odd obsession. But it's so *fucking clear* now." This time I did laugh, albeit mirthlessly. "No one's put me through it like you have. And still, all I want to do is… be with you. I want to sail with you. I want to see new places with you. I want to fucking read books with you and talk about them together. I want to teach you Huudari, so you can talk to your whores properly —"

That got a laugh out of *him*, which I took as a good sign that I wasn't about to lose a friend.

"I want to laugh with you," I released one of his shoulders so I could tip his muzzle up. "I want to drink together. I want to see what you're like when you *smoke*, if you've a mind. See you well and truly blissfully foolish. I just want us to *be* together, dammit. I have *never* found anyone, in all the world, I'm more fascinated by, who answers the siren song of my heart like you do —"

"Grayson," he said in a soft, warning tone. Shaking his head. He'd shut his eyes.

"Shut up, it's my turn to be dramatic," I snapped. "You don't get to make me sob for nights on end at the thought of your death and cut me off mid-pouring-out-my-heart, alright? Let me be goddamn poetic if I want to."

"Please," he pleaded softly.

"I've forgiven you," I said, leaning in close until our foreheads touched. "For every bloody wrong I've endured on your behalf. I don't want to go over it all anymore. I just want you to hear me now. And you owe me that. You owe me at least that."

"I'm listening," he insisted, his voice paper-thin. "I just… no one… says these things to me… and the last man who did —"

"I'm not Klaus Richter," I said. "I am alive, and here, and your friend, and… I love you."

He nodded silently. He made to speak but said nothing except a few exhalations of breath. And then he moved in towards me and —

Stopped. Pulled back. Blinked rapidly and visibly self-corrected.

"I-I'm sorry," he said quickly. "I-I know this isn't… I was just… rather overcome —"

"You're an idiot," I muttered. Then I leaned in and kissed him.

I met only brief resistance, then a bodily shudder, and his muzzle opened into mine. In the whole span of our tumultuous relationship, we'd only been this close but a few times. More kissing than most 'friends' I'd ever known, I'll grant you, but the moment I'd tried to push for more, up went the walls. Every time, without fail.

Not this time, I told myself. No more of this rocking about back and forth. I enjoyed a slow burn in my novels, not in real life.

I'd come in fast, no planning, just action, as ever. In the few seconds I took to reangle our muzzles, he gusted out a tumble of words. I was worried he was about to object, but —

"Fuck you, I'm bloody brilliant."

I laughed out loud, not just because it sounded more like something I'd say, but because I was relieved. "Yes, you are," I conceded, and moved back

in. He was more ready for me this time and surged into the kiss with an eagerness that made my jowls curl up. There was something raw about the way he kissed. I think it was the sincerity with which he did… everything that mattered to him. Including kissing.

Soft peach fuzz bristles pressed to mine, the wet heat of his mouth mixing with my own, tasteless at first, then as my tongue pressed past his teeth, like betel nut and peppermint. Some part of my mind registered that he'd clearly cleaned his teeth before he came here, likely this morning if he still tasted fresh of it, and while I doubted he'd been planning for any of this, I stowed that away to tease him about it later. Fastidious jackass.

The hot slide of his tongue against mine made something jolt down my jaw to my clavicle, waking my body up like no drug ever would. My stomach clenched all the way down, and my paws instinctively clutched tighter to him, claws sinking into the loose-fitting, black cotton shirt he was wearing. I tipped my head, and he answered in return, mirrored; I didn't have to see him to know, because then our mouths locked together, the soft, pliant edge of our muzzles sealing against one another's. I sucked on his tongue, and he danced it along mine, the flexible muscles fluttering as they curled and cupped one another. He dragged it along my gums and my teeth once I'd released him enough to do so, growling almost imperceptibly. *Fuck*, I think I *liked* that. I liked it when cats purred and growled, and I'd been with female canines before, but most of them were taught not to growl. It was unladylike. I couldn't remember the last time a canine had growled *into* my mouth. It was more familiar than a cat's rumble and pressed more against the warning centers in my mind. It made the fur prickle along the back of my neck just so. Especially a male growl, deep, low, and quiet for now. The barest hint of danger.

He was keeping his hands to himself, but I saw no reason to do so. My palms were already clutched around his bicep and shoulder, and it was oh so easy to release my hold and move each individually below his armpits to his ribs, sliding the claw tips as I did. Lazy and careless, but intentional, of course. Making someone fall apart under your hands was as simple as making the lightest touches count, whether it was for comfort or something more. In the few sparing moments I'd had to be more intimate in the past, I'd barely gotten past petting.

Right now, I just wanted — *ah*, and there it was, that bodily shudder again. My fingertips spanned over the swell of his ribs as he took a breath I could vaguely feel them through the thin cotton, and then, as my palm slid up the edge of his shoulder blade, there...

The distinctive, raised seam of a scar. And another. I'd wanted to touch them for so long now.

We were breathing together, snuffing out warm air through our nose against one another's muzzle, licking wetly and bumping teeth together. I could *hear* how heated the kiss had become, echoing off the walls of my cabin. He didn't seem to notice or care that I was touching his scar, that I'd gone from holding his arms to embracing him, pulling him in closer to me. We were both sitting with our legs off the bed, so we had to turn towards one another, and it wasn't... enough. It just wasn't enough.

But it was a quiet moan — my own, I realized belatedly, he'd bitten gently at my lower lip — that pulled us back. Pulled him back, anyway. His palms flew out to plant on my chest and push us apart those critical few inches, our muzzles disconnecting with a shared gasp and a wince in my case. One of his fangs had caught on my lip, not enough to break the skin, but enough to pull me with him briefly before it slipped away. I could still taste his saliva, cooling on the cleft of my muzzle just below my nose. I licked it, chasing that spicy, clean flavor. I had no idea what I tasted like, but I was certain it couldn't be as good as that. I'd always known he'd probably taste good. He *smelled* good.

"This has..." he stammered around a likely thick tongue. Mine certainly was. "Gone... beyond...."

"Yeah," I agreed, eyebrows lifting and a slight smile tugging at my muzzle. I leaned back in, bumping our noses together, and he let me. I brushed our muzzles together again, lathed my tongue achingly slow against the open seam of his mouth, and he let me. His gaze drifted, uncertainty creased his features, but when I eased him back against me, he let me. He released a shuddering breath, kissing me again, shallow, but open-mouthed, once, twice, a third time, and I tasted his tongue again, but then he was shaking his head, brows knitted, eyes closed tight as he pulled away once more.

"The hell are we doing?" he asked, his voice rough and lower in timbre.

It was a voice I'd never been privy to before. I wanted to hear him say my name in that voice.

"Fooling around," I supplied helpfully, rubbing my nose down the edge of his jaw, feeling him swallow as I nuzzled at his throat. "Thought that was obvious."

"I don't fool around," he said, the words sounding painfully honest. Almost as if it were a fact he was resentful of.

I snuffed. "Your predilection for brothels says otherwise."

"I can't even go into a brothel without wanting to change someone's life," he said helplessly. "I find paid men out of desperation, not because it's what I want. I'm after…"

When I found the soft spot at the juncture of his throat and clavicle, and bit into it gingerly, his breathing stuttered. I moved back up in slow nips towards the edge of his chin, where the fur twisted round in eddies at the base of his ears. I fully intended to stop before I got there… probably. Maybe. His ears were sensitive. I knew that from experience. But he hadn't stopped me yet, and I'd never been good at self-control if I'm being honest.

"I'm… after…" he swallowed again, "… I'm…ah-a… romantic. You know… that. We've entertained this before. You're not…."

"Mmhhh," I inhaled as I burrowed into the thick, dense fur along his neck. "God, you smell good," I say raggedly. "Some kind of oil in your fur?"

"Just soap," he answered quietly. "Vetiver. I use it when I go on land missions, too… blends in with most forests."

"It's fucking great. Always liked that you don't smell like some posh cologne. Not like the others."

"I'm not one of them," he reminded me. "I'm a cattle dog."

"Mm-hm," I nodded shallowly, my nose firmly buried in his scruff. I felt a tug, gentle, but there, and realized one of his hands had come up to find the dreads tumbling over my shoulder between us. Specifically, the largest, the one I'd know the feel of from anywhere. The one I'd tied his silk into. He was toying at it, fingers curling 'round it like I did when I needed to feel its presence.

I bit his ear. If he was going to tug on my dreads, it seemed only fair.

The noise *that* pulled out of him was a breathy gasp, *so* close to a moan I could almost imagine what he'd sound like if he did. I followed it up with a few more nibbles along the dark edge of his triangular ear, my tongue feeling the grooves of each little, long-healed tatter.

"Fuck!" he finally snarled and gave me a shove, for real this time. I swayed back and caught myself on my palms, pressing them down into the tangle of blankets I'd tossed about in my sleep.

I watched him catch his breath for a few moments, the pink tip of his tongue visible as he panted a few times. His fur was delightfully askew, one hand scratching at the base of his skull where it would never settle. He swallowed eventually, noisily. And then his eyes flicked up, pinning me with a scalding stare.

"What the hell kind of game are you playing?" he demanded. His voice was deadly serious, and I felt bad that I was still smiling, but it was impossible not to. He was misreading me, though. I'd need to clear things up. "If this is some…" he gestured at nothing, "…some… quid pro quo, you don't have to do that. Or if it's pity… if you think you need to throw yourself at me because I'm so low-down right now, I promise you, I will get up each and every day and do my duty, and I will fight until I am no longer capable of drawing breath. It isn't as though I've given up —"

"Luther," I said, almost shocked by how confident the words felt coming out of me. "When are you finally going to realize I'm doing this because I want to?"

A beat of silence. Those eyes were scanning me, looking me over like a battle map, trying to make sense of me. "No," he denied.

"No, you don't want it?" I tipped my head. "Because if that's the case, mate, just say as much. You seemed… enthused, but bodies and minds are two different things, I get that —"

"No, I mean," he bit at his lower jaw a moment, "*you* don't want this."

"Bold telling me that like you know better than I do."

"You've *never* committed to wanting this in all the time I've known you," he exclaimed. "You tease, and you flirt, you're always playing with me, but it's all a big sodding laugh to you."

I sighed. "You know I'm sorry about the teasing I've done in the past. I thought we were both gettin' something out of it back then, but that was cruel of me. I knew your interest in other men was genuine, and I toyed with that. I'm a shite person sometimes, what can I say?"

"You don't do things like this with men," he clarified. "You've always been clear about that."

"I mean, I'm a sailor." I rolled my eyes. "Don't matter to me who's got a turn in the barrel, and it is *always* a man, it ain't like I don't know that. I've shared women with other men before, too."

"That isn't the same thing as this." He pointed between the two of us. "It's masked by humor or it's plausibly deniable. You don't 'romance' men."

"No, I do not," I confirmed. "To be fair, I don't 'romance' anyone."

"Whether or not you realize it," he growled, "you're doing a damn good job on me."

The frustration when he said that, I… I felt guilty, and I knew I deserved it.

"It isn't a ploy, mate," I tried to assure him, keeping my tone as genuine as I could manage. "I mean, it ain't like I'm courting you, but I meant everything I said to you this morning. I'm a nasty blaggard, but I wouldn't dare fuck with your head like that. I don't have a death wish." I briefly stared down into my lap. "Not to mention it was… embarrassing. And not in the way I generally like. We've had more than a few false starts, and I understand why at this point you might be fed up of the idea."

"I didn't say that," he said quickly.

I lifted my gaze again to look at him. "Oh?" It was hard to hide the hope in my voice.

"Yes," he confirmed, vaguely. It wasn't *the* words. But it seemed to be close, and probably all I'd get for now.

"But," he said in a clipped tone, "you don't fancy men as I do. Yes or no?"

"No," I answered after one last moment thinking it over. "I don't think I do."

He let out a breath. "I've… wondered for years," he finally admitted. "Your reputation as a womanizer is infamous, but I've known my share of womanizers who… run in my circles. But I thought, with you, your infatuation always seemed like more of a fascination with me. Like pulling on a predator's tail or lighting a powder keg to see if you could outrun the blast. Thrill-seeking."

"Arrogant twat," I chuckled. "Who said I was 'infatuated' with you?"

"What would you call it then?" He lifted his chin, staring down at me now that I was slumped back on my palms. "Because I don't know. It's sure as hell more than friendship at this point. I've been trying to put a name to whatever it is that's between us for years."

"Yeah, so have I," I admitted. "Y'know what I ultimately decided on? Too much work. Why bother?"

"Because it is *very important*," he enunciated, "that I carefully map out the boundaries for myself with male comrades and friends. Know where the borders lie lest I catch myself yearning or worse yet, overstep." His voice got smaller for a moment. "I have made that mistake before, more than once. If you read someone wrong, you can end up in a work camp. Or dead."

"Bleedin'… shite," I groaned, scrubbing a hand over my eyes. "Mate, you make me *so* sad for you sometimes. Living like that sounds fucking *awful.*"

"You don't actually want this with me," he said softly. "You never have, and I won't take advantage of you now, *again*, when I've already made you suffer so much of late."

"I told you I forgave you," I said, my irritation rising. "Isn't that my right?"

"I just don't see how you could —"

"You can believe me when I tell you my own mind, for starters," I said emphatically, putting some power into my voice. I didn't want to tell him about the promises I'd made in a dark cabin to a dying friend. That was my oath to take to my grave. And I didn't regret it, anyway. "It's in the past. Then was then, and now is now. Anyway, sore as I may be, I don't see how any of it was your fucking choice. It's not like you were left with a lot of options in Serwich, and, as I said before, we'd literally all be dead if you hadn't done what you did, including hiring me, so…"

"You're not wrong," he said, regret laced in every word. I knew when he was putting on airs. He wasn't. Not about this. "But that doesn't mean you don't have a right to be angry with me."

I sighed. "To be honest with you, and this is gonna sound awful… I'm glad you had to make the decision, so I didn't. You're better at shouldering that kind of weight than I would've been. Or Shivah. Hell, even Johannes. I don't subscribe to your myths. I don't think there's some canine in the sky judging your decisions, so all that matters, ultimately, is that you can live with it. If you can sleep at night —"

Something in his eyes froze me up mid-sentence. It's like the light went out. He was staring at a spot on the bed, at nothing in particular, and I knew he wasn't seeing me or the room anymore. It was what I would've seen in myself all those nights I'd lain awake, recalling the sight of him ripped up and bleeding through five layers of bandages. Whatever he was seeing, it wasn't here. It was a memory.

"Luther." I sat up suddenly, reaching for him and finding a grip on his arms. "God, I'm sorry —"

"How cold you must think I am," he said, barely above a whisper.

"No," I said bitterly. "No, fuck — I don't — I know you've got a beating heart in there. It's just tougher than mine. That's all I meant."

He'd pulled his legs up onto the bed, was sitting on them, staring down at his knees. "I don't," he suddenly said, for some reason.

"Don't…?" I leaned in. "Have a heart? Now who's being poetic?"

"Sleep well," he answered at length. "Not most nights, anyway. I see the cliff raid nearly every night since I woke from the fevers that wound brought on. And I probably saw it then, too, I just… can't remember."

"You should stay here," I said, before I could think the better of it.

"Pardon?" he asked, finally looking up again.

Fuck it.

"Here," I repeated. "With me. In my bed. It's not like you're required to sleep on the ships when they're docked, man. Plenty of your boys go out and haunt the city most nights. No one'll care. Come here."

"Your bobcat wouldn't like that," he pointed out.

"She isn't 'my bobcat,'" I snorted. "And anyway, even *she* doesn't sleep here most nights. She has a," I tried to keep my lip from curling at the thought of the wolfhound, "paramour. A few actually, I think."

He seemed confused. "I thought the two of you —"

"Wow, you bought that?" I chuckled. "Figured you'd see right through that. Nah, that's mostly for her protection. Not like she can't protect herself most of the time on her own, but the crew's less likely to hassle the captain's woman, you know?"

He looked mildly shocked. And re-evaluating, if my guess was right.

"Was that one of the things hanging you up?" I queried. "Thinking you'd be some homewrecker?"

"You… have a reputation…" he said carefully.

"Yeah, I'm a cad," I didn't dare deny, "but most women I've been with know the score, including Shivah. Hell, she's working on brewing up her own scandals."

"Oh no," he muttered. "It's one of my men, isn't it? Someone married? In a position of authority?"

"Lord, you have *no* idea," I sighed. It would tickle me inside out to tell him, but it went against everything I stood for.

He cut a hand through the air, shaking his head. "No, best if I don't know. They afford me my privacy for the most part. I should do the same."

"I meant what I said, you know," I reached out slowly for him so he could back off if he wanted. The two of us were rough on one another, like puppies tussling. We didn't ask permission much. We just kind of… put our hands on one another. That's how it'd been literally since day one with us, and it wasn't likely to change. But right now, I thought to check myself. Everything about his bearing said he was on a knife's edge.

He let me touch him again, this time with a hand on his shoulder, the one with the scars on it. I thumbed the collar of his shirt and pressed a few of my fingers up beneath it, tracing the marks by feel. He kept his eyes on me the whole time.

"Come stay with me," I asked. *Asked*, not demanded, essentially pleading. "At least nights you're having trouble sleeping. Maybe the change of scenery or a big smelly wolf to share body heat with will help, y'know? Can't hurt. And anyway, if you want to make up for all the nights *I* spent up late worrying —"

"You started out good and then went straight to blackmail," he muttered. "*Again*. And this is Shanivaar. The nights are nearly as hot as the days."

"It's alright. We probably won't do much sleeping anyway," I said, cracking a lopsided grin.

"I don't understand what it is you want out of this," he said, frustrated.

"I *want* you to fuck me," I stated plainly.

I'd been rolling the words over in my head the way you do in the back of your mind, when you're hyping yourself up to say something or ask for something, since this encounter had started moving in that direction. It didn't take much for me to consider sex, really no more than a glance in some cases. But with him, not just because he was a man, but because it was *him*, I'd not wanted to act on impulse for once. It may not have looked like it to him, but I'd been considering whether I was going to ask all this time. If things had moved that way naturally, it would've been easier, but Luther wasn't an easy man. Asking for it was more awkward, but I found myself pretty confident by the time the words finally left my mouth. It's not like we hadn't gotten close in the past. It was an aching itch between us that needed scratching, even if we ended up regretting it. Ignoring the unrealized yearning would be worse, in the long run. Or at least, that's what my primal brain was trying to convince me of.

He stared at me, agape, through the next few moments of silence. His eyes were wide with shock when he finally said, "You don't fuck men."

"I said I wanted *you* to fuck *me* —"

"I know of your preference for submission," he assured me in a deeper-throated tone that made something quake inside me. "Most of the piracy world and the navy knows, in fact."

I made a frustrated noise. "Well that's… humiliating, but —"

"That's what you like about it," he filled in for me like he was dully reciting a known fact. Nothing about my infamous lechery seemed to bother him. He spoke about it more like a doctor diagnosing a common affliction. "You're not unique," he assured me with a sigh.

"Is that the problem then?"

"No." He shook his head. "In fact, it's… almost directly opposite my own inclinations, so…"

"We're a good fit. I sort of figured," I said with a wry smile. "But I really *did* stop looking into your private life after Dokuro, so I could never be entirely sure what the famed Cerberus Admiral got up to in the sack."

"Thank you for affording me at least that level of privacy," he muttered.

"If you really want to thank me, you can start off by saying the word 'submission' again in exactly that tone of voice."

"Forget love for a moment." He ignored my bait, his eyes drifting half closed as I moved my thumb and finger pads, squeezing and kneading at his shoulder where I still had purchase just under the collar of his shirt.

I'd not let up since he'd given me leave to touch him there. "I thought you weren't even attracted to men."

"I'm not. And trust me, I've entertained the possibility plenty."

"Then why — ?"

"Except for you, I guess."

That stopped him mid-thought, or at least that's what it looked like from the outside. "That's not —" he stammered. "It doesn't… work that way —"

"I know you've known men who like both, Luther," I reminded him. I didn't want to say as much, but I'd *met* one of his previous lovers in Debriss and sailed with him briefly. He'd given me more perspective on the matter from someone who had no particular preference on gender. It had become a subject of interest for me lately for… reasons. I wasn't certain he and I were the same, but it was enlightening nonetheless.

"Fine, yes," he agreed disinterestedly, "but that was usually because of a marriage forced on them, or because they were in denial, or because they were mollies for money. They always had a clear preference."

"I don't think it's as cut and dry as all that," I said, "but I guess in that case, my preference would be women. I mean, my history speaks for itself." I smirked. "Maybe all this time, I just had *really* high standards for men. And you're the first to meet 'em."

"That's a flattering sentiment," he said with a visible roll of his eyes, "but kissing is one thing, and it's much the same. I've been in your position before with my wife. It… it went disastrously," he admitted with no small amount of shame. "We weathered it, but I don't think you realize how different it is once you cross that barrier into unknown and… at least in my case… unwanted territory."

"I'm pretty fuckin' sure I know what I want with you," I said, clucking my tongue. "Haven't stopped thinking about it since Elrados, in fact."

"A kiss like that would get most men riled up," he reasoned.

"Fuck yes," I agreed wholeheartedly. "I had a feeling you'd be a good kisser. The passionate ones always are. And I *know* I'm pretty damn decent myself —"

"Yes," he agreed dulcetly, "you are."

"— but I was more referring to the… lord, probably half a dozen times now I've beat off thinking of what you'd do to me if I gave you the chance."

I watched as shock once again overtook his features, and I hummed thoughtfully. "None of my imaginings went exactly like this though. You were a lot more forceful in those."

I gave him a bit to recover, hoping he'd have something to say, but he still just seemed stunned. "Oh, come on," I egged him on. "You can't tell me you haven't done the same. We've known each other an age, and you *are* into men. And I'm not so bad on the eyes, I know that. You mean to tell me you've never wanked thinking about what you'd do to me if you had me at your mercy?"

"No comment."

I laughed, "That's as good as confirming it, y'know."

"A man's private pleasures are his own business, and no one else's," he muttered, "except in your case I suppose since you seem predisposed to expose yourself to ridicule at every given chance."

"That is kinda my thing, yeah."

"… you really have thought about me that way?" he asked uncertainly.

"How could I not?" I guffawed. "Like you said, I've been pulling on your tail for years now, we've been in a number of… compromising positions throughout that time, and you're exactly the sort of person that sets my loins on fire. If you were a woman, we'd've fucked on Dokuro when we first met, or you would've killed me."

"Don't assume I'm as easy as you are," he snorted.

"Of course, I've thought about what could've been if not for the… obvious barrier," I sighed. "I even tried something with a slinky molly boy once, y'know. Just to be sure."

He arched an eyebrow. I didn't miss the interest there.

"Oh yeah," I confirmed. "You think I haven't gotten curious? I've fucked inanimate objects, for crying out loud. Trying out the whole range of actual people wasn't even a weird one for me."

He pinched his brow. "If you're trying to seduce me, admitting you've stuck your dick in a… in a — I don't know, and I'm not sure I want to —"

"Was one of those big clay jugs they use for shipping," I said, scratching my chin. "It had a pretty wide mouth, and —"

"What are you, twelve?" He looked at me, exasperated. "I assume booze was involved. Is that what was inside it?"

"Olive oil," I corrected him. "And I'm sure I wasn't sober, but that wasn't it. It was more a gambling situation."

"I didn't need all these details —"

"Someone made an 'extra virgin' joke I think."

"Where did we lose the thread here?"

"Don't knot a bottle of olive oil. That's the lesson here. That was a long twenty minutes."

If possible, he looked the most horrified he'd looked all morning. "You *finished?!*"

"*Anyway.*" I cleared my throat. "The whore fellow I tried things with, I mean, it was just… paws, and it took me a damn long time. Can't say the lad got me fired up, but he put some effort in, and we got there eventually. Didn't try it again, though. Felt like I was forcing it."

"How you can be so easygoing about all of this, after we've spent nearly a decade's acquaintance dancing around one another is… beyond me," he huffed out, shaking his head. "I envy your fearlessness."

"I can't tell you what a relief the last hour's been," I admitted. "Fuck, it feels good to get it out, and you're still here, talkin' to me. This doesn't have to ruin anything, alright? We're still friends. We each had our say, and I think most of it was miscommunication, if I'm being honest. I told you I wasn't really mad at you. I guess I just felt… neglected. Like everything I'd done, everything I felt, wasn't being seen."

"I'm truly sorry for that," he said softly. "I suppose I *was* pushing you away. I thought I was protecting you by doing so."

"One of us is gonna have to die to be rid of the other," I said, quirking a lopsided smile.

"Now's a bad time to joke about that." He shook his head.

"It's not a joke, really," I leaned in, hooking my fingers in his shirt collar, my other hand reaching round to settle on the scruff of his neck, fingers splaying through the fur. I tugged, and he let me pull him forward, shifting on his knees beside me until he was precariously off-balance. His forearms found my shoulders, resting one on each. His muzzle was suddenly inches from mine, looking down on me.

"I know we're in a tight spot," I said, smoothing my palms slowly down his back. "All the more reason to take our pleasures now while we can."

"That's just," he gave a long sigh as my claws found his spine and traced it down to the base of his tail, "how you walk through life, always."

"Yeah, maybe you could learn a thing or two," I said pointedly. "Maybe stop thinkin' about what could go wrong, constantly, *all the time* catastrophizing, and just enjoy a moment now and again."

Luther sighed once more out through his nose this time. He closed his eyes for a spell, then opened them slimly and asked bluntly, "You're sure you want to try this?"

"I'm fucking sure."

"Mark your words," he said in a low, throaty growl that was nearly against my muzzle. He was that close.

"*Fuck,*" I groaned with a smile, "that was sexy."

"I have rules," he said.

"Of-fucking-course you do," my eyes rolled back into my skull, and I slumped.

"Everyone has rules," he reasoned. "I just prefer to be explicit about mine from the outset."

"Uh-huh," I grumbled. "Get on with it."

"The first goes without saying. No boasting or bragging or telling anyone in your fleet or mine, in any way, what goes on between us."

"I'm not trying to get you killed, mate," I assured him, and then glanced sidelong out the window. "Although I can't promise someone won't hear us in here. I can be, uh…"

"I fully assumed you'd be a mouthy bitch," he assured me. "Just don't yell *my* name, and it's fine."

"There's that arrogance again," I smirked. "So sure you're gonna make me cry out for you, huh?"

"Like I said before, I've only taken to a few things in life," he untucked his shirt as he spoke, "but I am *very* good at them."

I swallowed dryly. My sheath felt tight. "Promises, promises," I tutted at him.

"I'm not going to fuck you today," he said. "That's the second rule. So don't expect it."

"*What?*" I couldn't hide the disappointment in my voice. "Why the hell not? Isn't that the whole damn point? If I'm gonna do this with you, with a *man*, I want the whole package, mate. That's the one thing I can't do with women, I — I wanna try it."

"There are other things you can't do with a woman, and you're about to learn that. But full-on sex means… a lot to me," he said carefully. "I don't know exactly why, but it makes me… very, *very* emotional, and… I think even you'd agree this isn't some oath we're making to one another here."

"I literally confessed my love to you," I said, frustrated.

"Yes, and you also keep calling me your 'friend,'" he pointed out. "Neither of us seem sure what this is or what it will be, and I just don't think you're up for seeing that side of me. I can get… intense, and possessive, and I don't always like who I am. Maybe… maybe we can ease into it. Maybe once we've gotten more comfortable with this, as it is. Whatever this is."

I'm sure I was still making a disgruntled face, but I didn't argue the point with him. God, it was hard to imagine him *more* intense than he already was.

Possessive, I could see.

"Besides," he arched an eyebrow down at me, "when's the last time you had a thorough wash, anyway?"

I blinked. "…umm…"

"Wrong answer."

"Fuck you," I said good-naturedly, "I swim in the bay every morning."

"Not the same thing," he assured me. "Although…" he tipped his muzzle down then, pressing it through my dreads, down into my clavicle, his breath gusting warmth into the soft hollow of my throat. It made fire lick down my breast bone, inside me, setting my nerves alight.

"Mmmhhhh," he thrummed appreciatively. "I *thought* you smelled like the sea."

"Alright," I tipped my throat back, exposing more of it to his snuffling nose. "That it for your rules? I agree to them, but you'd better do every other damned thing you know how to do, alright?" There was, embarrassingly, already a hint of a whine in my voice. "This is new to me. I want to try it all. If nothing else, it'll be an experience."

"Impatient," he growled.

"I have never had a longer preamble to sex," I groused. "I should've figured with you."

"I'll teach you to be patient, wolf," he said, his muzzle peeling back against my throat, the hard shape of his teeth pressing to my nape. There were those warnings going off in my head again.

"God *damn*," I groaned, clawing at the edge of his shirt until I got my hands up beneath it. "*Please* do."

His teeth were *literally* at my throat, and he was teasing me with the scrape and brush of them, bobbing my primal instincts between dangerous territory and pleasure. It was maddening, and he seemed to know it, but then, far too soon, he withdrew slowly, looking down on me with half-lidded eyes.

He did something then I was utterly unprepared for. He surged forward on his knees and slid his thighs up over my lap, until he was sitting astride my legs, straddling me. He moved so spryly and with such confidence, slotting our hips together and not being shy about pressing his weight down into me. It was hard to believe this was the same man who'd been hemming and hawing over whether or not we'd do this until now. But it seemed once the dam burst…

He was a smaller man than I was, slimmer as well as shorter, but he was still a *man*, and he was dense, hard, his compact muscle tone like iron under velvet where my hands were still settled on his lower back and hips. I whuffed out a long breath as he pressed the heat of our bodies together where gravity bore down on us, and my hands scrambled to fist in his shirt so I could tear it up over his head. His muzzle came down on mine while I grabbed and bunched at the cotton, his mouth sucking my tongue into his maw. I struggled to perform the world's most basic task — there was literally no excuse for this, it wasn't even a woman's top I was less familiar with, it was a *shirt* — before he eventually broke off from the kiss with a hard nip at my whiskered lip, and the slick noise of our tongues uncurling from one another. Then, as I watched, he finished pulling the dark shirt up over his head, the light hitting his chest and shoulders in a bright stripe where the window cascaded over us. It lit up the planes of his gray, dappled fur and threw his anatomy into stark relief.

"How do you look like that at forty?!" I asked, mock angrily. "It's like someone fucking chiseled you out of quarry stone. What the actual hell, man?!"

He chuckled. "Thirty-nine, actually. And I'm slimmer than I'd like right now. The wound took its toll —"

"Oh, go fuck yourself," I grumbled, and then kissed him again. But my hands were already roving, making good on the offered meal. I'd known this man for so long now, and I'd only ever shared brief, companionable touches with him. At most, his shoulders, neck, ears. Nowhere as scandalous as his trim, clenching hips, or the hard divots of his stomach, the dense, tough mounds of his pectorals —

Oh, there. There I found a little give. I couldn't help that my instincts drove me to touch and toy with the same areas I would on a woman, and at first touch, his chest actually *did* have a little softness and spring to it. But the moment I cupped and squeezed at him there, he tensed, and the flesh in my palm went taut and hard again. It was fascinating, honestly. Muscle was soft until it tensed up, and he was almost nothing but muscle. It made touching him rather… fun… and led me to press and squeeze with my hands more to see if I could get that jump, that response in his body. If the guttural breaths into my muzzle were any indication, he didn't mind the rougher handling.

His hands finally descended on me, starting with my mane. Not a shock. It's where most anyone I messed around with tended to want to touch first. He palmed and stroked both sides of my cheek ruff first, smoothing it back gingerly while he kissed me, languid and slow, making good on his promise to drag this out. His claws carefully threaded back through the leaves of fur beneath my ears and along the base of my skull where my mane began to grow out. Manes were a distinctive mark of — usually northern — tribal lineage, and the traditional knowledge necessary to care and cultivate them stayed with our tribes insofar as we could manage it. The Amurescans saw them as a sign of savagery, of outdated barbarism, and a link to our feral ancestry (or so they assumed). Dyre had manes. Proper bipedal canine folk did not.

Luther had never said anything unkind about mine, and as we kissed, he touched it curiously, carefully, clearly trying not to snag or get his fingers caught up in it. It was sweet, honestly… and felt good, on top of that. Some women were put off by it, avoided it, and I couldn't remember the last time someone had touched it like this other than Shivah. But to be fair, she had her own (she was a tribesperson after all) and sometimes we helped one another with maintenance.

"It's really grown out," he murmured in between another kiss. "I think this is the longest I've ever seen it."

"It's been years since I cut it," I said, smiling against his mouth. "You're the only person I've ever cut it for. You know that's sometimes a tradition for a marriage ceremony in Carvecia, right?"

He tucked his head against my shoulder and coughed lightly, and I felt him smile. What's more, with his head where it was, I could see him flushing in his ears. "I, ah… yes. You told me then. I regret to inform you I am already married —"

I laughed. "I'm just playing with you, mate —"

"I'm aware," he said, lifting his head and pressing his muzzle alongside mine again. "And if you keep bullshitting, we're not going to get anywhere."

His fingers had sunk into the thick forest of fur at the very base of my mane, where the branches of my dreads began. His claws were blunt. He seemed to file them or wear them down naturally somehow, a trait I'd long known about him, but still puzzled over. But they still felt damn good carding into and teasing at my scalp.

I felt my body uncoiling, growing warm and lazy like I might if I were smoking. I was undoubtedly aroused by now, had been for a while if I'm being honest, but it was a calm, pleasant buzz in my body, like the start of waves lapping before the tide came in. If this was all I'd be able to get out of this, it would still be a good time, but I could tell already this was different than when I'd been with the molly boy. I wanted this, whatever it turned out to be. It didn't feel so forced. It was different than being with a woman, it all but had to be, but —

His fingers had been clenching slowly tighter at the nape of my neck, clutching my mane, and then, at once, he gave it a *tug*. And hell if that didn't wake a few things up.

"A-ah —" I gasped, craning my head back as he explicitly wanted me to, clearly. And then I was staring up at him, the dark mask of fur around his eyes making the gold stand out all the more. He'd pulled his muzzle back from mine fractionally, but still close enough that we were panting into one another's mouths. The tension on my scalp felt *so* fucking good. I wanted to tell him he could pull harder, but he spoke first.

"You like that, do you?" He brushed the whole of his muzzle along the side of mine, sliding it slowly upwards. I heard the clack of my gold hoop earring against his teeth. "Thought you might," he breathed into my ear with another tug at my scalp.

"Fuck — !" I bit out. Who the hell was this? This wasn't the anxious, guarded 'I have rules' fellow from just minutes ago.

"Alright," he said, his voice simmering and deep and still right against my ear. "Let's get started."

"Wh — we hadn't alre — ?" I began.

He rolled his hips down into mine, and I mean, like... undulated. Like a bloody belly dancer or a woman riding your cock. Fuck, I hadn't even known a man could *move* his hips like that. It was... something else. His doeskin leather britches were thin and soft, wrapping like a glove around his hips and doing very little to contain or conceal the hard shape of his cock when it pressed down into the groove of my hip. One thrust down —

"Ah-uhh," I wrapped my palms around his hips for purchase on something, anything, but that meant I felt the flex of his body as he ground down into me again.

Two thrusts, and he was kissing me again, swallowing any more gasps of surprise.

Three, and then he must have found the angle he was looking for, because he gave a satisfied hum, braced his arms where they were still resting over my shoulders, and lined our sheaths up. And when he rolled his hips down into mine again, I felt the hard press of his manhood all along my own, spear to spear, and damn if that wasn't... different. The pressure felt good though, satisfying, but unfamiliar. That was *definitely* another man's cock.

And a sizeable one at that.

My heart was thudding in my chest. I was greedily gulping down breaths between what was swiftly becoming frantic kissing, at least on my part. He was still irritatingly calm, or at least it felt that way. Some part of my mind was constantly firing that this was strange, new, that I didn't know how to respond to it and that came with an edge of panic. But that constant press and rut of his hips against mine, our cocks rubbing together through soft, inadequate fabric, was... working. I could tell I'd be fully unsheathed in no time. I could feel the low burning in the bottom of my belly, the clench lower down. It helped that I was sober right now. My body was always more responsive sober.

I'd been worried this would lead nowhere, that I'd disappoint him. I was beginning to worry about something else entirely as this went on.

I had been wiggling my hands up beneath the waistband of his britches. The fabric was soft and pliant enough that I eventually got them fully inside. I took full advantage, cupping his ass in both hands and kneading, feeling the flex and clench as he ground against me. He was wearing smallclothes, but I was an expert at getting my hands under *every* layer of clothing, thank you very much.

"*Fuck*, you're solid," I rumbled at him, trying to no avail to rut up into his thrusts. I just couldn't find a rhythm the way I was sitting, with his weight on top of me.

Perhaps sensing my troubles, or just because he wanted to, I don't know, he disentangled a hand from my mane and placed his palm on my chest, shoving me. I went down like a sack of wheat. I had no desire to fight him, but I also just genuinely had no way to stay upright with my hands on his ass, and I wasn't about to move them.

He lifted his body only briefly, but not to remove his trousers much to my dismay. I wanted to *see* what he'd been rubbing against me with this whole time. I was beyond curious. I hadn't felt this way with the only other man I'd tried this with, my only point of comparison. I hadn't *wanted* to touch him like this. And it might have just been fascination, but I don't know. It certainly felt like more than that.

Soon he was back atop me, but propping his elbows up now, affording me more freedom to squirm and writhe against him. I'm not too ashamed to admit, that's exactly what I did. He had me tenting my trousers, so he clearly knew what he was doing up there. I felt no need to take the wheel. I was able to squeeze his ass in my palms and play with the base of his tail all the more easily with his hips hovering over mine though, so I did. He was working his teeth over the edge of my ear when I stroked my index finger in a small circle around the very base of his tail bone and found out one of my secret spots worked on him.

This wasn't a new trick. The base of most peoples' tail was a good spot to try, but in his case, it was the underside, along where the fur got thin. He gave a hitch of breath when I found it and then rubbed my claw back and forth a few times, teasing him. His tail shivered and curled up. He rose above me, propping himself up on his palms, pinning me down with a smoldering stare, only somewhat diminished by the fact that he was panting. We both were. It was getting hot in my quarters.

No witty banter this time. He just pressed our muzzles together again, kissing me but briefly, then scraping his tongue and teeth over my lower jaw, nipping his way down my neck. I bore my throat for him — a gesture of utter submission in any canine culture around the world, but that was no longer up for debate, really — and he descended on me. He bit at my neck and clavicle, hard enough this time that I could actually feel it and soothed each bite with a swipe of his tongue afterwards.

I clutched at the scruff of his neck with one hand. The other stayed where it was, feverishly petting at his lower back and squeezing his hips as he continued to roll down into me, chasing that friction. His legs were partially entangled with my own, paws clawing at my calves. I could feel my tail wagging weakly where it was pinned beneath our combined weight, its only presence the occasional thump against the bedspread.

"Y-yes... fuck..." I shuddered, the hand I had on his head urging him in closer against me when he bit at my neck again. "H-harder," I urged breathlessly. "You can... bite... harder..."

He did, his next nip hard enough that I was certain I'd have a small bruise, which is what I wanted. Something to remember this by.

He was moving his muzzle down my chest now, and I guess I should've seen it coming, but for some reason I didn't. When his tongue found one of my dark nipples hidden amongst my fur, I wasn't ready. And he got his first shout out of me.

I arched up into the molten, wet slide of that tongue with a strangled, "Ffhhh-uhhh!" One of my arms flew down to my side, my hand grasping at the blankets for purchase, while the other clenched into his hip tight enough that he gave a low, warning growl.

I eased up my grip after taking a few moments to catch my breath, but his growl persisted. It was lower, more a noise of satisfaction now. And he set back to his task with a fervor, lathing at the dark little peak very intentionally. He did that for a while, driving me absolutely dizzy with need. The need to do something, *anything*, to alleviate the cresting tension in my body, was overwhelming. The newness of all of this was combining with the immense buildup and relief of everything I'd felt this morning, the surreal thrill of just exactly *who* was grinding on me like the world's most dangerous rent boy, and the innate knowledge that what we were doing would make literally everyone we knew outraged beyond imagining.

And then he bit down on one of my areolas and sucked. All that tension peaked and overwhelmed me at once. It was like touching a branding iron. I had less than a second before my nerves sung and my body caught up with what was happening to it. That was not enough time to do anything but clap my palm on his rear and slam my hips up into his.

Perhaps not realizing, just keeping with the rhythm we'd set, he responded to my desperation with a growl and an answering thrust of his own, forcing me back down flat on the bed and bearing down into me. The keening whine I gave turned into a long, helpless moan as he rode me through what he'd soon learn was a very abrupt, gut-clenching orgasm into my only good pair of sleeping pants.

Good fucking god, my eyes were nearly crossed. I had not been prepared for that. I hadn't even realized how close I was, and all I could do was shudder and try to warn him in the wake of it. He still had his bleeding streetwear on, and he was pressed down into me —

Yeah, nope. Those britches were *done* for. I'd have to lend him a pair of my own 'til I got them washed or something….

For some reason that's where my thoughts were at as I came down, lightheaded and riding the high my own body afforded me… when he finally realized what had happened. And I know he'd realized it, because he stopped grinding on me and started *laughing*.

It wasn't meant to be a mocking laugh either. It sounded genuinely amused. Low and throaty because he had his bedroom voice on, but earnestly mirthful. I mean, there was no getting around it. It *was* mockery, ultimately. It couldn't help but be. But we both knew I was into that.

"Yeah, get it out of your system," I groaned, flinging a hand up over my eyes.

"Ohhh, you poor darling lad," he chuckled, reaching down and running both of his palms over the expanse of my chest, letting his fingers trickle down along my ribs. One gripped my hip while the other traveled down my trail of pubic fur, utterly unbothered by the slick mess I'd made of my trousers, of his, and in streaks along my stomach where it had spilled through the fabric. He dragged his fingers through it and the wet fur there, already sticking together. He was hazy-eyed and smirking in that way that had made me feel all kinds of strange for years now.

His hand eventually found the hard, still throbbing outline of my dick, the pink of it clearly visible now through my soaked cotton, and he *gripped* it, wringing it slowly from knot to tip, milking the last of it out of me. I clapped a hand over my mouth, moans muffled into it because I had been half a second away from calling out his name. And *not* at a respectable volume.

"Wolf," he said, his voice rough, but affectionate, "I'm not trying to be an asshole here or anything, but I have to tell you, I think you might like men after all."

"You," I said between gasps, "are an exception… I will happily make."

"Mmmhhh," he rumbled, continuing to stroke me casually. He dragged his blunt claws up the ruff of my pubic fur again and gathered some of my seed on his finger pad before bringing it up to his muzzle to suck it clean. The subtle wet pop as he withdrew his finger from his mouth nearly undid me.

I groaned, wriggling under his palm, which was still cupping me through my pants. He squeezed at my knot like it was fruit he was testing for ripeness. "Sensitive," I whined.

"Petulant little bitch, aren't you?" he cut back, and squeezed me harder, until I was gasping. "You'd best not be tapped out. I have literally barely gotten started with you."

"Fucking… give me a moment!" I stuck my tongue out at him, both because I was panting and because I was, in fact, a petulant little bitch. "M'not in my thirties anymore."

"You're older than me?" he asked disbelievingly.

"Only by three months and seven days."

"My… given birth date, wherever you found it, likely isn't accurate," he said with an arched eyebrow. "In the highlands, we usually only go by season. So, we might be closer or further apart than you think, but still. I didn't realize we were the same age."

"Yeah, well," I said, "you clearly didn't go digging around, using every possible resource at your disposal to learn all you could about me."

"You've got it bad," he clucked his tongue at me. "Alright, maybe you really *are* infatuated."

"I told you I was fascinated by you," I shrugged. I basked in the wash of afterglow and the continued, almost-too-much, shiver-inducing sensation of his paw brushing back and forth over my cock. My knot was out, so it wasn't going anywhere, and it wasn't likely to retreat any time soon at this rate. "You outmaneuvered and flanked me on two separate occasions in the Tiraltic, fucking broad-sided me, and then let me run. You may as well've shown me your whole ass and spanked it. I had *no* idea what to make of you." I sighed.

He was looking far too pleased with himself as I spoke, either because I was recounting how thoroughly he could have trounced me on numerous occasions in the past or because he was touching — ah, and now holding — my cock in his hand. He'd undone my britches at long last, freeing it from its damp confines. He tore the loose, thin sleeping pants off me without much further ado, tossing them off the bed, and renewed touching my manhood. His paw pads felt roughened with use, and he was less gentle than a woman when he stroked me, more confident. Like he knew what I could take.

"Why *didn't* you sink me all those times?" I asked, my throat straining not to whine through my breaths.

"Honestly?" he answered distractedly. His eyes were purely on the task at hand now, half-lidded and pleased. "It wasn't out of pity, or mercy or fondness or whatever it is you're likely hoping for. We just didn't have leave to sink you. We didn't know whom you were contracted with, and we suspected, were certain of, in fact, each and every time, which merchant ships you were after. But we couldn't prove it. The desired outcome was for you to simply leave, and you did. You weren't one of the particularly bloodthirsty raiders out there, so I didn't feel like bending the law to make an example of you." He smirked. "Also, the crew got a real kick out of making you turn tail each time. Good for morale."

"I'm sure your Captains would've sent me to the bottom if the choice was theirs," I said wryly.

"Luckily for you, they are not in charge," he leaned down over me, pressing his nose between my ears and inhaling softly again. His voice was deep and reverberated off my skull, making me tremble. "I am."

He seemed to enjoy getting a noseful of me, for the second time now, which brought to mind another thought.

"What do I taste like?" I asked curiously. "I never ask the women."

"Like you've had a lot of citrus lately. Could be worse."

"Oh lord, I ate so many oranges when we got here," I muttered. "Scurvy's my greatest nightmare. I value my teeth."

"Altogether, you're less of a dirty blighter than I thought you'd be," he complimented, rubbing his muzzle down into my mane, mixing our scents. What a fucking dog thing to do too. I was hit with a sudden wave of fondness and moved a palm up to cup and rub at his free ear.

"I want to touch yours, too, you know," I said impatiently, trying to reach for the laces on his doeskin britches. "Move up a bit, would you?"

He placed a palm on my shoulder and *pushed*, forcing me back down with a thud loud enough that I heard it, even against the relatively soft surface of my bed. "Eager *slut*," he growled, the rumbling tone he enunciated the insulting — but accurate — description of me causing an immediate physical reaction in me like a whip crack. "You're not steering this ship. Shut your mouth and let me work."

I swallowed, wanting very badly to cup my cock all of a sudden, but he probably wouldn't want me touching myself right now, so I held off. Instead, I just gave a hesitant, "Yes, sir," through a bit lip and a smile.

"Good lad," he nodded, lifting his hips to begin undoing his laces himself. "See, if you were one of my men, I'd have gotten you in line a long time ago."

"I don't doubt that actually," I concurred.

"But what fun would that be?" he chuckled, shucking his britches and smallclothes down at once, at long last. His impressive cock sprung free once he had, and he shimmied and kicked the garments off with an efficiency most sailors who'd lived in crew housing were capable of, but as someone who'd always had their own cabin. It still impressed me to see. I was like a newborn foal trying to get out of my britches in the morning.

He slid back over me before long, and I won't lie, having a man like him kneeling over me at full mast, the weight of his cock brushing against my stomach, was a little strange. I didn't know how to feel when the utter, well, *maleness* of him was so hard to ignore like this. It set my mind reeling in a way that at once felt a little wrong, and a little exciting. I wasn't a bigoted man. I didn't believe all that heresy bullshit, but I'd still been *raised* in canine society. And there was, even now, after nearly two decades spent a criminal, outcast, and unwanted degenerate, a part of my mind that reminded me this wasn't how it was supposed to be.

I'd never had trouble with that like Luther had. I *loved* women, loved looking at them, flirting with them, taking them to bed. I was 'normal' in that regard, I guess. The standard, average canine male, except that I seemed to have developed a preference for felines. But it wasn't even their looks or the allure of the unknown in another species. It's just that canine women were brought up with more rigorous rules and expectations, to be soft-spoken, demure, keep sweet, and never impress their will upon men. And while I could appreciate a cute girl who earnestly just *was* like that by her very nature, I wanted to be with someone who wouldn't let me have my way all the time. I wanted someone who would challenge me.

And ideally, overcome me.

I'd never really understood why I enjoyed being dominated, but I was so far beyond caring why anymore. It wasn't just what got me off. I liked the adversity in *every* aspect of my interactions. It kept life interesting, kept me from getting bored. And in many regards, it also kept me humble, which was something I needed, I think.

The reason I'd kept answering in the negative when Luther had asked, again and again, whether or not I was sexually attracted to men… is because I wasn't. Even now, with a very fine specimen like the cattle dog atop me, that was true. I could appreciate him aesthetically, like you might a painting or some other work of art. He was a fairly standard-looking canine clothed, but he worked at his body. That much was clear once his clothes were off. And I'd known that before, had appreciated it before. But I'd been around every stripe (literally) of men, seen most of the ones on my crew nude by now, for years, and I can't say they got me hot under the collar. Not in the way Luther might feel about them, anyway. Or the way I felt seeing women nude.

When I'd gotten off to the thought of this before, in my paw and now in reality, it really came down to his bearing. His confidence, how he treated me, and the way he used his body. I hadn't been purely physically attracted to every woman I'd ever been with, either, looking back. I guess you didn't always have to be. As trite as it sounded, I was attracted to his personality. His swagger. His physical competence and composure.

Regardless, I'd been worried at the start of this that I'd disappoint him. It'd still be fun, but he struck me as the type to get upset if he was the only one getting off. Guess that wasn't a concern.

His breath ghosted over mine again, teasing me with a kiss that didn't connect, before murmuring softly, "The talk's just talk. Tell me if I overstep? Obviously."

"You're doing fine," I assured him just as softly. I brushed our mouths together. He returned the pressure twofold, licking his way into my muzzle and bringing his hips down again, this time with the addition of his paw lining us up. There was no barrier anymore. I could feel every inch of him pressed against my own manhood, and he was able to wrap his fist around nearly both of our lengths together. I say nearly because he couldn't quite connect his fingers, but that was no deterrent to his firm grip.

He took his time once he had us both in hand, stroking languidly and slowly, likely giving me time to rebound, but he was unhurried in general. Everything with Luther was methodical and even-handed. I don't know why I'd thought sex with him would be any different. He only acted swiftly or rushed when he needed to, and when he did, it was decisive. We'd get there eventually, I'm sure.

I panted and groaned into his mouth, returning the kiss far more distractedly and messily than before, but to be fair, I was still raw and shaking from the continued stroking of my throbbing cock. I could feel my knot had begun to retreat some, thank *god*, but he wasn't letting me lose steam entirely. He *certainly* fucking knew what he was doing with his hand, and I'd be more impressed by that, but I'd wager most men did. I guess that was one of the benefits of same sex relations: more familiarity with the parts in question.

I was moaning like a whore already; it didn't really take much with me. He didn't seem to mind, swallowing many of my noises and letting others puff out into his neck fur while he toyed with my ears or nipped at me. He hadn't told me I couldn't touch him, so I was, my hands roaming the hard planes of his body, feeling it bunch and uncoil as he rolled our hips together. I loved feeling him move and catching the little tremors and spasms. He was irritatingly quiet save the occasional growl or heavier breath, a fact I could've called in advance, but still… I wanted to feel, to hear, to know what I was doing to him. I knew he was enjoying himself. I wanted him to *lose* himself. I wanted to be the reason.

There's a power in giving yourself over to someone. You might be under them, which an outsider might see as surrender, as weak, but you're also *their* weakness in that moment. You're the one making them work for it, relinquishing physical control, but ultimately, you'll be the one reducing them to piteous whimpers when their pleasure overtakes them. I had no idea what the Cerberus Admiral would sound or act like when he came. It was literally the most private moment in a person's life, and I was excited and aroused by the thought that I'd get to experience it. I just had to figure out what pushed his buttons. He already clearly had *me* figured out.

He hadn't stopped my paws from roving yet, so I tried venturing into the unknown, dragging a palm around his ass, kneading and squeezing all the while… until I found his sac, and gave it an experimental grip and rub. He gave a punched-out whuff of a noise into my mouth, *so* close to a real moan, and I knew I was on the right track. My finger pads toyed and teased, winding their way around to the base of his sheath where the bulge of his knot was still barely restrained. He wasn't as close to climax as I'd been, so it wasn't out yet. Which meant he got *bigger*, good god. Alright, he might've been right to caution me against going straight to buggery right on the first go.

I was incredibly curious about having someone or something up under my tail because I'd heard a lot of good things that I had yet to experience. I'd tried it once with a woman using a strap, and it hadn't gone well. And the one she'd been using was smaller than his. While I was certain he'd likely know what he was doing with his actual penis a bit better than she had known how to use a false one, it was clearly a lot more complicated than I'd always thought. Maybe easing into that sort of thing with time was the right way to go, after all.

All these thoughts of having a cock inside me had distracted me. I'd apparently really gotten into fondling his sheath (wishful thinking, maybe) because he exhaled suddenly and broke off our kiss with a loll of his tongue, and the heavy, hot weight of his knot finally gave way into my palm. I'd coaxed him out.

Which meant he was getting close.

Unlike me though, he knew when to slow down. He pulled his muzzle off mine with a wet lick. "That's enough now," he growled and eased back. He leaned up first on his palms and then lifted his hips up off mine, reaching down to fist his hand in my mane. He used his grip to guide me up to a half-seated position, still lying down but up onto my elbows. And for some reason, that's where he stopped, and clearly where he wanted me.

"You're going to learn to suck cock now," he told me. Not asked. Told. "You can stay as you are or get on your knees on the decking. It doesn't matter to me."

Oh fuck. I kind of wanted to be on my knees... but, no. No. That'd likely hurt, and while that might be fun once I was a little more practiced at this, it probably wasn't great for a first timer. Speaking of....

"I might," I licked my lips, "benefit from a little live instruction, first."

He tugged on my scalp, sharply, but no rougher than before. "I'll instruct you plenty," he assured me. "But you're doing this first. If I put you in my muzzle, you'll come apart in less than a minute. And I doubt you've got three rounds in you. Besides, you'll be more... *enthusiastic* about this with a little inducement."

"I'm on my second go," I pointed out. "I'm a lot less pent-up. You really that good?"

"If I had to choose between my military career or sucking cock, I'd give up my career. Like that," he snapped his fingers crisply. "Yes. I'm that good. Now shut the fuck up already and use your mouth for something more useful."

"Only the... forty-seventh time I've heard *that*," I muttered, eyeing the flushed, slick tip that was bobbing in front of my muzzle. This would definitely be the most challenging part of this. I was pretty good with my tongue where a woman was concerned, and I certainly had enough experience having my cock sucked by someone else, but...

I had said I wanted to try everything. And this was male-on-male lovemaking at its most basic. For most of the men I had on my ship who engaged in this sort of thing, it was this *far* more than actual buggery. But I'd never tried to learn my way around a cock, not even with the molly boy.

He used his grasp on the back of my head to guide me in, and the first part was easy enough. I looked up at him as I opened my muzzle to take him inside and curled my top lip in an attempt to spare him my teeth.

At least the front ones. There was no avoiding my canines. But for the most part, they didn't press down into his swollen length, just sort of… slid alongside it. Alright. Doing well so far, I thought.

The taste hit me at a delay, and it wasn't… the worst, but I wouldn't say it was entirely pleasant, either. Luther was fastidiously clean compared to most sailors, but it was still the muskiest, saltiest part of his body and crucially tasted very different to my own. There was no getting around the unfamiliar nature of it or the unsettling sensation of suddenly having my mouth *so* very full —

It didn't take me long to gag. And he was careful about it, too. As soon as he felt me tense and choke, he eased me back. I felt the drool collecting in the back of my throat and looked up at him again, both to let him know I was fine and because I liked it when women looked at me while they did this.

He seemed to like too if the simmering stare he gave me in return was any indication. He loosened his grip on my mane for now and stroked his other hand up over my ears. "Start off using your tongue more than your muzzle," he instructed as promised. "You're not going to swallow me down right off, if ever."

Right, stupid. I should've started with my tongue. I leaned back a little and lathed the underside of his cock as I did, circling it round near the tip to feel the contours of the broad, flushed head. The salty taste was strongest there, but it licked off quickly enough, and anyway, I was a sailor. It's not like saltiness bothered me. I was getting used to the scent and taste of him, too. It'd probably never do for me what it did for him, but I liked that it was so *him*. And for some depraved reason, I rather liked the idea that this particular scent, the smell of his sex, would be all over me for a while. No one else would likely know exactly what it was, but *I'd* know. I liked scandalous secrets.

I'd have to be sure to make an excuse to talk to the wolfhound at some point today or tomorrow.

God, what was wrong with me?

He was pulling me forward again, pressing his cock back into my muzzle, while I frantically licked and tried my best to tease him with my tongue. I had zero technique and was probably mostly succeeding in making a slobbery mess of his dick, but when I looked up again, he had

that hooded look to his eyes. He wasn't laughing at me or smirking at my inadequacy. He was just watching intensely, probably committing this to memory.

I suddenly felt I needed to try harder.

I bobbed my head forward, faster than he was encouraging, opening my muzzle wider to try to accommodate him. I had a long muzzle thankfully, but once his tip hit even close to the opening of my throat, there came the gagging again. I squeezed my eyes shut and tried to force it, and I got him maybe an inch down before I couldn't stand it anymore and came up coughing. My own saliva was strung between his cock and my teeth, and I could feel tears prickling at the corners of my eyes.

He didn't scold me or do much of anything besides rub my head soothingly. When he spoke again, his voice was calm. "You're tense. Try to relax. Breathe through your nose."

I kept my eyes on his in between clenching them shut from discomfort. I felt him throb in my mouth as I tried a few experimental bobs up and down, going right to the brink of where I couldn't tolerate it any more, before letting my tongue do the rest of the work at his base. I was absolutely certain I was doing a piss-poor job at this, but his breathing was getting deeper, more audible, and soon, he started with… the talk.

"You know, I was never going to force you to swallow my whole fucking cock, wolf." His abdominals clenched, rose and fell with his breaths, the horizon I had from my current point of view. "I wouldn't do that to anyone their first time, but you just *had* to have it, didn't you?"

Shit, he was right. He hadn't pushed me to take him down my throat. That had been all me.

"That hungry for it, were you?" His paw continued to clench and stroke at the base of my neck, not guiding as much as just keeping his grip back there. "If your men could see you now. Half the bloody world knows you're a filthy rake, but I doubt they know how desperate you are for my fucking cock."

I gagged again around a wanton noise that didn't make it past my stuffed muzzle. He was all the way down again, or at least as far down as I could take him. I could feel saliva dribbling down my jaw, could taste the hint of something saltier at his tip, and when it dripped down my throat, I coughed again, desperately trying to keep him in my muzzle.

"Good god," he groaned, a real groan, finally! "You're a fucking mess. Look at you. Are you touching yourself again? Who the hell said you could do that?"

I stopped. He clutched at my mane tighter, actively directing my efforts more now. I could feel the minute shudders of his thighs where they were practically straddling my head now, his knees up beneath my arms, hips answering my pathetic attempts to bob my own head into some kind of appropriate motion. I felt the shape of his knot with my tongue, bigger than before — fuck, he was close. I was going to bring him off, and it'd be —

Down my throat, most likely. I shuddered a bit, uncertain if I was ready for that.

"*Fuck*," he said breathily, voice laced with a tremor. Everything, every sign he was nearing release, was subtle. He gave very little away. "You are..." his stomach clenched again, throwing his muscle tone into stark relief, "... terrible at this..." he breathed out, "...but damn if you aren't trying. Hells, you look... so desperate to please right now... if you could only see..."

I honestly did wish I could see myself. But seeing his reaction was better. Much, much better.

"Let's... ahhh... offend God, shall we?" he groaned, smirking hazily, one of his ears beginning to lose its battle with gravity. Oh shit, that was cute. "I could spend my seed down your throat, but I'd rather... see it painted across that beautiful dark fur. H-ah...how... would you like that?"

I couldn't respond so I only nodded, blinking slowly. Yeah, I was down with that. For multiple reasons. I think he was probably trying to spare me, too. But I liked what he said about my fur.

"Of course you would." He snuffed and reached down with his free hand to grab one of mine, bringing it up between his legs. "Eager slut. Use your paw and your muzzle. Both together. Like this."

Again, I'm not sure why I hadn't thought of that. It was just overwhelming, all of this, and I needed the guidance. He closed my fist around his knot and the base of his cock while my muzzle kept to the top half. I could swallow at least half of him before it hit my gag reflex, so I craned my neck in and began bobbing my head in time with the motions of my paw. It was obvious once I got a rhythm established and much less difficult. And it worked relatively fast, although that was likely because he was already so close.

I'd commit the sound of him coming undone to memory and distill it as a fine liquor if I could, then get drunk on it every night. It was a few shuddering, heavy breaths and a tight, soft cry that bled off into a deep, relieved groan. I hadn't expected that little, needy noise at the beginning of it, but I could hear *his* voice in it, the one I'd known for a decade, the one I so associated with strength and confidence. I'd brought that out of him. *I'd* done that.

I was grateful when he spurted on my tongue and then pulled back and began painting my muzzle and chest. Glad, namely, that he'd been going into town to see this jackal. It was enough, like this. I couldn't imagine how bad it would've been if he'd been pent up from months at sea and I was his first chance at emptying his balls. As it was…

I blinked my eyes rapidly once I was certain he was done, and licked my muzzle where some of it had drizzled down. He… also tasted citrus-y? Wow, I thought he'd been making that up, but no. I could taste it, too. And salty, obviously. Honestly it wasn't nearly as strong or abhorrent as I'd thought it would be. Now, a full mouthful, on the other hand…

Whatever had gone down my throat, I'd swallowed before I could really taste it. To be honest, I was okay with that. No thanks.

He'd slumped back down to plant a palm on the right side of my head and was stroking my cheek ruff and my ears feverishly. Before I could say anything, he leaned in and kissed me again. And if he cared that I tasted like his cock, he sure didn't act like it. He plunged his tongue in, no hesitation whatsoever, and kissed me deeply.

I closed my eyes and leaned back down onto the bed fully, both because sitting half-up like that all this while had been hard and because I was relieved. No matter what happened after this point, we'd both cleaved the pin with one another. No one could say it hadn't been mutually enjoyable. Successful romp by anyone's measure.

"I had…" I said, my voice rough from a misused throat, "… *no* idea you'd be this talkative. You've got a filthy mouth on you, Denholme."

"Mmhh," he rumbled, sounding relaxed and content. "Most of that was for your benefit. I always try to tailor how I act, to please my partner above all else. So they'll…" he paused, "…come back."

"I'm not going anywhere," I promised him.

"My own needs are honestly rather easily met," he murmured. "I hope I've done alright meeting yours."

There it was. The vulnerability, the halting uncertainty, the barest edge of fear. I'd been waiting for it. For all that Luther was death on the water, a demon with a blade, and possessing of a mind sometimes terrifying in its machinations, his weak spot was how he absolutely *handed* his heart over to his partners. Which I guess I counted among, now.

This was dangerous ground to tread. I'd known it when I'd invited him into my bed. While I could maintain our friendship with the occasional lewd scramble on the side, Luther would struggle with that. I wasn't going to say as much, but he was wrong about it being strictly relegated to penetrative sex or whatever metric he'd arbitrarily set.

The die had been cast from the moment I'd kissed him.

On a ship, there's a delicate, fine line between wind and water where the hull balances precariously at its proper depth. It varies most in storms, through rogue waves and dangerous tides, and if you're failing to maintain that balance, you're either sunk or beached. In this regard at least, Luther was worse at maintaining that balance than I was. I might need to keep his worst inclinations from ruining what we had, and my own careless behavior from doing the same. I just had to be careful. He'd given me a piece of himself here. I had to look after it. That's all.

I was a man more known for my failures than victories. But this… this, I just couldn't fuck up. He meant too much to me. I didn't want to imagine a world in which we hadn't met.

I mean, the *world* might be better for it, but I wouldn't be.

I leaned up and kissed him again, keeping this one relatively chaste and short, so I could murmur against his mouth, "You're so good, mate. Doing real good. M'happy we did this."

The affirmation worked instantly, his ears lifting slightly as his jaw shifted into a smile I could feel, if not see. We were still muzzle to muzzle, so I went back in for another kiss. He breathed in, filling his lungs, and slowly released it in a long sigh as we lazily kissed and, eventually, petted one another's bodies.

I was still hard, but I could easily let that bleed off, and that's basically what was happening over time anyway. If he wanted to end things here, that would've been fine. I'd be utterly content to lie in bed all day and touch someone and be touched in return. Even if it was just kissing and holding one another. But I got the feeling having a lover he didn't have to pay for was rarer for Luther than I, and he seemed in no hurry to put his clothes back on.

A sudden bang from outside brought the soft moment to a close. Luther's whole body went rigid. He twisted his neck up and caged his arms around me, dark ears pivoting towards the sound.

"It was just someone dropping a crate on the deck," I assured him. "Happens a lot since we're making repairs. It's getting later in the morning. The men've started working. It's alright, mate." I closed my hands around his taut arms, squeezing them. There was *no* give, they were like corded steel in my palms. He was primed for something to go wrong. For someone to burst in here and —

"I locked the door behind you," I thought to remind him. "It's a reinforced door, reinforced bolt, for if we get boarded and I need time to… destroy a few things," I chuckled. "No one's getting in here unless we want them to."

He relaxed some at that, then seemed awkward. "I-I'm sorry, I…"

"I know. I've got you covered," I said, reaching up to stroke one of his ears between my thumb and forefinger. "You don't have to explain."

Something overtook his features at that. His eyes got soft as he looked down at me, a wave of almost painfully strong affection washing between us like waves lapping back and forth. I smiled up at him, easily, and eventually he smiled back. Fragile and worried, but there.

"Is that offer still good?" he asked quietly, eyes slipping closed as I moved from stroking his ear to his cheek ruff. "To stay here? Tonight? I think I'd like that."

"You up for reading Lyefield?" I asked with a cracked grin. "Because that was my plan for the night." And maybe also something to drink now that… all of *that*… was settled.

For some reason, he guffawed into a breathless laugh at that. "Fine, but I hope you're up for robust debate. I bloody *hate* Lyefield."

"Yeah, he's got some shoddy takes on interspecies social orders," I agreed, "but his economic theories are what woke me up from the posh conditioning of my youth —"

"Later," he groaned, rolling his eyes. "Right now, I'd rather you not remind me I'm in bed with a neo-communist —"

"Neo-communist suggests I believe in a reform towards communal reallocation through existing governmental framework," I said with a 'tch' between my teeth, rolling my head back and forth a moment. "I personally think that's impossible without tearing the existing systems down first, which puts me more in the Neo-anarchist commun —"

"I am honestly sorry I got you started," he muttered. "Lord, you really *were* an academic at some point."

"I know, not particularly sexy," I grinned and rubbed our noses together. "Are you less attracted to me now? Now that you know my shameful bookworm roots?"

"Not in the least," he assured me, his chest vibrating with the rumble of his voice where it was pressed against my own. "I like that you constantly surprise me. I'm glad you're not the damn fool the rest of the world seems to think you are. I need a sharp mind and a sharper wit to cross swords with. I... love that about you, earnestly."

"You love... *that*, do you?" I teased, leaning in closer.

"It's... one of a few things... I love about you," he said carefully, but *very* intentionally.

"You're an asshole, you know that?"

"Give me time," he muttered. "This is harder than I thought it would be."

"Speaking of," I muttered, glancing down between us.

"Could you lie around with a fiercely attractive, naked woman without sporting a little wood?" he pointed out.

"That is not 'a little,'" I laughed.

"Were you serious about trying everything?" he asked rather suddenly.

I opened my mouth, then closed it, then opened it again, uncertainly saying, "Well... yes. But, you said you didn't want to go that far, and honestly —"

"You want to know what it's like, though."

It wasn't a question.

"I do," I confessed with a sigh, running a hand through my dreads. "I mean, there has to be something to it, right? I've been curious a long time, but I tried something similar with a woman, and it mostly... hurt. I can handle pain, but I don't exactly enjoy it. Nothing outside a little discomfort, you know? Is that really all there is to it? Gotta like the pain?"

"No," he said solidly. He sounded so very certain, I knew instantly I was missing something here. When he spoke again, it was gentler. "It shouldn't hurt. It can, and… it often does, because it's done with no kindness in mind. But it doesn't have to. And it's rather… *overwhelmingly good*… if you do it right."

"You've been on the receiving end too, then, I take it —"

"Yes," he said without a trace of shame. "It isn't my preference, but I'm not speaking out of turn." Silence stretched between us following that, until he quietly prompted, "So?"

"I-yes," I said quickly. "I want to know what I'm missing out on. I'm all about experiences. But your rules —"

"You're not ready for all of me, anyway," he assured me. "But I'll break you in —" *god*, there was that tone again, "— if that's what you want."

"Yes," I answered. I had no witty banter for this. My tongue was thick in my mouth, my cock was still hard, and him saying specifically 'I'll break you in' had featured in more than one of my imaginings.

Also, and I don't know what this says about me, I was rather glad this was happening while I could hear all the men outside, going about their day. Not just because it was loud out there, and that lessened the chances we'd be heard, but just the thrill of it. I mean, he'd said he was staying the night. We could *wait*.

But he wanted to do this *now*. And so did I. Fuck, if it went well, maybe we could do more of this later…

"I think I have —" His voice snapped me out of my lewd imaginings, and I saw him leaning over, rifling through the pockets of his doeskin britches, discarded in a crumpled heap, half-off the edge of the bed. He gave a sudden 'ah' and brought something out. Like a tin.

"I have my own, you know," I snorted out a laugh. "Why was that in your pocket?" I had to ask.

"I wear these when I go to the Crimson Divine," he explained.

"Right, they named the brothel after the drug they peddle," I remembered after a moment. "They don't provide — ?"

"I prefer my own," he shrugged. "Puquanah," he pronounced the fox's full name perfectly, which was impressive for an Amurescan, "recommended this particular oil mixture to me in Serwich, and it's the best I've ever found."

"I guess your rules don't apply to prostitutes, then?" I guessed. If he was bringing oil on his visits...

"I have him use it on me," he explained.

"Oh," I paused, "yeah, I guess that makes sense. That's why I have it, or at least partly why. Women love it too, y'know."

"Mnh."

I gave a slow smile, lying back and watching him apply the oil to his fingers. "So," I brushed my paws down through the blankets, palming and stroking my own cock with a free hand, "did you fuck the fox, too?"

"I don't kiss and tell," he said pointedly, glaring at me. "But... just out of curiosity... what makes you think I did?"

"I heard you and the coyote got into it."

"You're a worse gossip than a bored housewife," he muttered, his shoulders and the wound spanning across them flexing as he moved back over me.

"Information broker," I corrected him.

"Jealous?" he taunted in between a few brief, nipping kisses.

"Excuse *you*, I don't *get* jealous," I grunted, offended. "Monogamy is for men with control issues — nnh...ohhh..."

There was a hot pressure under my tail suddenly. It was unmistakably his cock, the broad tip pushing up into my cleft and... oh, god, just... rubbing there. Against me, pressing at my pucker, not enough to slip inside, but I could *feel* him there, could imagine now that it was tactile, and what an impossible stretch it would be...

Something inside me burned, aching, and I felt... empty. In a way I pretty much always was, but right now in this moment, it felt hollow. It was like a deep muscle was suddenly making me aware of its presence, yearning for contact. I'd tried fooling around down there once or twice myself, but I wasn't flexible enough to accomplish much, and it was awkward, uncomfortable —

"I could put you on your knees if you preferred," he said in a gravelly voice against my ear, punctuated by the slick sound of his tongue teasing my lobe. "But I do like that I can see your face like this."

"Maybe... for a bit?" I croaked. "I might... like that...."

Without another word, he got his arms around me and flipped me over with some kind of twisting, deft motion he must've learned from grappling or wrestling. It was so obviously low-effort, using leverage to his best advantage. I was on my stomach before I knew what was going on, and then he braced an arm across my back, pinning me down beneath him. I realized belatedly when I tried to wiggle against him that he'd just, like it was nothing, put me in a surrender hold. The innate knowledge that he was handling me like he would an opponent while doing this was unbelievably alluring.

"Nnhhhhfuck," I groaned when I felt his hips slot up against mine again, this time behind mine. He had the molten heat of his manhood lined right up beneath my tail with nary a spare motion a moment later. Again, he just… teased me with it, teasing himself in the process too, I'd wager. He ground under my tail, humming a tuneless noise of satisfaction as he did. All I could do was whimper.

"You'd take me well, wolf," he growled, the spade tip of his cock pushing against my button, making me gasp with the pressure, "but you'd pop like a cork, I can tell already. Are you always this quick?"

"I'm a better lay when I'm drinking," I muttered. "I'm not used to being sober. Everything's… sharper. Clearer. Too much. I need booze to slow down a little."

"That's got to be a fine line," he grunted. "Drink too much and you're useless."

"I've gotten pretty good at knowing where my sweet spot is," I said.

"Mmmhhh," he rumbled. His arm shifted, his fingers sinking into the fur at the nape of my neck, closing and holding me there, my muzzle pressed down into the bed. "Let's see if I can find it."

"Wh-oh — !" I yelped as he yanked my hips up with another firm hand, and rutted against me, the hard outline of his cock sliding back and forth beneath my tail. He was still stubbornly just dry humping me, but I got a taste of what it might feel like for a bit, being bucked at under him, and…

I'm not going to lie. I liked it.

"Nhhuhhh…" I groaned pitifully, my voice muffled by my own fur-covered, musky comforter. It mostly smelled like me, obviously, but it had begun to pick up his scent as well. I was *never* washing this blanket.

His hand tightened around the nape of my neck, buried between my dreads, clutching at me like he meant to drag me around the room. With his weight fully pressing down atop me, I was absolutely certain I wouldn't be able to move even if I wanted to. The restraint, the utter surrender, made my blood boil and my nerves light up all the way to my extremities.

"Fuck — gnhh," I groaned gutturally through my teeth. "You... bloody... cocktease," I got out between the rolls of his hips. "Gnhhh... fffhh... fuck me already."

"You are testing my restraint, wolf."

"Hehe-AH —" I hissed as he pushed *hard* against me, and I'm pretty sure the tip of him made it partially *inside* me that time, or it bloody well felt like it. "Fuck!" I swore. "Yeah, there's the pain I remember."

"Careful what you ask for," he growled, and then leaned in over top me and kissed the crown of my head. He dropped his voice to a rough whisper, promising, "I can make this good for you. Just stop getting ahead of yourself."

He eased off the pressure. I felt his cock slip away, and I whined. I couldn't help myself, it *had* hurt, but the absence made that hollowness come back. And the see-sawing back and forth was worse. Maybe this was like ripping off a bandage. Maybe if we just did it really fast —

I felt that he'd backed away from me marginally, I could still feel his weight on the bed, but he wasn't over me anymore. I was about to ask why, when his muzzle began nipping and nuzzling its way down my hips, the small of my back, and eventually my rear. The hand he hadn't coated in oil was squeezing at my hips where he found purchase. I was less slender than I used to be, so... he found plenty to play with. His slick hand had moved to where my cock was hanging between my legs, idly stroking.

"Spread your legs," he demanded, and then bit at the soft meat of my rear, getting a good and proper mouthful.

I did as I was told, widening my knees apart until the stretch burned my inner thighs. Lifting my tail was almost instinctive, which, I don't really know what *that* says about me... oh who am I kidding, yes I do. But it wouldn't have mattered whether I did it myself or not, because he'd launched an all-out assault biting and kneading my ass. Soon, the heat of his mouth was perilously close to the underside of my tail.

I wasn't too squeamish to go to town on a woman's rear, let me tell you. But I'd never expected *he* would, and I'd never been on the receiving end. When his tongue lathed up the underside of my tail, right where I'd teased him earlier, I learned a few things about myself *real* fast.

One, my blankets did very little to muffle the kind of moan that could apparently rip out of me. Two, I should have tried this a *long* time ago. All these long years wasted.

And three, I wanted him, something, anything, he could give me, inside of me, right the fuck now.

His hot, wet tongue tortured and teased my arsehole like he was playing a goddamn musical instrument, carefully plucking at me and making my body literally jump and twitch. I kicked out with my feet until I was having trouble staying up on my knees.

I begged him between hoarse moans. "What... th'fuck... are you *doing*... to me...?"

His only response was a hum, and then his hand left my cock, bereft, and I thought I could kill him. I could really kill him if he didn't —

But then came that press again, that burn, and it was smaller, more manageable. It was his finger, I realized, and his claws were blunt — oh, fuck! *His claws were blunt.* He must've ground them down *intentionally*. The motherfucker always had a reason for everything he did, I should have fucking *known* —

A brief pressure, and then — "AH-nhhh —" I whined as he slid the digit in, slick and with far less resistance than his cock had met. I'd gotten about this far before on my own, but he... did something... different. He got it all the way to the knuckle, for one. And then he — I swear he must've — curled it, inside, and —

It was like touching lightning. A quake passed through my entire body, forcing the air out of my lungs in an escalating, helpless moan. My back arched, my toes curled into the blankets, claws digging for purchase. I grabbed at anything I could, finding the headboard and holding on for dear life.

"Either," his breath was hot beneath my tail, reverberating with the low timbre of his sultry bedroom voice, "you're *very* sensitive, or —"

He took his time inserting a second finger, and this one stung more than the last with the addition of its partner. The pain was minimal, it was

just… strange and uncomfortable at first, but when he thrust them slowly in and out and did that *thing* again.

This time it hit me like the precursor to an orgasm, a ripple through my whole body like the pleasure from working a sore and wanting muscle, but *so* much stronger —

I straight-up sobbed out the moan this time, and I couldn't help it anymore… I said his name. I did my best to muffle it into the mattress, but I know he heard.

Oddly, when he spoke again, his voice sounded fond and relaxed. "Lad, I am *wasted* on you. You're a shallow mark."

As if to make his point, he hit that spot again. God, he'd picked me like a bloody *lock*.

"…Luther…please, fuck…" I begged, *begged*.

His other hand had come round to touch my cock again, and I wanted to warn him. I — he needed to know that if he did that —

But rather than stroking me again, he gripped me at the base and *squeezed*, and my breath hitched. My whole body froze up.

"Not yet," he warned at a growl. "You spill when I have you in my muzzle, this time." He continued to stroke his fingers in and out, lighting up that spot inside me with a casual brush each time. It never got any less alarming or overwhelming. And imagining what it would feel like if I were fuller, if he was actually fucking me, stretching me around that big cock —

Bloody hell, I didn't care what it took. We'd get there.

When he tried a third finger, that's when it tipped past the threshold of discomfort into pain again. But some part of me wanted it by then, yearned for that stretch, that feeling of *fullness*.

He didn't ask this time when he flipped me over again. He just withdrew his fingers, grabbed me by the hips, and did it. And then he wrapped an arm around my thigh and lifted one of my legs up over his shoulder, hunkering down between them. I spared a glance down my own body at him, and saw a flash of that confident, seductive smirk he wore so well, before his muzzle descended on my cock.

There was, obviously, not a trace of hesitance or uncertainty when *he* did it. He took me smoothly to the knot, not a hint of a gag, and swallowed, closing his throat around the top half of my dick, snugly. And then he slowly dragged back up, cupping the underside with his tongue the whole way. Like a fuckin bawd working her thousandth client.

I understood, obviously, that Luther was more in the position of a man who'd had a few very *dedicated* lovers over the years, not actually a whore like me who'd taken multiple lovers in every port, but still. It was fuckin impressive. I was sizable, too. A lot of my previous partners had struggled to take all of me in their mouths.

I barely had time to register how bloody good his muzzle felt before he'd slid his fingers into me again. He started with two, found a pace with the mind-blowing magic his muzzle was working on me, and then eased his way back to three.

All I could do was lay back with my legs splayed and buck my hips weakly into his merciless assault. I gasped in between ragged moans, babbling incoherently, mostly just 'yes' and 'fuck' and 'thereohfuckthere', and he *unraveled me*. The combination of his muzzle sucking and swallowing down my throbbing cock and his hand fucking me into oblivion was enough to make me question every hour of my life before this I'd spent doing literally anything else.

He wasn't holding back anymore, and since the man had to be right about goddamn *everything*, once he took me in his muzzle, I really did last less than a minute. But what a fucking minute *that* was.

I came crying and sobbing my pleasure at the ceiling, and I felt him groan as he sucked and swallowed it all down. He didn't stop pumping his fingers inside me either, answering some deep part of me I hadn't even known I had that wanted him there, wanted him deeper, mercilessly stroking me through the blazing climax.

I was dizzy and high in the wake of it, sparks dancing in front of my eyes, every sound and sense coming through hazy and vague. It wasn't like I hadn't experienced mind-blowing orgasms before, but this was new. This was a new sensation, a *new* way to feel this kind of pleasure, and briefly I felt like a teenager again. It was euphoric knowing I could still find new experiences in the world like this, let alone that I had someone to share them with.

I felt him roll me to my side, and I allowed him, boneless as a rag doll. When he moved up beside me, I tipped my muzzle towards his and wasn't disappointed. He kissed me again. But it wasn't a lazy, slow kiss. He still felt hard and trembling.

He slotted our hips together, lying beside me and behind, and I felt why. He was still hard. In fact, his knot was out. Doing all that to me had really worked him up. God, but I was so relaxed and spent. What could I —

He pushed on one of my legs to press it flat to my other and held my hips against his. I let him do as he wanted, uncertain what his goal was... until I felt the shape of his cock slip up between my thighs. Right against my sac, under my own spent length. I understood at once and clenched them together. He groaned approvingly.

He rutted up between my thighs, giving halting, breathless groans as he made use of the tight little nook I'd provided. He fucked into me like that, hands pulling my hips into his, cheek crushed against my shoulder, body shuddering with want. This was as good as being fucked by him, as far as I was concerned. I could hear the noises he made as he got close, feel his hips slapping into mine, thrusting with abandon... and when he tensed up and came, I could feel his knot swell under my own. I felt the slick heat as he painted my thighs and the cleft of my ass in messy spurts.

Knowing I'd made him feel that good was... satisfying. It was always satisfying regardless what person I was with to give them pleasure. But, in his case, it had come at the end of the longest burn I'd ever felt for someone. And it was a relief to know this hadn't been a mistake.

We lay there for a time, our senses returning to us. I was stroking his back and shoulder idly, and he had his muzzle tucked into my dreads. It could have stayed quiet and peaceful.

But nothing with us stayed peaceful for very long.

"Hypothetically. Would you..." he began to ask, and I knew, I could sense right off from the tone in his voice that whatever he was about to say, it would be problematic, "... would you... give up the women? If I gave up Amon?"

I sighed, closing my eyes. "Alright. First off. I don't *want* you to give up the jackal."

He lifted his head. "Why not?" he asked.

"Because you like him," I responded simply. "Don't you?"

"I... do," he admitted softly.

"You and I can't be the whole world for one another, Luther," I said, forcing the words out even though I knew they'd hurt him. In the past, I'd strung the women in my life along more times than I cared to recount, often by telling myself doing so was sparing their feelings. I was learning with Shivah, because she wouldn't let me get away with that shit, the value of honesty. Finally. And Luther deserved that, too. "He... or someone like him, I don't know... they could be something for you that I... can't," I said.

"It isn't as though we've really tried, yet," he said quietly, if defiantly. "This could work."

"No," I said with certainty and a sigh. "It can't."

His voice was tinged with the barest hint of envy when he spoke again. "You'd be enough for *me*. You really can't imagine being content if it's just... you and I together — ?"

"Honestly," I said, "I don't know if I could stay strictly loyal to one person, any one person, no. But that isn't it. Even if I did, you'd always wonder, and you'd be right to. I have a history, and you're a naturally suspicious person. Besides," I shifted, so that we could look at one another, "if I changed that much for you, you'd need to give up something, too."

"No, I wouldn't," he said stubbornly, knitting his brow. "We'd be equal partners. Equal, and both of us loyal to one another —"

"No, not that," I shook my head. "I mean, you'd need to give up the Navy, Luther. Amuresca. You'd need to sail with *me*."

His eyes widened in realization.

"I wouldn't ask you to give up your family," I said definitively. "I don't care that you're married. I'm fine getting to know them, and... I'm sure your kids are great. I like kids. We have a lot in common. But you'd *have* to be the one to give up your loyalty to your country, your ships, your command. Not the other way around. You must realize why."

His muzzle twitched, and his eyes went distant. He didn't fight me. He knew I was right.

"Tell me you're willing to do that," I said, touching his cheek. "Throw off the mantle... and I'll tell you what, at that point you can have my sole loyalty. I've been trying to get you to liberate yourself from those shackles for... god, *years* now. If you really wanted me to give up women, if *that's* the fucking price I pay so you get the hell away from the chain of command, the empire, the *church*, all the Pedigree who bloody *hate* you, and you come walk with me in freedom? Finally?" I sighed. "Fine."

"You wouldn't be happy with a compromise like that," he murmured.

"Not… entirely," I admitted. "But it'd be worth it. The seas are a better place with you on them. You and I? We'd be a force of fucking nature. And your people, your country, don't deserve you. I don't even know that I do, but I know what I'm offering's at least a hell of a lot better than what awaits you there."

"I can't abandon my fleet now," he said, his voice threadbare.

"They'll hang you," I said with certainty, even though that probably wasn't certain. The fact that it was even on the table was what was important here. "Once they find out what you did, and what you gave up to do it, they'll execute you. That will be how they'll show their gratitude for saving all their lives."

He gave the weakest, most trembling smile. "But," he breathed, "I'll have saved their lives."

I hugged him. Because I didn't know what else to do. And this time, he didn't just let me. He closed his arms around me tightly in return.

"I oughta steal you away," I muttered against his neck. "Save you from yourself."

"I have a duty —"

"*Fuck* your duty," I growled. "Your duty made you choose between thousands dead and committing war crimes. Look what they've done to you. Don't you fucking *resent* it?"

"I do," he admitted, his voice small. "But it doesn't change the position we're in, now. I love my men, Grayson. My ships. And… yes…" he sighed, his voice nearly inaudible when he said, "… you. I love… you… too. That's… why I need to stick this out. It's me they're after. But they'll not stop until they've killed all of us. And I haven't concocted a solution for this one yet. I don't know how to get us out of this. But I can't just run from it. That isn't an option."

It was like I'd gotten my wish granted by a cursed lamp. This wasn't how I'd wanted to hear that from him. But it was…

He was right. I was right. We were both right. We could both be right and still be unhappy because there were no good solutions here. The situation we'd found ourselves in was dire.

He may have had the right approach, doing as he'd been doing up until today. Dancing around the subject of fixing my ship, maintaining our friendship to the last moment, and letting me find my own way in the world. Releasing his hold on me, so that my fleet and I could disconnect from all of this. Honestly, as an Admiral, it might have been the best course of action I could have chosen too.

But it was impossible. My feelings forbade it. I was not about to sit here in the safety of this cove and watch him sail away from me for the last time, knowing what waited for him out there.

"We'll… come up with something," I said, stroking a hand through his neck scruff. "We always do. But whatever we land on, we do it together."

He rolled to his side, facing me, and wrapped an arm around my chest, resting his head over my heart. I kept my own arm around him, and we lay there, listening to the sounds of the bay and the creaking of my aging ship.

"I love you," I reminded him after a long time spent in silence.

"Now it just feels like you're competing with me to say it more often," he murmured.

"I was giving you a chance to follow me up properly, mate." I said wryly. "Seeing as how you seem to need instruction on how this is generally done."

"I thought you were lacking in experience as well," he pointed out.

"I read a lot of fiction."

"Yes, you mentioned your fondness for utopian philosophers before."

"You're a horrible paramour," I said around a snort. "You're supposed to *compliment* the things I like —"

"I do love you," he interrupted me. He was hiding his head in the crook of my neck when he said it, but he still said it.

I patted his back. "There you go."

* * *

We were mid-raucous debate, speaking between a dinner of drinks and flatbread sandwiches, when we were paid a nighttime visit. Luther had stayed most of the day, save a brief walk around the inlet that I'd joined him on and a swim in the bay. Followed by another round in one another's muzzles in a little private nook by the rocks I'd found weeks ago.

I think I was getting better at it. He'd probably disagree.

This time, the knock that came at our door was not quiet, nor cordial. It was a loud pounding, followed by an all-too-familiar voice. God, I was starting to hate that brogue.

"I know you're here, *sir*," the last part was said with particular frustration. "You could have bloody well told me you'd be gone all day. I've had Singh up my arse since dawn."

I glanced at Luther, who held a straight face for all of a few seconds before snorting a laugh into his palm.

I turned towards the closed door, raising my voice. "That sounds like a personal problem, mate! Although I respect that kind of endurance. Didn't know the bastard had it in him."

"*Open the goddamn door!*"

Luther started laughing flat-out at that, and I grinned at him. "Shit, he's taking the lord's name in vain now. I think he's mad."

Luther made to get up, but I waved a paw at him and did so myself instead. I headed to my cabin door and undid the deadbolt before I turned the brass handle and leaned in the door frame, greeting the irate wolfhound with a smirk. Looks like I'd gotten my wish after all. Sometimes the dice fall your way.

I leaned in far too close into his personal space, and he swayed back, curling his muzzle. "Out of my way, you sodding criminal," he groused, throwing an arm to the side of me to shove me.

I stood firm. "Now, now," I chided. "This is my ship, my *quarters* in fact. There's no call to be so rude."

He snuffed. "Ugh. You smell like…"

I lifted my eyebrows, waiting for him to continue.

"…I don't know, and I'd… rather not," he muttered. I opened my mouth, and he cut me off. "No. Please. Spare me. Sir!" he called past me. "Am I to run the fleet myself, then?"

"I finished my work with the purser this morning," Luther said from the table, clearly eating another sandwich square. "And I spoke to the scouts again. What have I neglected, exactly?"

"Your presence," Johannes said, sounding exhausted. I almost felt bad for him. Almost.

"We're grounded," Luther stated the obvious. I extricated myself from the doorway and drifted back towards him, grabbing up my rations cup and draining it. "Most of the men are in port. Is it really that important I get squawked at by Singh all evening?"

"It's either you or I, sir," the wolfhound said, frustrated.

"Why? He just wants someone to tear down right now." Luther shook his head, lifting his own cup to his muzzle to drink, before continuing. "Man's afraid of death, and he's not handling it well. Let him tire himself out with Addison."

"He's insisting some of his crew have come down with dysentery from the food here," Johannes muttered. "I've spoken to the physician, and he says otherwise."

"It's the fish," I spoke up, pouring myself another cup.

They both looked at me, so I explained. "Sorry, one fish in particular. There's a type of parrot fish in these waters that's not actually safe to eat, but the locals have been eating it so long, they know how to handle it. If it's prepared wrong, which I'm guessing your boys are handling themselves if they're doing their own fishing, it'll make you sick. But they're probably eating it in port and then catching it on their own without realizing there's a difference in how you have to prepare it. And the damn things are everywhere, so your boys are *definitely* catching them."

Johannes gave me an appraising look, and Luther snapped his fingers, pointing at me. "There. Good man. Pass that on to the physician, alright?"

"Yes, I... will," Johannes said, still looking at me. "How exactly did your crew figure this out?"

"We... talked to the locals," I said, as though it were obvious. Because it was.

The wolfhound's shoulders slumped, and he spared a glance at the table covered in books, drink, and our meal. Almost... wistfully. "Lyefield?" he said, while looking over one of the covers.

"Your Admiral has piss-poor takes on philosophy."

"There are no good utopian philosophers," Luther muttered. "The world's a dark hole of shite. There's no room for optimism when examining the psyche of men."

"Good luck to you convincing him otherwise," Johannes said to me, of all people. He sounded tired and dismal, but not angry any more. He looked back to Luther. "Will you be returning at *all* tonight, sir?"

"No, I don't think I will," Luther replied, chewing on another bite of sandwich. I felt my chest lift a little. He hadn't even hesitated.

"Better here than the brothel," Johannes muttered, then made to leave. "I'll handle Singh."

I felt… *bad* for the man, which was a weird feeling, considering it was him. So, before he could leave, I called out, "Uh, hey. Wait."

He turned and gave me a long-suffering look. I considered whether or not I wanted to go through with what I was about to do, about to facilitate, before I did. But ultimately, I reminded myself I wasn't an asshole. And I shouldn't be the only one alleviating my misery with good company, right now.

"You wanna repay me for the advice on the parrot fish?" I offered.

"Not particularly," was his dull answer.

I pressed on anyway. "One of my scouts is missing." I sensed a bolt of alarm from both of them, before I waved my hands about. "Sorry, not… missing, per se. I'm sure she's fine. She told me she'd be 'taking a walk' before she left, which for her can mean, you know. Days. She wanted to get the lay of the land. It's a small enough island, and she can handle herself. I saw smoke up in the nearby bluffs last night, so I think she's just camping up there. Getting some time off the boat. Could you just… check up on her? You're one of the few men I know that could probably find her."

"Lady Shivah," he guessed.

"Only woman scout I have," I confirmed. "Only… woman on the crew, actually. I don't want to intrude on her privacy, but I know she trusts you…" I cleared my throat, and he narrowed his eyes at me, "… specifically. So. You're the only man for the job."

He gave me a long, searching look. No words passed between us, but I could *feel* his ire. He probably saw this as a threat. My way of telling him I knew what was going on between them. Amurescan men are so fucking suspicious and pessimistic.

I just smiled at him, saying nothing. And eventually, he consented with a quiet, "I will tell Lady Shivah, if I can find her, that her captain is looking for her."

"Thanks, mate," I said. "But there's no rush. She can return on her own time. Just… pay her a visit, aye?"

He glared at me, but ultimately couldn't ask me what my game was in front of Luther. So, eventually, he just turned with a 'hmm' and made his way out. I shut the door behind him.

"I'm glad he's made a friend or two," Luther said from the table, stretching his arms above his head with a sigh. "But won't the bobcat resent you sending him after her?"

"Not as much as you might think," I said quietly, before drifting back over towards him. Instead of sitting at the table again, I moved in behind him where he was sitting and shoved my hands beneath the collar of his shirt, working open the laces in the front so I could get my paws in there properly.

He groaned when I began to work the bunched muscles at his neck. I realized belatedly that I was rubbing around the scars, but he hadn't cared before, either.

"They don't hurt?" I asked, tracing them with my finger pads.

"They've healed for the most part," he answered. "The broken collarbone was more of an issue, but that's deeper. I'm still not sure how it will affect my sword arm."

"We can spar tomorrow if you want, but I have a feeling you'll still hand me my ass," I shrugged.

"I'd still enjoy that," he hummed contentedly, tipping his muzzle up to look at me.

I quirked a smile back down. "Do you think he could tell?" I asked him.

"He's a Templar," he shook his head. "We'd never know. Their *oath* is to keep our secrets. No matter how much at wits end he is right now, he'd never break his composure in a way we'd catch. And anyway, this whole room smells of the two of us, Shivah, and sex. I don't think he'd put the two of us together as the cause."

"Maybe we ought to try harder."

He smirked slowly in that way that I loved. "Maybe we ought to, yes."

Azimuth

Azimuth

"Lord, the husbands are fighting again…"

I heard it murmured in voices I could not yet put faces to on the main gundeck. Canine and a rat, I think. That wouldn't have narrowed it down, aboard one of my vessels. Here, that was barely one-quarter of the crew, so I had less of an excuse. I should know their names by now. Normally I was a quick study to learn the men on any vessel I found myself crewed aboard, but I was out of practice and out of my element. I wasn't really crew here, not yet, perhaps not ever, and the only time I'd spent on the ship thus far, I'd spent grounded. It was harder to fall into the rhythm of a vessel that hadn't set sail yet.

And this was no Navy ship.

These men moved to the beat of a different drum, not as chaotic as I might have imagined, but harmonizing in a way I could not match. It was new now in the way it had been new back then. I felt like I'd stepped backwards two decades, unmooring myself from the stable foundations of my life. Back then, that had been the greatest relief I could have imagined, leaving my childhood life behind.

But I'd put blood, sweat, and tears and lost several people who mattered to me in the process of earning my place and comfort in the familiar rhythm of what my life had become in my adult years. In rank, in coin, in privilege. Even when I'd known I was bedding down in a nest of vipers, I'd buried myself willingly in those coils. When the vipers whispered, I towed the line and did their bidding because of that security. I had people, again. People I didn't want to lose. A life, while imperfect, was a life that I had fought hard for. I had felt the poison glands grow inside of me, and my fangs lengthen. And I'd done terrible things.

Terrible, unspeakable things.

More than once over the course of a decade, this eclectic, unfamiliar, aggressively rogue band and their infuriatingly brilliant Captain had offered me an outstretched hand into a life that was antithetical to all I knew, but free from the vipers. And I had told myself for years that I'd rejected it because of the most self-flattering reasons. I had people to take care of. Family. A legacy I'd promised to protect. Loyalty to my men.

This had been a long time coming. And it would have gone down smoother if I'd gotten out in front of it. But I hadn't. I'd been a coward and clung fast to those ill-tailored vestments of civil society that did not suit a ditch-born heretic and murderer like me until they'd been torn away by force. At the worst possible time, in the worst possible place.

The few men whose loyalty to me eclipsed their loyalty to the Navy were here now, defected, alongside me. And much to my shame, finding their place here faster than I. There was no going back, this I knew. But enough of my mind clung to Johannes's assurances that the Court Marshal imposed upon me by the coalition of Officers who'd commandeered control of my fleet was temporary, and we'd have it all smoothed out once we returned to friendly waters. He had more faith in the Board of Admiralty than I did. Some part of me clearly believed him, though. Because I kept expecting I was going to wake up in my cabin.

The Navy could suspend my rank and privileges, but they could not force me off my own ship. Our family owned them. No… this had been a decision. Made by others on my account while I was wounded, but it was a decision I'd stood by because I was not safe on my own vessel any more. And that stung like the lash, but it was the only right call. It wasn't just about my health and security. The Cerberus Fleet was precarious, on the brink of mutiny, and I was the spark that would light that keg. It was better I remain here for now.

The men here didn't even hate me. They didn't all seem to know what to make of me just yet, and that was fair. I'd tried to kill some of them in the past. Or at the very least, menaced them. Honestly considering that, they were being downright amicable. They treated me like one might treat a pet feral, a predator their Captain was keeping aboard because he was fond of it for some reason. And crazy. But then, they must have come to terms with him being crazy long ago.

They didn't harass me, but they whispered about me. They whispered about… us. They knew. I was certain they knew. Something like this didn't happen aboard any ship — no matter how large — without the men finding out. And knowing my secret was all it had taken for me to lose the loyalty of nearly all of the men who'd followed me in the Cerberus fleet. Even some I would have called friends. Even some who would have died for me, and I for them.

Even some who — I was certain — had known for a long while already. It was one thing to overlook it, to never speak of it. But one could not be seen to stand beside a Heretic Admiral. God's disfavor was too high a cost for superstitious, pious men like these to pay. Especially when they were clinging to every lifeline they could find in a desperate situation most felt I'd put them in.

There was a sentiment amongst my crew that this was God's Wrath upon the Cerberus Fleet. Punishment for the grave misdeeds of one — namely me. And regardless of my own beliefs on God, I could see how my men had arrived at that conclusion. I wasn't even certain they were wrong.

But that sentiment was absent here. None of the hatred and bile that had nearly cost me an eye and my command. What replaced it here in this strange, more liberal-minded place was a wary curiosity, it seemed. And an almost dandy, effeminate atmosphere of clucking gossip and bitter mockery. These men weren't going to knife me in my sleep; they were too entertained by my situation. They enjoyed watching me squirm and stumble on my unsteady footing here and whispering about my personal life.

It reminded me of Court. And I hated it.

It was fair play, I had to remind myself. There was a gauntlet, a hazing process aboard any vessel, and I was a previous enemy, to boot. Honestly if this was the worst of it, I was getting off light. And I knew why. It was due to no credit of my own.

My… unique relationship… with their current Admiral was what protected me. In the past, I might have been in real danger amongst these men. But right now, we were allies, and more than that. Besides, it wasn't as though Privateer crews were unaccustomed to taking on ex-patriated, excommunicated, discharged men. There were dozens of souls on this crew who'd been Navy men once. Including fourteen who'd come with me. I wasn't unique.

But none of them spent entire nights in the Captain's Quarters. None of them bucked and growled in his bed, fell asleep with his claws carding through their fur, bled into his satin sheets, hissed and hollered in passionate arguments with the man... none of them but me.

Or at least, that is what I'd believed. Until tonight. Until I'd smelled another man on him.

The leopard, I knew. I knew his scent, I knew the color of his fur when I saw it on those very same sheets. I even knew his name. Taarush. I don't know how I hadn't seen it coming. He was not his First Mate, but he *was* his shadow, his attendant, nearly always at his side. One of his personal guards, I'd told myself. And indeed, the wolf had called him thusly on more than one occasion. I had no reason to doubt him. Given his condition, it was natural and justified that he kept a retinue close when he was out and about to look after him. On more than one occasion in our past, he had left his honor guard behind and paid for it. It was fine. I was fine with it.

I was... fine with it. Having the constant reminder that I could never truly be alone with him, never really have him to myself. That was understood.

It was *fine*.

But part of our arrangement was that at the very least, I was the only cock of the roost. I might have to dine on humble pie on his ship, start over from the bottom with his boys. But I was the only *man* in his bed. And I didn't have to vie for my top position there. He *wanted* to be under me. More so than I was even willing to allow, and that had been a bone of contention, let me tell you.

That was due to an old wound. A gap in my armor I was not willing to bare, not yet. He couldn't understand why, and I couldn't seem to explain it to him in words. Not to his satisfaction.

But then... this was new... and not the way either of us preferred things. The situation as a whole was less than ideal, in predilection and temperament. I'd begun to worry it was amongst our worst blunders. Which, knowing our history, was saying something. Our relationship had always been fraught with clashing egos and wounded feelings, and I'd thought — in light of that and the fact we'd *changed* the nature of said relationship — we'd both decided to *take our time*.

I should have known. He was a liar, a traitor, and patience was *not* amongst his virtues. You could say worse things about me, and they'd be true, but I didn't fuck around on the topic of loyalty. Not at this stage of my life, and not with the few people I trusted.

Maybe my mistake had been trusting him in the first place.

* * *

I hadn't kept careful track, mind you, but I don't think I'd ever kissed anyone quite so much as I kissed this blaggard.

We were at it again, hot and heavy and entirely too drunk once more, but I liked him better that way because it took him longer. For someone who claimed no attraction to the male sex, he popped like a cork far too fast once I got *my* muzzle around him. And granted, I was no slouch, but for the first time in a very long while, I had two lovers at the same time, and the wolf's endurance was a laughable thing in comparison to my jackal, my skills aside.

The problem is, if I laughed at him, he only came faster.

The man's penchant for humiliation seemed matched only by his insufferable pouting at having the fact pointed out. I couldn't even decide if he was at peace with it, and the petulance was all an act meant to incite me to further put him in his place, or if he earnestly *was* ashamed at how easily he was debauched and how eagerly he took to it. If there was any real offense taken there, he'd certainly never complained about it after the fact.

Which could make it hard to find the line.

We were sailors, the both of us. From wildly different backgrounds, but the sea has a way of leveling the playing field. It doesn't matter where you were born or what echelon of society you're from when you face a storm at sea. You weather it or sink to the depths together, and all that separates you from the ones who join that inky grave is skill and luck.

I saw Grayson Reed as an equal in skill. An argument could be made for our luck, either way. He'd escaped being sunk by my Cerberus fleet more times than anyone else of his vocation, which most would call lucky. He'd been born wealthy and given it up — I'd found my way into wealth instead of prison due to the happenstance of knowing the right man. But he and I now shared the same dire situation on this isle, and we'd succumbed to a decade of violent foreplay and given in to passions here that would tether us together for the foreseeable future, and that was poor luck indeed for the wolf. He could have stepped aside this conflict if he wasn't so invested in my fate. He *should* have.

But... we were sailors. Stubborn, intrepid, never settling, ever looking for a creative solution to every problem where we got *everything* we wanted. And rough. We had always been rough with one another. I meant nothing by it, I was hardly a sadistic man, but it was my natural state of being, and he *liked* it. He... he brought it out in me.

But sometimes, as I said, it was hard to find the line. Tonight had been one of those times.

I did not usually abuse drink as much as I had these last few weeks. Nearly always with him, of course, he was a bad influence... but also for medical reasons. The pain from the laceration I'd endured in the brothel attack made it difficult to sleep, if my troubles were not reason enough for that already. I was not willing to drug myself into unconsciousness, but I needed rest at least a few hours of the day, and there was one tried and true method the wolf was more than happy to offer to assist me with. If I was going to drink myself into oblivion anyway, it may as well have been with company. There was nothing quite so miserable as drinking alone. Especially without even the comfort of doing so on your own ship.

Grayson was a lusty, rambunctious drunk, but I could not say the same. It brought out a sourer side in me, an angrier man than I preferred. I had no trouble *fucking* under the influence... which was good as it seemed to nearly always be where the night progressed when we were in our cups if he got his way... but it made the sadness, the hopelessness, harder for me to ignore. And with it, the uglier facets of who I was.

I had him under me, panting and wrecked already, his dark mane spread around his head like a mantle gilded in gold and turquoise. The single dread threaded with red lace that he kept pulled around the front nearly all the time now, that he toyed, twirled, and played with when he knew I was looking — always with that cockeyed grin on his face — was partially plastered to the side of his muzzle from saliva. His or mine, I couldn't say. A strand connected our teeth when we parted.

I pressed my nose down into his neck, briefly catching an odd scent on him, but it was hard to immediately pin it down. My head was spinning from the delayed effects of the spiced rum we'd drunk entirely too quickly tonight in our rush to get one another in bed. The bobcat was out for the night — not an uncommon occurrence, but he was always especially restless when she was away — and I'd taken my bandages off fully for the first time today, which seemed to have riled him up. He said he liked the scar. It was a paltry attempt at lining this whole event in silver, but God love the man for trying, at least. I just wanted to sleep well tonight if I possibly could, and strong rum and a good rut would go a long way towards that.

I hadn't seen Amon since the incident save to assure him I was alive, and Grayson's time had been consumed by ship repairs and whatever other skullduggery he was getting up to on this island for several nights now. And he had other lovers, of course… I didn't stay in his quarters except on the nights he wanted me there.

I'd convinced myself the distance was good for us. We grew frustrated with one another swiftly if over-exposed, and no one *exposed* me quite so efficiently as the disarmingly clever wolf.

I'd gotten used to having sex available to me with two very different men remarkably quickly. Especially given how I'd starved of it my whole life, lacking so long for even one committed lover. Perhaps I was gorging myself while I could. I'd grown spoilt on it, I daresay. So, a few weeks apart from the jackal, and even a few days apart from the wolf, and I was hungry for it tonight.

He was always greedy for my affections. Whether it was time spent arguing over philosophy or my cock, the man was eternally seeking satisfaction and never satisfied with what he got. Even tonight, with our rum-spiced tongues tangled 'round each other's teeth and three of my fingers buried to the knuckle under his tail, he was bitching and begging for more than I was willing to give, and he knew it.

"Fucking hell, mate-!" the wolf's jaw fell open, eyes squeezing shut in rapturous bliss, as I curled my fingers inside of him. "Aahh-uhhhhlord fuck'n be praised, thas'where I wannit — FUCK! Please fuck me, I'm ruttin' beggin' you, mate. I'll get on my knees, I'll suck y'on the deck in front of all m'boys, just please fuck me-!"

I clucked my tongue at him, licking a canine. "That'd please you more than me, honestly. Have some bloody self-respect, wolf. Not tonight with this."

"*Please* fuck me…" he begged again in a thready whisper, opening his eyes enough that just a hint of the striking blue stared back at me in the dark.

The man had no respect for my boundaries, I swear. I didn't want to argue with him when I was ornery on rum and nursing an injury. I just wanted to paw him off, then unload down his throat, and go to sleep. That should have been good enough for both of us, right? But if I said that aloud, I'd be a beast.

No, he deserved… slightly better. So, I leaned down and kissed him again. That always softened him up and brought him back around to my side, even when we were arguing. I tried to be gentler about it, even… but he took it differently than I'd intended. He must have taken it as acquiescence because he surged up into me, clutching at my biceps until I felt his claws pulling him down into me, and his thick thighs locking around my waist.

I withdrew my fingers from him and tried to dislodge my muzzle from his, but he nipped at my lower jaw, dragging me back in. I tried to say something into the kiss, but it came out garbled. I tried to shake my head while lifting up off of him, but he bucked his hips up into mine, pressing my cock into the warm cleft of fur between his legs. I felt the heat of his taint and the full, soft pillow of his sac against my nearly exposed knot, and I had to blink repeatedly to keep my eyes from rolling back into my skull.

God, I was drunk. For so many reasons, but perhaps especially that one, this was not how I wanted this.

The path from my mind to my body was one I prided myself on maintaining control over. I was not prone to bouts of angry temper or fits of rage as I had been in my idiot youth. But, I was less exact in exercising restraint when my senses were muddled, and that's a bad thing when you hone your body like a weapon's edge, as I do. When I gave way to my frustration and put my strength into gripping the man by the scruff, rolling and shoving him off of me, I overdid it. I can admit that in retrospect.

His eyes snapped wide, and he flailed to grab at the loose blankets, only barely avoiding tumbling off the edge of the bed. His head thunked into one of the bedposts, hard enough that it struck the boards of the cabin wall. He blinked, dazed, then gave a somewhat understated, "Ow…"

I sat up quickly, fingers dug into the bunched sheets, swinging my legs over the edge of the bed and catching my breath for a moment or two while my head stopped spinning. I tried to will my erection away faster than it was already retreating, but that was hard, we'd already been at it a while, and it'd be stubborn, I knew. I began to open my muzzle to say something but chanced a glimpse at him and found to my dismay that he was taking this all better than I'd hoped.

He snuffed, grinning toothily and getting on his hands and knees, leaning back as though to pounce. "S'that how you want it, now?"

"Grayson, no," I stammered out between huffs, "I don't think I'm feeling up to th —"

But he was on me, palms pounding into my shoulders, shoving me first to my ribs, then using his bulk to his advantage to bear me down until we both tumbled off the edge of the low bed onto the floor, taking half the blankets with us. One of them wrapped around my legs, and a bolt of genuine, long-deferred panic coursed through me. I was out of time and place for just a moment, the blankets were the biting twist of rigging rope, I was a teenager, found in my smalls with another man, dragged kicking and howling towards the railing, off the side of the ship where the barnacles would flay me raw-

"ENOUGH!" I screamed and brought my arm up to lock around his, twisting with a leg between us and throwing him away from me after releasing the lock. I held nothing back, and even sober the man wouldn't have stood a chance against me in hand-to-hand, so drunk, he went rolling across his rumpled carpet onto bare planks like a sack of flour.

I lay there splayed on the floor while he groaned several feet away, breathing raggedly and trying to convince the room to stop spinning. I smelled blood and coconut oil. I wasn't sure where the blood was from, yet. But glancing to my right, I saw something beneath the bed. A clay pot with the lid cast off. Some of it was smeared on the leg of the bed, like someone had wiped it there.

My mind would fixate on odd things sometimes when I was dazed or overwhelmed, and that must have been why. I vaguely heard the wolf grumbling something to my left as he grunted and tried to right himself, but I was focused on that pot. Why was the lid off? Why had I never known it was there? Was it new? I couldn't recall ever having used it with him. I'd always either brought something myself, or we'd used spit. Not sufficient, but it wasn't as though he was taking my cock yet, so-

My thoughts came to a halt.

"Fuck, you're a killjoy," I heard him mutter, and then in a more concerned tone, suddenly, "shit, you're bleeding. Luther..."

I felt it. My cheek had split and began to trickle from overextending my jaw, when I'd yelled.

I batted at the pot, knocking it in his direction, the tilt of the *Manoratha* ensuring it rolled towards him. I watched him carefully for a moment and saw the moment he realized what it was. And there it fucking was. The look. The way those blues widened. It was a flash, but I could not mistake it for *anything* else.

Guilt.

"Using that with your women now, are you?" I asked, stone-faced.

"Yes," he said unsteadily. Like it wasn't a lie, but also wasn't the whole of it. "Works the same way with women, y'know. Sometimes there's a need. I told you before I've kept the stuff on hand, s'just a new pot. Calm down."

"You think I can't tell when you're hiding something from me?" I said, my muzzle twitching as the rivulet of blood reached its edge.

"I'm not hiding anything from you mate, fuck…" he groaned, running a hand through his dreads to push them out of his face.

"You're a fucking *liar*," I snarled.

"You're drunk, Lu," he said in a deliberately softening tone. He was looking at me with those pretty eyes, speaking in that same lulling, gentle tone he'd used when they'd been pulling glass shards out of my face, and he'd wanted to comfort me. Using his stupid pet name. In this moment, I fucking *hated* it. How dare he?!

I stumbled to my feet unsteadily for a second, then propelled myself towards him with a speed that must have scared the fuck out of him, based on the expression on his face. I grabbed him under the armpits and hauled him to his feet, and before he could get a word out or react to being handled like a ragdoll, I had my nose in his neck again, buried in his fur.

"Ah-ahhh…" he sounded uncertain. I felt the ghost of his hand up near my neck, hesitating before embracing me. And he was right to. This wasn't an apology or an olive branch.

I inhaled slowly, filtering the scents on him I knew through my rapidly focusing mind. Making an inventory. Sand, musk, brine, wood smoke and incense, my own saliva, rum, coconut…

Feline. Mature, powerful, sub-tropical or equatorial, with a distinctive sage undercurrent.

My eyes snapped open, and I shoved him away from me.

I stepped back slowly on the tilting floor, swiping a hand over my cheek, and snuffing the scent out of my nose. He watched me warily from where he was still kneeling, hands limp at his sides, looking at me for all the world like I was acting like a maniac. He looked worried. Maybe scared.

Scared he'd been caught. Yes.

"We need t'get that re-stitched," he ventured gingerly. He sounded more lucid than I felt. He'd always handled his drink better than I did.

"Taarush," I said, the name falling between us like a stone, the moment it left my mouth. His ears fell back. I shook my head, sniffing, letting my eyes fall from his. "You're fucking your bloody *bodyguard?*"

"Lu, please sit down," he begged, struggling to his feet, "you're not handlin' your drink well, an' I'm worried about that wound."

"I saw all the goddamn gold fur in your bed, and I thought it was your bobcat," I said, gesturing in a sweep at the tangled sheets. "Shit, wolf. How long?"

"It isn't what you think," he said with a hand held out.

"His scent's all over you, and he's the only man here who reeks like sage all the goddamn time. Don't fucking deny it. How long?"

"Mate, that is... a long story I can't get into with you right now, not 'til he and I talk —"

"*How long?!*" I demanded, raising my voice.

"Stop yelling, you daft fool," he growled, "you're tearing your cheek. Shite... I'm getting a cloth..."

He made his way knock-kneed over towards the wash basin, and I couldn't stop the torrent of words that left me. "You made me the barest minimum promise I could have demanded of you when we set our boundaries. I didn't ask for your loyalty," I said, cutting through the hurt in my voice with raw, liquid anger, so it wasn't as obvious. I didn't want to give him that.

"An' I didn't offer it," he said, not turning while he wrung a cloth out. "Nothin's changed, Luther. This's all for naught, you're just pissed and in your cups. Gonna feel like a right tosser when you sober up —"

"You're not even fucking denying it anymore," I snapped, grabbing twice for my britches before I successfully got them in my hand. "Did you even wait until your bed was cold before you brought another man into it? Women. Only. That was the agreement!"

"That was *your* demand," he turned when he said that, glaring at me. "An'I *did* offer you loyalty, mate. If that's what it took t'keep you happy, despite it bein' against my nature. You just didn't like my terms."

He turned fully, approaching me warily with the cloth as I pulled on my clothing, presumably feeling safe enough to do so while I was in an awkward state. "It's real self-righteous of you to get up-in-arms over the leopard, though I can't say I'm surprised," he sighed. "Man pre-dates you, and I don't just mean this arrangement of ours. I've 'ad him aboard my crew since you were just a legend whispered on the wind t'me. Things've changed in that time between us... a lot of things. Things that I'm gonna be honest, don't bloody involve you at all. It's fuckin' complicated, mate."

"You said you hadn't been with another man before me, nothing that mattered," I hissed between my teeth, narrowing my eyes at him when his palm came up carefully to dab at my cheek.

He had trouble maintaining eye contact with me. "I... hadn't. Not. I mean. Not like we do."

"Sex is sex, wolf," I snapped. "What'd you not count it 'til now, when you wanted someone to start *fucking* you?"

"I said it's fuckin' complicated, alright?!" he blinked rapidly, gritting his teeth. "I can't — it ain't somethin' I'm free to talk about, not *right* now, not til he and I —"

"Were you lying to me then or are you lying to me now?" I growled, slapping his arm away. "It's not *complicated*, Grayson."

The first real signs of hurt crossed his features. I felt perversely satisfied. The dark-furred wolf was hard to wound with words, resistant to sadness in a way I envied. Even if it was usually through denial and drink. I was glad I'd penetrated both. Let him feel it. In this case, it felt warranted I share it.

"Neither," he said quietly. "It's... it's hard to explain. And now seems like a bad time t'try. You're not listenin' to me."

The last words were barely whispered. I felt my wound bleeding again and snapped the cloth out of his hand, pressing it to my cheek. I pulled my shirt on over my head, removing the compress only briefly to finish, then stared down at the red streaked cloth in my hand and discarded it harder than necessary back in the wash basin with a splash. I started towards the door.

"I'd rather you lie down right now," he said, falling in behind me.

"I'm not sleeping in the bed you broke my heart in," I said before I could process how stupid that sounded.

"Luther, I'm sorry," he said, surprisingly, instead of laughing at or mocking me. "I love you, mate. I fucked up here, not talkin' to you about this earlier… I can admit that. Please stay and we can talk in the morning."

He sounded genuine. I didn't care.

He tried to put his hands on me again, I don't even know why, probably to turn me to face him, but I'd reached my limit. I spun with a shoulder and knocked his arm aside, then arced one of my arms around him to grab him by the thick of the back of his mane, and pulled downwards until his eyes squeezed shut in pain, and he had no choice but to drop down lower than my eye level.

I held him there, staring down at him while he hunkered, suspended in my clutching grip. I wanted to strike him. I think he was bracing for it. And he wasn't fighting me… not really. He was nearly on his knees. Like he was waiting for it.

It was red, ultimately… a flash of color… that stopped me. A hue that didn't belong amongst all the dark fur. Faded with time, unraveling, and ragged in places. Lace, forever now interwoven in one of his dreads.

It was the memento he'd taken when I'd nearly died. And it made me think of how many times I'd already hurt him. How many times we'd already hurt each other.

But for some reason, I knew if I hurt him in this moment, it would be different. It would be wrong in a way we had never wronged one another before. And no matter how angry I was, no matter how drunk, and hopeless… I was not willing to be that wrong. Not to him.

I released him, turned, and fled.

* * *

I was long hungover when dawn broke.

Lacking any better options aboard this ship that wasn't my own, and unwilling to go back to the — admittedly spacious, for a 'new' hire — quarters that I shared with three of my own defected men, I'd done the second most stupid thing I could have done in my angry, addle-brained haze. I'd climbed the main mast and tried to sleep in the nest for the night.

The first most stupid idea would have been to make my way through the forest trails, drunk, and into the city in the midst of the night to find the Crimson Divine. I considered it briefly. Dismissed it as perhaps the most ignoble way I could have chosen to die. Climbed the mast instead.

No one else was here, obviously. Not only was the ship at a permanent fourteen-degree tilt now, there was no reason to keep an eye on the sky on this side of the island, let alone grounded. Especially at night. The mountains caused a lee effect that kept this cove darker longer than even the main coastline, blocking most of the sunrise. In essence, it was the safest place on the island from drakes, and there wasn't much else that could threaten the behemoth or her crew, even grounded. Her guns still worked, after all. Grayson had been certain to position her broadside towards the sea, just in case. And if any locals dare come to pillage from the forest, they'd be shaking up a hive of hornets.

The *Manoratha's* fore mast still lay cracked in half in the shallows, abandoned to the tides, now. From up here, I could vaguely make out the debris collecting around it, wreaths and wild bouquets rotting in the surf, a few idols made from eroding sand, and even some wooden grave markers, tied with twine and ribbons. The sailors of this beast paying their respects to the tarred backbone of wood that had seen them through so much.

The new fore mast was being shaped and weather-guarded at great expense right now in the city proper. I'd seen it in the shipyard; it stood out, given its size. They'd had to import it off the mainland. It had cost me a King's ransom and very nearly broken my ranks, thanks chiefly to one of my Captains. I was glad at least I'd seen that through before the hammer dropped.

I'd never be able to do Grayson any such favors ever again for so long as I lived. Really, no, it was a debt repaid. But regardless what you called it, my power, my privilege to make such calls, was at an end. In fact, regardless how the future shook out for me, whether we survived this or not, whether I was dishonorably discharged, sentenced, or hanged… my ability to dictate my own future, let alone the future of my fleet, was over.

If… I went home.

It seemed pointless to even consider the possibilities past this island, past this month, this week, each *day*... but I was a planner at heart. It was difficult for me to accept defeat, even when it was so clear. And I couldn't *sleep*. So instead, I considered all unlikely futures. Again, and again, and again.

Was the mess I'd made of this night even worth fixing? Did I really have a choice? It was insane to consider any outcome of our situation here where I survived, but didn't return to Amuresca. My life, my family, my whole identity was moored there. Giving it all up would mean reinventing myself at forty, and I feared I was too old, too tired, and too calloused for that. If I went home, Johannes would try to protect me — as would some of my allies at Court. But even if they succeeded, would a life under house arrest at my estate, in social seclusion, landlocked, be any better than a death sentence?

What was the alternative? I had royally fucked up my friendship with the wolf by allowing it to become more, I'd known it when we'd begun this, and it was panning out almost exactly as disastrously as I'd feared. Even if we could smooth this fight over, there'd be others. We'd been sparring for over a decade now. I'm not sure we knew how to be at peace with one another. Maybe it was folly to think our relationship could be anything other than a series of pitched battles.

But I liked that he challenged me... I even liked fighting with him when it was sparring and neither of us really had our steel out. No, that wasn't really the problem, was it? I was scapegoating our bickering when that had never been the main issue.

The fact is, I couldn't love halfway. Everyone else I'd opened that door to had walked out of it before I got my arms around them. Either death, disinterest, or another man had stolen them away from me. And Grayson came pre-claimed by the sea, his ship, his women...

And apparently another man.

I wouldn't lie to myself. That one stung the most. Because it was so familiar. I wasn't even certain he loved the leopard, but it didn't matter because I'd always wonder, now. Until the day *he* left me, too.

Realistically, I had so little time left. *None* of this should have mattered. I should be getting my affairs in order instead of agonizing over this, helping those I could help, and taking every man to bed who would have me. Live as Reed lived, with whatever days were still afforded to me.

But I could not.

The hope — and thus the fear — was too sharp. The minute possibility, the sliver of light through the cracks of the coffin lid, tantalized me. And if I had a future, there was the possibility of a future where I was left behind. Again. And this time it wouldn't be like Mikhail or any of the other courtesans or prostitutes I'd foolishly formed an affection for. Even Amon, I'd measured my relationship with. I wanted to help him. I would consider a future with him... but if he turned me away, I would not be surprised. We'd only just begun our tryst. I was fascinated, yearning, but if he walked away from me, I would already be braced for the sting.

But the Privateer...

If Grayson Reed finally grew tired of circling me, lost interest in me, or worse yet, began to resent, to truly *hate* me... not just our snapping and bickering... if he genuinely loathed me... left me...

It would break me as only Klaus had broken me. A man's heart can't rot away like that twice. I'd painstakingly regrown the ability to feel that way again after half a lifetime of difficult, costly work. If it happened again, none would be safe from the daemon I would become.

Thanks to Serwich, I had plumbed the well of my capabilities past the ice line. I knew now that which no man should know — how cold I was capable of becoming when the need arose. I was frightened of myself. If I couldn't return to my family, couldn't return to my command, and I had no place even here, amongst perhaps the most liberated crew in the world? Then what was left to me...

I had no choice. I had to defeat these fears, or they'd cost me the last safe harbor I had left. If I couldn't make things right with Grayson, whether I died on this island or not, I would die alone. And I was a desperate, hollow, merciless man when I had no one to tow my line in.

But God, I felt betrayed. It was a fool's errand ever expecting the wolf to be entirely honest with me, but on this at least, I'd really tried to trust him. It hadn't been much of an ask. He could have at least told me.

My head was throbbing, so I almost didn't notice the sound of heavy footfalls on the pegs below. Almost. I'd never entirely shed that battle-readiness. Some might call it paranoia.

I knew it was the leopard before I smelled sage, and well before his dappled hide clambered up over the side, settling remarkably quietly beside me for someone so large. Cats…

"Cowardly of him to send you instead of coming himself," I said before I could prevent the acidic words. To hell with civility. My head hurt. And the wolf *had* wronged me, I reminded myself.

"Shut the hell up," the feline said gruffly, sidling in beside me to fold his arms over the side of the basket and face the sunrise, where it was finally breaking over the top of the mountains.

"That's just how you all talk to me now, is it?" I sighed.

"Yes," he replied curtly. "Best get used to it. You're a low boy here, you know. Special case, being as everyone knows what you're capable of and is piss-scared of you, *and* you're the Captain's favorite, but… you're no one important, otherwise. So, you can shove that attitude right up your ass. I'm here as a courtesy."

"I don't think I've ever heard you speak so many words at once before," I said, glancing at the feline. The early morning light caught briefly, throwing shine in my eyes from the collar around his neck. I'd noticed it before, but he wasn't the only collared person on Grayson's crew, so I'd never considered the implications of what it meant. Who he had likely been before he crewed up. To be honest, I'd never taken very much stock of the man at all, other than that he was tall, strongly-built, preferred to dress simply and masculine, and was always at Grayson's side. He wasn't the usual, ostentatious sort that the wolf might have fancied.

But then I suppose I wasn't, either. If he *had* a taste in men, it was dissimilar to his taste in women.

"I've never had very much to say to you," Taarush said flatly. "To be honest, I've never really understood your relationship with the Captain, and I didn't feel it was my place to intervene. He has a *lot* of troublesome friends. I only involve myself when his choices threaten his safety, the safety of the crew, the ship, or myself."

"I'm no threat to you, if that's why you're here," I muttered, leaning my chin against my arm. "I'm not interested in cockfighting over the man. You 'pre-date' me apparently, and I'm not about to make waves like that on a crew predisposed to hate me already. Rest easy."

"I'm not worried about myself," the leopard clarified. I could feel his eyes on me.

I turned to regard him and felt the accusation, the weight, now that I had to stare him down. And then I remembered…

"I didn't hurt him," I insisted, too quickly. Too defensively.

"You're a shit person, you know that?" the feline said, showing the tips of his fangs when he said it through a grim smile.

I let my gaze drop. "… I do," I agreed.

"You're a shit person, but so are most of us," the leopard continued. "There are worse people in the world than us. Much worse. Men who beat unmercifully on their partners. Matriarchs who sell their own kin into slavery. Pirates who sink ships just to watch people drown. Sometimes, if rarely, Captain *really* fucks up and finds himself involved with people like that."

He moved closer in beside me, leaning down over me. "But you, Luther. You're not a person like that. Are you?"

I swallowed. "Not… like that, no. I'm not so far gone, as of yet."

"See to it you never are," the leopard said with a finality to his words. "Because then? I get involved. And I'm not afraid of you, cattle dog. One on one, you might think you can take me. You might even be right. But we are never alone on this ship. We look after our own. And we don't fight fair. Honor here means the most amount of us survive the day, profit, and live well. Honestly, it isn't a bad way to live. You ought to consider it."

My eyes widened marginally. "You still want me here?"

"Captain likes you for a reason. You're crafty. Knowledgeable. Not just on the water, but you've got insights about the people who sail it. Insights no man here's had the experience and the privilege to gather. This is a wager on Reed's part, but I could see how it could pay off in the long-run. Also, he likes you. *Fuck* knows why, but that isn't my business."

I narrowed my eyes, leaning in a little closer. Something about the feline's voice was odd. Thicker, intentionally. Pitched down. I'd never noticed it before because he didn't usually speak much.

"And you…" I hesitated, "… personally… don't mind me being here? I have to ask —"

"*Effas amondi,*" he swore in an unusual dialect of Huudari, but I knew that one because it was a common enough phrase. He was essentially calling me an infuriating child. "Say what you mean," he said a moment later.

"Grayson and I had very few rules for one another, at least compared to what I'm accustomed to," I relented.

"What you're accustomed to is Amurescan High Society, so that means nothing."

"I am *trying* to broaden my concept of what's acceptable in relations," I said, frustrated. "Have mercy on me, this is all very bloody *new*, I am not accustomed to the liberal eccentricities of a group of people like… you. I need…" I gestured at nothing, "… *boundaries*. I need to know there are some lines in place that won't be crossed! Is that too much to ask?!"

"What boundary do you feel he crossed?" he asked. "You have another lover as well."

"And he has the women he takes to bed," I insisted. "I don't deny him that, not even prostitutes, I'm aware it would be hypocritical. I have one, he has… many. And still, I allow that."

"How magnanimous of you," the leopard gave a lazy smirk.

"There are practical concerns here," I growled. "He keeps to felines for the most part, at least. That limits the issue of disease, but it is *still* a potential issue."

"Your lover is canine," he said with an arched eyebrow.

"He *spies* on me and my lover," I bit out. "He knows he's clean and exclusive, at least for the moment."

"Alright, granted."

"Other lovers means more people potentially vying for his time, his trust, and if they're on the crew?" I pointed out. "That introduces more problems than I can list."

"Trust me, that's a subject of conversation all over this ship right now," the leopard confirmed. "But it's not his female bedmates the men are concerned about."

My shoulders slumped. "Good God, does everyone know? I told him not to talk about… us… with his crew."

"He didn't need to, you two are not as subtle as you think."

Irritated, I gripped the edge of the basket, willing back a wave of nausea and anger. Being outed had cost me everything not a few weeks ago with my own crew. I had to keep reminding myself it wasn't exactly the same here. But it was hard. A lifetime of fear…

"None of this is the point," I went on. "I had… one main ask. One thing I thought wouldn't be a promise he'd have trouble keeping. No other *men*."

I let out my breath slowly, awaiting another snappy reply. But none came. Silence was my only answer..

"He swore it to me," I said quietly. "Regardless of whether or not you think it was fair of me to demand it, he *did* agree to it. He didn't even hesitate. And then he took *you* to bed, and… he didn't tell me…"

The leopard's shoulder bumped mine, and when I looked up, his expression was mildly kinder. Not soft, but more open. "I'm sorry. I didn't know," he said.

"I believe you," I relented, relaxing marginally. "But that isn't any less frustrating. That means he was hiding this from both of us. Which is… very him. I don't know why I'm surprised."

"There's an angle to this you don't understand."

"So he said," I muttered. "Look, either he lied to me now, or he lied to me about his past. I get that relationships are complicated, especially between men. I don't think I'm entitled to the details, but if you'd care to enlighten me as he apparently didn't feel permitted to —"

"I was once a woman."

Of all the things I'd expected, that had *not* been on the list. I turned to gape at him, confused, and he chuckled.

"Go ahead, do the once-over. Everyone does."

I couldn't help myself, I was. "I don't…" I stammered, "… know what you mean," I finally confessed.

"I was born a woman, or rather a girl, at least in body," he explained. "My mind and soul is that of a man. I've known it since I was very young. Sometimes the Gods misplace us. Somewhere out there is a male leopard with a woman's soul," he said with a laugh, building on his chuckle from before. "I've long wondered if I'd meet them… if we could set this whole mess to rights."

I had nothing to add, so I just listened. I'd never heard anything like this before, and I wanted to hear every word.

"When Grayson first met me, I was still wearing the trappings of womanhood," he continued. "I was not all that unlike your jackal, back then. Seeking to escape the Charic. My port was not nearly so militantly patrolled, and I stowed aboard the largest vessel I could find. It was difficult, being discovered as a woman aboard a ship full of men who didn't want me there… but the Captain was fair. He offered me safe passage to the nearest free port, in exchange for the only services I had to offer, at the time."

I must have reacted because he glared at me. "Don't shame he or I, you've never been in either of our positions. He was new to commanding this ship, morale was shakier back then, and I was a prostitute. It's work. It's the only work I was allowed, even on a ship like this."

"It's coercive," I said distastefully. "You had no choice."

"I wanted to work," he said, bumping me with his elbow. "And I could have left at that first port, but… I didn't. This was still the freest place I'd ever known, up to that point. Was it ideal? No. The world is an imperfect place, and we are imperfect vessels, all of us. Opportunities narrow even further when you are a woman. But I didn't mind my vocation. Captain wasn't the only man I serviced, and one of my other regulars became my mate, eventually. We're still together to this day."

I must have grumbled something because he gave a long-suffering sigh and pressed, "You *hire* prostitutes, Amur. If this changes your opinion of me, you had best re-center. My *work* was no reason for shame in my previous life. The issue was that I was *enslaved*."

"Yes, fine," I agreed quietly.

"I outgrew my role as ship whore in time," he said easily and admittedly — without a trace of shame. I envied him in that moment. It didn't matter what rank I'd achieved throughout my life; I'd always lived in shame.

"I've always been tall," he continued, "and strong. I wanted to work like the other men, and… in time… after proving I could, Captain was willing to allow it. I began to dress like the men, too. I bound my breasts and put in as much time as I could doing manual labor. My body began to change, grow broader and more… muscular, and I…"

I looked over when his voice had cut off for a moment, almost choked, pitching softer. I couldn't help but feel he'd let me hear it, rather than losing his cadence. He looked slowly back at me, his black jowls curling up into an expression of raw, genuine joy. "I began to look as I'd always felt myself to be. I cannot describe the relief. The bliss, waking and finally feeling like a man each morning. It is an ongoing challenge, but one I relish. Most men feel bound to the body they were born with, whether by species or pelt. My barriers were difficult, but I worked to re-shape myself — defy the Gods!" he said that with particular relish.

"I've seen you without a shirt on, and I didn't know," I confessed. "Although, explains the sage, I suppose. Covers your natural scent."

He grinned toothily at me. "The fur and my pelt patterns help, but I'll take that as a compliment all the same. Nowadays if anyone notices, they don't dare contradict me. I do a lot to look the way I do."

"As do I," I said, my eyes roving him, again. "From one fellow bent on fitness to another, it shows."

"When the crew began to call me a man… I knew this was my home," he said, blinking and dragging a thick breath through his nose. His gold eyes found mine at that, and his smile lengthened. "It could be your home, too. But, you'll need to prove your worth. Not just to him… to all of us. Just as I did. And that may not mean hauling rigging for you, as it did for me. You don't need to prove you're just as capable as them physically, you've the benefit of being born like them, but… respect. Respect may come slowly. They're afraid of you, now. That isn't the same thing."

"I know," I said, sighing. "Maybe hauling rigging *is* the answer. Show them I'm not above the work."

"You going to patch things up with the Captain?" I looked again to him, and he shrugged, moving on. "Not that you need to. You'd hardly be the only companion who's moved in and out of his bed through the years. Captain Lotus can't seem to decide if she's done knocking paws with him, and they do that dance near every time they share a port. Shivah's disgusted with'm more often than not, and they still bed down sometimes. You could stay here, and I'm sure he'd still be fair to you, even as an ex-lover."

"I don't think I could manage it," I said, setting my teeth tightly together inside my muzzle. "I'm not good with this being… transient. I need to know he won't discard me. I need to know I matter. That whatever it is we have matters to him."

"Then tell him that."

I turned to regard him. "You say it like it's so simple."

He thudded a paw into the center of my back, then gripped my shoulder and gave it an affirming shake. "Trust me, mate. It is. Just stop being so bloody stubborn, and say everything you said to me, to him."

I blinked into the sun as the seabirds began their morning cries. Digested what the feline had said for a few seconds, then gave a contemplative and highly eloquent, "Huh."

"You're both lucky your enemies think you're brilliant," he muttered as he produced a cigarette from his pocket. "If they knew how fucking stupid the both of you really are..."

"Blessed thing we're all so good at keeping secrets then, I guess."

He laughed uproariously at that and lost his cigarette over the drop.

* * *

The wolf was a vision, spread out in the starkly-lit sand, the usually ebon leaves of fur covering his body revealing the subtle hints of mahogany and even red residing in his undercoat. Normally I only saw them when I raked my claws through his fur, plying it apart to find purchase on the skin beneath.

The hints of gray peppered along his muzzle, his eyebrows, and through his mane were also more visible in the beaming afternoon sun. Precious stones and metal beads lay littered like constellations in the black of the wet locks. I could have stood there in the surf, staring at him, for the rest of the day.

He was such a fussy peacock every moment he was awake, bedecked in his baubles and fine clothes, gold and silver-handled weapons and pistols, still touting the finery of his wealthy lineage, but with a carefully-crafted veneer of scum and villainy. He wanted people to know where he'd come from, and whom he had decided to be despite that. He cultivated a certain image, and it had seen him through a long and illustrious career for a Privateer.

But all of that was for the masses. I got him in his rawest, most honest form. Dirty, ill, vulnerable, underconfident... it wasn't always pretty, or well-balanced, but sometimes it was...

... the wolf splayed in the warm sand of a hidden inlet, beneath the tossing shadows of the nearby palm, wearing nothing but his soaked smalls and drying in the sun. Here, I had to assume, because he knew I'd come here looking for him. This sight was for me and me alone.

He was asleep, his chest rising and falling almost in time with the lapping of the waves. He hadn't heard me, yet. My approach had been hidden by the sound of the surf.

I'd only guessed he'd be here because we'd been coming here since we'd started our tryst. It was moderately private, in that I was certain other men had discovered it as well by now — the occasional charred remains of a fire or a discarded bottle said as much — but the swim to get here was difficult, so we were usually left alone.

I couldn't just stand there staring at him all day. I'd pickle myself in the brine, eventually. Relenting, I pushed through my fears and waded ashore.

His eyes opened when I got close. The same color as the sky. He blinked at me blearily at first, then sat bolt upright.

"Easy," I said softly, settling down into the sand beside him, still dripping. I shook my ears out, wicking the water off my tail in a pinched fist. All the while, he watched me, his expression tipping between hope and worry.

"I'm sorry I woke you," I said. "We could both use the sleep, I'd imagine."

"Please forgive me," he said immediately, skipping any preamble. He turned towards me, nose and ears down, contrite. "Please…"

I was humbled and frustrated by my own cowardice then. The wolf didn't really seem to struggle with admitting when he was wrong, like I did. He'd experienced ego death so many times, falling on his sword was a natural inclination.

Accusations, shame, and guilt had been laid at my feet my entire life, both for good reason, for choices I'd made, and for fundamental parts of who I was, that I could not change. My birth, my desire for partners, the many dead end moral decisions I'd been forced into by the powers that be… *my* natural inclination was to fight. To defend myself. To double down.

But, I had to remind myself, this was not one of those intractable facets about myself that others took offense to for no reason. This was an aspect of my character that was hurting someone I… cared for. And regardless who was more in the wrong here, I *did not want to keep hurting him.* This was not fundamental to who I was. This was something I could change.

"The way I handled you last night was... not right," I said, having trouble looking at him as I said it. It was weak, but it was essential to me getting through this. And maybe it was alright to be weak. With him. "Regardless how hurt I was. I don't like who I was in that moment. You didn't deserve it, no one deserves that side of me, and..." I breathed out into the humid air, "... I'm sorry."

I got the nerve to look at him and found his expression bemused, more than anything. "You mean," he stammered, "the... rough handling? I'm alright. You'd told me you were a miserable drunk, and I didn't listen. I thought it'd help you relax, like it does for me, and I leaned on you. Shouldn't've done that. You know yourself better'n I do."

"No excuses," I said sourly. "I've struggled with anger my whole life. That isn't your burden to bear or suffer for." I looked up at him slowly. "You're important to me. I can't imagine my life without you in it, and I nearly ruined that. Over nothing. Nothing that should have come between us in any meaningful way."

He seemed poised, nervous. When he spoke again, he was almost trembling. "Did Taarush come to speak to you?"

"Yes," I replied plainly. I turned my body towards his, reclining on my side in the sand, so that I could more comfortably face him. "I'm going to ask you something important, Grayson. I need you to be honest with me."

He nodded and chanced moving a bit closer to me.

"Taarush is a man," I stated that part. "But, do you yourself see him that way?"

He blinked, quietly considering my question for a bit. He eventually said, "Yes, I... for a long time now. Yes."

"Then don't class him as something else," I said. "Not with me, not even in your own estimation. I know this... must be more complicated, as someone who knew him before and after. But, it doesn't have to be. He doesn't seem at all uncertain about who he is, and I know better than to question a man like that. It's cut and dry, far as I see it."

"Right," he agreed.

"Did you ever consider how he might feel," I asked, "knowing you thought of him as some kind of exception?"

"No," he admitted, ashamed. "I just… didn't… I thought perhaps, I should talk to you about him at some point, but there never came a right moment for it."

"You should've talked to both of us," I sighed. "Taarush deserved your honesty, too. He's a good man… a loyal man. You're lucky to have him, take it from one who knows, men who are loyal to the quick like that are *rare*. He feels he owes his current life to you, and he's likely right, but that doesn't mean you should take that for granted. You should have told him about our arrangement, and if you wanted to carry on with him, *asked me*. I'm certain you already had his consent."

"I'm sorry," he said soft as a whisper, tipping his muzzle to lean up towards mine at a submissive angle.

I gave a rough groan. "Don't think that just because it's working on me, I'm not aware of how well you beg, wolf."

"I'm begging in earnest," he insisted. "We are… *so* close to what I've wanted for so long now. I don't want to fuck it up."

"What is it you've wanted so long that you feel we're closer to now than we were before?" I asked airily. "You cannot mean the sex. If you've been waiting all these years to ask to suck my cock, wolf, I am going to tear your *new* mast down. I *asked* you back then —"

"Not… that," he said quickly, "damn you. You're so bloody smart, figure it out."

I stared down into the sand. "You mean the two of us, sharing a ship. Grayson, this is temporary —"

"It doesn't have to be," he insisted, shuffling up onto an elbow. "This was a mistake… a big one. I… I can admit that. I can make excuses to set your mind at ease, explain myself more, but —"

"Taarush told me it's not romantic," I filled in, "and never has been. He… told me you hadn't even done anything like that in a long time," I said carefully, remembering the leopard's words. "This was, what, more of a professional visit?"

"You've worked out a few things with hired pros over the years, I'm sure," he said guardedly. "Sometimes, it's just better to learn from someone who knows what they're doing, you know?"

"He used the strap on you."

He blanched. "It... it's always hurt in the past. The few times I've tried. I thought he might know how to do it right. So... if we..."

I closed my eyes. The fact that even during this indiscretion, he'd been thinking of me... pleased me more than I cared to admit. And simultaneously filled me with guilt for my reaction. I pushed through it for now.

"And?" I asked around the lump in my throat.

"And...? O-oh," he said in realization. "Uh. Yeah. I guess I... it was instructive. I don't like how unyielding it is, though. I never have. I keep thinking maybe I just don't like the strap because it's... not..."

"The real thing," I said, opening my eyes.

"I don't know," he said into his own arm where he was leaning. "Maybe. I've never... it's hard to say."

"Do you know why I've never relented on that front?" I asked directly.

"Your rules," he responded more than a little bitterly.

"I have the rules for a reason," I said. "A few reasons..."

"Honestly, Luther," he said with evident frustration in his voice, "I don't know what your internal reasoning is, but it's hard not to feel — especially since I know you're buggering the jackal, now — that I just don't make the cut."

I leaned up on one arm, looking down at him, startled. "What?"

"I know I'm not exactly your type," he gestured at himself.

"I'm not *yours*," I pointed out, sparring back. "That clearly hasn't stopped us from indulging in one another. You think I don't find you, what, attractive enough?"

"You've said as much before. You can't blame me," he said.

"We weren't exactly considering this as a real possibility, back then," I countered. "That was banter — God, wolf, is this even at question? My 'type' is canine, male, and preferably not inbred Pedigree tossers."

"No promises on the potential inbreeding," he muttered. "Knowing my family."

"You know what I meant." I narrowed my eyes. "No limp, soft men. I've been with foxes, fuller-bodied men, older men — you are *well* within my wheelhouse, trust me."

"I wonder sometimes," he said in a profoundly catty way. My eyes could have rolled out of my head.

"You are the most effete straight man I have ever known," I bit out. "You want me to flatter you again? Fine. I couldn't stop staring at you just now from the surf. You're stunning, bloody gorgeous, it has been a *problem* from the first moment I saw you in that cantina. I get hard just thinking of you — I'm hard right *now!*" I said angrily.

He looked. Of course, he did.

"Happy?" I demanded, and I was certain I was red in my ears. "I am not holding back because I do not want to *fuck* you, Gray, I'm scared that if I do, you'll *leave* me."

His ears fell back. "Why the hell would you ever think that? I can't stand being apart from you. I followed you across the bloody *world*, mate."

"Because every man I've ever loved fucking leaves me!" I said, louder than I'd intended. The surf covered my outburst, though. From anyone's ears but his.

He looked at me in silence with more pity than I would have liked. It fed the anger. But, it wasn't at him anymore, at least. I don't know where it was pointed. The world, perhaps.

I couldn't look at him as I went on. "I know it's superstitious horseshit, Gray. I know. But it's… the rules because, so far… it's worked. Johannes is still with me. My closest men from the *Cerberus*, those that defected with me…" I felt my breath failing me and pushed out a final word, "…*you*."

"Lu," he said quietly, his unfathomably blue eyes dragging my gaze back to his, kicking and screaming against my instincts. "People fucking die, or walk out of our lives, or the winds just don't blow us in the same direction. It has nothing to do with the depth of your feelings for them. Your love isn't a *curse*."

"I'm not an atheist, Gray," I reminded him softly. "I wish I were as certain as you are that there's no powers beyond this world, punishing us for our transgressions, taking our happiness away out of bloody spite… but it feels like a forced repentance every time it happens. Like I'm already in Hell. Paying for my sins."

He scoffed, "If that were the case, your god is making the people around you pay, and that's no benevolent deity. Fuck'm."

"They're at peace," I said in a whisper. "Or moved out of my radius. Happy and content with another man… another life. Safe from me. The ones who ran are the lucky ones. The punishment is mine. It's this. Being left. Abandoned at the pier. Waiting for a ship that will *never* come in."

"You tried to force my hand," he pointed out with an edge of anger in his voice. "Pushed me aside, almost wouldn't fix my ship. Because you thought it'd be better for us to fall out. Maybe you're bloody *manifesting* this, mate. Ever think of that?"

"Maybe that's the right call," I said.

"It is *not*," he said, his brows drawn tight. "Not just for you, but for everyone fuckin' else. Look, no offense Luther, but you make *shit* calls when you isolate yourself. When you think no one else but you should be handlin' the horror of your reality?" He chewed on his lip a moment, then sighed. "You can be a real bastard. You need people in your life to be your guiding stars. To find your bearings. I'm the same way. Lonely, desperate, I… I've done things I really fuckin regret. Haven't you?"

I must have paused too long because he pressed me after a time, worriedly. "The answer to that is 'yes', Luther. It better be yes, or you're lying to both of us."

"Yes," I said obediently. I meant it. I felt a bitter smile tugging at the corners of my muzzle, but it seemed inappropriate, so I tried to suppress it. It must have twisted up my face something awful because he leaned in, concerned. "It's not…" I insisted quickly, then cut myself off, "…God, you've a knack for knowing what's been on my mind. It's uncanny. I hate who I am when I'm alone. I'm aware how brutal that creature is, I experience the nightmares he wrought nearly every night."

"Shit, mate," the wolf sighed raggedly. "You think I don't know? I've slept next to you before. Watched you sob in your sleep, wasn't sure *what* I should do. Wake you, hold you, leave you be, I-I… I don't know."

I gave him a wry smile. "You've an inkling of how I feel when I watch you seize, then."

"Yeah," he said with a weak smile. "We're a mess you and I, huh?"

"Indeed," I said, slowly sitting up and dragging my knees to my chest, looping my arms around my legs. I could feel the sand getting into my fur already. I liked the familiar feel of it, however inconvenient.

"Why didn't you just tell me all of this?" he asked quietly, still lying down.

"Same reason you didn't tell me about Taarush, I'd wager," I answered. I turned to look at him. "Fear. Not having the right words maybe, afraid I'd fuck it up. You know, back before you and I started… this thing we have… whatever it is you want to call it —"

"My men call it a 'matelotage,'" he said, reaching an arm out, his claws brushing over my thigh. Not purpose-driven, the wolf just liked to touch and be touched, I think.

"No, I've heard that one passed about by buccaneers," I cleared my throat. "That's more like marriage. And isn't it mostly for asset-sharing? It's not always sexual, either."

"Naw, sometimes it's more like what we had before," he concurred. "Bosom brothers. Mates. Friends. Platonic-like, but still life-mates."

"Like what we had before…" I said, and I must've sounded wistful because his expression became concerned.

"You got regrets?"

"Of course I do," I answered immediately, giving him a sharp look. "Don't you? This was less complicated before. And we knew it would be like this, too. I certainly fucking knew. I warned you…"

"I don't regret it," he said with an easy smile. His hand traveled up my leg to find one of mine, linking our forefingers in a loose hook. "It's alright if you do, though. Most'ah my bed partners regret gettin' involved with me, and honestly, that's fair. I'm trouble."

I stared down at him just long enough to be certain he wasn't actually aggrieved, but as usual, the wolf was letting this wick off his fur like water. Man could really take a hit on the chin and just keep on smiling.

I laughed, hoarsely, tiredly. It bubbled up into several, and between them I coughed out, "Yes… yes, you bloody well are."

He pushed himself up finally, stiff and slow, and tossed his mane to clear some of the sand out of it, before leaning into me and putting his big, stupid head over my shoulder.

"God, you're heavy," I grumbled. "And still wet."

"I don't dry off as fast as you do," he said, close to my ear, keeping his voice low in consideration for my hearing. The gravelly, wolfish nature of it when he dropped it like that was annoyingly alluring without him even trying. I suppressed a shudder, keeping my countenance.

"I'm not goin' anywhere, Lu," he said, tucking his nose into the scruff of my neck. "If you can stand to be with me, you've got a mate fer life. I've wanted to sail with you since the first day we met. There's somethin' strung between our hearts, like a current, pullin' us back towards a single point no matter where we go. We keep finding each other. I don't care what we call it. Tired of fighting it. I don't ever want to be apart, for so long as I've got left."

I let out my breath in a shudder, speaking quietly, myself. "I have no idea how you say things like that, so unashamedly, then claim you don't believe in romance. You're a walking contradiction."

"M'I wooing you good, then?" He grinned, the edge of his fangs pressing against my neck. "You gonna give me what I want?"

"You *always* get what you want," I growled. "Was it ever in doubt?"

"Not with you," he said. "I rarely get what I want when you're involved."

That point was both true and had darker implications than what we did in the bedroom. I knew he didn't mean it in anger, but my own conscience was a merciless force, and right now it was serenading me with a cascade of my many misdeeds where the wolf was involved.

This — all of this — was so little to give of myself in comparison to what he'd given me throughout the years. Willingly, knowingly, or otherwise. He'd put his entire fleet on the line for me, and God knew how that would ultimately turn out. He'd risked everything he was and everything he had for me.

I could risk this. For him.

I shoved him off me, and he fell back into the sand with a dramatic 'whoof' of a noise, hands grabbing for me as he fell. He didn't need to, I'd rolled onto my knees and straddled him before his back had fully hit the sand, boxing his hips in with my legs and pinning him down by the wrists.

"Ha-ahhh..." he rasped out, amused and grinning up at me. "So... I take it we're good, then?"

I leaned down slowly, until our noses touched. Then rumbled, "We're good."

"While we're on a tear admitting uncomfortable truths," he said between heavy breaths. We'd hardly exerted ourselves much, but I'd begun rubbing our sheathes together where our bodies were pressed. "Can I admit somethin' to you?" He went on without waiting for me to give him the affirmative, of course. "I know the whole mess at the brothel was downright awful for you and fucked up your life… but honestly, the first thought I had after I found out you were alright, you were gonna live and not even lose yer eye? Was relief. I was… glad… glad it went down the way it did."

I gave him a moment to explain, and he did. "This was always gonna happen, mate," he said, his gaze a plea as he looked up at me. "One day or another. I'm just glad I was around when it did… was here to give you refuge. I'm glad yer singuard brought you here because I *knew* how it'd go down with your boys. He must've, too. Watchin' you rest it off here on my ship, all I kept thinking was…"

Here he paused, mouth forming around unspoken words a few times. I urged him to go on, soundlessly. He did, but not without adding, "See, you say I got no shame, but I do. It just takes somethin' like this to bring it out." He sighed, finally saying, "I kept thinking… 'he's ours now'. All these years, I knew eventually the Amur Navy would spit you out. I was just hoping when it did, you'd survive it. And then you'd be…"

"One of you," I finished. "Free."

"Mine," he amended quietly. Perhaps the most ashamed he'd sounded yet.

"Oh," I arched an eyebrow, "and here I thought I was the possessive one."

"I don't care who you bed, Lu," he said, "or who you love… but as for your allegiance? *Fuuuuck* the Crown. They have *never* deserved you."

"I might like your possessive side," I admitted.

"Oh yeah?" he grinned, one fang peeking out from beneath a dark lip.

"It's good to feel wanted," I admitted.

"Givin' me ideas, cattle dog," he growled, as he ground his hips up into mine. "You'd better watch it."

"Oh please, you dandy," I tightened my grip on his wrists. "I'm not afraid of you. You beg for what most men charge me for."

"Fuck, yeah, call me a whore," he groaned, rubbing his now-exposed cock against mine. "That'll get me there. I'm tired, and I want to cum, then pass the fuck out."

"God, you and me both," I agreed. "Finish just like this, then sleep until the tide comes in?"

"Sounds grand, mate."

* * *

The galley was belching spicy smells, the wafting steam from rice and soup cooking, and what was most certainly the bread that would be served with the evening meal. It — like the rest of the food served on this ship — smelled more like local fare than an Amur sourdough or a Carvecian cornbread. It made sense, in most ways, really. The *Manoratha's* crew was a more varied lot than my own had been, they traveled to foreign ports more than colonial, and they were accustomed to a broader palate. It was easier and less expensive to prepare local dishes sourced from the island than rely on stores, and they had no such restrictions as our own vessels did. It was one thing if the men wanted to dine on native fare when they went ashore, but onboard a Navy ship, protocol was tight on what was right and proper to nourish a crew.

And... predictably bland. But safe, usually. Our crew was primarily canine, and certain dishes prepared in places like this could lead to mass illness. Onions and more acidic vegetables, for instance.

I'd been here several weeks, and I'd been... somewhat forced... to broaden my horizons. To mixed success. The local curries burned my mouth and didn't always sit well even if I could choke them down. Grayson had assured me I'd 'get used to flavor in time'.

Like all things here, it was an adjustment. Tonight though, I was hungry. And the wolf had convinced me to be bold on multiple fronts. I generally ate my meals in my own quarters with my closest men, or — on a few occasions — with the wolf himself in his quarters. But he apparently preferred to eat amongst his boys. Specifically in what had once been the Officer's Dining Hall on the middle deck. It was where the room I shared was located and was amongst the better quarters on the ship.

But this ship, strictly speaking, *had* no Officers. Not in the traditional sense. And Grayson didn't like to stand on decorum, so other than a few chairs being saved for himself and his two Captains, the privilege to dine at the big table was apparently a rotating position. Although he'd assured me... only trusted men.

Grayson trusted *most* of his men, though. So, I might be walking into a nest of vipers, sitting with him tonight. Time would tell.

The wolf snapped up a few slices of some kind of raisin… swirly… bread, then a heap of rice and curry, which the cook was more generous with him than me, I noted. Not a problem. I wasn't even certain I'd get through my portion. We filled our rations cups, and headed through the throngs. We'd changed after our swim, and the Privateer had chosen my wardrobe. He kept putting me in red and black, and eschewing what he called my 'drab, Navy-look'. He insisted it'd help me fit in better here, but really, I thought it just made me stand out more.

When I told him he reminded me of my wife, he got the *biggest* grin, and I immediately regretted it.

"You'll be fine," he assured me for about the dozenth time, draining half his drink before we got across the deck. "Just, you know, stand your ground. Don't let 'em smell weakness."

"Mmmhh-huh?" I blinked.

He grinned at me. "What, you too chickenshit to face 'em down without a few cannons between you? You'll be *fine*."

"It's precisely because we've traded shots in the past that I'm uncomfortable breaking bread with these men," I said, glaring. "Don't be dense."

His tail brushed mine, presumably because his hands weren't free to do so. "I wouldn't bring y'here if you were in danger, Luther. You know that, right?"

I found myself glancing around and tucking my tail away from his. We were surrounded by men milling about and filing in for supper, but other than a few of the same wary looks I'd gotten since I'd come aboard, nothing.

"Relax," he said in an easy tone. "I know that's a big ask, but trust me. These lads aren't out to end you over whatever mischief you get up to twixt the sheets. Most of 'em don't care, and those that do won't harass you over it. We've got a woman aboard, for fuck's sake."

"The bobcat is a sharpshooter with feather-feet," I muttered. "They're afraid of her. As well they should be."

He just laughed. "Yeah. Alright, here we go —"

He swung open the door to the dining hall with an elbow and a bellowed, "Evening, ya cunts!"

"The fuck 'ave you been all day?" a voice belonging to a man I hardly knew called out from the farthest end of the table. He was a big, broad fellow, an otter with white fur speckled down his chest and a nasty facial scar. He was one of Grayson's Captains, I knew that much. Clever fellow — otters often were — and I think he'd been a part of his crew since I'd first come to know the man, so a veteran. He was seated beside a black and white rat who said nothing when we entered, only took brief note of me, then got back to his food.

Magpie. I knew that one, at least. Another of Grayson's bodyguards. Quiet, serious, deadly. A friend of Shivah's I think, and the two of them were seated together now, so that confirmed that. Two severe people like that only sat together if they were close.

A few 'Evening, Cap'n's came from around the table from the friendlier folk, including Taarush, a painted dog I'd seen around Grayson quite a lot, a hippo who stood out if only because of his size and how infrequently you saw them out in the world, a black fox who I'd gathered was something of a seneschal or purser for the crew, and a few other canines.

"And to answer your question," Grayson pulled out the chair at the 'head' of the table and dragged up one for me beside him while he was at it, "talking shop with the cattle dog, here."

"Oh yeah?" the hippo spoke up, "got any idea how to un-fuck us from this predicament, yet?"

I think he grinned, but it was hard to tell. I had to remind myself that the enormous, sharp tusks were not — in and of themselves — a threat display.

I realized the question had been asked of me, so I answered while settling into my chair, trying to sound as casual as possible, "Not as of yet, I'm afraid."

"Think we can count out the Amur bastards as any help, a'this point," the otter said, not looking at me specifically, but the sentiment was obvious. "We oughta' be running this blockade joint-like, but they're more like to cut us outta any plannin' or lie to us, an' use us as fodder once they're ready to make their run."

"It isn't as though that wasn't already the case," the fox snorted, swirling some murky red wine in a chipped glass in front of him.

"Aye, we barely limped t'shore from the barrage we took protectin' their ass on the way to berth here," Magpie agreed.

A sudden chuckle, and the painted dog said, "Don't look now lads, but I think you're making the Amur at the table uncomfortable."

I must've been showing it on my face despite my best efforts, but I swallowed some of the rum I'd had and shook my head. "Don't hold back on my account. You're not even wrong, and it's good speaking openly about it. For whatever my opinion is worth at this table, I concur. Our best chance is unified, but the possibility of negotiating a plan we were all agreed on was poor before. Now, it's…" I twisted my muzzle up, and not just because of the taste of the food, "…well, I wouldn't sit down at a table with them and expect you'll like what you hear. Nor should you trust it."

"Damned, outta the mouth of their Ex-Admiral hisself," one of the canines, a mixed-breed tan dog, said. "We are on our own, gents."

"Not like we aren't used to it," Grayson reasoned, chewing a big piece off his bread. "We're palm bugs, boys. We've gotten back up after worse stomps. We'll endure."

A few laughs went 'round the table, like that was some kind of known joke around here. The mood was good, energetic, but not aggressive. And then someone — I don't know who — called out in our direction, "So you two husbands settle yer fuckin' row, then?"

I set my spoon down perhaps too hard and half hid my face in a hand, trying to disguise it as settling my fur. It didn't work.

"Oh *shit*, lookit'm flush like a wee damsel!"

A round of raucous laughter lit up around the table, chairs squawked and a fist or two pounded the wood, someone choked on their food briefly. I kept my eyes on my plate, tipping my ears back in a vain attempt to hide the way my blood was rushing to them.

Grayson's hand settled on my shoulder, his fingers inching up just a bit beneath my collar to settle on the nape of my neck. "S'just ribbin', mate. Means they like you."

"Oh aye, y'best settl'im down like one of your bloody birds, Cap'n," the same dog chortled. "Lest some unlucky bastard gets the talons."

"I prefer the Amur to those fuckin' birds," the otter grunted. "Better table manners."

"Honestly, Cerberus," the mutt — clearly the talkative sort — continued with a gap-toothed grin, "if you embarrass easy, y'oughta try to keep it down in thar better. Gag the wolf or somethin'. You'd be doin' us all a favor."

"Suck my dick, Ian," Grayson rolled his eyes, finishing off his drink.

"Oh, don't rob the cattle dog of the privilege, Ian," Taarush parried back with a smarmy smile. "Lad's possessive, way I hear."

I glared across the table at him at that and nearly got out of my chair. A chorus of excited, entertained 'Ohh's and swearing went up around the dining room, and someone who'd been relieving themselves in the wash room came stumbling out still buckling their trousers, obviously hoping for a show. I heard at least a few whispers and coin purses being rifled through.

Taarush grinned at me, and I stared him down, but Grayson's hand clenched on my shoulder. "C'mon, lads. No blood at the table, them's the rules."

"Ayyy, c'mon!" the otter flung his hands up. "I could'a done good money on that, Cap'n!"

"Odds on the cattle dog," the painted dog said around a bite of curry. "He's quick, I've seen him."

"I'm… better with a blade than bare-knuckle," I relented, settling back into my chair not only because the mood at the table was still proving to be congenial, but because Grayson's hand was kneading my neck. "Honestly, I think the leopard would have me. Don't you fight for sport?"

"Aye, you've seen," Taarush said. "All but undefeated."

"Ain't much else t'do while we're stranded," the otter pressed, leaning forward on his bulky arms. "We should get some matches goin' tomorrah. Cerberus, can I write y'in?"

It took me all but a moment to decide. I chewed on my second piece of bread, then leaned back in my chair and nodded, "Sure. Why the hell not?"

"You're gonna tear your bloody face open again," Grayson said irritably from beside me. "That's why."

"I'll go easy."

"No, you fuckin' won't," he muttered back at me. "This time tomorrow I'll be stitchin' that wound back up, sayin' I told you so."

"Listen to Cap whingin' on like a fussy wife," the mutt 'Ian' cackled around a mouthful of food. "We got us this'un, boys. We *got* the bloody Cerberus Admiral *whipped-*!"

"I'm not about to pass this up because the wolf gets faint at the sight of blood," I insisted. "I'll be there."

"Cap'n, don't you worry now," Taarush smirked, "you can kiss him for good luck."

"And watch from the crowd with yer goddamn tricorn clutched in yer paws like the missus you are!" the otter howled with laughter.

"When... exactly... did this turn into you lot barbing *me?*" Grayson asked, dropping his paws down heavily on the table.

I smiled despite myself, and from somewhere amongst the busy table, someone shouted, "Kiss'm *now*, you coward!"

"Aye, I need to see this fuckin' heresy for myself to know it's real," the otter agreed.

"Alright, lads, alright. Enough now," Grayson put his hands out, palms down, indicating for the level of noise in the room to drop. It had the opposite effect.

I wasn't sure what to make of all of this, it was completely antithetical, absurd, like a mirror world of what I knew. I looked to the wolf, who didn't seem at all... surprised... by the sudden throng of shouting, whooping, and catcalling in the room, but he *did* seem worried for me. We couldn't have possibly heard one another over the laughing and cajoling from the crowd, but he mouthed 'Are you alright?' at me.

I wasn't. I really wasn't. But it's not that I was afraid, or angry, or embarrassed, or any of the things I thought I'd be. Something inside me had unhooked. Something about... all of this... was so overwhelmingly new, it was almost too much.

I felt...

... free.

He leaned in, giving me a questioning look, glancing back to the rest of the table, before looking again to me. And... there it was. That final snap as the chain to the anchor broke, and I lurched forward into something. Open waters.

I gripped him by the collar of his jacket, the same time as he grabbed me by the scruff of my neck, and we kissed.

The room erupted into a cacophony of cheering, laughing, noises of disgust, and swearing in a half dozen languages.

But all I cared about was him.

* * *

I've never finished my dinner so fast.

We couldn't get back to his quarters in time. We didn't even make it halfway before I had him backed into a shadowed nook somewhere away from prying eyes. Mostly, anyway. There may have been one or two people who saw us clinging at each other as we walked, and the brief wrestling match that preceded us ducking away. I could tell myself it would probably just seem to an outsider like we were drunk, but honestly? I wasn't sure any of the excuses fucking mattered any more. Not here. Not on this ship. If the crewmen didn't know already, they would soon. And it was essentially just fodder here for lewd mockery. It was like another world.

The wood shuddered under his weight when I shoved him against the wall, his throaty chuckle filled the darkness we occupied, and then strong hands and claws were gripping into my shirt, pulling me to him.

"I ain't even sure any more when we're fightin' and when we're playin'," he admitted, the cold of his nose brushing my muzzle. "Are you mad at me, mate? Or just horny? You sorta' initiated that one."

"You set me up," I countered, grinning with my teeth to keep him on his toes. "Don't act like you didn't manifest all that, you were loving every second of it."

"You assume I've got *way* more control over my crew than I actually do," he said with a wry smile.

"You feign incompetence so often, I think you've begun to believe it," I said in a softer tone, leaning in and pressing my hands up beneath the gaping collar of his coat, claws sliding over buttons and gold thread, pushing the heavy fabric aside to enter the inner heat from his cotton-covered chest. The soft brush of the fur escaping at his neckline grazed my knuckles as my palms cupped and travelled around the mounds of his masculine breast. While I admired a trim figure, there was certainly something to be said for how much of the larger man there was for me to get ahold of, when the mood struck.

"You ain't mad," he surmised with a grin and a wet, eager kiss. He hummed and then growled contentedly as I bit at the edge of his lip to keep him there longer, curling my tongue 'round his and dragging him in deeper. I crushed him against the wall, my palms finding purchase beneath his shirt now more easily that I'd untucked it from his trousers. I got a good and proper handful, finally, and gave it the rough-handed squeeze it was due.

"You like tits more'n I thought you would," he mumbled into my mouth, the words nearly lost in the sucking, obscene noises we were somehow managing to fill the creaking silence of our hiding spot with. Really, I had never been so despicable, so improper, so disgustingly *wanton* as I was with this man. He was dragging me down into the depraved muck with him.

And I was enjoying it. Lord help me.

"You are once again talking too much," I muttered. "Take the win, wolf. You'll get what you want tonight if you don't distract and annoy me too much until then."

"Really?!" He pulled back from the kiss long enough to grin excitedly at me, his eyes sparkling in the dark. I could *hear* the swish of his tail against his coat. "Y'gonna mount me right and proper? Ah'm in *heat*, Lu, the day's got me ridin' so many highs and lows, I can't *think* of a better topper. I'm so riled up…"

I fought the urge to roll my eyes. "You're making me regret my decision already. Relax. *Please.* I can make this good for you, but you're setting your expectations a bar too high, I fear. You may not like this at all. Trust me… it's not always good for everyone."

"I'm relaxed," he lied. While almost literally quivering. That couldn't have *just* been the wind.

"Maybe it's better you go into this rearing," I sighed, toying with a dread with my free hand, "for you, anyway. You're balls to the wall on everything, and if it's over fast, it'll at least be… over fast."

"Oh, pile on the romance, why don't you? What confidence you have in the both of us," he *did* roll his eyes. "We've been fuckin' around for a while now, cattle dog. Why's this so different? It's not *near* as uncomfortable as

I thought it'd be, when we first tangled. Yeah, that... part... isn't always pleasant for me, but I like it when *you* do it. A'least so far. You seem to know what you're doin.'"

"I don't want to hurt you," I said, kissing him again more sweetly, which I knew from experience now nearly always got his hackles down. It never failed.

He leaned back slowly after we parted, the softness back in his features. He wasn't like me... never had been. His resting state was gentle, empathetic. *Gentlemanlike*, you might say. He'd never really entirely shaken his roots, and honestly, I was glad for him that the hard-living years hadn't hardened his heart. It wasn't natural for him. The few times in my life I'd seen the man forced to be brutal, it hadn't suited. He was a softer soul.

"A little pain for pleasure's sake ain't the worst thing in the world," he said with a curl of his dark lip upwards, looking down at me with hooded eyes. "You think that mightily of yourself, eh?"

"I'm the wrong man to break you in," I said ruefully. "My first was... unpleasant, to put it mildly, and he wasn't packing near so much firepower. It's *going* to hurt like hell, no matter what I do."

"I wouldn't want anyone else," he said simply, brushing his paws down my arms and cupping my elbows to hold me close. "And, uh, mate..." he cleared his throat, "... y'know I've spent more than half my life sleepin' around, right? You keep acting like I'm some virgin damsel here, you're gonna give me a complex."

"You know what I mean."

"Y'know what I think?" he asked absolutely no one while patting my rear.

"I'm certain you're going to tell me," I sighed.

"I think you kinda' get off on the thought of it, honestly," he grinned. "Being the first to stake your claim in me? 'Breaking me in'? Whoahh," he made a dismissive noise, "what's that about, then? Could've said that *any* other way, really, but no, you —"

"Oh my God," I groaned, pushing away from him.

"— you're here acting like you're taking my cherry because you're gonna plant your flag in just about the *one* place in my body ain't no one's penetrated yet, at least not in explicitly this *way* —"

"I'm leaving," I growled, turning around. "Follow me or don't, but I'm not listening to your aspersions anymore."

He jogged up behind me, looping an arm around my shoulder. "It's an Amur thing, right? This obsession with virtue? Mate, I'm as unvirtuous as they come, I'm sorry to tell you. But if it gets your rocks off, thinkin' you're defiling me or something —"

"*Please* don't use that specific word," I said.

"Sorry, right, just saying, if you wanted to hang a sheet out our window afterwards or something —"

"You are trying to bait me into getting aggressive with you again because you're nervous," I said, leading the walk to the cabin. "And for whatever reason, bickering and being aggressive with one another seems to be where we're most comfortable."

He made a face like he was mulling that over, as we finally reached his door. His guards were absent tonight, I noticed. He'd probably called them off discreetly at some point over dinner. Affording us some privacy. Considerate of him, especially since I knew for a fact it was for my benefit. He didn't care if the whole world knew his private business.

"That's... I mean..." He seemed flummoxed by my calling him out. I stopped and gave him a moment, but he genuinely did not seem to know what to say now that I'd derailed his trying to get a rise out of me.

"Relax," I repeated my sentiment from earlier, keeping my tone steady and calm. It wasn't a façade — I had made my mind up about this at the beach, and generally once I had a course I was confident in, it was hard to shake that confidence. The wolf was all over the place, as always. Chaotic. Excited. Perhaps more nervous or worried than he was letting on. As someone who knew these waters, it was my job — as I saw it — to instill some of that confidence in him. To soothe him, show him serenity, and guide the night.

"I don't want to fight, tonight," I said, turning against the door as I pushed it in, stepping backwards and reaching up to brush my claws over his chin, leading him inside as though by a lure. He did so obediently, transfixed on me. "My first time, as I said, was... rough. Rushed. Unpleasant. I don't want it to be like that with the two of us. I have a chance here, later in life, more experienced now, to spare you the mistakes of my own youth."

I let my claws slip away from the whiskers on the bottom of his chin, as the door swung shut behind us. "I want to make good memories with you, Grayson," I said. "So much of my life has been a battle. I can't spare you pain, not entirely, but… I can try to be as good to you as you deserve."

He opened his mouth, and I cut him off. "No." I said firmly. "Not a self-loathing word about whatever it is you *think* you are worth. Tonight, I decide what you deserve. Understood?"

His ears splayed, but he didn't frown or cow. In fact, his tail was swaying, almost imperceptibly. But I knew his mannerisms by now. I could read him.

"You liked hearing that," I said. It was not a guess.

"I was worried when you got talking mushy," he admitted with a breathy laugh. "I like… I like the way you push back against me. Never afraid to tell me off, bicker with me, be a little… forceful with me." He began to shoulder out of his coat slowly. "But you're still being firm. You just… don't want to argue?"

"Bantering back and forth is fine for foreplay," I said, approaching him and slipping my hands up beneath his coat to help him remove it and tossing it over a nearby chair. "But tonight, there will be no arguing with me." I tipped my nose down, locking my eyes with his. "Alright? Trust me. Do as you're told, let me lead, and I'll make this good for you. For both of us. I know the ropes."

He gave a slow, heady smile. "Yes, sir."

I nodded and undid my belt, looping it and my sword over the side of the chair alongside his coat, untying my sash a moment later and leaving it on a chest he kept near the side of his bed, where he stowed some of his possessions. I saw his eyes briefly flick over to where I'd settled it, as I sat down on the edge of the bed.

"Wh… what's that for?" he asked, impishly.

"Gagging you, if it comes to it," I muttered. "Don't worry about it, for now. We bathed in the sea earlier, so that's one thing less to worry about. You've still got the oil under there?"

He nodded. "Plenty of it."

"Good," I said, reclining back on my palms. "Light the lanterns and undress for me."

He took but a moment to acquiesce. He set to the task of lighting the lanterns first, starting with those by the door.

"All of them?" he asked.

"Yes," I said in case he couldn't see me nod. "I want to see you."

When he'd finished, he stepped into the center of the room and began undoing his belt. He wasn't near so clumsy or functionally-minded about the act as I'd thought he might be, either. I could pull out of most of my clothes, or into them, at a moment's notice. Decades now in the Navy had seen to that. But I wouldn't say the way in which I did so was particularly… alluring. Not like any of the professionals I'd seen over the years. There was an artistry to disrobing, no doubt.

The wolf was — whether he realized it or not — deeply enticing with the careless laziness he displayed while shrugging out of his shirt or peeling off his trousers. He clearly seemed to think otherwise because midway through, he said, "Always feel I look the fool, stumbling out of my clothes. You're so much faster at it."

"It's not all about speed," I said, my chin resting in my fist.

"Guess not," he said when he was clear of his smalls — which he was actually wearing today! Amazing. Kept a man cleaner… down there… so it spoke to him trying, at least, to be fresh for me after we'd bathed in the surf earlier today. The man *could* be taught, apparently. Especially when you dangled something he wanted in front of his nose.

His gaze, I realized suddenly, was fixed very specifically on my waist. Rather, the undeniable bulge making itself known in my britches. His own sheath, now fully on display, was only modestly swollen. Its pink tip pressed out enough to be noticeable, but was still acting far more demure than the state my own body was giving away.

I kept my composure, at least externally. I wasn't even frustrated with myself; it couldn't be helped. The wolf was standing before me, nude and eager like a meal begging to be devoured. I was a mortal man, for the love of God. Maybe my obvious desire would be a boon — give him some confidence. He'd clearly been worrying he wasn't my physical ideal. Let him say that again.

"You got it bad, huh?" he said with a smug smile as he sauntered towards me. I couldn't even hate him for it, he was right. "Y'like what you see, cattle dog?"

"Even a beautiful piece of art could always stand a *little* improvement," I said, and before he pouted at me, I pointed at the decking at my feet. "Knees. I think that would improve the view for me somewhat. The angle of the ship right now is not quite doing it for me."

He grinned wider and bent down to go to all fours, his dreads tumbling around his shoulders and settling over his back, gold and silver catching the lantern-light, and making soft jingles of noise as he crawled the final pace towards me. He settled there, between my legs. I'd been kinder to him on our first night together, but for a long while now, I'd had him service me from the floor. It... honestly didn't matter much to me... I suppose there was *something* novel about it. But it certainly seemed to awaken something in him.

I stroked a palm from his nose all the way up between his eyes, his forehead, between his ears, and down the waves of his beaded mane. And then I repeated the gesture, petting him as he settled with his nose resting just over my bulge. His eyes kept moving between it and me, the request unspoken, but obvious.

"Do not touch yourself," I said as I stood, untucking my shirt and dragging it up my chest, then down over my arms in one fluid motion. I tried to draw it out, unsure if he got the same thrill from watching a man undress as he might a woman. But it seemed only fair, given what I'd asked of him. He certainly wasn't *bothered* by it.

"At all?" he asked uncertainly.

I considered that for a moment. "Yes," I settled on eventually. "At all. I'm going to take my pleasure of you tonight, and I'd like to give it in return. Let me get you there... alright?"

He nodded. If he was concerned I'd fail and was robbing him of the chance to find release on his own, he didn't say as much. I hoped I wasn't making a mistake, but... it felt right. With him.

I wasn't usually one for this much control. Earnestly. I could be a controlling man in many other ways, but I preferred to tailor myself in the bedroom to the tastes of whomever I was with. All that mattered to me was that we both enjoyed ourselves and woke the next day with as few regrets as possible.

Grayson liked having his control taken away. There was freedom for some men in submission. He wasn't the first I'd known like this, and now that I knew him as well as I did, it wasn't honestly all that hard to understand. There were many times throughout my life that I'd had difficult, life-altering decisions laid at my feet that I would have rather given to another. For the Privateer, that clearly included intimacy. I could give it to him, and it suited my natural inclinations to assume the 'male' role with my partners. So why not?

I'd barely gotten my trousers off before his nose was buried in my navel, his teeth scraping at the trail of fur down below it. He was moving too fast again, snuffing his way down towards my exposed cock, and I fisted a hand in his mane and squeezed to slow him.

"Easy," I soothed. "Paw first. Build me up proper, the way I like. Aye?"

He nodded, leaning back as he lifted a hand paw to wrap around my length, squeezing me with a long swallow, before his tongue unfurled and fell from his muzzle again. He panted while he stroked me, managing to keep it slow, at least at first. His breaths were the only noise in the room other than the creaking of the ship... and the occasional soft 'plat' of saliva dripping from the end of his tongue.

"Hell's fire, wolf," I shook my head at him, "you were *made* to suck cock, you know that? I enjoy it more than anyone I've ever met, I love everything about it, and the fervor with which you've taken to it still gobsmacks me."

"Have I gotten better at it?" he asked, lifting his blue eyes to mine while his fist continued to pump me.

"Immeasurably," I assured him. "You're still a mess, don't get me wrong... you drool more than anyone whose muzzle I've ever fucked before. But you're a mess in general," I patted his cheek, "so that's rather to be expected."

He gave a whuff of breath when I finally led him with a grip still in his mane to my tip. He took it in all too eagerly, looking up at me as he slowly eased me inside, inch by inch. There was the brief shudder as I hit the barrier of his gag, and then a rapid blink, wince, and I was down his throat. He'd gotten better at relaxing that reflex over time — an effort which he himself had been most enthused to pursue. He liked it when I stood over him and fucked his face. Used him, he'd call it. He settled in for it readily, curling his whiskered lip to cover his front teeth, craning his neck up and locking eyes with me while I began pumping slowly in and out of that long, dark muzzle of his.

It was the best bloody seat in the house. I couldn't put to words how satisfying it was, filling the Privateer's mouth with my cock. Stifling any of his clever comebacks, stuffing the root of my manhood down his wet, willing, *eager* maw.

Oh, the noises, as well… he still choked occasionally, gave slick swallows and muffled whines, as the saliva pooled at the corners of his mouth and unshed tears prickled in his eyes. And the brushing broom sound of his tail against the floor, clearing dust and sand in its wake… God, he fucking *loved* this, and it was hard not to brought right along with him.

I was directing the night, I reminded myself. I could do as I wished with him, and a quick glance down confirmed he was now as hard as I was, bobbing between his thighs, probably *aching* for the feel of his own fist. But he was obeying my ask and holding off.

"You're not close yet somehow, are you? You've cum without touching yourself before," I said, stroking one of his ears, while my claws danced along his opposite cheek, feeling the strain of his jaw muscles as I pressed in deep. "Still pent up, even after our round on the beach? You aren't allowed to spill before I've gotten inside you either, for the record."

He swallowed, or at least tried to, the walls of his throat closing around my cock and squeezing it until I was humming in pleasure. But he did eventually manage to nod slowly.

"You fuck like a twenty-and-some man," I sighed. "No patience." I stroked back his ears, both of them. "I want you right on the line before I fuck you. Not over it. So, you're going to tell me if you're getting too close, yes?"

He nodded again, more readily this time.

I dragged him to his feet, and he nearly stumbled into me in the process, but I caught him while he was dizzily panting into the warm cabin air and recovering his strained jaw. I found his muzzle with my own all but immediately, the both of us groaning as we threw our arms around one another and licked the taste of my precum from one another's tongues. He dug his fingers into the small of my back and my ass for purchase, and I steadied the two of us with my arms under his, wrapped around his midsection. How we'd been aiming for the bed and ended up on the wall nearby, I do not know, but we were too wanton for one another to care. Once his back hit the wall, I grabbed for his wrists, eventually finding them and pinning them back against the planks. His cock was heavy against my thigh as I leaned into him and rutted up into the warm crux of his thick-furred thighs. I couldn't possibly fuck him against the wall unless he bent double — he was too tall — but I found a good spot to grind into the soft meat of his inner thigh, where his fur was downy and plush, and I could *feel* the heat from under his tail from there.

The reality that I was about to fuck this man… the Privateer Grayson Reed, whom I had struck an unlikely alliance with over a decade ago and carried on a long and often fraught friendship with over the years, despite every good reason not to… finally landed in my mind. It was surreal and strange, but also, somehow, felt inevitable. Like we'd spent our acquaintance navigating towards this heading, detouring, and delaying, but always knowing this is where we were going to end up. We'd been flirting since the very first day we'd met.

I didn't exactly believe in fate, but if I had one, it was Grayson. No other person in my life had been so constant a fixation. In this life, in any other my path may have taken me down, he and I were meant to be together. In one form or another.

And now, I'd have him. Whatever we were to one another from here on out, however my life unfurled, I'd know he'd been mine, this night. He'd begged for it, cajoled me into it, and if I was a man of my word, he'd enjoy it. There was neither good nor bad in those facts, only truth. What we made of it was up to us.

He gave a long, shuddering breath when we pulled apart for but a moment, the heat and friction building between our bodies. "I love you," he said, before I could.

"Bastard," I could have laughed. "That was my line."

He smiled like he did when he was drunk. "Sorry to jump the script. You can still say it. I like hearing you say it."

"I love you," I said without fear. I wasn't as comfortable saying it as he was, but I wasn't about to be a coward in this moment. Especially as the few simple words brought the peace over his features I had been hoping for. I wanted him loose and calm, for what was to come. Comfortable… and yes… I wanted him to feel loved.

It's what I had always wanted. And I wanted to give him what I had never had.

We navigated ourselves back to the bed, and I began kissing him, starting at his paws. He seemed confused at first, leaning up on his elbows… but I soon reached up, pressed a palm firmly into his chest, and shoved him back down into his blankets. He gave a surprised huff, but didn't argue. And he didn't object physically, either, lying down and stretching out while I worked my way up his inner leg.

He was doing as I said. I'd sort of paid lip-service to this submission play of his in the past, but honestly? I could get used to an obedient Grayson Reed.

When I nuzzled at his balls, his legs twitched and splayed, and his tail shuddered and tickled at my ears as it flopped about. I smiled a bit at how puppylike he was being, but I doubted any of it was intentional. Which made it all the more charming, really.

I curled my tongue beneath the two soft, hefty mounds, and nibbled, then dragged them into my mouth, gingerly. He sucked in a gasp, and I sucked on his sac, while the hands I'd been kneading up his thighs with found his sheath and protruding length. I squeezed the knot still encased in his sheath, while my fist finally touched his overheated, slick manhood.

I gave him a few steady, slow pumps, while suckling wetly at the truly impressive mouthful I had. When people said the Privateer had balls, they didn't know the half of it. I'd *never* admit aloud how envious I was… but at least I got to play with them.

I finally thought to get the oil, somewhere between moving my muzzle from his sac to his cock and forcing his legs further apart with my elbows. It was right where it had been before, perhaps a little closer to the edge of the bed even, which meant he'd prepared for the possibility that we might be fucking tonight, even back when we were still fighting. It was presumptive, arrogant, and got me a little hotter under the collar than I'd like to admit.

I could see his button, inky black as his paw-pads, only pink when you pushed inside and opened him up. I got as much slick on my fingers as I could, and wasted no time, sliding two fingers in to the knuckle, while his cock was still down my throat.

He arched his hips up and keened for me, begging, "Awwhhhmate, fuck, please-!" One of his legs kicked down against the blankets, his claws pressing into the wood of the bedframe. I could hear the strain and pop of the old timber. "M'so ready, Lu… god, please… I need you… Don't even warn me, I-I'll tense up."

"You'll do no such thing," I said after releasing his length from my muzzle and licking my chops. I pumped my overly-slick fingers, easing him open before adding a third. "You see how loose you're getting for me? Good lad, there… you're doing so good. God, you take this so well. You're going to love my cock, aren't you?"

"Y-yes," he groaned headily. "I can't fuckin' wait any longer…"

That was the mark. I gave him one last, long lick, a bead of precum sliding down the tip as I pulled away. I left it, letting it bead and gather, while I leaned up on my knees to take in the sight of him, one last time.

"You look so bloody good," I said, leaning down over him to brush aside some of his cheek ruff, kiss him, and show him how much I fucking *adored* him.

He smiled softly up at me, rumbling a masculine, pleased growl into my palm. I smiled back… and the distraction worked. I'd lined myself up without him noticing, and before he had a chance to realize it, I'd pressed past the resistance of his pursed hole and sheathed myself near to the knot inside his heat.

He sucked in a gasp and cried out, nearly choking on his own saliva. He immediately tensed tight around me, locking me in place, but I eased down atop him so my weight was pressing into his — a sensation I knew by now he enjoyed — and nuzzled his throat with a soft, "You're good, lad… so good… try to relax…"

"Fuck!" he finally uttered, giving a full-body shudder, his heartbeat thundering beneath me. "Fuck, that's… ahhhh… s… s'much more…"

I just nodded and leaned up on my elbows, pressing our noses together. "The pain will fade. Relax…" I kissed him, "… you're doing good. It'll feel more right, soon."

"Ahh… uh-huh…" He nodded quickly, squeezing his eyes shut for a moment, before opening them again, breathing out in short pants. I could see the discomfort and, moreover, the fear, growing there. He was worried he'd disappoint me or himself. That this wouldn't be what he'd wanted it to be.

"Remember how much you wanted this," I reminded him softly in between kissing him. "Wanted to feel us joined? We've done it… we're as

close as we can ever be, wolf," I smiled a little against his muzzle, then moved my mouth up to his ear. "And I'm going to make you cum. Just give me room to maneuver."

I slowly… slowly withdrew as his body began to uncoil. He was trying to steady his breathing and rub his hips up against mine. He didn't know how to move, but that was alright. That was my job.

Satisfied now that it was the right time, I reached down slowly and curled my fingers around his cock. He'd not lost any of his fervor there, I'd gotten him *far* too close beforehand, and he was still slick. I drifted my grip up and down, as I rubbed steadily back and forth at my current depth inside of him. I had to blow out a breath or two of my own, steadying my want. I wasn't made of stone, and the man was tight, molten hot, and *begging* to be fucked deeper. Although I'd taken him almost to the root on my initial push, rather than dragging the whole affair out, I had not yet begun to drill down with my hips. I could have been unmerciful… as the man who'd first taken me when I was a teenager had been with me.

But, I was a better man than that bastard had ever been.

"Nnhhh-ahh-!" the wolf whined softly, and I focused my gaze down on him, watching his expression go weak, his brows lifting, the tip of his tongue protruding. I was keeping my pace steady but shallow for now… and that's when I remembered.

"I'd forgotten how shallow a mark you are," I chuckled between pants. "Already feeling it, are you?"

"O-ohhh… fuuckkk…" he lilted, hips straining up to answer one of my thrusts. I saw it the moment the understanding passed over his face.

"There you are," I smirked. "That's the rub, sailor. You've got it… now just ride that out…"

I could tell he was on that fine line, wrestling between discomfort and the razor's edge of the very specific and unique pleasure this act could bestow. I was better with my muzzle than I was at finding that fine line, being as I just didn't… *do* this often, at least not any more. And God, why was that, again? Bloody fucking *hell*, I had wanted this. I wanted nothing more now than to see this sight before me, the beautiful black wolf beneath me, taking my cock pumping beneath his tail, his sac and length bouncing with my thrusts, while he slowly came undone and learned the meaning of fucking *life* at my behest-

He grabbed a fistful of the blankets and threw his neck back, sobbing out a sudden, "Fuck, Lu! Thassit, right. There! Oh god, do that again, do that again, I'm beggin' you, it's so... I feel so fuckin' full, but I want... I-I want —"

I rutted in harder this time, and it must have struck the chord he wanted because he barked out another cry, and his cock wept in my hand, and I could tell he was close, but we kept at it for a while, and he didn't break. He seemed on the verge, he was crying — quite literally now, his cheeks were wet — and I didn't want to hurt him, God I didn't want to hurt him, but he wasn't *quite* there, and he wanted more of me. He begged me hoarsely to fuck him, to *really* fuck him, and I hoped it was earnest because it's all I wanted in the world, too.

I kissed him. I kissed him deeply and pounded my hips into him, and he took it. He wasn't a fragile man, I had to remind myself. He liked it rough... we had always been rough with one another... and I'd done all I could to get him this far.

We finished as we'd started. Swearing and yearning and going hard at one another, and on the thrust that finished him off, I saw his eyes roll back, and his hips strain beneath his fur, his whole torso tensing until he erupted in my paw. Spilling, and spilling, and spilling.

I didn't follow immediately in his wake. I was overwhelmed, and sometimes when I'm overwhelmed, it can actually be hard for me. Besides, I was struck watching him... the beauty of him, gasping into the hot, musky air between us, with his spend painting his dark chest and glistening in the lantern light. And altogether, feeling so... deeply...

... fulfilled.

The truth is, I'd been far more afraid to do this than he'd been to receive me. I'd been the one who'd needed to calm myself... to let come what may and accept that whatever the outcome, this would not change what we had. That we loved one another, were too tightly-bound and locked in our course together to drift apart because of one bad night. Or even discovering we were fully incompatible in this way. He would have been there in the morning, regardless.

We always found one another, somehow. We were the point on the horizon for one another. We were each, to one another, how we found our bearings. Through the worst of it.

Whether lovers or friends.

"I want all of you," his voice cut through the din of my thoughts, and I found my visage of him bleary. I swept an arm up over my eyes, clearing them, and hoping he hadn't noticed.

The look on his face said he had.

"You have me, utterly," I said, wondering if he'd remember the context. That one, he missed. Perhaps for the best.

"*All* of you," he repeated, tugging at my arms to pull me back down. "Tie me. I want your knot."

"Why must you *always* dive in to the deepest possible depths?" I huffed, grunting as the push and pull of his body still throbbing in the wake of his orgasm caused the first of the shudders I knew too well to course through me. I was not long for this world, and I'd not stopped moving. My hips moved of their own accord, at this point. It was instinct.

"I deserve all of you," he said, with the sincerest confidence I think I'd ever heard from him. "And I can take it. Please."

I braced my arms, that shudder passing through me again as I crushed our muzzles together. Before the last push that did me in, I growled a rough, "You know I can never deny you anything."

He sobbed when I gave him what he wanted, with a final hard, unyielding thrust. It was bliss. It was everything.

It was the start of a new chapter for us. Not the end of what we'd had, as I'd feared. Not by a long shot.

* * *

Grayson Reed was infamous for reaping what he sowed, but I doubt he'd put much thought into certain decisions he made that night, regardless of the many, many warnings I'd given him since we'd started all this fuckery. One of these days, he'd learn to listen.

Maybe. Perhaps.

The chances were slight, if I was being honest.

I slept fairly soundly sharing a bed with someone else, almost regardless of who it was. I liked sharing the master bedroom with my wife when I was home, and despite our admittedly mostly platonic relationship, we both enjoyed holding one another at night. It was warm and comfortable, and I wasn't too proud to ask for it when I truly wanted the company. In a different world, I would have liked to share my marriage bed with a man, bury my nose in his fur each night, and tolerate whatever snoring or kicking he put up, just to feel less alone while I slept. That... that would be nice.

Grayson did not like to share his bed. He had admitted as much to me on more than one occasion. He was willing to and often did, owing to the women he hired (and himself) being far too inebriated to do much else besides pass out whenever they were fed up with or finished their nightly activities. The bobcat stayed with him frequently, I knew that much. Although one morning I had found them together, and she'd had the absolute lion's share of the bed, splayed out like a starfish. The wolf was hanging half-off his own side with none of the blankets.

I had also found him on the floor, more than once. Sometimes with a pillow, suggesting it had been an intentional choice... sometimes not.

I don't think it had anything to do with him disliking the idea of a warm body next to his because he *could* be rather clingy. A fact which I didn't mind. We'd fallen asleep entangled around one another, thankfully managing *not* to nod off while I was still knotted in him, although that had been a near thing. As far as nights like this in my life — rare enough as they were — went, all was well. Very... very well.

But Grayson was a light sleeper, frequently rousing, tossing and turning, mumbling in his sleep, and in the case of this particular night... grumbling. About something *I* knew to expect, but he clearly hadn't thought through all that much.

"Bloody hell," he rumbled from behind me, his arm shifting where it was draped around my midsection to reach around, presumably under his tail. "Alrigh-yeah... thas'what I thought. Ain't just... m'fuckin' leaking, ain't I?"

I didn't even bother opening my eyes, only chuckled sleepily, deep in my throat.

"Don't sound so smug, y'bastard."

"I said nothing at all," I pointed out, my voice coming out gravelly.

"I could hear it in that throat laugh o'yours." More rustling. He was pulling back the comforter to get up.

"Where exactly did you *think* it went?" I asked, content to stay put while he fussed about.

"I don't know!" he exclaimed, his tone irritable and something else. Husky, thicker. I didn't have to turn around to realize he was probably probing at himself, I could tell in the way the weight shifted on the bed. "Just thought… inside?"

"If you've got a womb you're not telling me about, we need to have a talk," I muttered against my pillow. "M'too old to raise any more pups."

"Not that I know of," he hissed softly, then shuffled off the bed with a light laugh. "Too bad, though. Little cattle-wolves would be cute, eh?"

"The world does not need any more of the two of us," I said with complete sincerity.

"Amen to that," he agreed, his weight shifting. He was moving slowly, stiffly.

"Oh, if you're sitting or standing up, you're going to want to…" I began, finally turning to address him.

"Oh, holy hell, it just got *so* much worse!"

"Uh-huh," I said, flicking one of my ears that never seemed to want to stand up straight when I was half-asleep. "You should — hang on, no, don't bother stumbling across the room, Gray."

I pushed myself up to a sitting position while the wolf vainly searched for something — anything — to clean up the mess presumably leaking down his inner leg, before I reached for something I knew was there on my side of the bed on his footlocker where I'd left it.

"Here," I offered him the folded cloth.

He took it without a moment's hesitation, and while he cleaned himself up, I could not help but notice the bobbing protrusion between his legs, half hanging out of his sheath. He was ignoring it — seemingly annoyed, more than anything else — trying to focus on the task at hand.

I watched, leaning my cheek into my palm. He didn't even turn to address me when he did, I presumed he could feel my eyes on him in the dark.

"Like what you see, mate?"

My voice came out odd thanks to the pressure of my hand on my cheek, but that didn't stop me from being cocky. Not one bit. "The evidence of that is dripping down your balls as we speak, so… yes."

"No, it's n — oh, shit, it is." He quickly remedied that, before lifting the cloth I'd given him into a thin sliver of the moonlight and *finally* realizing what he was holding.

"Bleeding hell, is this your Amur red?" he asked, turning to hold the folded, and now very stained, sash up for me to see.

"It is," I confirmed.

"Did you *mean* to give me the signifier of your national pride to wipe my arse with?" he asked, flummoxed.

"I did."

"I mean I know you're on the outs with your fleet," he said, crawling back onto the bed on his hands and knees, approaching me, "but you've been here a few weeks now, and you've still worn it every day. I didn't think you were giving up on your *people*. Or is this really not all that deep for you?"

"No, it is," I said, taking it from him, re-folding it and tossing it onto the nearby chair with the rest of my clothing. "It's fabric, wolf. It'll wash out."

"Still..." he said uncertainly. He looked rather fetching, crouched beside me, ears tipped back, looking a bit demure, a bit aroused, and altogether rather... cute.

I sighed, reaching up to brush my palm over his cheek and stroke back his ears, dragging him towards me by the chin with a leading claw. He followed, just as I'd hoped. He always followed me.

"Do you know why we wear it?" I asked him first.

"Something akin to a spirit talisman," he said automatically. "I grew up in Carvecia, you know. My family's Kadrushian and Carvecian, but we're both pretty well intertwined with Amur culture. I know most of the signifiers. It's to pay homage to your dead, right?"

"The red represents the blood of those who've been injured or killed at sea, serving the Empire," I said. "Land forces wear them sometimes, but its roots are in a Navy tradition. It helps identify us in times of boarding, too... so it serves a utility. The average Navy 'uniform' amongst most of the ranks is nondescript. There are standards, but anything more formal was abandoned in the last century, save the coats and sash."

"Noticed you saved that, too," he pointed out. "Saw it amongst your things when we were tending to you in your cabin."

"It isn't mine," I said. "Not… entirely, anyway."

"Right," he nodded, "belonged to your Shepherd lover."

I ignored the minor sting of Klaus being referred to so casually. It wasn't fair to blame Grayson for that… the man had been dead a generation now, and the wolf had never known him, except by reputation. And they would *not* have gotten along, that was for certain. God knew what Klaus would think of me now, but I *was* certain how he'd feel about the company I kept. The only thing the man had hated more than Kadrushian wolves were pirates.

"It was passed into my care by Lucius Denholme," I said. "My father-in-law. And even if I've forever disgraced his family's name, I still see it as my duty to look after an heirloom he entrusted me with. Klaus would want to be remembered, too… even bitterly. He was self-important like that."

I must've smiled a bit because he hummed, smiling back pointedly. "Chose the right protégé, then."

"I hope he'd feel that way," I said, then flicked my eyes up to his. "Please, if you make no other grand gestures in whatever time we have left together, do me one favor, Gray."

"I can try," he said, listening.

"Don't die before me," I pleade, quietly.

"Sorry, mate. Can't promise you that," he said sadly. "The world's a hellish place, and I'm sick, remember. It won't have to be violence. I can't avoid the clock tickin' away inside me. I've already outlived all the Physicians' estimates."

"I know," I said quietly, tracing the length of one of his dreads between my thumb and forefinger. "It wasn't a fair thing to ask. I'm just…"

He leaned in against me, bumping our noses together. His fur smelled good, and I inhaled slowly.

"I'm so tired of outliving the people I love," I finished somberly.

He didn't say anything. Only moved a hand up to the ruff of my neck, carding his claws through my fur and eventually rubbing my ears. He was beginning to learn all of my weak spots… it was a problem.

"You know, this," I said, gesturing at the folded red cloth I'd tossed into the pile of my clothes, "was a tradition of his. I've kept it going."

"Dis… gracing your Navy tradition by using it to literally wipe yer ass on?" he guessed, eyebrows lifting. "Or someone else's, I suppose."

"Klaus didn't have the highest regard for our country's traditions," I summarized. "But the way he explained it to me, men have been fucking one another and loving one another in the Navy since we first began going to sea. The red represents blood, and we've all bled on our sash, at one point or another. He'd use his to… clean me up… when we were done. Any time he took a Navy man for a lover, he said. He swore even after he washed it, he'd always be able to find their scent on it."

"I don't know how to tell you this, Lu," he smirked, "but your shepherd was a bit filthy."

"It's no worse than blood," I shrugged. "And anyway, I'm not about to shed my love for my kin and country just because they've lost their love for me. But some parts of home… of the Navy and everything it represents… might warrant wiping your ass with."

He laughed. "Fair enough, I guess."

"I haven't really carried on the tradition with most of my other lovers through the years," I confessed, "because it was just… never safe… to take up with other Navy men. Especially not once I had my command. I don't know. Maybe that was never the point, but…"

"You put me in the same echelon as your Admiral lover?" he asked. "Rare company, sounds like."

"It is," I said very seriously. "And why not? You're not Navy, but… you *are* an Admiral. And we share our love of the sea. Of all the misgivings I had about you, that's not something I've ever doubted."

"Well, I'm honored to warrant such, uh," he paused, "care. Truly. Ugh…"

Before I could say anything, he twisted up his muzzle and assured me, "No, it's not you. Or anything we just talked about, this is… absurdly vanilla, all of this, compared to the depravity of my twenties. No, I'm just… there's more…"

I barked a laugh, then glanced at the cloth on the chair at least ten feet away, where I'd thrown it. He followed my gaze, moaning, "I know. It's so far away."

I moved to lie on my back and spread an arm out towards him. "Come here."

"Over you? Alright," he said uncertainly, moving still a bit sleepily and *so* trusting me to know what I was doing. I almost felt bad. "You got another one of those stowed away, or you just want me to get it all over you?

Because I'm fine with either, honestly, as long as I make it your problem. This's all your fault."

"You asked me to knot you," I said, "nay, *demanded*."

"I didn't know there'd be so much *more* of it than usual…"

"Take it for the compliment it is," I said, lifting the blankets. "Under. Come on."

"You just want to cuddle, don't you?" he smirked, ducking under, then rolling on top of me, careless of his weight. He was bracing a mere fraction of it on his elbows and knees, but he wasn't trying all that hard. "You could've just said."

"Still slick back there, are you?" I asked casually.

"Oh, it's *bad*," he groused, his tail thumping between both of our legs. "Now I get why all the girls go off to the privy afterwards or throughout the night. Maybe it's my just rewards for all the times I — nnhhhagh-! The hell?!"

I grinned up at him, fangs and all, and clamped my palms down on his hips, while I thrust my own hips *up*, letting gravity do the rest. I'd gotten myself pretty well positioned while he was blathering, and it hadn't taken much more than trying to seat myself up under his tail and sink to the hilt inside his — indeed still very slick — and recently knot-loosened hole. Earnestly he'd been rather too tight at the start of the evening, both owing to his inexperience with the act and nerves, I'd wager. I liked him better warmed-up.

"Oh, you slick bitch," he groaned, squeezing his eyes to slim slits, fighting back and failing to prevent his tongue from pressing out between his teeth. "God *damn*, Lu…"

I chuckled, slowly releasing my hold on his hips to rub my palms up and down his shuddering thighs. "Any easier, this time? You feel good… more relaxed."

"Oh, fuck, you're deeper like this." He lost his battle against his tongue lolling out and any dignified face he could've held. He slowly leaned up on his knees and ground his hips down into mine, loosing a long, seemingly relieved groan. "Bloody hell, thas'the ticket, mate. Oh shit, that's good, right off…"

"Mmhh," I hummed. "You just needed to be broken in."

"You ain't kidding," he moaned, rubbing his hips back and forth inexpertly, his expression twitching and going lax intermittently as he tried to satisfy himself.

"Sore?" I asked, gingerly dancing my claws down the fold of his belly towards his bobbing cock.

"A little," he confessed sheepishly. "You could've asked *before*."

"You don't like it when I'm hesitant," I said, gripping his length and squeezing.

"Nnnhooo… I don't," he agreed, jerking his hips once, then twice, finding a staggered and imperfect rhythm. "I like that you didn't ask, honestly. Fuck mate, you look good in the moonlight…"

"As do you," I said, pumping his now fully-hard dick in my palm. "You're not going to last, are you?"

"No," he whined, his breath coming faster, now. "Been hard since I woke up feeling your spend leaking out of me like I'm your bred bitch."

"In essence, you are," I said, giving him a single good, hard thrust of my hips.

"Oh, fuck!" His eyes rolled back, and he braced an arm on the wall above us. He panted out, "Y-yeah. You gonna give it to me again, cattle dog? Knot me, like the bitch in heat I am?"

"You're being loud again," I smirked up at him. "Dinner tomorrow ought to be interesting."

The thought of his imminent public shaming must've been what did it… I think we hit under the two minute mark this time, but to be fair, the man was easy to work up when you knew his vulnerabilities, and I didn't actually want to drag things out the second time around, or he really *would* be in pain all day.

He came shaking and whining, my cock pounding up under his tail through the throes of it. He painted my hand and chest, and I kept stroking him through it until he was all but begging me to stop.

Then I turned his weak, limp body over onto his belly and climbed over top of him, taking hold of his tail so that I could sink home once more. I was not usually one for brevity, but I could finish myself off fast if I had a man chewing the bed, spread, and presenting for me.

God, he felt good, and I didn't feel I needed to hold back nearly so much when I crested my peak this time. I didn't knot him, once was enough for a night, I decided. And if he'd wanted me to, he didn't get the request out in between the baying moans.

I'm not sure who shared a wall with the Captain's quarters, but someone was banging on it and shouting obscenities at us by the time we'd both finished.

The both of us dissolved into fits of laughter, when we'd finally come down enough to realize it. It was the middle of the goddamn night, after all… and whoever they were, they'd been good enough not to complain during our first round. I didn't even blame them, at this point.

"I tried to warn you," I said fondly down at the wolf, pressing a kiss to the back of one of his ears. "You're so bloody *loud.*"

"You were ruttin' on me so hard the bed was hitting the wall," the wolf objected and flipped me an obscene gesture from where he was laying. "Kindly go fuck yourself, mate."

"I'd rather save my energy for you," I said, settling my weight atop him. We weren't tied, I just… wanted to feel close to him. And he didn't seem to mind, at the moment.

"You'll stay with me the next few nights, won't you?" he asked, peering up at me from one small sliver of blue, amidst all the dark fur.

"If you'd like." I smiled. "You really want to get in that much practice, do you?"

"Hell yes, I do."

"I don't honestly think you need it. You were made for this."

"Mate, that might be the nicest thing you've ever said about me," he said warmly.

"I am also falling rather deeply in love with you," I said offhandedly.

"Shit, you beat me to it this time. You're getting better at that," he complimented me.

"I certainly hope so," I sighed, resting my weight against his back, my palms drifting down over his body, feeling how warm, how solid, how very much he was… there. "I'm not letting go of you. So… we're going to make this work, you and I. Come Hell or high water."

"Aye, mate. God help anyone who gets in our way."

About the Author

Rukis is a Writer/Illustrator with a focus on Historical Fiction and Romance, exploring social issues, relationships and history through the eyes of Anthropomorphic characters. When not nose down working on a book or art, Rukis enjoys hiking, gardening, mountain biking, and tabletop gaming, as well as caring for five enormous dogs and a bustling flock of chickens.

About the Publisher

FurPlanet Productions is a small press publisher serving the niche market that is furry fiction. They sell furry-themed books and comics published by themselves and most major publishers in the community. If you can't get to a furry convention where they are selling in the dealers room, visit their online stores:

FurPlanet.com for print books
BadDogBooks.com for eBooks